OVERWATCH

OVERWATCH

MARC GUGGENHEIM

MULHOLLAND BOOKS

Little, Brown and Company
New York Boston London

Mulholland Books / Little, Brown and Company
Hachette Book Group
237 Park Avenue, New York, NY 10017
mulhollandbooks.com

First Edition: April 2014

Mulholland Books is an imprint of Little, Brown and Company, a division of Hachette Book Group, Inc. The Mulholland Books name and logo are trademarks of Hachette Book Group, Inc.

The publisher is not responsible for websites (or their content) that are not owned by the publisher.

The Hachette Speakers Bureau provides a wide range of authors for speaking events. To find out more, go to hachettespeakersbureau.com or call (866) 376-6591.

ISBN 978-0-316-21247-2
LCCN 2014932101

10 9 8 7 6 5 4 3 2 1

RRD-C

Printed in the United States of America

For Tara. My North Star.

The real rulers in Washington are invisible and exercise power from behind the scenes.

— U.S. Supreme Court Justice Felix Frankfurter

OVERWATCH

PROLOGUE

OVER YAZD, IRAN
2330 HRS. ZULU

THE DESERT sand stirs for a moment before coiling up like smoke in the direction of the blowback created by the Sikorsky MH-53J's titanium-and-steel rotor blades. The Sikorsky sails just a few feet above the sand dunes, flying low to avoid radar detection. In whisper mode, the helicopter makes a sound more evocative of a golf-course sprinkler than a 38,238-pound troop carrier. Inside, the men of the 21st Dust Devils Special Operations Squadron of the 352nd Special Operations Group wait without a word of chatter passing between them. *This* silence, however, is not tactically mandated. This silence is a function of the fucking heat. On a night like this, the stale, hot desert air can push the mercury well over one hundred degrees, which is uncomfortable, at best, when one is completely naked but almost intolerable when wearing thirty pounds of ordnance and Kevlar. Even with years of training, these soldiers have to concentrate simply to keep from passing out. That kind of effort takes focus that's best not wasted on talking.

Not that the Dust Devils have much to talk about in any case. The pre-op briefing they received in Iskenderun has been repeated and reviewed so many times, the mission objectives are as familiar to them as their home phone numbers. These objectives were applied to the general insertion-and-extraction scenario the men have drilled on so often that muscle memory will do more than half the work for them. So long as the hostages are where the intel indicates they are, the Dust Devils think, this op will not be unlike going to the grocery store to extract a quart of milk, a confidence shared by every man in the unit, even the more historically fluent who recall Captain Edward A. Murphy's famous remark "If anything can go wrong, it will."

But then, Captain Murphy was air force, not Special Forces.

◈

The Sikorsky's two rear wheel sets kiss the roof of Ardakan Charity Hospital. A falling leaf makes more noise. Less than two seconds later, five pairs of boots spill out. In one fluid move, Sergeant First Class Robert Gundy takes the point as his men fall into a standard two-by-two cover formation behind him. The deployment is only slightly more coordinated than a ballet you might see on any given night at Lincoln Center.

Gundy shoots a look to his right to find that the roof-access door is precisely where the briefing given by his CO said it would be. With a sharp jab of his finger, he gives Sergeant Bellamy the signal to unlock the door, which Bellamy does with practiced efficiency and the aid of a hydrosulfuric acid mixture that bubbles and hisses through the lock like a destructive Alka-Seltzer. After a few seconds of chemical activity, Bellamy pops the lock as easily as if he were walking down a flight of stairs.

The Dust Devils navigate the utility stairwell, taking the steps two at a time, and arrive at their designated floor. Gundy places a gloved hand on the bar that their briefing indicated would open the door into the intensive care unit, the lone barrier now separating him and his men from the rest of a hospital staffed and occupied mostly by civilians. He hopes he won't have to kill any of them but knows that such hope is futile. The thought gives him pause for maybe half a second.

Gundy pushes the door open to reveal the ICU. The room is both dark and quiet, two things no hospital anywhere in the world is. *Shit's wrong,* Gundy thinks. *Too damn quiet for a hospital. A hospital in the States, at least,* he corrects himself. *No electricity's just SOP for a BFC like Iran.* "Standard operating procedure" for a "backward fucking country." He gives the signal for the men to don their AN/PVS-22 Night Vision goggles.

Gundy taps a button and the view through his goggles shifts from murky blackness to the ethereal green light of infrared. Activating the infrared also toggles the settings on the mini-cam mounted to each man's helmet, so the video feeds transmitted via WiFi back to the Sikorsky are simultaneously shifted to Night Vision. The Sikorsky, in turn, uploads the data — after encrypting it — to a KH-11 satellite flying in geosynchronous orbit directly overhead. It takes approximately 1.68 seconds for the bird to decode, re-encrypt, and relay the video back to Earth, where the data stream can be unencrypted yet again and displayed on an LCD flat-screen. "As good as the feed is, it's not much good," a professorial-looking Paul Langford mutters, scrutinizing the video.

Behind Langford, the Operations Center is abuzz with focused activity. A cadre of a dozen men, all wearing nondescript business suits, dutifully attend to their jobs at workstations consisting of computer displays, ebony keyboards, and touchpad interfaces. There is no reason other than personal habit that Langford is peering at the LCD monitor. The same footage plays on a matrix of flat-screens arrayed on the op-center wall, almost as large as a movie screen. With the overhead fluorescents dimmed, the green-tinted night-vision imagery provides most of the lighting in the room, casting the entire space in a ghostly emerald hue.

Watching the images come in from Gundy's helmet cam, Langford takes all of eight seconds to verbalize his misgivings, which he does in three syllables: "Call it off."

"Misplaced your balls, Paul?" William Rykman, a taciturn man five years Langford's senior, says. He has a military bearing to go with his thick, marine-like physique. A Brillo pad of hair tops a severely angular face that frames eyes as cold as a New England winter. He's got a knack for simultaneously criticizing Langford and challenging his manhood with the most economy of words.

Langford and Rykman aren't on each other's Christmas-card lists, but what they lack in friendship, they make up for in mutual respect. They share a bond that's closer than blood, even closer than marriages lasting for decades. It's the type of bond born of holding another man's intestines inside his torso with your bare hand while concussion grenades explode over both your heads.

"Balls have nothing to do with it, Bill, and you damn well know that. Something's not right here."

"We're not going to get another chance at this," Rykman reminds him in a level voice.

"Jahandar got wise to what we're trying to pull, Bill. It's time to go to plan B."

"Agreed. Soon as we get the men from plan A back."

"Those men are acceptable losses. An entire division of Special Forces troops is *not*." Langford tries to keep his voice as even as Rykman's but can't quite pull it off. At the end of the day, that's what really distinguishes the two men: Langford's heart may have grown cold decades ago, but Rykman's has always been at absolute zero. Assuming he has one to begin with.

"I hope I don't have to remind you that I'm in command here," Rykman replies. "I make the tactical decisions. I define the acceptable level of loss."

"Bill—"

"Green light." Rykman says this not to Langford but to Tyler Donovan, a short but stocky crew cut of a man who had any trace of independent thinking removed by time and training long ago.

Donovan glances over to Rykman's seat, slightly removed from the table, before repeating the "Green light" order into the system that keeps him in real-time communication with the Dust Devils, half a world away.

Those two syllables are all Gundy needs. He flashes the signal to commence the next stage of the operation, extraction: His index and middle fingers in a V-for-victory sign, he points to his goggle-clad eyes and then pulls the fingers down. *Night Vision off.*

Bellamy is up next. He throws a flash-bang grenade down the hospital corridor. The hallway lights up like Times Square on New Year's Eve, blinding and disorienting the armed guards keeping watch at the other end. It takes only three silenced shots — which sound like someone spitting out watermelon seeds — to send the guards to Allah. The corridor now secure, the Devils continue their practiced attack, moving down the hallway and into the room where their pre-op briefing told them the hostages would be.

Gundy switches on his Maglite, tacitly giving his men permission to turn on theirs. The high-wattage flashlight beams cut the room into sections. Light dances around before coming to rest on the faces of six men, all strapped to gurneys. *Faces,* however, would be inaccurate. One of the men has been relieved of his right eye. Another is missing a nose. A third has had his skin peeled off, and an eyelid, which exposes a milky white sphere that glows in the reflected light. The eye, like those of the other men, has no spark of life.

None of the Devils blanch. They've seen worse done to men, and worse still done to women and babies. If they have an emotional response at all, it's not disgust or sorrow, but rage. And the rage is fueled not by the depravity done to their countrymen but by the realization that comes too late: *They've been had.*

◆

Langford and Rykman watch the grainy video images being sent back by the Dust Devils and reach the same conclusion. The six hostages weren't prisoners; they were bait. The epiphany hits hard, like a slap in the face from a betrayed lover.

Langford notices Rykman leering at the gory images. He's made a habit of turning a blind eye to Rykman's tendencies toward the sadistic. Instead, he focuses on the six dead hostages. It's worse than he feared and just as he'd warned them all, but Langford doesn't revel in being proved right. He's not the type of man to celebrate, under any circumstances, the death of even a single American.

Nothing but the static from the Devils' radios prevails, blanketing the Operations Center in a thick hiss that sounds like driving rain. After a few seconds — the kind of seconds that unfold with the speed of hours — Rykman takes a step toward the monitors that still display the video feeds of the mutilated hostages. He continues to stare at them, neither angry nor sad, like an auditor looking over a tax return. "All right," he mutters, his voice barely above a whisper. "Let's get them home."

◆

Gundy hears Donovan convey Rykman's evac order. He raises his index finger in the air and whirls it around three times. "Bug out."

Sergeant Murphy is the first to speak. "We taking them?" He points to the six dead hostages.

"They're Americans."

With that, the Dust Devils start to release the hostages from their confines. The men work quickly, each using his Colt Commander utility knife to slice gurney straps with the precision of a Japanese *teppanyaki* chef. With the hostages dead, there's no need to be gentle about it. There's no time to be either. "Two-six over," Murphy calls out. They're already twenty-six seconds behind their op schedule. Gundy doubles his speed, and as a result, he doesn't see the wire cable that's wrapped around the neck of the hostage he has in his arms. As Gundy lifts the dead man, the upward motion pulls the cable taut. Gundy barely has a second to register the cable's resistance before it flies free of a hidden gas canister with the sound of a cork popping.

Then comes the screaming.

Olive-green gas carpets the entire room within seconds. Gundy takes a breath, and it feels like a colony of army ants lines his throat, each one trying to burrow its way through mucous membranes to freedom.

Murphy is the first to remove his goggles, revealing the cracked, blistering skin around his now-bloodshot eyes. There's a deep, dark recess of his mind that has always been curious about what it feels like to have your face burn off. Now he knows. The agony continues for twenty seconds before he mercifully passes out. Death follows thirty seconds later.

Gundy is next to die. *This can't be fucking happening,* he thinks over and over again as he suffocates. When he finally drops, the thirty pounds of equipment he's carrying makes a resounding smack on the hospital linoleum.

A third Dust Devil, Roger Pruitt, places his SIG Sauer P226 under his jaw and fires a single, self-euthanizing shot.

With Pruitt's death, Bellamy and a fifth Dust Devil, Edwin Hodge, are the last men standing. As the ranking officer, Bellamy should be the one to give the bug-out order, but it's hardly necessary. In any case, he can't speak with the fucking gas choking the life out of him. The two men make their way out of the hospital room and race back to the utility stairwell, where they take the steps two at a time up to the Sikorsky waiting on the roof.

The helo's pilot sees the soldiers and notes they're about three men and six hostages short of the group he's supposed to be lifting off. But Bellamy barks at him, "Abort op! Abort op!," which prompts the pilot to stab a series of buttons that start the copter's twin props and readies them to fly the hell out of Dodge.

◈

In the Op Center, Rykman turns to Donovan. "Cover our tracks."

Langford looks to Rykman, who doesn't meet his gaze.

Even Donovan, who always obeys without question, glances up at Rykman.

"Scorched earth," Rykman confirms.

Donovan types in a string of commands that send a concert of electronic signals into space to be retransmitted back down to the Sikorsky...

◈

It takes only one pound of military-grade M112 C-4 plastic explosive — the same explosive al-Qaeda used to bomb the USS *Cole* in 2000 — to cut a one-inch-thick piece of steel in half. The belly of the Sikorsky is packed with almost thirty pounds of the stuff, needing nothing other than Donovan's signal to ignite it. Within milliseconds, the signal reaches the receiver hidden away in the Sikorsky's bowels and triggers the C-4. The chemical reaction that occurs releases a cornucopia of gases. The nitrogen and carbon oxide storm expands so fast that the force released is the equivalent of a car slamming into a concrete wall at 300 miles per hour.

Bellamy, Hodge, the Sikorsky's pilot, and the Sikorsky are ripped apart in seconds.

The return-trip jet fuel joins the gas and chemical orgy, the whole thing blossoming into a fireball that consumes the upper six floors of the Ardakan Charity Hospital, destroying all evidence of both the Dust Devils and the six hostages they were charged with recovering.

Scorched earth.

"We'll need cover stories for the hostages," Rykman says. "Car accidents, house fires, whatnot."

"What about the op team?" Donovan asks.

"Training exercise."

Without waiting for confirmation from Donovan, without exchanging a glance with Langford, Rykman turns and marches out of the room. He's barely at the door before all thoughts of the Dust Devils, the hostages, and the Sikorsky are expunged from his mind. *There are more pressing matters to deal with.* Langford was right about one thing: His enemies figured out what the hostages, Rykman's assets, were doing in Iran in the first place. As Langford said, it's time for plan B.

Rykman pushes open the steel door and is greeted by a thick blast of humidity. He takes a deep hit, filling his lungs before slowly exhaling in a practiced attempt to clear his mind. He's not troubled by what just happened — no more than an oncologist is troubled by a spot on an x-ray of a patient he's just met — but he wants to give himself one last reprieve, a few more seconds of calm reflection, before pulling the trigger on the decision he made in the elevator ride up from the Op Center.

Rykman takes one look at the nondescript industrial park surrounding him — gray warehouses with gray doors and gray roofs, a monument to the unexceptional — and removes his phone from his pocket. The custom firmware on the phone's touchscreen scans his thumbprint and biometrically confirms it belongs to General William J. Rykman, U.S. Army, retired.

The phone on the other end of the line rings only once before Rykman speaks. "Rykman. Ident code six-niner-alpha." A series of harmonics — three overlapping chimes — indicate acceptance of Rykman's call. Seconds later, a voice drier and more world-weary than Rykman's croaks out a simple question: "Yes?"

Rykman pauses. The encryption needs a second to work its magic, so it's best not to reply too quickly lest he cut the other caller off. In that brief moment, Rykman reflects on the fact that while the man's question — "Yes?" — may be simple, the answer is anything but. The answer is damn complex and nuanced, as all good answers are. But that will be fodder for a different conversation in a secure location swept of any electronic eavesdropping devices. For now, pure naked information will suffice: "Vanguard's dead."

"All of them?"

"All of them."

"Any consideration given to replacing the assets?"

"It took thirteen months to set Vanguard's cover. And the target blew through it anyway."

"We go with plan B, then. Solstice."

"Green light?" Rykman asks, more out of habit than a genuine need to confirm.

"Green light."

The line goes dead. Rykman swallows another gulp of humidity before he makes a new secure call. The voice on the other end is female and unfamiliar. He's fallen behind on his review of the personnel files of his ever-growing staff. Again. He makes a mental note to catch up — tonight, over a glass of Macallan — before acting on his elevator-ride decision. "Send a cleaning crew to eight sixty-three M Street, Georgetown. Langford, Paul."

ONE

Jesus Pena leans back on the metal chair he's sitting on, glances over at his attorney, and then returns his attention to the bandage on his hand. He picks at it, giving it a flick, flick, flick with the nail of his index finger, as if to suggest he's far more interested in whether the bandage will stay on than in how many years of his life he can expect to spend in prison. In addition to the bandage, Jesus wears a bright orange DC DOC jumpsuit. The outfit would have had the effect of making him look nonthreatening, bordering on silly, were the sleeves not rolled up to expose the intricate multicolored tattoos covering both arms. They complement the two additional tattoos in the shape of teardrops under his right eye. The face tats, each the work of a different prison artist, represent two different murders. However, neither homicide is the reason Jesus is sitting in the concrete-floored jailhouse conference room.

Jesus looks up from his bandage again, this time to eye-fuck the prosecutor, Sandy Remz, although he knows the man only as "the DA motherfucker." Remz is sitting across from him at the bolted-to-the-floor metal table. He has the kind of smug look that comes with knowing he has Jesus dead to rights. It's a look Jesus has daydreamed at length about wiping off the DA motherfucker's face from the skin on down ever since first meeting him at his arraignment six months ago. It was at that hearing that the prosecutor argued, with the kind of fire-and-brimstone self-righteousness you'd expect from a southern preacher and not from some 50K-a-year civil servant, that Jesus was a flight risk and should therefore be left to rot in jail until he was convicted. And that, Jesus recalls with venom, is why he's wearing this fucking orange jumpsuit and why he has already served six months for a crime he hasn't yet been convicted of.

Worse still is the fact that Jesus has had to spend those six months in jail instead of prison. Prisons, at least the kind of prisons Jesus is accustomed to, are built to house inmates serving sentences measured in years if not decades, and they have the facilities to meet those needs. Jails, however, are designed for housing misdemeanors, people serving out sentences of 365 days or fewer, and those awaiting trial, like Jesus. As such, their amenities are minimal and their cells small, which makes jail a much deeper circle of hell than the worst of prisons.

"Murder two. Fifteen to thirty," Remz throws out.

"*Man* two," Jesus's state-appointed attorney counters, as if the two men are dickering over a used car. "Seven and a half to fifteen."

Jesus regards his lawyer, a chill enough guy named Alex Garnett. When Jesus first met him, he got up in Garnett's grill. "You my lawyer, you figure out a way to get me off. 'S'not my problem no more," Jesus hissed.

But Alex didn't back down the way most civilians did. He just shrugged his shoulders with the same kind of apathy Jesus prided himself on. "Actually, it *is* your problem, 'cause I'm not the one facing life in prison. You wanna go in for all day, that's cool. I get paid either way, man." It was a show of sack that Jesus could respect.

Remz scoffs theatrically at Alex's offered plea bargain and turns to his partner for confirmation that the public defender is barking up the wrong tree. The partner, whom Jesus has come to think of as "the bitch

DA," is much younger and more attractive than the DA motherfucker. She shakes her pretty little head. Her wholesome expression is contradicted by eyes that are a little more come-hither. She catches Jesus looking at her, not for the first time. He puckers his lips in response. He knows from long experience that she's only pretending it doesn't make her want to vomit as she keeps a dead stare on Jesus's smug face. "Mr. Pena shot a man in cold blood."

"Point of fact," Alex counters, "his running buddy did. This accomplice — a Mr. Luiz Grenados — already pleaded to man one and is currently serving a fifteen-year sentence in one of our finer correctional institutions."

"Mr. Grenados's plea arrangement doesn't interest me," Remz rebuts. "That deal was negotiated by a different — and clearly more accommodating — *assistant* district attorney. More to the point, who fired the fatal bullet is irrelevant due to the application of the felony murder rule."

"*Bonhart* issues," Alex says with a dismissive wave. "I can get past felony murder. Plus, the vic was another gangbanger. So I could go self-defense."

A felony repeater of some years, Jesus has enough experience with the criminal justice system to detect public-defender bullshit, the same way a meth head can tell if the crystal's been cut with too much baking soda. That experience, however, tells him that PD bullshit won't get it done. Not this time. Not with all the evidence, both forensic and ballistic, plus an eyeball witness, to say nothing of Luiz's testimony against him. The bitch DA is pointing out exactly that as Jesus commits to doing something he's not so much daydreamed about but planned. It's a strategy he started formulating shortly after his arrest, on the ride to Central Booking in the squad car with the busted shocks, his hands still cuffed behind his back with the metal bracelets digging into his wrists. Its penultimate step was cutting his right palm on a cell-made shiv this morning. The jail infirmary bandaged it up, but Jesus has kept at the wound enough to prevent a scab from forming. Now, it's oozing just a bit. Just the right amount.

Thanks to the natural selection of the street, most gangbangers, including Jesus, have the bodies and reflexes of at least farm-team-level athletes. That's why it takes only three seconds for him to vault over the metal table, hockey-check aside the DA motherfucker, and get his arms wrapped around the bitch DA. Both prosecutors, completely unaccustomed to dealing directly with any type of violence, are frozen by the sudden display of aggression. All they can manage to do is suck in huge lungfuls of air. This paralysis buys Jesus the half second he needs to rip off the infirmary's bandage, exposing the gash on his palm he's so carefully maintained over the past few hours. Another half a second is all he needs to claw the side of the bitch DA's face with his fingernails. It's a pretty face and it's a damn fucking shame to mess it up like this — it's like keying the side of a brand-new Escalade — but drawing blood is the important element, the critical element, of his plan.

It takes three tries to open the bitch DA's skin because she's so busy crying — Jesus can't believe she's crying already — and the tears have made her cheek slick. Complicating matters further is the fact that she's screaming — hysterically — practically in his goddamn ear. The DA motherfucker is screaming as well, starting with "Get away from her!" and then, perhaps realizing it will take more than that, turning away and yelling, "On the gate! On the gate!" He's not shouting to the door but rather to the guards he hopes are within earshot beyond. If they are, they're ignoring him, because no guards come in.

Jesus grips the female prosecutor tighter and raises his voice. "I'm positive. HIV, hoss. You lemme outta here or I'll do her!" Then, as if more explanation were required, Jesus brings his bloody palm dangerously close to the girl's bleeding face.

"Get your client under control!" Remz screams at Alex. As Jesus's attorney, Alex is clearly the one best suited to bring Jesus under control, but Alex is showing no indication he plans to do anything of the kind.

Instead, he's taking notes on his yellow legal pad and he seems far more interested in whatever it is he's writing than in the well-being of Remz's partner, a fresh-out-of-law-school trainee. *What is her name again?* Alex wonders. Michelle Something-or-other.

"I'll fuck her up!" Jesus yells. "I'll do it! Sure as shit, I'll do it!" His voice is trembling a little now, suggesting he might be just slightly unnerved by the fact that his own lawyer doesn't seem to care he's taken a prosecutor hostage.

"Let her go!" Remz bellows repeatedly over Michelle's sobs. "Let go of her now!"

Jesus's eyes flash back to Alex, who continues his scribbling. To the extent that Jesus had a plan here, it included at least some effort on Alex's part. Specifically, Jesus was counting on Alex, as his attorney, to negotiate for him, to act, in essence, as the good cop to Jesus's bad cop. But Alex does not seem interested in participating. He doesn't even appear to be paying attention. He just writes away, like he's working on a goddamned novel. Finally, without looking up from his pad, Alex remarks, "You're wasting your time here, Jesus." The room goes quiet. Alex continues to scribble on his pad. "I don't know what you were thinking, or if you were thinking *at all,* but there's no way they can let you out of here. Not alive, at any rate. In fact, I figure you got about thirty seconds before two guards burst in." Two guards charge in, right on cue. "Okay, maybe a little less than thirty seconds."

One of the guards' hands is trembling and Alex is certain it's not from the coffee the man consumed during his break. Alex intuits that neither guard has seen any action in his entire correctional-facility career up to this point. This is evidenced by the fact that neither has as yet remembered that he's carrying an OC pepper-spray canister and a PR-24 baton on his hip. Despite having these weapons, the guards can't seem to manage anything other than variations on Remz's ineffectual commands. "On the floor!" is a favorite.

Finally, Alex rises from his seat, the very picture of calm. Jesus's eyes dart to Alex and then to the guards and then all around the room—his street-honed instincts calculating his best chances for pulling this off—before settling back on Alex. "Go ahead and do it, Jesus," Alex says. Silence descends on the room. "Go ahead and do it," Alex repeats. "You might as well. 'Cause whether you infect her or not—and, let's be honest, we don't really *know* that you're infected—whether you do it or not, you've well and truly fucked up your defense. This is kidnapping, Jesus. Plus attempted assault with what I'm going to take your word for is a deadly weapon. And now that the guards are here, we've got two impartial witnesses. My point being"—Alex pauses for effect—"if you're going to do the time, you might as well do the crime. Am I right?"

Jesus's heart is beating so hard that all he can hear is the sound of the blood surging—*whump-whoosh-whump-whoosh*—in his now-throbbing head. His pulse is racing so fast that it feels like blood must be pushing through the gash on his hand in tiny spurts. He looks again to Alex, as if the answer to why Alex is actually arguing in favor of infecting the bitch were written on his cavalier face.

"Except," Alex says slowly, with the suggestion of offered hope, "*except* maybe you don't want to do it." Jesus's trembling eyes lock with Alex's, emboldening Alex to take a cautious step toward his client. And then another. And another. Until he's standing less than a foot away from Jesus. "Maybe you know this girl hasn't done anything to you. Maybe you know that hurting her is wrong. Even in this…this game of ours. Maybe you know it's wrong."

An eternity passes. Michelle's not crying anymore. The room is still.

The locomotive heartbeat in Jesus's ears finally subsides enough for him to hear himself think. He looks at his lawyer, who's nodding slow, silent encouragement…and lowers his bloody hand. With his good hand, he pushes the bitch away from him. The moment he lets her loose, she starts sobbing again for reasons he can't understand, but the issue is made moot by the two guards leaping over the metal table to get at him. The two screws finally remember their batons and set to work on Jesus, literally beating him to the floor. Jesus hears a gunshot-like sound that is actually his kneecap fracturing, setting his leg ablaze with agony.

Alex's voice cuts through the chaos, louder, forceful, and commanding. "Hey!" Alex jabs a finger toward Jesus, now immobilized on the floor and wincing in kneecapped agony. "Cut that shit out. That's my client."

◈

Alex docs his best not to reveal the extent to which the hostage situation has unnerved him as he walks down the long jailhouse corridor. Remz and Michelle are walking beside him. Michelle's eyes are red. She's filled with the conviction that she won't be coming to work tomorrow. In fact, if her silent promises to herself are to be believed, she won't be returning to this particular job ever again. Alex places a hand on her shoulder, feeling for the first time just how small she really is. "You okay?" he asks.

Michelle nods. Alex figures she's silently cursing herself for losing her shit, thinking that he'll tell this story, including the details of how she handled herself, to his fellow PDs, and all hope she ever had of gaining their respect will be lost. Another good reason, he thinks, for her to leave and take the corporate job she should have said yes to in the first place.

Alex turns to Remz. "Back to the case for a second. To be blunt — and I'm sorry about this — but what just happened in there, it puts you in a bit of a jackpot." Remz's eyes go wide. Is Alex really going to talk about Jesus Pena? Now? After what just happened? "Because of what transpired back there, if you and Ms. —" Flailing for her last name, Alex gestures over to Michelle. "If you and Michelle don't recuse yourselves, Jesus has a slam-dunk appeal on prosecutorial bias."

"You've got to be kidding," Remz blurts out.

"Unfortunately, your department is shorthanded these days, and it's gonna take time to bring a new ADA up to speed, which, consequently, would step on Mr. Pena's right to a speedy trial." Alex lets this notion, a legal Hobson's choice, sink in. Remz can either proceed against Pena, knowing all the while that any conviction he wins will be vulnerable to appeal, or hand Pena a virtual acquittal in the form of an unconstitutionally delayed trial. Alex watches, with some enjoyment, as these thoughts play across Remz's face. He sees the prosecutor checking Alex's legal math, probing for holes, not finding any. "You can take this to trial, but I can guarantee you it's gonna be more trouble than it's worth," Alex says.

"What are you thinking?" Remz asks, his tone dripping with acid.

"I'm thinking man two. Eight to sixteen." It's only one year more than his last counter to Remz and half the sentence Remz was trying to get Alex to take, but Alex can tell from Remz's resigned expression that he's got himself a plea bargain.

❖

DC PUBLIC DEFENDER SERVICE
6:20 P.M. EST

Alex looks at his desk in the DCPD bullpen and surveys the remaining items: a stack of legal files, a stapler, a desk blotter, a desk calendar, a desk lamp that hasn't worked properly for months, and a chipped coffee mug filled with half a dozen pens. Everything else that was in or on his desk now resides neatly in the single banker's box at Alex's feet. Alex didn't commit a lot of personal items to his meager workspace over the past two years. He'd always been, as they say, just passing through. Not that this troubles Alex much. At thirty-three, with his own share of personal baggage, he's given himself permission to spend a few more years finding himself and figuring out what he really wants to do with his law degree from New York University. Perhaps next year, he thinks, will be the right time. After all, he'll be facing down the business end of thirty-five.

Probably the only personal item of note in the box is the framed photograph of himself and his fiancée. The photo, taken on vacation a year ago in Costa Rica, is so perfect it almost looks like it came with the frame. Alex's blue eyes look particularly cobalt against the setting sun, and his close-cropped hair lends a distinctive squareness to his jaw. Because he's sitting on the bow of a catamaran, it's hard to tell how tall he is, but the way his fiancée folds her svelte form into his hints at Alex's six-foot-three frame. Her face, framed by long locks of black hair, defies categorization. Indeed, in person, she is capable of such metamorphoses — depending on light, angle, hair up, hair down, and so on — that Alex often wonders if he's marrying a girl who's part chameleon. But the way she looks in this photo, captured in the Costa Rican splendor, most closely matches the picture of her he keeps in his mind's eye.

Alex lifts his banker's box. He's thankful that the office is empty. It means a clean getaway, free of maudlin good-byes and halfhearted *Good lucks*. Just then Paula Jobson, Alex's bureau chief, walks in and blows the promise of a quiet exit all to hell. Of course she's still in the office, long past the hour when five-figure employees should go home. A severe woman of forty-two, Paula doesn't have anyone to go home to. It'd be easy to assume her solitude is the result of the fifteen extra pounds she carries in her waist and thighs, but it could also be due to the hundred-pound chip she carries on her shoulder. As to which came first…well, that's a riddle for the ages.

"Exciting last day," she says.

Alex nods as he discreetly slips his public defenders' office badge into his pocket. "I'm pretty sure," he says, "that Remz will plead out on Jesus Pena. Eight years, out in five."

"Not bad for second-degree murder" is all that Paula, who abhors doling out praise with a fundamentalist's fervor, will give him.

Alex hands her the first file off his stack. "B-and-E. Seventeen-year-old, first offense. DA'll cop to a mis," he says, referring to the breaking-and-entering case he's already plea-bargained on behalf of the client. It took less than a day's worth of badgering and more than his usual amount of charm for Alex to convince the ADA to let the accused plead out to a misdemeanor.

Without further preamble, Alex drops the rest of the files, one by one, into Paula's hands. With each file, he rattles off a different charge. "Rape. Assault. Assault with a deadly. Possession. Possession with intent. Search is bad on this one," he interjects. "Rape. Rape. Agg-battery. Possession. Possession. Possession. Possession."

Paula holds the files in her thick arms. "You know, if two years ago someone told me I'd actually be sad to see you go, I wouldn't have believed it."

Alex tries, without success, to come up with a reply that won't make him vomit.

"Honestly, I'm pretty much screwed without you to help shoulder the load around here," Paula admits.

Alex points to the stack of cases now in Paula's custody. "Bench trials on top." He punctuates this with a smile he hopes will signal an end to both the conversation and his relationship with Paula.

"Truth be told, nobody's more surprised than me. I mean, with you being Simon Garnett's kid…y'know, the whole silver-spoon, to-the-manor-born thing…" she continues. "Well, I guess you couldn't fault me for having low expectations."

"Don't worry about it," Alex manages.

"I guess this new gig's more suited to your pedigree, huh?" she asks, reminding Alex that his new job — his next job — is also on the list of things he'd rather avoid talking about. "The Office of General Counsel. Dad really pulled the right strings this time."

Alex stiffens. "My father hasn't said one word to me since I left Garnett and Lockhart to come work for *you*." Then he adds, without really having to, "I got the OGC job on my own steam."

"Right," Paula says. "I didn't mean to hit a nerve. I hope the new gig suits you, Alex. That's the truth."

"I hope so too, Paula. But if it doesn't, you can bet I'll be back, résumé in hand." He offers a polite smile and heads out of the office without waiting for Paula to respond.

❖

New Hampshire Avenue NW
Washington, DC
7:00 p.m. EST

Alex unlocks the door to his condominium and ambles into the Clive Christian décor. Setting down the banker's box, he's greeted by the sound of running water from the bedroom shower and chatter from the TV.

" — Supreme leader of Iran, Ali Jahandar," the talking head on TV is saying. To the extent Alex has heard of Jahandar, it's been under circumstances such as this: cable-news reports or cocktail-party chatter taken in with only one ear. In this, Alex is not unlike the vast majority of Americans who know very little of Jahandar or the position he holds as supreme leader of Iran. Most Americans think of Iran's government as being like America's, where the position of president is the pinnacle of authority. But in Iran, the president is outranked politically, religiously, and militarily by the supreme leader.

The graphic on the TV shifts from a file photograph of Jahandar to the black-and-yellow oval seal of the U.S. Army Special Operations Command. The anchor shuffles some papers and moves on to the next story of the evening: "Five Special Forces soldiers died yesterday in a training exercise…"

Something on the floor captures Alex's attention. A red ribbon. Long. Starting in the living room, where Alex is watching television, and disappearing underneath the closed bedroom door. Behind it, the sound of a running shower continues unabated.

Alex smiles. He employed a very similar trick during their weekend away in the Hamptons. It was Grace on Alex's side of the ribbon then, with the other end tied to a small box containing an engagement ring. And now here Grace is, ripping off his idea—well, co-opting it, at least—a mere six months later. Alex smiles. *What happened to originality?*

He opens the bedroom door to find that the ribbon terminates not at an engagement ring or a rose-petal-festooned bed but at his Armani tuxedo. And on top of that, a jewelry box similar to, though larger than, the one that contained Grace's engagement ring. "You can't propose to me, honey," Alex calls out over the shower. "I've already proposed to you, remember? Besides, it's not supposed to work that way."

Once again, the only reply is the shower, so he opens the box resting on the tuxedo. Inside: a gorgeous metal watch. It has heft to it. Substantial. A man's watch. A man of means' watch. A Krug Baümen, if Alex is reading that correctly. Smiling, Alex removes it for closer inspection. His fingers detect a roughness breaking up the otherwise smooth metallic back, and he flips the watch over to reveal an inscription:

CONGRATULATIONS ON YOUR LAST DAY
GOOD LUCK ON YOUR FIRST
I'M IN THE SHOWER
LOVE, GRACE

Noting the watch's claim to water resistance to a depth of thirty meters, Alex strips off his old watch and replaces it with the new Krug Baümen. As he does, he spots a card of some kind sticking out from under the satin lapel of his tux. He snatches it up, feeling the thick stock and letterpress embossing of an invitation.

G & L

Please Join Us to Celebrate the 70th Birthday of Simon Garnett,
Esq.
MAKOTO RESTAURANT
4822 MacArthur Boulevard NW
Washington, DC 20007
November 6 at 8:00 p.m.
Please RSVP to lockhartasst@garnettlockhart.com

Alex tears the invitation neatly in two. He eyes the bathroom door, with the shower running behind it, and his fiancée, the love of his life, standing naked in the warm water. As he undoes his tie, heading for the bathroom and all that it promises, he tries to force thoughts of his father, his father's party, and Grace's obvious expectations that they'll attend from his mind. Alex has never fully understood Grace's fetish — his term — for trying to reconcile Alex and his father. There's nothing, he's explained more times than he cares to think about, to reconcile. The relationship has simply atrophied.

Alex shakes his head. Simon Garnett will have no place in what the next forty-five minutes will bring…

TWO

The Potomac River passes under Alex's Lexus ES 350 as it shoots over the Theodore Roosevelt Memorial Bridge that joins Washington, DC, with Virginia. He drives, pumped for his first day at a new job, with his MP3 player blasting. Bruce Springsteen's "Thunder Road." A good first-day-of-work-in-a-new-job song if ever there was one.

The northbound section of the George Washington Memorial Parkway is, somehow, always free of traffic, so within ten minutes he's turning onto Route 123, where signs begin to appear: George Bush Center for Intelligence. United States Government Property. Authorized Persons Only. After passing these, he stops at a traffic light before making a right turn into the main entrance of the Central Intelligence Agency. Yet another sign warns, No Cameras or Video Equipment Permitted on Premises. The exception to this rule is the video camera and accompanying monitor that greet Alex at the gate.

"Alex Garnett," he tells the security guard he sees on the video monitor. "I'm starting today in the Office of General Counsel."

"Social Security number?" the guard asks. Alex provides it. There's a short pause before the guard instructs, "Pull up to the right of the building and show your ID."

The gate blocking Alex's Lexus swings up and he drives forward to the small security building. *This* gate is manned by an actual guard who exits the security building and approaches Alex's open window. Alex provides his driver's license as instructed. "Wait here," the guard says.

As Alex waits, he looks around, taking notice of the several security guards walking the grounds. Each is armed with an M4 carbine assault rifle. They carry the weapons almost casually, as if the guns weren't capable of firing up to 950 deadly rounds per minute. Redwoods blanket the area in an attempt to obscure a towering fence, well above ten feet high, and conceal dozens of CCTV security cameras. In his two years as a public defender, Alex has spent more than his fair share of time in secure facilities like jails, prisons, and courthouses, not to mention a federal building or two. None of those places, however, made Alex feel the way he does now. It's an almost electric sensation, a feeling so deep it can be described only as primal: *This is the safest, most secure place on Earth. No one can touch you here. If anyone tries, we'll see. We see everything.*

The guard returns with Alex's license and a red VISITOR badge. "Wear this at all times. Drive ahead and park in any available lot. You're gonna enter through the New Headquarters Building. Look for a white water tower. It's close to the NHB entrance."

Alex nods his thanks and gives a polite wave. As he drives onto the grounds, he passes a nondescript marker indicating the nonsecurity entrance. The *real* entrance. It sits to his left, a few feet from the outbound lane, near a walkway leading to a small courtyard framed by two wooden benches that bookend a three-foot-tall wall of carved Dakota mahogany granite. Inscribed in the granite is a simple message:

In Remembrance of Ultimate Dedication to Mission
Shown by Officers of the Central Intelligence Agency
Whose Lives Have Been Taken or Forever Changed by Events at
Home and Abroad
DEDICATO PAR AEVUM
May 2002

As Alex drives, he begins to understand why the guard told him to park in "any available lot": There aren't any. Half of the Agency's workforce live way out in western Virginia and are in by six to beat the morning traffic. Consequently, he finds parking only in the outer-perimeter purple lot.

It's a ten-minute walk to the New Headquarters Building. The headquarters of the Central Intelligence Agency sit on 258 acres that call to mind a college campus, not the nerve center of the world's most clandestine organization. As Alex makes his way across the grounds, he passes a section of the Berlin Wall, which has been repurposed as a kind of monument. He notes with some interest that the western side of the wall is covered in graffiti while the eastern — Communist — side is whitewashed and unremarkable.

His path takes him past the Old Headquarters Building. He walks only a few feet away from the structure's cornerstone. The term *cornerstone,* however, is misleading. *Cornerbox* might be more accurate, given that it's actually hollow. But an even more correct designation would be *time capsule.* Inside the box are numerous key documents and memoranda related to the establishment of the CIA, including all of the executive orders concerning the management of CIA operations before the commencement of the OHB's construction in 1959. This collection includes Executive Order 9621, titled "Termination of the Office of Strategic Services and Disposition of Its Functions." It's a document few Americans have ever heard of, but it lays the foundation for the corruption of American government as securely as the cornerstone lays the foundation for the OHB.

◆

Alex walks into the New Headquarters Building and is surprised not to find the CIA seal inlaid on the lobby floor. Nor can he find the Memorial Wall, with its 107 commemorative stars set in marble. He'd been looking forward to seeing both — the most well-known images of the CIA's interiors. But Hollywood takes its inspiration from the décor of the *Old* Headquarters Building. Alex walks up to the closest guard station and introduces himself to the green-jacketed man on duty. "Hi. I'm Alex Garnett. I'm supposed to be starting today in the OGC's office."

"It's just OGC," says the man, whose name is Ciampa, according to his Agency ID. "The *O* stands for *Office*. So you just said the 'Office of General Counsel's office.' It's like saying 'HIV virus,' y'know?"

"Or 'CIA agency'?"

"Exactly," Ciampa says, as he finds Alex's name on his computer. "Yup. You're supposed to go to three B twenty-two NHB. That's vault twenty-two in the B corridor on the third floor of this building. You're reporting to Leah Doyle. You know her?"

"She was in one of my screening interviews."

"Great. Because you've got a red badge, I've got to have someone escort you." Ciampa turns and waves over one of the other men in green jackets standing nearby. "He'll take you where you need to go. At some point today, you're gonna have to head over to the Badge Office to get your permanent badge. The Badge Office is right off the Old Headquarters Building entrance."

"Thanks."

"You have a good one, Mr. Garnett."

Alex's chaperone leads him deeper into the building. They pass a sixty-something man who looks like he just stepped off Air Force One.

"Garnett. Alex Garnett?" the ruddy-faced man asks. "I thought I read something about you starting today." Alex's blank expression conveys he has no idea who the man is. "General Counsel Arthur Bryson."

General Counsel. Alex blanches a little. Bryson is the man whose office he's working for now. Alex swallows, then accepts Bryson's offered hand and shakes it firmly. "Alex Garnett," he says. "It's a pleasure to be working for you, sir."

"We're happy to have you. Particularly with your experience. We don't get many refugees from the public defenders' office around here."

"Well, I appreciate the opportunity."

"It's the least I could do for Simon Garnett's boy." Bryson's warm grin grows to a legitimate smile. *You didn't think you got this job on your own steam, did you?* "Give your father my best, Alex," Bryson says and continues down the hall.

◆

Accounts and opinions differ on the question of when Leah Doyle first showed up on the CIA's recruitment radar. She graduated summa cum laude from Stanford Law and promptly went to clerk for Supreme Court Justice Ruth Bader Ginsburg. The high point of Leah's clerkship was her authorship of Ginsburg's majority opinion in *Olmstead v. L.C.,* a landmark case in which the Court ruled that mental illness is a form of disability and, therefore, is covered under the Americans with Disabilities Act. Initially, people believed it was Leah's work on *Olmstead* that drew the CIA's attention to her, but in the ten years Leah's worked at the CIA, she's watched that story grow into the belief that the CIA had targeted Leah for recruitment the moment she scored a perfect 180 on her Law School Admission Test as an undergrad at Harvard University.

Like much of CIA lore, neither story is true (although Leah did, in fact, go to Harvard and did, in fact, score a 180 on her LSAT). In reality, Leah became intrigued by the OGC when she saw Arthur Bryson argue the CIA's case in *El-Masri v. Tenet,* a suit brought by Khaled El-Masri, a German citizen who had the misfortune to share the exact same name as a member of al-Qaeda's Hamburg cell, a coincidence that resulted in his being abducted and transported to the Salt Pit, a covert CIA prison in Afghanistan. Bryson was able to get the case dismissed by relying on the rarely cited precedent of state-secret privilege, and he still managed to preserve the plaintiff's dignity. Leah was so impressed by the legal and ethical balancing act—*victory with grace* was how she'd thought of it at the time—that she became determined to work for the man who had pulled it off. It just so happened that he worked for the CIA.

The fact that the legend of Leah's recruitment into the CIA has grown in the telling doesn't surprise Leah in the slightest. The CIA has always cultivated its own mythology like a garden. When Allen Dulles, the Agency's fifth director of Central Intelligence, an attorney and the first civilian to hold the post of DCIA, was asked by reporters what was in the OHB's cornerstone, Dulles replied with a wink, "It's a secret." Leah has followed Dulles's lead, responding to any questions about the origins of her hiring with a curt yet always provocative "No comment" or a more enticing "I can't talk about it." (She'd always despised the worn "I'd tell you but I'd have to kill you" cliché.)

Alex Garnett doesn't seem curious about Leah's history with the Agency, and that suits her just fine. She's content to merely give him his introductory tour of the General Counsel's offices.

"The Office of General Counsel—we tend to shorthand it as the OGC—has a group of attorneys inside each of the Agency's area divisions and centers of the NCS. That's National Clandestine Service."

"You guys like your acronyms."

Leah ignores him. "We assign attorneys to departments like the Near East Division or the Counterterrorism Center. Those attorneys work only on issues specific to their divisions or centers. But it's highly unlikely that we'll be putting you in one."

"Why's that?"

"You don't have any operational background," Leah answers. "Instead, you'll be working within the OGC proper. There are four divisions: Ops and Intel, Ad Law and Ethics, Logistics and Procurement, and, of course, Litigation. You'll start off in Ops and Intel and rotate through divisions, one per quarter. That'll give you a chance to see each division and give each division a chance to evaluate you. Then we'll sit down with General Counsel Bryson and figure out the best fit."

"Is this typical? The whole rotation thing?"

"Are you asking because you think you're being singled out for special treatment?" Leah says, her voice edged with accusation. Alex doesn't take the bait. "If so, you have either a persecution complex or an arrogant sense of entitlement."

"I honestly don't see any reason I couldn't have both." *This* joke earns a slight smile. "I'm guessing my relationship with my father came up in the background check you guys did on me."

"Once or twice," Leah says, but what she really means is *very often*.

"I asked out of curiosity," he assures her. "I mean, it can't be easy, rotating that many lawyers through every department." He gestures to the large office area. It's arranged like a newspaper's bullpen, a sea of desks partitioned by sleek metal and glass dividers. Black placards with white lettering hang from the ceiling, indicating the four divisions Leah laid out: OPERATIONS AND INTELLIGENCE, ADMINISTRATION LAW AND ETHICS, LOGISTICS AND PROCUREMENT, and LITIGATION.

"We have about a hundred attorneys. And that's just in the main office. Each one undergoes a thorough interview process, background check, and psychological evaluation. That's a lot of effort to expend to not place someone in the right department at the end of the day. The job of the OGC is to provide the rest of the Agency with all manner of legal advice and support. This ranges from counterintelligence to counternarcotics, from civil litigation to criminal litigation, and from foreign intelligence to intellectual property." Alex knows all this from his application process, but he lets her continue. "So, for example, if one of our case officers uses advanced interrogation techniques in the questioning of, say, a suspected member of al-Qaeda, he or she does so under guidelines devised and overseen by the OGC.

"This morning's particular problem," she continues, "concerns a law-suit filed by the Vietnam Veterans of America. Have you read about it?"

Alex shakes his head. "That's not classified?"

"Not at all. Public filing. Therefore, public record. The VVA is accus-ing the Agency of exposing soldiers to a variety of psychotropic drugs in the course of the MKULTRA program."

"I thought MKULTRA was, like, an urban myth," Alex says.

"Oh, no, it was quite real. We've been dealing with the legal fallout for decades now, this case being only the most recent example. For the past year and a half, we've been trading discovery and holding deposi-tions and we're finally at the point where it looks like we can hit them with a Rule Twenty-Six motion. Am I boring you, Mr. Garnett?"

Leah asks because Alex appears preoccupied by the sight of a guy — a kid, actually, from the looks of him — fidgeting nervously at a com-puter stationed in the bullpen. " 'For the past year and a half, we've been trading discovery and holding depositions and we're finally at the point where it looks like we can hit them with a Rule Twenty-Six motion,' " Alex parrots back, syllable for syllable. "You then asked if you were bor-ing me. Which you're not. By the way, I wouldn't bother with a summary judgment motion under Rule Twenty-Six."

"You seem a little preoccupied with one of our computer techs," she says, nodding in the fidgety kid's direction.

"He looks kind of young to be working for the CIA."

"He's nineteen. And while currently the youngest person employed by the Agency, he's not the youngest in its history."

Alex struggles to put a name to the face.

"It's possible he was in the news at some point. We recruited him a year ago and already his talents rival anyone's at the Agency, even the cybersavants in the DS and T," she says, referring to the Agency's Direc-torate of Science and Technology. "According to those guys, the only person on the planet who can match Gerald's skill is Free Radical."

"Excuse me?"

"Free Radical, the twelve-year-old Ukrainian hacker. We don't know his real name. That's how good he is. But Gerald's better."

It clicks for Alex. "Gerald Jankovick," he says triumphantly.

"You know him?"

"Yeah." And in an eye blink, Alex is ten feet away, closing in fast on Gerald. "Hey, Gerald!"

Gerald, who's tightly wound even when medicated, nearly jumps out of his skin. "Jesus!" the nineteen-year-old shouts, turning it into a two-word sentence—*Jee-zus*—and breaking the quiet hum of the office. People look up from their desks and workstations, clock that it's just Gerald—his anxious outbursts are already familiar occurrences—and return to their work.

Gerald glares past Alex to Leah. "I thought I told you I need that kinda scare-the-crap-out-of-me shit kept to a minimum."

"Relax, Mr. Jankovick."

"I would except I *can't*. I *told* you. I have a psychiatric condition. Diagnosed."

"Generalized anxiety disorder, if I'm remembering right," Alex offers. "I represented Gerald in a little something when I was at my father's firm."

"Small world," Leah notes dryly.

"It was back when I was at school," Gerald explains. "Can you believe I could do anything that would merit the involvement of an attorney?"

"Yes, Gerald, I can."

Gerald shrugs. *Guilty as charged.* "The principal just didn't have any kind of sense of humor, is what it was."

"Yeah, well, I'm not all that sure humor should reasonably have been expected after you hacked every machine in the school that had an Internet connection and made 'em all start displaying porn," Alex observes.

"*Free* porn," Gerald corrects. "And you got me off with some First Amendment free-speech bullshit." Gerald smiles, savoring the memory. It had been impressive, watching Alex in the principal's office, Gerald dutifully sandwiched between his parents, dressed up for the occasion in a sports jacket and tie, as Alex promised that if the school expelled Gerald for exercising what was, after a fashion, a constitutional right, then he would rally the ACLU to dump more difficulties and scrutiny on the school than all the free pornography in the world could bring.

Alex can feel the lack of interest rippling off Leah like heat off asphalt, so he looks for a graceful exit. "It's good seeing you. Leah and I have to get back to work."

"You're working here? *Here?*"

"Wonders never cease. I'll see you around."

"Cool. Peace out," he adds in an attempt to sound street that's so pathetic it borders on charming.

"Like you said, it's a small world," Alex remarks as they walk away.

"Actually, it's an extremely *large* world. That's why the intelligence community works so hard to make it small. You know what does that? Information."

"I think you lost me."

"Our business is information. Data. Research. We do our homework. Everyone is a subject of investigation. Consequently, there are no coincidences."

Alex stops and turns to Leah, genuinely surprised. "You knew I represented Gerald."

"It's what got you on our radar. Like I said, there are no coincidences in this line of work. We'd been looking at Gerald and you came along as a kind of unexpected bonus."

"You consider me a bonus," Alex muses.

"Provisionally. Speaking of which, before you spotted Gerald, we were discussing the VVA case."

"Yeah. I think I was telling you that summary judgment is a waste of time."

"Trying to get the case against us kicked is a waste of time?"

"No judge is going to grant summary judgment here. The Vietnam

Veterans Association litigating against the CIA. The case may not be national news yet, but it absolutely will be the second a judge hands down a ruling on your motion. Under those circumstances, why would any judge smart enough to make it to the bench in the first place rule against war veterans? Why would he expose himself to public scrutiny like that? Public scrutiny," he adds, "*and* appeal. There's zero upside for the judge. None whatsoever." This last part he punctuates with a dismissive shake of his head. "Instead, what you do is, you let the case go forward, right up to jury selection. Then you hit 'em."

"Hit them with what, if not summary judgment?"

"Motion *in limine*. All your grounds for summary judgment, you convert into reasons to exclude evidence. Now you're asking a judge to make an *evidentiary* ruling. That gives him political cover. He grants the motion…"

"And I've limited the evidence the plaintiffs can use at trial."

"Severely. You let 'em keep their fire, but you take away their oxygen. And with all that evidence excluded, the trial becomes either impossible or extremely difficult for the plaintiffs to prove their case. Either way…"

"They're inclined to settle."

"At a substantially reduced amount."

Leah smiles. "Very smart. Come with me."

"Where to?" Alex asks, thinking he's just won himself a place on the VVA/MKULTRA trial team.

"I want you to sit with a guy." She points to a glass-enclosed conference room. Inside, Alex notes, there's a bespectacled man sitting at a polished oak table looking at an open laptop; he has the kind of distinguished air typically found only in Oxford professors. "One of our staff psychologists."

The only thing less palatable to Alex than talking to a psychologist is talking to a CIA psychologist. He gave in to the requirement during the recruitment process only because he'd been told, in no uncertain terms, that it was a deal-breaker. The fact that Alex had been willing to spend time telling an absolute stranger things that he hadn't even shared with Grace spoke volumes about just how badly he wanted this job. But now that he has it, he feels no inclination to catalog his sexual fantasies, personal insecurities, hopes, dreams, and nightmares for another stranger with a psychology degree.

"Actually," Alex demurs, "I already had a psych eval as part of my SBI."

"The standard background investigation is just that." Leah smirks. "Standard. Working in this office requires you to have a more thorough evaluation."

"Why do I get the feeling that only the sons of White House royalty get the special treatment?" Leah doesn't answer. "I went to law school. If I wanted to jump through hoops, I'd have joined the circus."

Leah nods. Alex is about to ask what's next when she stops him with five very unexpected words: "Hope you enjoyed the shower."

Alex actually takes a step back, he's so startled. He wonders if he heard her correctly. Sensing this, she adds, "Nice watch." She's pointing to the new Krug Baümen on his wrist. "From your fiancée, right?" She steps forward, cutting the distance between them to inches. "This *is* the NFL. Last week, the OGC dealt with a coup in Jordan, an assassination in Belgrade, and the arrest of five terrorist cells in Karachi. I report to the general counsel, who reports to the DCIA, who reports to the president of the United States of America. So when I tell you I want you to sit with a guy, it's not a hoop. It's your cue to say, 'Where's the chair?'"

THREE

DR. DAVIS Fordes sits across from Alex, resting his hands—palms up—on the table and exuding a practiced warmth that Alex's SBI interrogator didn't possess. Alex notes that the man is taking pains to avoid any body language that could seem judgmental (a hand on the chin) or guarded (arms folded over his chest) or skeptical (finger on the nose). Much to his surprise, Alex finds the approach very effective. He's breezed through the questions of the last two hours with greater ease than he had expected. Or perhaps he's just growing accustomed to answering questions about masturbation.

Ultimately, however, the subject comes up, as it inevitably must: "Did you respect your father?" the psychologist asks.

Alex shrugs with practiced indifference. "He was chief of staff to Bush One and solicitor general under Clinton. It's kind of hard not to respect a man like that."

"But you've tried. Tried not to, I mean." Offered without a hint of judgment. On the contrary, Dr. Fordes sounds like a co-conspirator sharing a dark secret.

"I didn't say that. I respect my father."

"But?" Fordes doesn't give Alex any more rope than that one syllable. *But?*

"I'm not sure what you're asking me."

"Your father cast a pretty big shadow."

"Not really," Alex says with another shrug.

"Your father was a very powerful man. He still is, in fact."

Alex doesn't offer anything more in response than "That's true." He may be the fish here, but that doesn't mean he can't struggle against the line a little.

"So, growing up, you didn't feel any pressure?"

"Pressure to do what?"

"To individuate yourself. To step out of your father's shadow, be your own man."

"I don't think so. I hadn't really thought about it."

"It's Oedipal."

"I thought Oedipal issues were strictly mommy-related."

"On the contrary. Oedipus killed his father, remember? Surely, there's no greater act of individuation of son from father than *that*."

"Well, killing my father wasn't an option," Alex quips. "For one thing, there was a lot of Secret Service around him when he was White House chief of staff."

The psychologist nods at that, amused. "Besides — barring patricide — true distinction can come only from playing on an even field. Isn't that why you became a lawyer?"

"I became a lawyer because I found it interesting."

"And what *I* find interesting is that you chose to work in the same field where your father initially distinguished himself. In fact, you chose not only the same field but the same *specialty* — litigation."

"Maybe it wasn't really a choice. Maybe me becoming a litigator wasn't psychology at all. Maybe it was genetics. Like father, y'know, like son."

"So you're your father's son."

"Sounds like I didn't 'individuate' myself very well, then, did I?"

"I couldn't say one way or the other," Fordes says, shifting gears. "What type of parent was your father?"

"What do you mean?"

Fordes throws out possible answers like a croupier dealing cards. "Strict? Controlling? Lax? Cold? Affectionate?"

"He was focused on his work most of the time."

"Most of the time," Fordes repeats. "Not *all* of the time." Alex nods. "So, what about the times he *wasn't* at work? What type of father was he when he was home? With you?"

"Demanding." Alex's defenses must be weakening, because the word is out of his mouth before he even realizes it.

"In what sense?"

Alex snorts back laughter. "In every sense." Fordes makes a note on his computer. "This isn't an area I'm comfortable talking about."

"Alex, you don't have to be uncomfortable. I know it may not feel like it, but you're among friends here. I can virtually guarantee you that there's nothing you can tell me about your father that would disqualify you from working for the CIA."

"Then what's the point of this little exercise?"

"For you to understand yourself better. To understand what drives you. Perhaps that understanding will make you a better attorney." The psychologist waves at the air. "You're driven to gain the respect of a man you've admitted you don't respect. It's a bit of a paradox."

"I said I *did* respect him."

"And your conviction was extremely persuasive." Fordes's sarcasm is palpable.

"It was a complex relationship." This is all the ground Alex will cede.

"Tell me about it."

Alex considers for a few seconds. "Before my mother died, it was just the three of us, me and my parents. Everything revolved around him."

"How so?"

"My father is all about my father. He had an edge. And a temper."

"Had," Fordes repeats. "Past tense?"

"After I went off to college he…mellowed. I think he's tried to have a closer relationship with me."

"Which you've denied him."

"You make it sound petty."

"Oh, it's not," Fordes assures him. "Your father damaged his relationship with you when you were a child. It's not surprising that you'd deny him a relationship once you departed the family home and became an adult." Fordes spreads his hands as if to suggest a lack of judgment.

"All this is really going to help with my job at the Agency?"

"I hate the term *emotional baggage*," Fordes says. "It sounds like magazine psychology. But it's a useful visual metaphor." He swipes away the digression with a wave of his hand. "At any rate, everyone has emotional baggage. It's part of the human condition. Working for the Office of General Counsel for the Central Intelligence Agency, you find yourself at the nexus of two key components of the human condition: secrets and justice." Fordes leans back and shrugs, as if all of this is obvious. "You're a lawyer for spies, Alex. You'll be placed in and called upon to evaluate some very unique circumstances. It's helpful for Ms. Doyle and your other superiors to have a sense as to how you'll respond — emotionally, psychologically — to these circumstances."

"And how do you think I'll respond?"

Fordes just grins. He'll never tell.

◆

GEORGETOWN, WASHINGTON, DC
8:00 P.M. EST

Paul Langford didn't go home last night. Instead, he'd checked himself into a room at L'Enfant Plaza Hotel under one of the several aliases he maintains. Yesterday, these precautions seemed more than prudent. It wasn't so much that his exchange — actually, Langford would have called it a dustup — with Rykman had been tense. The two men have decades of history, and the last two have been spent shouldering the weight of the world. Dustups were to be expected, were even necessary. They offered the opportunity for both men to let off a little steam. But yesterday's disagreement had occurred in front of an audience, and, worse, it had made Rykman look bad. In his rational mind, Langford doubted Rykman would send a cleaning crew for him purely out of spite, but his less rational, more animal instincts — instincts honed to a knife-edge by years of working in the military and intelligence communities — had prevailed. But the fuel of instinct is adrenaline, and adrenaline's effects, while powerful, are temporary. So Langford checked out of L'Enfant. And now he's disarming his condo's security system, chiding himself for being so fucking paranoid.

Who was it who said, "Just because you're paranoid doesn't mean they're not out to get you"? Langford wonders. *Kissinger? I think it might've been Kissinger…*

He enters his renovated Georgetown brownstone to find it stripped clean. The handwoven afghan rug he bought in Iraq is gone, exposing the floor of polished cherry. The bookshelves stuffed with tomes on foreign policy and the works of Dan Brown and Tom Clancy are missing. The Samsung LCD wide-screen that hung over the mantel is nowhere to be found. Even the television's metallic wall mount is gone, the hole in the drywall patched up expertly. The apartment didn't look this pristine the day its construction was completed. To say the effect is disconcerting would be an understatement. It produces a feeling of nausea that even Langford's practiced stoicism can't overcome.

He immediately reaches into his suit jacket, presses his palm against the reassuringly cold grip of his Beretta 92SB 9mm. Then the adrenaline kicks in. Langford wheels around to the front door, less than seven feet away. His actions are the product of pure instinct, much like the previous night's hotel stay. Were he given the opportunity, Langford would gladly trade his Beretta to be back in that hotel right now, just to have the chance to —

The world goes cold and black with all the suddenness of a power failure.

◆

The first thing Langford feels when he comes to are the straps. They press into his wrists and ankles, dig deep channels in his flesh. There's another restraint around his neck that makes it impossible for him to lift his head and get a better look at his surroundings. Not that he needs to. He knows enough about the cleaning crew's debriefing assets to recognize what's going on. He's been in several such debriefings, but this is his first time as the individual in the chair. It closely resembles the kind of chair you'd see in a dentist's office. In fact, the entire space — a small room no larger than the interior of a moving van — has a clinical look to it, right down to the intravenous drip that snakes its way into Langford's arm. It's hard to tell what has Langford's heart racing right now: self-supplied adrenaline or the IV's cornucopia of amphetamines. The purpose of this little cocktail is to keep the subject from passing out from severe pain. Immobilized by the leather restraints, he focuses his efforts on using the parts of his body he *can* move: his eyes. They dart around furtively, like anxious spiders, as Langford tries to seek Rykman out. He knows he's there. Rykman wouldn't miss witnessing his debriefing, and if Langford can just talk to him, make a human appeal, *explain* things, this would all be over. Yes, he could salvage this. It's stupid to throw away years of productive collaboration over a small difference of opinion. A minuscule one, really. He just needs to have the opportunity to *explain* that, to look Rykman in the eye, soldier to soldier, man to man, friend to —

Then he sees the video camera perched in the upper right corner of the room. It might as well be screaming at Langford that there will be no human appeal. Rykman's not coming. Whether he doesn't want to risk letting sentimentality turn to mercy, or whether Langford simply isn't worth the effort to him, Langford can't be sure. The only thing he *is* sure of is that Rykman will be watching the tape tonight, probably adding it to his personal collection. Goddamn if that fucking video camera, silently staring at Langford like a fucking Cyclops, doesn't confirm his long-held suspicion that William Joseph Rykman, U.S. Army, retired, is one truly deranged sadistic motherfucker. And the acknowledgment of what Rykman is — not a soldier, not a colleague, not a friend, but a monster on the order of Mengele — makes a dam burst in Langford's mind. It fuels a rage that shakes his body with such force that the dentist chair actually moves, as if his anger might provide the fuel necessary to rip his body from its confines. The leather straps moan in protest — though the sounds may be Langford's, he really can't be sure — but they hold. He feels a slickness on his wrists where blood seeps from his skin, moistening the leather straps. But his anger passes like a cloud, revealing a blue sky of recognition that this cold and narrow room, this clinical space, is the last place he'll ever see.

Whoever's watching the feed from the video camera must have seen Langford surrender, because that's when the man in scrubs walks in. Although the man is wearing a surgical mask, Langford recognizes Tyler Donovan's eyes. And although Langford's rational mind knows there's no point to pleading, rationality has long since left him. "Donovan, please —"

"I need to debrief you, Paul," he says. "It's standard operating procedure. Nothing personal."

"Tyler, we —"

"It's necessary to make sure you haven't told anyone about the Overwatch," Tyler says, his voice as cold and austere as the room they're in. Langford's eyes follow Donovan's latex-gloved hand to a tray containing a selection of gleaming metallic instruments. Each one looks more medieval than the next. Forceps, wire cutters, and a scalpel are the only tools he can recognize. His mind races to come up with something that will get Donovan to reconsider. But getting Donovan to disobey an order from Rykman is like trying to convince the pope to renounce Jesus. He finally gives up his planning and strategizing and trades all his hopes for the prayer that Donovan's work will be quick.

"Let's begin," Donovan says, and selects the wire cutters from the metal tray.

FOUR

————

CIA, New Headquarters Building
8:24 a.m. EDT

Funny how it never gets old, Alex thinks as his blue keycard — referred to in the Agency as a badge — gets him through security at the New Headquarters Building. He's been working at the Agency for six months now, gone through this specific security checkpoint multiple times, and he still gets a charge from entering the headquarters of the CIA. He also never fails to think of the NHB's entrance as resembling an airport security line. All belongings need to be passed through one of two x-ray machines and everyone — blue badge or not — is required to enter through the metal detectors. But somehow all the security procedures combine to make the feeling more real: Alex Garnett works for the Central Intelligence Agency.

Alex takes his Johnston & Murphy leather messenger bag off the x-ray machine's treadmill and says to one of the green jackets — as the security guards are known, due to the dark green sports coats they wear — "So did they pay up yet?"

The man shakes his head. "Not yet."

The green jacket's name is Tom Ciampa and this exchange has been repeated as faithfully as a catechism between the two men for some time. About two years ago, Ciampa's wife was in a car accident that shattered her hip. Her convalescence took several agonizing months, during which she was unable to work at her job as a librarian. That was income that Ciampa and his wife depended on to support their three children. Fortunately, they had insurance for that sort of thing. The CIA was good about benefits and Ciampa believed in supplementing them when it came to important things like insurance. However, after filling out all the right forms, answering all the right questions, and providing all the right documentation, Ciampa couldn't get the insurance company to pay what it owed. Ciampa was long past the point of knowing what bullshit excuse the company was now offering. The only thing he knew, all that he *understood,* was that he'd done his part, he'd paid all the premiums and jumped through all the bureaucratic hoops, and now the insurance company was failing to live up to its end of the bargain. It was a mugging, pure and simple — or, perhaps, more accurately, a con job. Either way, after a year and a half of haranguing without success, Ciampa would have marched into the insurance company's fancy DC offices with his Agency-issued Glock 20 if he thought it would do any good.

Three months ago, Alex happened to catch Ciampa after he'd gotten off a particularly vexing call with one of the claim Nazis, as he referred to them. Ciampa's poker face was pretty good, but Alex saw the genuine distress beneath. Perhaps Alex was the only one who saw through Ciampa's façade, or maybe he was just the only one who cared to ask if Ciampa was all right. Either way, it was the first bit of luck Ciampa and his wife had had since that Camry T-boned her.

Since then, Alex has been navigating Ciampa through the insurance company's maze of bureaucracy. "So did they pay up yet?" has become the opening volley in a humorous call-and-response. Ciampa usually replies with the latest update, often a variation on "left a message." But today's a little different. Today, after Ciampa says, "Not yet," his polite, professional smile is a little wider.

"Yesterday was a good day, Mr. Garnett," he explains. "I made it through voice-mail hell to speak to an actual live person."

"You never know, Tom. Those automated call centers are getting pretty sophisticated. You might've still been talking to a computer."

"That's a fact," Ciampa admits. "When I finally got a human voice, I was so surprised, I almost didn't know what to say. But then I remembered what you said—I had it all written down, actually—and I told 'em everything you said to tell 'em."

"And?"

"And the claim's still under review. I gotta admit, though, it felt good just to speak to a human being."

"I bet. But still not good enough. Time to drop the hammer, Tom." He produces a thick stack of documents from his bag and hands it to Ciampa, who looks the papers over with confusion.

"What's all this?"

Alex points to each document as he explains. "This is a complaint. This is a first set of interrogatories. This is a request for production of documents. You'll need a process server to serve all these." He points to the business card paper-clipped to the top of the stack. "That's the name and number of a guy I like."

Ciampa eyes this gift with equal parts gratitude and abashment. "Don't get me wrong, Mr. Garnett—"

"Alex," he corrects, and not for the first time.

"I want to sue those fuckers back to the Stone Age, but…" He shrugs, a little embarrassed. "I can't afford an attorney."

Alex knows. Just as he knows the CIA's code of ethics prevents him from pursuing the claim on Ciampa's behalf, even pro bono. "There's a difference between filing a lawsuit and taking the case all the way to trial, Tom." Ciampa nods, a dutiful pupil. "Insurance companies have the time, money, and manpower to process only ten percent of claims. Ten percent. So they stonewall, like they've been doing, knowing all the while that *ninety* percent of people will get fed up, take less than what they're owed, and go away." Alex taps the complaint with his finger. The caption at the top reads *Molly Ciampa v. Equix Insurers, Inc.* "You're not suing anyone. You're just telling them you're in the ten percent they have to deal with and that continuing to blow you off is gonna be more trouble than it's worth."

Ciampa considers that…and smiles.

◆

Alex enters Leah's office but starts to make a U-turn when he sees her on the phone. She keeps him planted, however, with a raised index finger in the universal sign for *Give me one more minute.*

As Leah listens to whoever it is droning away on the other end of the line, Alex takes in her office. It's clean to the point of immaculate, a paragon of minimalist organization that borders on Zen. The only concessions to the existence of a life outside the office are framed pictures of her nieces.

"The extradition-order draft looks good and we've got grounds for the injunction in Jerusalem," Leah says. Alex assumes she's talking to her counterpart in the Mossad, the Israeli intelligence agency. "I understand your concern, Avi. But if you're so inclined, you can confirm this with my superiors. My AIN is four-five-eight-seven-nine-six-three." She pauses to listen, frowning. "Tell you what, why don't I get back to you with a memo. I'll have one of our guys put something together." She ends the call with a perfunctory yet polite "Thanks, Avi. Talk to you later." She sets the phone down with less exasperation than most people would but still more than she cares to show in front of subordinates like Alex.

Before Alex can ask about the call, she hands him a Redweld file folder. This is what she summoned him into her office to discuss. *"Harling versus Harling?"* Alex asks.

"One of our case officers is getting divorced. Case officers are what other people might call spies or secret agents, but we obviously don't use those terms. You can imagine how common marital problems for these men and women are. The divorce rate hovers around eighty-five percent." Leah points to the file. "CIA case officer Harling is getting deposed by his wife's lawyer today."

"I've got absolutely zero family-law experience. None."

"You don't need any," Leah says. "Harling is already represented by counsel. An actual divorce attorney."

"So then why am I —"

"All you need to do is sit there and make sure Harling's testimony doesn't cross into any classified areas."

"Like Agency-enhanced lovemaking techniques?" Alex jokes. But the humor is lost on Leah.

◆

BEIT RAHBARI PRESIDENTIAL PALACE, IRAN
1605 HRS. ZULU

Ayatollah Seyed Ali Hoseyni Jahandar looks up from his tea at the spy sitting across from him. He looks competent enough. Jahandar places the man in his early forties — old enough to have seen something of how the world works, but young enough to play the game of espionage. He wears a neat Savile Row suit and was polite enough to remove his Ray-Ban sunglasses upon entering the presidential palace. All in all, there is nothing remarkable or, for that matter, memorable about the man. Jahandar supposes that's entirely the point: Members of Iran's secret police and primary intelligence agency, the Vezarat-e Ettela'at Jomhuri-ye Eslami-ye Iran, or VEVAK, should come and go as ghosts.

Jahandar makes it a point to keep his interactions with the VEVAK — or Ministry of Intelligence and National Security of the Islamic Republic of Iran, as it's also known — to a cautious minimum. But it's been over three months since the agency uncovered the six American spies within his country's borders and it's time for a report. The VEVAK agent hasn't brought any files or notes. But this is not surprising. Secrets are best not committed to paper.

The operative sips his tea and observes, "Good tea." He takes another sip.

Jahandar nods, acknowledging the compliment, and prompts, "The six Americans."

The operative sets his tea down. His emotionless affect doesn't shift. He speaks with quiet deliberation. "They each worked for an American company, Vogle Electric. Its headquarters are in Lansing, Michigan. It is a wholly unremarkable corporation."

"Any corporation that constructs nuclear power plants should not be described as wholly unremarkable," Jahandar says. The operative nods. "What were they doing in Iran?"

"Officially, providing consultation services with respect to the operation of our nuclear power plant in Bushehr."

"The Americans' capacity for hypocrisy never fails to astonish me. Their Congress rails against our nuclear ambitions yet permits their citizens to aid us in them."

"They do value capitalism above all things."

"So, were the consultants in Bushehr there merely to earn money?"

"No, Supreme Leader. They were spies."

"You sound quite certain of that."

"I am."

"Might I ask why?"

The operative leans forward, picks up his tea, and takes another sip. It's a small gesture, but it's the first outward sign of discomfort Jahandar has detected in the otherwise collected man. "Once we developed our suspicion that they might not be all they appeared, they were taken into custody and questioned."

"Questioned?" the supreme leader asks, sensing something more to the story.

"Subjected to enhanced interrogation techniques," the operative allows, retreating into the in-vogue euphemism for torture. "Despite what many Americans contend, the intelligence gained through such measures is extremely reliable."

"They confessed to spying on Iran?"

"They admitted that they didn't work exclusively for Vogle Electric," the operative confirms.

"The CIA?"

At this, the operative shakes his head. "These Americans were well trained. Although they were quick to surrender information about their activities within our borders, they were particularly obstinate with regard to their real employer's identity. After two weeks of interrogation, however, the last one gave us the name of the agency they worked for."

"The last one?" Jahandar asks, confused.

"Before dying, Supreme Leader."

Jahandar offers a sage nod. He's troubled by the taking of any life — much less six — but acknowledges the necessity for the sake of his country's security. In truth, he cannot muster more than feigned sympathy for the death of Iran's enemies. "I see," he says, "but I do not understand. These six did not work for the Central Intelligence Agency, and yet you say they were spies…" Jahandar spreads his hands to indicate his confusion.

"Don't be misled, Supreme Leader," the operative cautions, "the United States maintains twenty-two separate agencies with intelligence-gathering duties and capabilities." He pauses for a moment to let the truth of that sink in. "Of greater concern is the fact that this spy claimed to work for an organization previously unknown to us."

Jahandar raises his eyebrows in surprise. As if Iran doesn't have enough to contend with. The CIA, the Israeli Mossad, and a host of other foreign intelligence services operate against his country, and the thought of yet another agency is almost as troubling as the fact that the

VEVAK didn't know about it until a few months ago. "An American organization?" he asks.

The operative nods. "The man said it is called the Overwatch."

Jahandar takes that in, considering the word. "What is an overwatch?"

"It's a military term, an article of U.S. military doctrine. An overwatch is a small unit that supports another unit, often taking a position that permits observation of the terrain ahead."

Spies working for the American military are of even greater concern than those working for the intelligence community. "And what is the connection between this agency's designation and its mission?"

"We're still gathering intelligence," the operative demurs. "We are compiling a full analysis of this new intelligence agency and its suspected capabilities."

"I want to go to Darkhovin," Jahandar announces. He sees the color drain from the operative's face. He'd anticipated the man's concern. Both men know that Jahandar isn't requesting merely to visit the Khuzistan Province.

"There are numerous security concerns that must be considered before undertaking such a visit," the operative observes.

"I understand. I trust the VEVAK implicitly. With both," he adds, "my safety and the security of our country's secrets." His tone remains polite, his voice level, but his face and eyes make it clear that this is not a topic he will debate.

"With respect, sir, may I ask: Why do you want to visit Darkhovin?"

"I want to see the future of our nation." But this is only partially true. He is suspicious about the six American spies and their specific objectives in Iran. But those suspicions are unfocused. He has an instinct, however, that they will be sharpened once he sees Darkhovin with his own eyes.

Alex sits in an impressively large conference room overlooking Washington, DC. It's the kind of room he grew up in, bearing a strong resemblance to the White House and private-practice conference rooms that are his father's domain and sanctuary. The plush leather seats, the long table of walnut polished to a mirror-quality shine, and the credenza stocked with pitchers of water and coffee feel as familiar to Alex as his family's living room.

He sits off to the side, a passive observer in the domestic legal drama playing out before him. On one side of the table sits the case officer in question, Jim Harling, flanked by his attorney, a middle-aged man with salt-and-pepper hair. Harling appears focused and engaged.

Harling's wife is not present, but it's typical for each party to sit out on the depo of the opposing side. Instead, Mrs. Harling is represented by her attorney, a sharp woman named Evelyn Moreno. She's familiar to Alex, either from law school or from one of the many Bar Association functions he attended while he was an associate at Garnett and Lockhart. She questions Harling with a tone that is pure detached professionalism, neither friendly nor cold. "Your job was to persuade foreign citizens to work for the CIA."

"No, it wasn't. I work for the State Department. I've never been employed by the CIA," Harling responds.

"At this point, Mr. Harling, I'm going to remind you that you're under oath," Moreno asserts.

"I understand."

"And *I* understand that you're lying. You're perjuring yourself. I know for a fact that you're a nonofficial-cover case officer for the Central Intelligence Agency."

At this, Alex leans forward. "Mr. Harling's testimony is that he works for the State Department. Let's move on."

"No, Mr. Garnett, I'm afraid I cannot. Your client is committing perjury."

"And you've made that allegation for the record." Alex gestures to the stenographer sitting off to the side of the table, dutifully taking down every syllable on her steno machine.

"Did you advise your client to lie in this deposition?" Moreno asks with incredulity.

I advised my client to follow CIA policy and regard his status as an Agency employee as classified information, Alex thinks but doesn't say. Rather, he turns to the stenographer and notes, "Objection. What instructions I've given to my client are privileged."

Checkmated, Moreno switches gears and picks up a clipped stack of documents from the selection neatly arranged in front of her, like a legal buffet. On the bottom right corner of each is an alphanumeric stamp, known as a Bates stamp, that indicates the papers are official documentary evidence in the divorce proceedings. "Let the record reflect that I am presenting the witness with a series of documents Bates-stamped HAR0036 through HAR0038. These documents were obtained from a third party via subpoena." She slides the stack of papers toward Harling's side of the table. "These are your bank statements from February, March, and April of last year," she says, picking up a duplicate set to read for herself. "You had a total of nine thousand dollars in February." Her finger glides down the rows of dates and figures. "Then eighty-nine point eight million in March. Almost *ninety million* dollars." She clearly considers it highly unlikely that a government employee would come into possession of that much money through legal means. "Did you win the Powerball, Mr. Harling?"

"Objection. Ask a question. A legitimate one."

"Well," she says, turning a page of the bank statements, "that was March. By April, you were back down to nine thousand." She looks up and stares at Harling; the import of these numbers is obvious. "Where did the nearly ninety million dollars go, Mr. Harling?"

Harling holds up the April statement and points to a notation near the top of the second page. "It was a bank error. The bank found it and fixed it. The bank says so right here." He taps the notation with a finger.

Moreno flips to the page in question in her own copy of the bank records. "Actually," she says, "the bank's statement specifically reads" — she turns to the steno for the record — "and I'm quoting from it now, 'Fund incongruity noted and corrected. First Federal apologizes for the discrepancy *but claims no responsibility*.'" Moreno sets the paper down with a theatricality normally reserved for addressing a jury.

Surprisingly, Harling's lawyer remains silent. Although Alex isn't a divorce attorney, he's enough of a litigator to know that when your client is in trouble, as Harling clearly appears to be, you step in and, if nothing else, stall the other side's momentum. But Harling's attorney, who bills out at four hundred an hour minimum, is like a statue.

"I need a minute with Mr. Harling." The words are out of Alex's mouth before he realizes they're his. Nevertheless, now committed, he stands up from the table. "Jim?" he says, looking over to Harling.

"This isn't a good time to stop," Moreno protests.

Alex waves this off. "Just a minute. Jim?"

Thirty seconds later, in a small alcove serving a dual purpose as a copy/coffee room, Alex asks Harling how it is that a midlevel CIA case officer has almost ninety million dollars in his bank account in a given month. Even if Harling had saved the money, which was unlikely, that didn't explain why it showed up in his statements one month and disappeared the next.

"It was a bank error," Harling says with a rather convincing shrug. "These things happen." The fact that Harling appears completely sincere and believable isn't lost on Alex. But neither is the fact that Harling is a covert operative and, therefore, a professional liar.

"A mistake of ten or twenty bucks might happen, sure. A rounding error is more common, yeah. But ninety million dollars?" Alex shakes his head.

"Tell me, how is this any of your business?" Harling asks.

"I work for the general counsel. If a NOC is embezzling Agency funds —"

"I didn't take a nickel." Harling cuts him off, his face turning red.

Alex adopts a less confrontational tone. "Look, I'm not saying you *took* money, exactly. But a spook like you, nine years in the field…" Alex shrugs and adds a friendly grin for good measure. "Money has a way of falling into your lap. Am I right?"

"You're right," Harling says, but he doesn't soften. On the contrary, he takes a confrontational step forward, holding back the outrage behind his eyes like a horse straining at the bit. "And I turn my head away. Watches, cars, off-the-books cash, outright bribes." Another step. He's talking through gritted teeth now. "I turn my head away."

"But a cute Iraqi passes, you stare straight ahead." In seconds, Harling has Alex on his back on the coffee-and-copy room's linoleum floor, his Brioni loafer pressing on Alex's throat. Alex stares up at the muzzle of Harling's Browning Hi-Power 1935, poised just a few inches from the bridge of his nose.

"I have to take that shit from my wife's lawyer," Harling says. "I understand that. I have to let her do her thing. What I *don't* have to do is take that kinda shit from *you*. Do we have an understanding?"

"That's a nice move. They teach you that at Langley?"

Alex can't tell if Harling is amused or impressed that he'd crack wise under these circumstances, but it doesn't matter once the gun disappears beneath Harling's suit jacket.

"Let's get back in there" is all Harling says.

FIVE

THE REST of Harling's deposition passed without incident, albeit with painful slowness. By the time Moreno finished excavating the microscopic details of Harling's professional, personal, and marital life, Alex was wishing Harling had pulled the trigger on his Browning back in the copy room.

Nevertheless, Alex retains the presence of mind to conduct his own inquiry down in the parking garage of the building that houses Moreno's law firm. He politely confronts her about the $89.8 million that appeared in and disappeared from Harling's bank account as swiftly and silently as Harling's gun had back in the copy room. It was Harling's reaction, clearly an indication of some inner tension, that has Alex thinking there's no bank error. His job today was to safeguard the CIA's secrets, but he feels like he's stumbled onto something else entirely.

Reading the bank documents himself does not quell this feeling. The actual numbers cement the reality that last year, CIA case officer Jim Harling was a temporary custodian of almost ninety million dollars without any good explanation.

"The bank wouldn't tell you who initiated the transfers?" Alex asks, his eyes compulsively scanning the bank records.

Moreno shakes her head. "That wasn't covered in the scope of my sub-poena."

"So do you have *any* idea where the money came from?"

"I'm a divorce attorney, Mr. Garnett. All I care about is where the money *went*."

Alex is considering his next move, if any, when a red 1965 Ford Mustang, lovingly restored to mint condition, rockets past, its engine roaring like a vengeful god, laying down rubber on the garage's cement floor. The Mustang's driver, whose *fuck-you* stare to Moreno is visible as he blazes past, is unmistakably Jim Harling.

◈

RESTAURANT MONTMARTRE
8:17 P.M. EDT

"You're an asshole," Grace observes after Alex tells her about the day's events. She's the smartest person Alex has ever known, and that's including his very accomplished father. He told her the story about Harling's depo in the hope that she might be able to offer an innocent explanation for Harling's month as a multimillionaire. Being called an asshole wasn't exactly the explanation he had in mind.

Still, the reaction wasn't entirely inappropriate. In the months since Alex joined the CIA, the evenings when he's made it home in time for dinner have incorporated a recitation of the day's events. Alex relates the stories against a backdrop of his fitting fairly well into the Agency. (Although, he has to admit, he's grading himself on the curve of his previous lackluster employment experiences.) Nevertheless, there have been times when he can sense disapproval lurking beneath the surface of Grace's expression, threatening to break free.

Alex has no desire to wake this sleeping giant, so he decides to play Grace's observation off as a joke. "This is support?"

Grace lights up the room with her megawatt smile. "C'mon, Alex," she says, almost amused, "you accused your client of embezzlement —"

Alex cuts her off right there. "He's not my client. And the divorce lawyer accused him first."

She smiles again. Alex has always considered Grace's smile to be like a musical instrument, capable of a thousand different notes. Now she's playing a piece that might best be titled *Don't Bullshit a Bullshitter*. He knows the tune well. "You were kicking up dust again."

Kicking up dust is Grace's expression for "making waves" or "rocking the boat," all of which Alex has a tendency to do with gleeful abandon, most often where his job — whichever one he happens to be holding at that particular moment — is concerned. But that's the whole point. "I'm a lawyer. Dust-kicking is part of my job. One could even argue it's in the job description."

Grace looks like she's about to laugh hysterically. "Last month, you called Senator Hollings a Rotarian bureaucrat."

"I was being kind —"

"My point," she says gently, "is that I doubt insulting members of Congress is part of your job."

"No. Insulting members of Congress would fall under discharging my duties as an American citizen."

"Okay," she allows. "That's fair. But what about insulting the Intelligence Oversight Board last month? That's the president's board, Alex. The president. Of the United States."

Alex offers a shrug. "The IOB's been reduced to an ineffectual rubber stamp. Someone had to stir things up."

"And you were only too glad to volunteer."

"What does that mean?" Alex asks.

He watches her shift uncomfortably in her chair. She picks at her tuna tartare, moving it around on her plate. "You're a lawyer. You're always going to make an above-average income."

"Okay…" he says, not knowing where this is going.

"And once my loans are paid off —"

"You went to medical school," he says with a smile. "Your loans will *never* be paid off."

"Once my loans are paid off," she reiterates, pressing past the joke, "I'll be able to make a pretty decent living too."

"Okay."

"My point is, I'm not worried about money. But it might *seem* like I am when I say that I'm worried about you. I'm worried about your career choices, your professional trajectory." Alex sours a bit at this, a topic he finds barely more palatable than his relationship with his father. "I thought the CIA would be the perfect job for you. Being a lawyer for spies, in an arena free from your father and his connections."

Alex decides not to dissuade Grace by reiterating the exchange he had with Arthur Bryson on his first day. "I've quit more than my share of jobs. My father's firm, then the public defenders' office." Grace nods. "And you're worried I'm going to quit this job too."

Grace shakes her head. "I'm not worried you're going to quit. You seem to be putting yourself on a path to getting fired, though." She leans across the table, taking his hand. "You're not your father. You could never be like your father." Her eyes find his, probing. The bottom line: "Even if you find success."

❖

GEORGETOWN, DELAWARE
9:31 P.M. EDT

William Rykman stares into Paul Langford's eyes. They're wide with horror and agony, and not just because his eyelids have been surgically removed. Tears tinged with blood pool in rivulets beneath them as they dart around furtively. The image is remarkably lifelike. And it should be. It was recorded on 1080p hi-def video.

Rykman takes a sip of his Macallan. Aged eighteen years and smoky. He toasts to Langford's memory, holding his glass up with a grin to no one in particular. And why not? It's been a good day. In fact, it's been a very good day for the Overwatch and, therefore, a very good day for William Rykman. More important, it's been a good day for America. All the right assets are now in place. It took six months, but Rykman is ready to pull the trigger on plan B.

It's not easy, Lord knows, to make history, but the work has its moments of satisfaction. It's like having the power of a god. It's that feeling of omnipotence combined with the disturbing images on his TV that produce the sensation Rykman now feels between his legs. On the plasma, Donovan is inserting a catheter somewhere it doesn't belong. Although Rykman would never admit it, it's his favorite part of the recording. Deciding not to let it go to waste, Rykman reaches for his laptop to bring up a website he favors and give himself some relief. Then his secure cell phone rings.

It's Donovan. Now that Langford has "retired," Donovan is the only one with this phone number. Rykman answers the cell. The TV is already on mute out of concern for the neighbors, who wouldn't approve of Langford's animalistic screams.

On the other end of the line, Donovan relates information that makes Rykman lose his erection. Rykman takes a deep breath, considering his options, calculating odds and angles. It's a pure numbers game, a computation done in terms of human lives, and Rykman engages in it with dispassion. And when he's done, the math is very simple. He relays his instructions to Donovan, confident that Donovan will execute them flawlessly. He's a good man, that Donovan. A very good man.

Rykman ends the call and finishes off his scotch. On the TV, Langford has passed out, despite the drug cocktail formulated to keep him awake. Rykman looks at the man's lidless, unconscious eyes. He should get some sleep himself. Tomorrow will be an eventful day.

SIX

BETWEEN THOUGHTS of his own troubled relationship and Harling's possibly ill-gotten gains, Alex had a fitful night's sleep. The combination made for an interesting stew once he started dreaming, his subconscious devising disturbing encounters among himself, Grace, and Harling in a variety of odd locales. At one point, the three of them stood on a rooftop overlooking the Capitol. It was rotated at a 180-degree angle, so the tip of the Washington Monument was digging into the top of Alex's head, threatening to impale him. When morning finally arrived like the cavalry, Alex couldn't get out of the condo fast enough.

After he's caffeinated, he makes the now-familiar morning commute down George Washington Memorial Parkway to Langley. He usually spends the time listening to NPR or an audiobook, but this morning he's hoping to call Evelyn Moreno early and catch her in her office. Even if he had the standing to subpoena Harling's finances, which he doesn't because the CIA isn't chartered for domestic activities, he would have to get up the ass of a local bank. And a formal investigation would take too long and send up too many red flags. Despite what Grace thinks, there actually are limits to how much shit he's willing to stir. And even if he were willing to launch a formal investigation, he doubts a single bank statement is enough to provide grounds for one.

His best bet is to convince Moreno to pressure the bank as part of the divorce case, he thinks as he dials her office number. If Harling came into possession of several million dollars once, then it might not have been the only time. And that fact would certainly be of interest to Moreno. Alex is optimistic he can use her doggedness to his advantage. The protracted ringing on the other end of the phone, however, suggests that Moreno hasn't shown up for work yet. But to Alex's surprise, when the receptionist comes on, she doesn't offer to take a message. Instead, she murmurs a polite, but uncomfortable, "Is there anyone else who might be able to help you, sir?"

"No," Alex responds. "Could you leave word for Evelyn, please?"

A long silence follows. Alex starts to wonder what the hell could be going on, but he doesn't wonder for long. "I'm very sorry, s-sir," the receptionist stutters. She sounds like she's struggling to keep her emotions in check. "But Ms. Moreno passed away this morning."

Alex opens his mouth to ask the obvious questions—the first one being *What the fuck?*—but no words come out. Maybe the receptionist got the name wrong. On the other end of the line, she drones on about a heart attack, very sudden, everyone at the firm is still in shock, et cetera.

Alex is still trying to absorb this when a car shoots past his, close enough to nearly clip his driver's-side mirror. He looks up to see that the speeding bullet, already racing two car lengths ahead of him, is a red 1965 Ford Mustang, the same automotive vintage, make, and model favored by Jim Harling.

The Mustang slaloms—threading between traffic with practiced skill—until the driver finds himself trapped behind a long-bed truck carrying a load of steel poles, each at least ten feet long. The Mustang shimmies—the driver is angling for a route around the truck—and then the truck's brakes seize. The long-bed's taillights are suddenly lambent with crimson. Doubled-up tires skid. Black streaks of rubber trail, drawing parallel lines along the asphalt. A rooster tail of smoke accompanies a horrific whine that sounds like a wild animal dying.

The long-bed lurches to a stop, its inventory of steel pipes jangling with the momentum of the Mustang colliding with the rear of the truck. Metal meets metal with a violent crunch as the Mustang's front, so carefully restored, accordions up against the truck's back end. The collision dislodges the truck's cargo, sending piping spilling onto the highway. Oncoming traffic swerves to avoid the onslaught, causing a secondary series of collisions, some of which send the vehicles pinwheeling off the asphalt and into the shoulder and the woods beyond.

Alex wrestles with his steering wheel, jerking it right and left, working the gas, swerving to avoid the oncoming cars. Up ahead, the Mustang continues its inexorable forward momentum. Two cars part, providing a view of one of the long-bed's longer pipes lancing the Mustang's windshield, which seems to explode, raining pebbles of glass down on the road. The ensuing cacophony of tortured steel sounds like the end of the world.

Suddenly, Alex is at ground zero, wayward automobiles and metal piping flying toward him like a meteor shower. Some miracle of navigation allows him to wend his way through the deadly metallic obstacle course. When he finally manages to beach the Lexus on the island of green that divides Route 123's opposing lanes of traffic, he can feel the death grip his hands have on the steering wheel. His heart jackhammers in his chest, providing the convincing evidence that he's somehow still alive.

"Breathe," he commands.

He looks over his dashboard to see an almost postapocalyptic landscape. At the farthest point is the Mustang, still joined in a union of steel and glass with the flatbed. Behind it is a trail of vehicular devastation, drawing a line down the highway as clear as if the Mustang had been a meteorite whose landing cut a swath through the earth. Automotive metal and plastic litter the highway. The brightly colored pieces suggest that some very wild party has just been thrown. Broken and twisted cars rest at odd angles in groups of two and three. Some movement as their owners begin to venture out, still shaking off the shock of what's happened.

Alex emerges from his car and takes it all in. A few of the cars are so twisted they resemble modern art more than automobiles. The cars that arrived latest to the accident lie scattered across the road, forming a barrier that prevents him from getting hit by oncoming traffic. Nevertheless, Alex finds walking in the middle of a highway unsettling. His brisk pace morphs into a sprint as he races toward the broken Mustang, hoping against reason that Harling isn't the driver.

But when he arrives at the car, he can't tell if it's him. Can't even come close. There's a long metal pipe where his face used to be. A marriage of steel, blood, and gristle rises from the man's slumped, lifeless shoulders. It's not grief but rather the sight of the man's left ear, dangling from a bloody sinew, that causes Alex to double over and vomit.

It won't be until the Virginia medical examiner issues the official autopsy that Alex will know for sure what he now suspects: Central Intelligence Agency field officer James Dennis Harling, who survived six years as a nonofficial-cover case officer in such places as Somalia, Yemen, and Afghanistan, was killed in the middle of his morning commute on Route 123.

❖

DARKHOVIN, IRAN
1330 HRS. ZULU

Supreme Leader of Iran Ayatollah Jahandar's movements are closely tracked. Not only by the watchful eye of the VEVAK, but also by the various foreign intelligence agencies whose operatives have infected Iran's borders. The list of penetrating agencies is long—much longer than the VEVAK would care to admit, even to itself—but clearly, America's CIA, Israel's Mossad, and this new Overwatch top the list. Of greater concern are the American-made KH-11 U.S. NRO surveillance satellites flying in geosynchronous perpetuity over Iran, making Jahandar's movements subject to constant monitoring. At least, that's what the VEVAK fears. Accordingly, the VEVAK's security and protection procedures account for the fact there is nowhere the ayatollah can travel without Iran's enemies learning about it. Meaning he doesn't go anywhere in Iran that might threaten to draw the wrong kind of foreign attention. But like many assumptions made for the purposes of security, this one is wrong. Jahandar isn't under round-the-clock surveillance, by satellite or otherwise, by the CIA or by the Mossad, but the VEVAK has long since decided it's better to overestimate their country's enemies than underestimate them, particularly where the Great Satan is concerned.

Still, when Jahandar heard about the project's completion, he insisted on seeing the final product for himself. Photos were presented, of course. They looked quite vivid on the iPad. But he needed to see it with his own eyes. He wanted to touch it with his own hand and, if so moved, say a prayer over it. It's not every day your country builds something that will change the world. Under such circumstances, photographs simply will not suffice.

The process of secretly moving Jahandar from his residence in the Beit Rahbari Presidential Palace in Tehran to Darkhovin in the Khuzistan Province took two months to devise, practice, and execute. Despite his status as supreme leader, and in part because of the security restrictions placed on him, Jahandar rarely leaves the confines of Tehran's borders and almost never goes as far as Khuzistan. Should the Americans or, Allah forbid, the Israelis learn that the ayatollah visited this place, a simple town as far from Tehran as one can get without crossing into Iraq, they would certainly grow curious as to why, and the answer would threaten everything Iran's government has been working toward, if not the country's very existence. Given those stakes, there was nothing the VEVAK could leave to chance.

An eight-year-old Iranian postal service van was selected for the trip. The Iran postal service might be one of the world's least reliable ways to send a message, but an IPS van is a near-perfect way to secretly transport someone from Tehran to Darkhovin, because no one will look twice at it. The only downside — for Jahandar, at least — is that the van is several orders of magnitude less comfortable than the Lincoln Town Car in which he is typically chauffeured. Still, the thirteen-hour pilgrimage over what can barely be considered roads in temperatures that prompt the van's aging engine to overheat three times will be more than worth it.

The waiting is the hardest part. Jahandar's VEVAK handlers refuse to offer specifics on exactly how long it will take them to assure themselves it is safe for him to visit the site. Their maternal caution is starting to grate on him, but Jahandar is nothing if not patient. After all, he has dedicated his life — his very existence — to following the teachings of the Koran, and the Koran counsels, "Be patient. For your patience is with the help of Allah." Jahandar knows that this principle, known as *sabr,* is as true as every other dictate of the Koran. And even now, he feels Allah soothing him, whispering into his soul. His wait will not be long…

Route 123
8:58 a.m. EDT

Alex doesn't know how long he spends staring at what he's sure is Harling's body. It must be a few minutes because three Virginia sheriff cars and an ambulance have arrived and he can't remember hearing their approaching sirens. Everything sounds different, as if he's underwater. He reasons he's in shock. And that's when it hits him that Harling's death wasn't the first gut punch he took this morning. What was it? Just before the accident, what happened? He was being told...the receptionist was telling him that Evelyn Moreno was dead. Heart attack.

Then he sees the long-bed's driver. The man sports a lumberjack's flannel shirt and a well-worn Orioles cap. He's talking to two sheriff's deputies. He looks shaken from the accident but otherwise unharmed. Alex can't tell if the man's apparent shock is an act for the police's benefit. It's hard for him to imagine how it would feel to be the cause of a ten-car pileup and yet survive without so much as a scratch.

Alex moves to his car with renewed purpose. Adrenaline restores mental clarity like a fan blowing away smoke. He unlocks the passenger-side door and reaches into his glove compartment to find his public defenders' badge. He keeps it there so he can grab it when he needs it, usually to get out of speeding tickets.

The badge is enough to get him past the deputy guarding the accident site as paramedics use the Jaws of Life to get to Harling's near-decapitated body. One of the sheriff's deputies talking to the driver spots Alex approaching and moves to cut him off, leaving the driver a tantalizing few yards away with the other officer. Alex raises his badge with a forced casualness he hopes comes off as legitimacy. "I'm with the public defenders' office."

"DC office, looks like," the officer says. Alex hoped he wouldn't notice. "This is Virginia."

"What are you, the Bar Association?" Alex asks. He points to the driver. "I want a word with that man."

The second deputy approaches Alex, getting a bit closer than necessary. "Our badges are bigger than yours, Counselor. So your word's gonna have to wait till arraignment." He returns to the long-bed's driver.

"Arraignment?" Alex shoots his gaze over to the man. "If the driver is getting arraigned, it's because he's under arrest. And if they're arresting him, it's because he committed a crime."

Following Alex's eyes, the first deputy points at the driver. "Yeah, arraignment. The guy's liquored up like a frat boy at his first kegger."

Alex's mind kicks into an adrenaline-fueled overdrive. Sure, it might just be a coincidence that the drunk-driving accident that ended Jim Harling's life happened to occur right on the heels of Evelyn Moreno's fatal misfortune. But that would challenge the definition of the word *coincidence*. The only way he can resolve the conundrum is to have a pointed conversation with the flatbed's driver. Unfortunately, it doesn't look like that's going to happen here or now. The second deputy lowers the driver into the backseat of their cruiser.

Alex turns back to the first officer with urgency and whips out his smartphone. "Where is he getting arraigned?"

◆

Virginia Superior Court
11:00 a.m. EDT

On his way to the courthouse, Alex calls in to the Agency, asks for Leah's assistant, and explains that he was just in a car accident. "I'm fine," he assures her. He fails to mention Harling. Leah will find out about him soon enough. "But the paramedics told me I should visit an ER and get myself checked out anyway. I could have a concussion and not know it," he adds for good measure. "Can you tell Leah I might be here for a while?"

"Of course, Mr. Garnett."

"Please. It's Alex." Confident his whereabouts for the day have been accounted for, Alex races into the courthouse and locates the courtroom where the flatbed driver will be arraigned. All courtrooms in the country are the same. Some are state courts, others federal. Some smell like a fresh coat of paint, while others have linoleum tiles that date back to the Carter administration. Some are reserved and stately while others endure an architecture more befitting a modern art museum. All are unlike those depicted on television. But they all possess the same electricity generated by the wheeling and dealing, hustle and bustle, the give-and-take of the American legal system in action. It is amid this energy that Alex feels most at home.

The clerk is just starting to call the long-bed driver's case when Alex enters. "Docket ending two-seven-oh-seven," she says. "*Commonwealth versus Alan Miller,* vehicular homicide." She continues reading the charges as Alex eyes the defense table. Sitting there is the man in the now-familiar Orioles ball cap and flannel shirt and his defense attorney, who, judging by his comb-over and off-the-rack suit, probably advertises in the Yellow Pages.

Alex steals a quick glimpse at the prosecution table to his right. The attorney sitting there is maybe a year out of law school. Judging from the height of his file stack, Alex figures he's juggling about twice the caseload he should be. Both are very good signs.

"Alex Garnett of Garnett and Lockhart for the defendant, Your Honor." Better to ally himself with his father's firm for this proceeding than drag the CIA into it. "We can waive the remainder of the reading. Mr. Miller pleads not guilty."

Yellow Pages is suddenly awake and shooting to his feet, seemingly unable to tell whether he should be angry or embarrassed. Has he shown up in court for the wrong client? "Your Honor…" he croaks.

Alex swivels around to cut off Yellow Pages' objection. But as his eyes find the defense table and settle on his would-be client, he freezes. The defendant, the man in the flannel shirt and Orioles cap on whose behalf Alex just entered an appearance, isn't the same man Alex saw at the scene of the accident.

His mouth goes dry. His mind races through the list of possible explanations. He's not in the wrong courtroom. How many flannel-draped Orioles fans can be arraigned for DUI in a single day? Coincidence and misunderstanding now ruled out, Alex finds himself left with conspiracy. One of the flanneled men was responsible for Harling's death. To be sure, it takes two to conspire, but it's obvious from the man at the defense table's disconcerted expression that he isn't one of the conspirators. Therefore, the police's taking the actual culprit into custody was less an arrest than a sophisticated getaway. But in order for this to be true, the sheriff's office had to have been involved. Or, at least, two of its deputies. And how did they switch one man for the other anyway?

"Your Honor, there apparently has been some kind of mistake," Yellow Pages says. "But I'm not the one who made it." He speaks with the conviction of a lawyer who is in danger of losing a client. "The court appointed me to represent Mr. Miller. I have the paperwork right here." He holds up a sheaf of documents and waves it around.

Alex knows that the only way he'll start finding answers is by getting the driver alone in a room. He also knows with equal certitude that that's not going to happen unless he's the man's attorney. "Every defendant has a right to counsel of his own choosing, Your Honor," Alex reminds the court. "The fact that Mr. ..."

"Morewitz," Yellow Pages obliges.

"That Mr. Morewitz happened to have been retained by the defendant first is irrelevant."

The judge looks to the driver, inviting him to speak. The driver's eyes dart between Alex, who stands confident and sharp in his neat Armani suit, and his for-the-moment attorney, with his comb-over and inability to say his own name with authority. He points to Alex. "I'll take him."

❖

Two hours later, Alex paces the length of one of the rooms in the courthouse set aside for private attorney/client conferences. The driver sits at the room's lone table and anxiously taps his fingers against the cheap pressed wood. Alex has confirmed two things. First, the driver's name is Alan Miller. Second, Alan Miller is the owner of record of the long-bed truck that killed Harling. Miller stares at Alex with glazed eyes as if he expects to wake up at any moment from a trying nightmare.

"It's like I told you," Miller says. "I passed out."

"And you don't remember anything."

Miller shakes his head, starting to get exasperated. "I got up this morning, I shaved, I showered, I had some coffee, and I got in my rig."

"And then what?"

"Then I really don't remember." Miller stares at his hands, palms spread out in front of him, as if they hold the answer to his missing morning.

"What's the first thing you remember?"

"Some police officer taking a mug-shot photo of me. I was pretty out of it…"

"Did you feel inebriated? Drugged?"

"I was definitely off, I can tell you that much."

Alex sits down so he and Miller are eye to eye. "You can tell me more. Everything you tell me is protected by attorney-client privilege. Absolutely everything."

Miller knows what Alex is getting at. "I don't have a problem with alcohol, Mr. Garnett. Sometimes a beer after work. If it's been a tough day, maybe I'll do a shot of Jack. But I've always" — he knocks the table with his knuckles for emphasis — "*always* known when to stop. Always." He taps the table again.

"The police think you were drunk."

"Mr. Garnett, my right hand to God, the strongest thing I had this morning was Folgers."

Alex leans back and considers. "Let me tell you something, Mr. Miller. Attorneys, particularly ones with criminal-law experience, are more reliable than polygraphs." Miller stares back, confused. "Lie-detector tests," Alex clarifies.

"Yeah? So what's your detector saying?"

"That you're telling the truth. But in this case, it's as problematic as any lie."

"I'm not following you." Miller shrugs.

"It very much appears that you weren't behind the wheel when the accident occurred. Which means the driver who was arrested at the scene was dressed to look like you, and you were drugged at some point this morning then swapped for him prior to his arriving at Central Booking. I don't see how that happens without the sheriff's office — one deputy, at least — being in on it."

"What you're talking about, it sounds like science fiction or some horror movie or something."

"I know. It sounds crazy."

"Me lying makes a lot more sense," Miller allows.

"This is my concern." Alex watches Miller shrink an inch in his chair, his hope deflating like a popped balloon. "But I believe you're telling the truth, Alan."

"So where does that leave us?"

Alex fishes in his pants pocket and takes out a pack of gum. He pops a piece in his mouth and begins to chew. He offers the pack to Miller, who just shakes his head. In between chews, Alex says, "By the time I get a serologist down here, whatever's in your system will probably have metabolized." Miller stares blankly, as if Alex just switched to another language. "If you're telling the truth," Alex continues, "then you were *drugged*. Most likely with GHB. Y'know, the date-rape drug?" Miller nods. *That* he's heard of. "And we have to get an expert to analyze your blood for any traces before your body metabolizes it." Miller nods cautiously. Alex removes a Montblanc pen, a gift from Grace, from his suit jacket. He starts to take it apart, chewing his gum as he does. "Fortunately, I've handled more than a few DUIs, and one former client of mine gave me a few tips on how to smuggle bodily fluids in writing implements." Alex shows him the disassembled pen. "Roll up your sleeve." Though clearly confused, Miller does as instructed. Alex holds up the pieces of the pen. "This is probably gonna get a little messy."

SEVEN

Alex leaves Alan Miller in jail with the twin promises that everything's going to be all right and that he'll check in tomorrow. It was arguably malpractice on Alex's part not to win Miller's release on bail. Hell, it was malpractice not to *request* it. Apart from a drunk-and-disorderly charge—a suspended sentence in college, which means it might as well have occurred in the Paleozoic era—Miller's record is spotless. But Alex suspected that Miller might be safer in jail.

Alex has twenty-eight minutes to ponder his choices as he completes the drive to Washington, DC, and up to the Hoover Building. With its 1960s federal-bureaucracy architecture and imposing concrete exterior, the building resembles a beige-painted airport terminal. As such, it seems thoroughly out of place among DC's more stately buildings, with their Queen Anne, Richardsonian Romanesque, and Gothic Revival architectural styles.

Alex strides across the black marbled lobby, over the FBI seal embedded in the floor. His CIA credentials get him past the gauntlet of security guards and metal detectors and he's directed up to the third floor.

Alex has to fill out a sheaf of paperwork and answer more than a few pointed questions before he is able to unburden himself of the Montblanc pen that's burning a hole in his suit jacket. The pen's business end is plugged with the wad of the chewing gum. The pen's middle seam is tinged a bloody brown. After two hours' worth of paperwork and bureaucratic legerdemain, he finally dangles the pen in front of Pamela Voytek.

Voytek is one of the veritable army of forensics technicians the FBI houses at the Hoover Building. A Bureau lifer, her career will never grow beyond what can be seen under a microscope or held in a test tube. But she appears quite content with that. Alex can't decide what makes him more envious: that Voytek seems capable of long-term professional fidelity or that she feels no pressure to climb the ladder of success.

Voytek stares at Alex with a look that asks if this is some kind of a joke. A CIA lawyer with a pen full of blood that's stopped up with a wad of chewing gum, and he wants her to run a full chem panel and toxicology screen? Voytek remembers the newbie last year who was given a sample of liquid soap to analyze, only to discover the pearl-colored liquid was, in fact, the very opposite of liquid soap and had been "donated" by the lab's more immature male forensic scientists. Lord only knew what was really in this pen.

"Sorry," she says. "Tell Bill he can blow me."

Alex smiles, taking this in stride. "I don't know who Bill is. And even if it were biologically possible for him to blow you, I think I outrank Bill on this." He taps the signed ticket that authorizes the lab work he wants done.

Voytek blanches a little. "And what case does this relate to?"

Alex shrugs. "It's classified," he says. The voice in his head warns that he has doubled-down on his hunch that something pertaining to national security is going on; something that will justify the trail of white lies he's been leaving in his wake lately.

Voytek takes the pen and carefully unscrews it. "If I'm getting punked here," she warns, "I'm gonna make you drink whatever's *really* in this pen." As she pours the pen's contents out, however, Alex can tell from Voytek's expression that the fluid is clearly blood, even if it has coagulated a bit during its voyage from Miller's vein to Voytek's Hewlett-Packard 6890 gas chromatograph. The machine whirs quietly for a few minutes.

A monitor set off to the side of Voytek's tidy workstation comes alive with a conventional-looking bar graph. Alex is surprised at how easy to decode it looks. At least, it would be if he understood the chemical equations on the screen. Fortunately, Voytek is on hand to translate: "Your subject's testing positive for trace quantities of GHA." She delivers this news with about as much interest as a librarian announcing closing time, waiting for the other shoe to drop. "GHA is gamma-hydroxyarsenate." For all Alex knows, gamma-hydroxyarsenate is no more sinister than something Miller's taking to lower his cholesterol. This is obviously playing across his face because Voytek elaborates, "GHA is a reformulation of GHB, which you might have heard by its mainstream name —"

"The date-rape drug," Alex says, but it comes out as almost a croak.

"That's right. What's going on here?"

"Can I ask you, have you ever heard of any incidents where GHA has been accidentally ingested?"

"What, you mean, like in the absence of foul play?" Alex nods. "I can't imagine a chain of circumstances that would lead to that."

"What about an organic formulation?"

"Organic formulation?" Voytek raises her eyebrows.

"Is GHA found naturally? Y'know, in nature?"

"No. Like I said, it's a reformulation of GHB. The reformulation is deliberate. And rare. The DOD's been monkeying around with it for a few years now —"

"DOD," Alex interrupts. "The Department of Defense?"

Voytek nods. "They've been trying to come up with a formulation that has the same effects as GHB."

"How do you know what the DOD's been up to with this?"

"I worked a homicide case about a year ago. The suspected cause of death was GHA. I studied up."

Alex shakes his head as he tries to get the jumble of thoughts to make sense. "Why would the Defense Department try to monkey around with the chemistry of GHB?"

"They were trying to replicate the side effects of GHB — sluggishness, blackouts, what have you — but in a formulation that would be reliably toxic, as in fatal."

The word *fatal* has Alex reaching for his cell. He quickly Googles the phone number of the Virginia jail where Miller is being held. He navigates the jail's automated directory and finally reaches an actual human being. "My name is Alex Garnett," he tells the civil servant on the other end of the line. "I need to talk to my client Alan Miller. He's currently incarcerated in your facility. I need to speak with him immediately."

"Hold on."

As Alex waits, he turns back to Voytek. "If someone's been exposed to GHA, what measures should be taken to treat him?"

"I'm not a medical doctor," Voytek is saying when someone comes on the line.

"Mr. Garnett? I'm a doctor at Rappahannock Regional Jail's infirmary—"

Alex cuts him off. "Doctor, my client needs medical attention. He's been exposed to a toxic and potentially fatal chemical known as GHA."

"Mr. Garnett," the doctor says in a measured voice, "I'm afraid it's too late for medical attention. Mr. Miller passed away twenty minutes ago."

❖

DARKHOVIN, IRAN
1700 HRS. ZULU

Jahandar's predecessor, the Ayatollah Ruhollah Khomeini, was a severe-looking man with sullen eyes topped with dark, caterpillar-like eyebrows, perpetually arched in sinister malevolence. His dour appearance made for great American propaganda; the Ayatollah Khomeini's visage seemed the very personification of evil. Perhaps that's why, as far as the American media is concerned, Khomeini was the face of the Iranian government in the 1980s. However, when Jahandar succeeded him at the end of that decade, the Americans shifted their attention to Iran's president. Looking at Jahandar, it isn't hard to see why: He has a kind face, a professorial smile, and warm eyes that betray a hint of whimsy.

That professorial smile is nowhere in evidence now, however. Yes, he'd seen the pictures, but that was nothing compared to being in the same room as the device. He's in a hidden basement beneath one of several ramshackle houses in Darkhovin. It was dug out over a span of several years, so as not to attract the attention of nosy neighbors. Amazingly, it's far enough underground that the space is naturally cool, at least compared to the oppressive desert heat.

Jahandar reaches out to fulfill the promise he made to himself, to test the reality of what he's seeing with the touch of his own skin. It's a powerful moment. Jahandar doesn't understand the object. All he sees is a rough assembly of plastic and metal whose construction he cannot begin to comprehend. But just like someone doesn't need to be a mechanic to know he's looking at a car, Jahandar is an expert in knowing the import of what he's staring at.

He turns around to face the three men standing behind him. One is his personal SAVAK bodyguard. The other two are, he assumes, the lead engineers of what's been designated Project 110 for several years now. *"Alhamdulillah,"* one of the engineers says. *"Alhamdulillah,"* his counterpart echoes with a concurring nod. *Alhamdulillah. All praise is due to Allah.*

Jahandar isn't entirely sure. He keeps his thoughts to himself, but the engineers misread his stoicism as disapproval. "It will fit in the Fajr-Three," one of the engineers assures him.

"And the X–One Fifty-Five and the Shahab-Three," the other adds.

"The effective range is three thousand kilometers." This is offered with a hint of pride and with the expectation that Jahandar, being a man of Allah, is ignorant as to weapons of war. But he isn't. And he knows that at least two of the three missiles mentioned are not capable of flying farther than twenty-five hundred kilometers.

He pushes aside that thought. He has much graver concerns on his mind. Iran has joined the United States, United Kingdom, Russia, France, Israel, China, India, Pakistan, South Africa, and North Korea as a nuclear power.

◆

J. Edgar Hoover Building
12:19 p.m. EDT

"Do not throw up in my lab," Voytek commands.

Although Alex looks like he's about to vomit, rage is keeping his bodily fluids in check. The anger is directed inward. He rages against himself: Miller is dead. And he might have been alive if only Alex had gotten him out on bail.

"Seriously, are you all right?" Voytek asks.

Alex barely hears her. His mind roars along like a freight train. There's no way three related people die under suspicious circumstances less than twenty-four hours after some divorce lawyer finds out a CIA case officer might have been embezzling money. There is another explanation, and concentrating on what it could be is what's keeping Alex from collapsing on the sterile laboratory floor right now.

He opens his mouth to ask Voytek a question, but nothing comes out. She's looking at him like he's having some kind of breakdown. Maybe she should call the paramedics? Or security guards? But before she can, Alex manages to get out, "You said…you said the Department of Defense was working this up."

She nods. Tentative. "Why the army needs a drug that'll knock people out and then kill them is beyond me, but…" She punctuates the remark with a shrug.

"Was it just the DOD working on this as far as you know?"

"The Bureau used to be ignorant about these kind of things, but believe it or not, the federal government's found its Rolodex since 9/11."

"I don't understand."

"We're actually sharing information now," she says. "The FBI has seen the most GHB, has the most experience with it, even more than the FDA, so someone over at Fort Eustis reached out to us when people at Defense decided they wanted to start fucking around with the stuff."

"Why?"

"Guess they wanted our expertise." She shrugs again. "Like I said, we have the most experience."

"No," Alex says, "I mean why would our government get into the business of inventing a fatal date-rape drug?"

"That's a damn good question. Know what they told me when I asked it?"

"What?"

"'Don't ask.'"

◈

The three-hour drive to Fort Eustis gives Alex's jangled nerves time to settle down. Once they do, he curses himself for being thrown in the first place. He's an attorney, damn it. A former defense attorney. If he can stand up to gangbangers like Jesus Pena and remain perfectly calm, what has him so goddamned unnerved now?

It occurs to Alex that he could easily head back up I-95 to Langley. He could march straight into Leah Doyle's office — hell, Arthur goddamn Bryson's office, for that matter — and come clean about everything. Publicity is his best protection. But as he thinks about what he would tell Leah and/or Bryson, the words start to sound ridiculous.

Three people dead from some grand conspiracy to…what? Conceal almost ninety million embezzled dollars? It makes no sense.

What Alex lacks, he realizes, is what lawyers term *the theory of the case.* He has evidence, sure. He has the toxicology report, the accident, and the circumstantial evidence that three unrelated deaths of three related people defies any innocent explanation. What he *doesn't* have, however, is a theory to draw it all together into a single narrative. The theory of the case. *The Why*.

Lawyers don't have to prove the Why in order to meet their burden of proof. The How, the Where, and the When are all that the law requires. In theory. In practice, however, it's different. An attorney wouldn't be able to convince a jury that water is wet without offering up at least a theory as to why. Without a *why,* the deaths of Harling, Moreno, and Miller amount to nothing more than a coincidence, a hypothetical flight of fancy. And it's pretty clear to Alex as he merges onto VA-105 that they weren't murdered to cover up some relatively unimportant embezzlement scheme.

It occurs to Alex that this is the first time he's permitted himself to use the word *murdered*.

Fort Eustis is a military installation the size of a small city located within the larger city of Newport News, Virginia, on the banks of the James River. It began its days as a military post in 1923, and in 1931 it became a federal prison. Because the majority of its inmates were convicted bootleggers, the repeal of Prohibition led to a sharp drop in the prison's population. It wasn't until World War II that it became a full-fledged military facility. Today, it's one of sixteen U.S. Army Training and Doctrine Command (TRADOC) bases. One of its charges is to oversee the procurement and development of new weapons systems. Alex wonders whether R & D on a fatally toxic drug fits that particular bill.

The truth is, it's hard to tell exactly what kind of work is done at Fort Eustis, as it doesn't resemble any kind of military installation Alex has ever seen. Rather, it looks like a not-so-small town, complete with a hospital (McDonald Army Health Care Center), a museum (U.S. Army Transportation Museum), a fast-food restaurant (Burger King), and a racetrack. The place is so large, so expansive, it takes Alex the better part of an hour to figure out where to go once his CIA identification gets him on the base.

Fort Eustis's administration building is an unremarkable one-story structure. The inside is all polished linoleum and government-issue furniture. A latte has more color to it. Nowhere is this truer than in the office of the base's post commander, Peter Walczac. Alex has been told that Walczac is the officer responsible for the base's interactions with outside federal agencies like the FBI.

Walczac, judging from the way his fatigues billow out around his midsection, looks like he's been behind a desk for most of his military career. He wears a hangdog expression that serves as a constant warning to visitors that whatever they want to talk to him about better be damn important. And as far as he's concerned, gamma-hydroxyarsenate doesn't qualify. "Honest to God, I've got no earthly idea what the hell the stuff is," he asserts.

"According to the FBI, this is something you guys were working on," Alex says.

"According to *who* in the FBI?"

"A lab tech named Pamela Voytek. According to her, someone at Fort Eustis requested information on GHA from her."

"If we did, I don't know anything about it. If anyone would, it would be the keeper of secrets."

"Excuse me?"

Walczac grins and sits down at his computer. His fingers go to work for a few seconds. "We requested absolutely no chemical data from the FBI. Not with respect to GHA. Not in this past year. Not ever. Quite frankly," he adds, "I don't know what we'd do with that kind of information even if we had it."

"The FBI is under the impression you're developing a version of a GHA here." Alex sweeps his hand dramatically, as if to suggest the entire base is involved.

Walczac shakes his head. If he seemed put out before, he appears genuinely annoyed now. "We're a training and support installation, Mr. Garnett." He sighs. "We don't have *any* kind of R and D facilities on-site."

"I thought this was a TRADOC facility," Alex says. "Don't you guys research new weapons systems and—"

"First," Walczac says, cutting Alex off, "a fatal toxin is the stuff of Baldacci novels, not a weapons system. Second"—he sucks in a lungful of air—"we may be a TRADOC facility, but we only handle transportation and deployment. You were outside. Maybe you saw the few hundred helicopters, trucks, tanks, and jeeps. That's the Fifty-Eighth Transportation Battalion. My point being, we're too busy *moving* weapons to be inventing them."

"It's a pretty big base," Alex says.

"It is," Walczac agrees, but not in a friendly way.

"So big that maybe it's possible you don't know everything that's going on here," Alex offers as delicately as he can.

The canyon forming on Walczac's brow deepens. "It's my job to know, Mr. Garnett. Have a safe drive back to Langley."

❖

Alex makes his way to his car. He takes in the hive of activity around him, noticing the wide variety of vehicles coming and going for the first time. Now that he knows Fort Eustis's purpose, it *does* seem ridiculous to think it houses some clandestine program to weaponize GHB. Alex trusts his gut more than any polygraph and he's confident he would have sussed it out if Voytek had lied to him. Which means that someone lied to *her*.

Behind Alex, a Sikorsky MH-53J helicopter flies overhead, its rotors kicking up enough noise and dirt to derail his train of thought. His eyes follow the Sikorsky past a chain-link fence where a phalanx of soldiers load jeeps and equipment into a Douglas C-133A Cargomaster. All of the men, vehicles, and equipment sport pixelated shades of brown and gray.

A sign hangs from the chain-link fence:

7TH TRANSPORTATION GROUP
58th Transportation Battalion, 51st Transportation Company

An attractive female soldier, a private if Alex is reading her fatigue insignia right, jogs past. He flags her down. "Hey. Can I ask you a question?" The private turns around, stopping in front of him as she continues to jog in place. He flashes his CIA credentials and gestures over to the Seventh Transportation Group. "That doesn't look like a training exercise."

The private, still jogging in place to keep her heart rate up, nods. "It's not. That's a deployment."

"Deployment to where?"

"I don't know for sure." She looks up to the sign. "Seventh of the Fifty-Eighth. They're Middle East. Iran mainly."

Alex points to all the soldiers. "That's a lot of guys and gear. Did we go to war with Iran and I missed it?"

She shrugs. "Mine's not to reason why, you know?"

By the time Alex returns to I-295, the sun is setting fire to the sky. After less than a mile, he spots a black Escalade looming in his rearview mirror, two car lengths behind him. It's been following him for a while. Har-ling's and Moreno's deaths weren't a paranoid delusion. And he was in the same conference room with them, working on the same case, privy to the same bank account information. He needs to find out the name of the stenographer and make sure she's still alive. And what if she isn't? What if she was in a car accident too? Or was clipped by an oncoming car — a black Escalade perhaps — while crossing the street on her way to work this morning?

He jerks his wheel hard to the right, crossing three lanes of traffic in a single move, cutting off cars and trucks on his way onto the shoulder. The Escalade flies past. Alex watches it disappear into traffic, along with any hope of confirming whether it was really following him.

EIGHT

New Hampshire Avenue NW
Washington, DC
9:36 P.M. EDT

THERE'S A 1997 Napa Valley cabernet Alex has had lying down long enough for it to have had a bar mitzvah, and '97 was a phenomenal year in Napa. Though Alex knows he should save the wine for an occasion, he's spent the last forty minutes thinking about pouring himself a glass or four. It's been that kind of day. Actually, that's an understatement of epic proportions.

When he gets to the door, however, he's surprised to find it unlocked. No, not just unlocked, *ajar.*

"Grace?"

No answer.

"Hello?"

Still no answer. His mouth goes dry. His heart gallops. It takes an eternity to reach the bedroom. The door is open and the lights are off in there too. The room is eerily quiet. All Alex can hear is the hum of traffic outside.

Something under the bed catches his eye: an errant piece of black cloth peeking out. Slowly, he crouches down, feeling a low tide of panic rise in his chest. Tentatively, he reaches toward it. His fingers start to graze the light fabric when he hears the noise. It's as loud as an explosion going off and it shoots him to his feet. The primitive part of his brain knows that if he's not alone in the apartment, he's moving too slowly to save his life. He fully expects the next sound he hears to be his last.

Which makes it all the more ridiculous that it's the unmistakable sound of his toilet flushing.

There's an interval of hand-washing, and then the bathroom door opens and a distinguished man in a dark blue Zegna suit steps out. At seventy, although he looks as if he were still in his sixties, he's older than your average hit man.

Not that Alex would ever mistake his father for a hit man.

Alex forgot about his father's key to the condo, left over from when he'd bought the condo for him and Grace as a gift. That was the word his father had used, *gift,* as if cars and condominiums fell into the same category as books and clothing. Alex didn't want to accept it, gift or not, didn't want to be beholden to his father in any way. But Grace fell in love with the place, with its clean lines and postcard-perfect view of the Potomac, and she convinced Alex to capitulate. She didn't grow up with the kind of privilege Alex took for granted and he couldn't deny her something that would obviously give her such joy.

Alex pours some Glenlivet into two bar glasses until each is about a quarter full. The Glenlivet's aged eighteen years and it's not the cheapest scotch, but it's still not the '97 cab Alex was hoping to enjoy. No force on earth could compel him to waste that vintage on Simon Garnett.

"Missed you at my birthday," Mr. Garnett is saying, sitting down.

"I figured the invite was perfunctory," Alex replies, handing his father one of the scotches and quickly taking a large gulp of his own. He sits down and closes his eyes, feeling the medicinal-tasting liquor hit the back of his throat with a burn. The entire glass is polished off in that single gulp.

His father savors the scotch like a sommelier. "Between the two of us, Alex, I'm not the one with the problem."

"Why are you here?" Alex asks, making a mental note to get the locks changed.

A grimace passes across Simon's face. He takes another sip of scotch. "This afternoon, I received word from the Virginia Superior Court that my firm had filed an appearance in a drunk-driving case," he explains in the most measured of tones. "On behalf of an Alan Miller. And that you were the attorney of record." The way his father says Miller's name, it doesn't sound like he knows Miller died in custody. At least, Alex hopes that's the case. But then, Simon Garnett is nothing if not inscrutable, particularly where his son is concerned. "I thought you were working for the CIA these days."

"I am."

"No need to thank me for the recommendation to Arthur Bryson, by the way."

"Thanks." Alex chokes the word out with as little gratitude as he can manage. "As for Miller, it's not something I can talk about. It's classified. CIA business. But I needed to make the appearance and I couldn't do it as an attorney for the Agency. You being such a patriot, I figured you wouldn't mind me using the firm's name."

"Alan Miller died in custody," his father says. Alex can feel his father's eyes burning into him, poring over his face for signs of whether this news has come as a shock. A litigator's probing gaze, hunting for tells like a card player at a poker table. "The jail called the firm. You weren't there, of course. So the call was forwarded to me."

"I hope it wasn't too much of an inconvenience." But Alex really could not care less about inconveniencing his father. He's just focused on maintaining his stoicism, keeping his poker face.

His father's eyes, gunmetal blue and piercing, look him over, the litigator's gaze giving way to a cross-examiner's stare. It's a look that says, *I can tell if you're lying*. What Simon actually says is "Alex…is everything all right?"

His father's tone surprises Alex. There's something in it that he hasn't heard since…childhood? Probably. He almost doesn't recognize it: genuine concern.

"If you're having some kind of problem," his father ventures, "you know I have resources…"

"I don't need your help. Everything's fine." Alex doesn't intend for this to come out as defiant as it does, but frankly, he'd like to be free of his father's resources for once in his life.

Fortunately, it appears Simon Garnett's not in the mood to fight tonight. "That's fine. I expected that. But don't tell me everything's fine. You're pretending you still work for me, your client is dead, and you're acting…" His voice trails off. "You don't look well."

Truth be told, Alex doesn't feel well. He feels tired to his bones. He wants Grace. He wants to fall asleep in her arms. And all he can manage right now is to repeat "I don't need your help." This time, there's no defiance in the words. Just exhaustion.

Simon Garnett has made a successful career out of knowing when to cut his losses. So he stands up, sets his empty glass on a nearby table, and offers up a nod that suggests surrender. He pauses at the door. "I understand you want to be your own man, Alex. Whether you believe it or not, I've always respected that about you. But a man knows when the water's at his head. And a man knows it's okay to ask for help when he needs it."

Simon Garnett then shuts the door behind him. It's not until the next morning that Alex notices he left his spare key behind.

◈

OGC, NEW HEADQUARTERS BUILDING
9:15 A.M. EDT

After his father left, after Grace got home, after they made love, after Alex felt Grace's body tremble and then fall asleep in his arms, he decided to let all thoughts of multiple homicide, conspiracy, and troop movement rest for twenty-four hours. The pause would give him some much-needed perspective. Problems are always clearer, puzzles more solvable, when they're put aside for a while. And after yesterday's unrelenting series of revelations, dealing with a routine evidentiary matter for The Hague, as he's doing now, is as welcome as a cool drink in a desert.

Then his phone rings. "Hello?" There's no response. "Hello?" Again, there's nothing on the line but silence. Alex is about to hang up when he hears a modulated, mechanical voice that sounds like a robot underwater, neither male nor female, not even human. It says three words, lending inflection or importance to none of them: "Stop asking questions."

His stomach dive-bombs into his intestines, but his mind remains razor sharp. He holds the phone's receiver with one hand and opens a desk drawer with the other, grabbing for the cell phone he should have left in his car. Phones are prohibited within two miles of headquarters. But old habits are hard to break, and Alex, like most people, is accustomed to always having his phone — it's like another appendage. Fortunately, Tom Ciampa is usually working security and gives him a pass. Alex offers a silent prayer of thanks for Tom as he find the phone, digs it out, turns it on, and thumbs one of the numbers stored in memory.

"Yes," Gerald Jankovick answers. He's doing his best impression of a radio DJ. "This is WCIA. Playing the best music from Mel Tormé, Neil Diamond, and Barry —"

"Gerald, it's Alex," he interrupts, hissing into the phone.

"Dude. Long time, zero speak. Which is odd, considering we're now working for the same spook shop. What up?"

The modulated voice on the other end of Alex's desk phone ticks off names: "Evelyn Moreno. Jim Harling. Alan Miller."

"I'm getting a call right now at my desk. Right now. Can you trace it?"

"Brenda Zollitsch," the voice says. Alex searches his memory for some association with the name but comes up empty. *Who is Brenda Zol-*

litsch? Is she alive? The caller certainly seems to be implying that Zollitsch was one of his—her? their?—victims, along with Harling and Moreno. The voice pauses for a few seconds before adding a fifth and final name: "Alex Garnett."

"What do you need this for?" Gerald is asking on the cell.

"Just tell me."

Alex can hear Gerald working his keyboard six floors underneath him at his workstation in the New Headquarters Building's subbasement. It feels like an eternity is passing. Although his life has just been threatened, Alex ignores that, too focused on his silent prayer that his anonymous caller won't hang up before Gerald completes the trace.

"Office G-eight," Gerald reports, mercifully coming back on the line. "Seventh floor."

"Of what? Seventh floor of *what?*"

"Of headquarters," Gerald answers. "Your call is coming from *inside* the building, hoss."

Reflexively, Alex looks around the bullpen surrounding his desk. Is he being watched? His head starts to swim. Without warning, the voice returns, bringing with it Alex's clarity, shattering his disorientation with the force of a steel pipe barreling into the windshield of a '65 Mustang. "Do you understand, Mr. Garnett?"

He drops the receiver on his desk without answering the question. The phone is useless to him now, anyway. But he needs to keep the connection alive so this mysterious caller won't realize he isn't on the line. That's assuming the caller isn't watching Alex sprint from his desk and run like a lunatic to the nearest elevator bank, still white-knuckling his cell phone.

"Is there any way you can tell if the caller's still in that office?" Alex asks Gerald as he slides into the elevator, its doors mercifully open.

"Well, the computer node in the room's still active," Gerald answers.

"Computer node?" Alex punches the button for the seventh floor repeatedly, willing the elevator doors to shut.

"Somebody's running spyware on your system," Gerald tells him. "Every keystroke you make, every file on your drive. It's elegant code, really."

Alex is about to ask if this kind of cybermonitoring is normal in the CIA, but the elevator doors open — finally! — and he bounds out like a thoroughbred from the starting gate. He doesn't get more than twenty feet before he realizes he's never been to the seventh floor. Its warren of offices and cubicles might as well be a labyrinth. His eyes dart around for some signage or directory, but there's nothing. He's in the tall grass without a compass and his window of opportunity is closing. Fast. His mysterious caller won't stay in G-8 for long. He presses the cell to his ear again. "I'm at the elevator bank on seven. Where's the office?" He doesn't hear anything, not Gerald's voice or the telltale click-clack of his computer keys. Did Gerald get off the call? "Gerald! *Where's the fucking office?*"

More silence. Alex is about to launch his cell down the hallway in aggravation.

"This takes time, y'know," Gerald says, finally coming back on. "You don't have to get pissy."

"Gerald —"

"Again with the pissy. Go to your right."

Alex bolts down the corridor to his right and finds that it T-bones at the end. A fork in the road. On the cell, Gerald tells him to hang a left, and Alex takes the turn in a sprint, disregarding the Restricted Area sign and promptly crashing into a wall of bulletproof Lexan glass. Pain shoots through his head and shoulder as he hears a siren that sounds like it heralds Armageddon. Then a flashing light bathes the entire corridor in red. Before Alex can react, a second wall of glass comes sliding down behind him.

Trapping him.

He better start working on his explanation for running around the restricted halls of the CIA. Of more immediate concern, however, is getting out of this security box and into that fucking room with the fucking spyware. The motherfucker in that room *threatened* him. And if there's anything Simon Garnett's only son learned from his father, it's that when you're threatened, you man up. In this case, manning up would also have the virtue of getting him some answers, perhaps allowing him to confront an actual person instead of a mist of theories, suspicions, and inhuman voices.

Alex barks into his cell phone — "Gerald!" — only to hear that Gerald, God bless the little geek, is already trying to fix the problem, judging by the sweet, reassuring click-clack of his keyboard.

"Working on it," Gerald says, sounding surprisingly calm. The virtual world of computers is the one place in which Gerald Jankovick is a Zen master. "I'm working on it," Gerald says again, "but security got wind of some nutbar tearing through the complex, and they've got the whole place on lockdown. Some coincidence, huh?"

The sound of footfalls, and Alex spins around to see three CIA security guards bearing down on him. They're running fast and carrying M4A1 carbine assault rifles. Alex looks to his cell to push Gerald again, but the line's gone dead. The cell's LCD, glowing an eerie pink in the light of the security lamps, is no longer receiving a signal.

The trio of guards approaches the glass wall in front of Alex. One of them has his walkie out. Despite the thick glass and the din of the security-alert siren, Alex can hear the guard calling for the wall to be retracted upward. Once that happens, Alex'll be taken into custody, and the guards won't be gentle about it. Hoping to avoid that fate with a show of goodwill, Alex puts his phone in his jacket pocket and starts to raise his hands above his head just as . . . *the wall behind him slides up.* The first wall still separates him from the guards. Alex bolts.

He shoots down the corridor, counting off the numbers on the placards outside the ghetto of offices — *five, six, seven* — until he reaches the eighth. *G-8.* He grabs the handle, throws his shoulder against the door like a linebacker. By some rare stroke of good fortune, the door isn't locked. Alex goes flying in, hoping to catch whoever's inside off guard. With his enemy disoriented, he fantasizes, Alex'll find the nearest heavy object and knock the guy out, and then when he wakes up, the guy can explain to Leah what the fuck he thought he was doing. In fact — fuck it — he's bringing Arthur Bryson in for the explanation too.

But there's no one in the room.

There's not even the computer Gerald said was there. Instead, all there is is dust. Dust and old file cabinets of rusted green metal filling the room, reaching to the ceiling.

Alex's gaze crawls over the cabinets, and he has the growing sense that no one's seen the inside of this room in months, if not years. The cabinets are marked with alphabetical ranges or simply letters: *A–F, B, A–G, A–M, D–L, E–M, F–Q, N–O, N,* and on and on and on. Rage building inside him, Alex starts pulling drawers at random, which takes no small amount of strength. The drawers protest with rusty, metallic groans. Clearly Alex is the first person in decades to open them.

Inside, he finds hanging folders with handwritten plastic-covered labels. The dust has even managed to get into the drawers, and he is soon choking with every breath. He covers his mouth with one hand while with the other he pulls out random files. They all look like employee records, with names, dates of birth, Social Security numbers, and pay-grade levels, relics from the days when the bureaucratic flotsam and jetsam of the CIA was kept on paper instead of stored in massive underground EMP-proof computer farms.

Alex opens a file labeled "Parking Permit Requisitions." He stares at it briefly, hoping its dry, bureaucratic contents somehow hold an answer to the mysteries of the past twenty-four hours. Then, oddly, a red dot appears on the file. It lingers for a beat before it slides off the page and out of view. Alex turns around and finds the red dot again. In the center of his chest. Suddenly, two more join it. All three generated by the SureFire laser sights mounted on the M4s that three green-jacketed guards are pointing straight at him.

"Very slowly, sir…place your hands behind your head."

Alex doesn't need someone carrying an M4 to tell him anything twice. He puts his hands behind his head as instructed, taking care to move as slowly as possible. "I've got an explanation for this," Alex says, hoping he can come up with one by the time he's asked for it.

"This area is restricted," the green jacket says.

"Right…" Alex lets the word trail off, his mind racing to come up with a line of bullshit to get him out of this mess. "Yeah, sure, but…see, the thing is, the GC…" Again, his voice trails off; he's stalling, trying to buy time until his cleverness kicks in. "GC — that's my boss, the general counsel — he asked me to pull all the KH-Eleven satellite tracks for Burma." He shakes the parking-permit requisition file he's still holding, hoping his thumb is covering the label, hoping that the file looks like it contains photographs taken by an Enhanced CRYSTAL KH-11 imagery intelligence satellite.

Alex sees the guard consider, his eyes darting up to the file, then back to Alex. Alex is watching the man's finger relax, ever so slightly, on the gun's trigger when a shrill beeping cuts through the room and the tension.

"My phone," Alex says flatly.

"Cell phones are prohibited at headquarters."

Alex ignores that. With glacial slowness, he lowers his hand, the hand that isn't clutching the file, and reaches slowly into his suit jacket. His eyes are pleading, *It's cool. I'm not going for a gun.* The guards seem to believe him because they don't open up with the M4s. Just as slowly, he places the phone to his ear.

"What the fuck happened?" Gerald screams on the other end. He's loud. Loud enough that Alex is afraid the guards might hear, so he presses the phone against his chest to muffle the speaker.

"That's Arthur Bryson," Alex lies, indicating the phone.

"Mr. Bryson's calling you on a cell phone you're not supposed to have on the premises?"

Alex holds the phone out to the guard. "You wanna talk to him? He wants to know what's keeping me. He sounds a little pissed." He holds the phone out farther. Gerald has, mercifully, fallen silent. "Go ahead."

The guard says nothing. The minute yawns. Alex's heart races. He's no longer afraid of being shot, but he's pretty sure he's going to be fired.

After an eternity, the guard shakes his head. "I don't need to talk to Mr. Bryson." Alex notes that the man isn't looking to his partners for approval, suggesting he's the one in charge. Which means he's the one Alex has to convince. He relaxes his grip and lowers the proffered phone. A relieved smile threatens to break out across his face and it's all he can do to suppress the grin. Until the guard speaks again. "But *we're* gonna have a talk with your immediate superior."

Alex deflates, knowing the conversation the guard is suggesting won't be a pleasant one. "That would be Leah Doyle," he says.

"Let's go see Ms. Doyle, then."

NINE

LEAH SAYS nothing as Alex waits in her office. He stands at attention while she stares at him, inscrutable. The green jacket lingers near the door, curious to see how this drama is going to play out. It's almost as if Leah is daring Alex to say something, but Alex knows that's the wrong way to go. The guard brought Alex straight to Leah's office and told her the whole story, like a cat proudly placing a dead mouse at its owner's feet, and now it is Leah's turn to respond. Instead of laying into Alex, however, she wields her silence like a club. He would prefer being yelled at.

After what feels like forever, Leah asks, "What were you thinking?" Apparently Alex takes too long to reply, because Leah follows up with "Running around the CIA, running through a restricted area...you could have gotten yourself shot. You *should've* gotten yourself shot. In fact, I have half a mind to have the sergeant here shoot you now like he should have ten minutes ago." The green jacket grins slightly, as if suggesting this is not an entirely unattractive idea to him, but Leah remains cold.

Seconds drip past. After a painful interval, Leah shakes her head. She's obviously angered but still hasn't raised her voice a decibel. Instead, she just turns to the guard and, in a level tone, says, "Thank you, Sergeant."

The guard nods and exits, knowing a dismissal when he hears one. He closes the door behind him and, once the two are alone, Leah motions for Alex to sit. She sits across from him, her interrogatory gaze unrelenting. Once again, the silence is painful. But now that the green jacket is gone, Alex fills it, speaking slowly and choosing his words with care. "I'd like, if you don't mind, to explain —"

"Except you *can't* explain." Leah cuts him off. "Because if you did, that would mean you'd have to either lie to me or tell me the truth, and if you told the truth, you'd be contradicting the lie you told to Sergeant Powell." She fixes him with a look. "Because we both know you weren't in that file room on Bryson's orders." Alex resists the urge to nod and just meets her steely gaze instead.

"Leah —"

But Leah looks away and cuts him off again. "Shut up." There's another pause and Alex realizes that this time, it's not deliberate. This time, Leah is trying to figure out what to do. This, Alex thinks, is good. When she looks back at him, she says, "People in the office said you got a phone call just before lockdown…"

"That's true —"

"I know it's true," she says, interrupting him yet again. "I had the phone logs checked." She exhales, exasperated. "On the incredibly unlikely off chance that Bryson did, in fact, call you on your cell." Leah shoots Alex a *checkmate* glare, having caught him in a lie. But then it occurs to Alex that it might not mean *checkmate* so much as *strike one,* because now Leah softens. "People in the office said you got a phone call and that you looked unwell. That you looked *ashen.*" She waits for Alex to reply. Wisely, he doesn't. "I'm going to assume those two events are related." Alex's expression confirms that they are. "I'm going to *assume* your running around the office has a legitimate explanation of a personal nature. I'm going to *assume* it was a onetime thing."

"It was and I'm —"

Again, she stops him, holding up a cautioning finger. "Actually, I'm *not* going to assume this was a onetime thing. I don't *need* to assume it. Because I *know* it. This was a onetime thing." There's no question mark at the end of that statement.

Alex has a multitude of potential responses here, but he chooses the safest one. "Thank you." Leah doesn't say anything. Alex takes this as his cue to leave.

But just as he gets to the door, Leah adds, "Don't forget that I read that psych profile we did on you your first day here. Don't think I don't know how professionally self-destructive you can be. If I'm being honest with myself, the only reason I'm not firing you right now is the possibility that on some level, that's exactly what you want." Alex looks back at her, defiant. "And I think you're better than that."

◈

Alex's mysterious caller mentioned a fourth victim, Brenda Zollitsch. Armed with that information, he heads for one of the building's stand-alone computers. For security purposes, the Agency's computer network is a closed system. Connections to the outside world of the Internet—with all its Trojans, viruses, and phishing schemes—are understandably limited to specific computers, and one must have special authorization to access them. Fortunately, Alex's position as a lawyer in the Office of General Counsel affords him said authorization.

A quick Google search immediately identifies Brenda Zollitsch as a stenographer, which leads to a conclusion as firm as bedrock: She was killed because she was present for Jim Harling's deposition. Alex knows this with the same surety as he knows that the transcript Zollitsch took of the deposition has, by now, disappeared.

Although there are no articles reporting Zollitsch's death, Google tells him that she lived in Arlington, Virginia. Back at his desk, Alex places a call to the Arlington County Sheriff's Office and navigates his way through several layers of bureaucracy. His CIA bona fides are helpful in this regard, but the process still takes nearly half an hour. He manages to get confirmation on Zollitsch's passing before he's eventually handed off to a weary-voiced homicide detective.

"My name is Alex Garnett. I work for the CIA's Office of General Counsel," Alex says. "I was told that you're investigating the Brenda Zollitsch homicide."

"It's not a homicide," the detective rebuts. "And what's an Office of General Counsel?"

"It's the CIA's legal department. Two days ago, I oversaw a deposition. I have reason to believe that Ms. Zollitsch was the stenographer for the proceeding."

"Okay." Clearly, the detective has lost both interest and patience.

"Ms. Zollitsch died yesterday."

"Yup. Coroner ruled it a suicide this morning. She overdosed on Ativan. She'd been taking it for anxiety."

"Detective, are you aware that an attorney and the witness in this deposition *also* passed away within the last two days?" The long pause on the other end of the line confirms that the detective was not. "Jim Harling died in a car accident, and Evelyn Moreno had a heart attack."

There's another pause. "Were they in the same car?" the detective asks.

"No. What difference does that—"

But the detective interrupts him. "I'm not seeing how those two deaths could be related to each other. Or how Ms. Zollitsch's suicide could be related to *them*."

Alex swallows bile. "I told you. They were all present for the same deposition two days ago."

Alex thinks he's done a good job of camouflaging his frustration, but the detective's response implies otherwise. "Mr. Garnett, I understand that you're agitated," he says. The cop takes a deep breath. "But try to see this from my perspective for a second, all right? You're telling me about three unrelated deaths. One from natural causes, another from a vehicular accident, and a third from a suicide." Alex decides it would not be a good idea to bring Alan Miller's death into the mix, so he lets the detective continue. "You're *also* telling me that these three individuals have nothing whatsoever in common apart from the fact that they were all involved in the same legal proceeding. I gotta be honest with you, Mr. Garnett: That looks a whole lot like coincidence to me. I heard of a case once, commuter plane crash, six fatalities, all of 'em were Libras. It didn't make me believe in astrology. Just coincidence."

Alex sighs into the phone. He starts to consider his options and realizes he has none.

"Is there anything else I can do for you, Mr. Garnett?"

Now it's Alex's turn to pause. "No, Detective. Thank you for your time."

◆

The restaurant, 2100 Prime, in the Fairfax Hotel in Dupont Circle is a throwback to the steak joints of the 1950s. Alex moves briskly through the restaurant. The *Mad Men*–like décor is all but lost on Alex as he practically sprints to where Grace, a friend of hers from medical school, and the friend's husband are already seated. He doesn't check his phone, but he estimates he's a good twenty-five minutes late. Although his life was threatened and his job nearly lost, there were filing deadlines he had to deal with. The business of the court continued, even in the face of death threats and dinner obligations.

"Sorry," he says as he takes his seat. "Killer day at work."

"Are you feeling okay?" Grace asks. "You look terrible."

"Thanks."

"I mean, you look pale. Are you sick?"

"Just…an extremely tough day at the Agency."

"Alex is working for the CIA, believe it or not," Grace explains to the other couple.

"Feel free not to believe it," Alex offers. "I barely do myself."

"I thought you were an attorney," Grace's friend says, a little confused.

"I am. The CIA needs lawyers too," he says as his phone rings. He removes it from his suit jacket and notes the Virginia area code on the incoming number. "I'm really sorry," he says as he rises from his seat. "It's work."

"Work already made you a half an hour late," Grace notes.

"It's been that kind of day." He heads toward the restrooms and stands in the corridor.

"Hello," he says into the phone.

"Mr. Garnett? I'm Dr. DeVeau with the Virginia Department of Health. I'm a coroner in the chief medical examiner's office."

Alex knows that already. He's the one who called DeVeau in the first place. "I was told you performed the autopsy on Alan Miller?"

"Yes. That's right. His attorney requested it."

"I know. I'm Mr. Miller's attorney. *Was*," he corrects. "Can you tell me what the cause of death was?"

"I'm afraid you're going to need a court order if you want to review the autopsy findings, Mr. Garnett."

"Off the record."

"I don't do off the record. That's how people lose their jobs."

"Doctor." Alex works to keep his tone level. "My client passed away while in the custody of the State of Virginia. The lawsuit I will file can drag in a large number of state employees or a focused group." DeVeau doesn't respond, which suggests to Alex that his threat may have been too subtle. "People mired in lawsuits also have a tendency to lose their jobs."

There is a chasm of silence on the other end of the line. Then Alex hears DeVeau suck in a breath that's followed by an exhale of surrender. "*Off the record,* sir, Mr. Miller died of cardiorespiratory arrest."

"I'm not a doctor, but isn't heart and lung failure pretty much what *everyone* eventually dies of?" Alex chides himself for letting his frustration get the better of him. He won't get much cooperation if he continues using this tone.

DeVeau sighs. "I don't know what to tell you. That's the result of my findings."

Alex wills patience into his voice. "Did you run any tests that might point to the cause of the arrest?"

"Of course we did," DeVeau responds with the same exasperation Alex is struggling to avoid displaying. "We ran a toxicology screen and a chem panel, and we did a full blood workup. There were no findings of note. Nothing unusual, in other words."

"What about gamma-hydroxyarsenate? Did you find any traces of that chemical in his system?"

"What? There is no such compound."

But Alex knows there is. He wonders if the Department of Defense had managed to devise a variation on GHB that was both fatal *and* undetectable by standard medical tests. "It's a reformulation of GHB, gamma-hydroxybutyric acid."

"I know what GHB is. But it's not something we test for. I mean, it's not part of the standard tests."

Now we're getting somewhere, Alex thinks. "Could you please test for it? Could you run a screen or something to determine whether there was any GHB or GHA in his system?"

"GHB is very difficult to detect, Mr. Garnett," DeVeau says sharply. "It's cleared out of the body extremely quickly."

"Please, Doctor. This is important."

DeVeau sighs a final time. "It's late. I'll look into it tomorrow. Don't worry; Mr. Miller isn't going anywhere, believe me."

DeVeau ends the call. Alex is about to go back to the table when Grace comes up to him in the corridor. "Everything okay at work?" she asks in a tone that is definitely below room temperature.

"Like I said, tough day," Alex answers. That much, at least, is the truth.

"Are you all right? You look stressed."

"I am stressed," he allows. Again, the truth. But the truth can conceal a lie if it's rendered incompletely. *Why don't you just tell her?* he asks himself. *Someone threatened your fucking life today.* But another voice in his head answers, *And if you tell her that, she'll freak out too. Assuming she doesn't take the opposite view and decide you're a paranoid nutjob.* "Things got a little tense at work today," he says. "Someone outside the Agency made a threat."

"What kind of threat?"

"Long story. It has me a little thrown, but I'll shake it off. Sorry I'm not the greatest company tonight."

"I just want you to be okay."

"So do I," he says, knowing that whoever called him today doesn't share that sentiment.

TEN

TEHRAN, IRAN
1600 HRS. ZULU

AYATOLLAH JAHANDAR and President Tehrani stroll leisurely past the White House — not the one in Washington, DC, but the identically named building among the eighteen structures dotting the grounds of Sa'dabad Palace. Tehrani's mood is ebullient, as it has been ever since he received word that Iran's first nuclear warhead had been constructed. The only thing that prevents him from taking to satellite television to announce Iran's grand achievement — and make the not-so-veiled threat of its use — is Jahandar, the one man in the government who outranks him.

"We could wipe Israel off the map," he says eagerly. Tehrani has made no secret of his desire to annihilate Israel. In fact, the entire world is aware that once Iran has the bomb, it will be only a matter of time before it destroys its vilified Jewish enemy to the west.

"Israel has its own nuclear arsenal," Jahandar cautions. "Surely you haven't forgotten it."

"They'd be hard-pressed to mount a counterattack if they're all dead."

"You sound like one of those Cold War zealots, my friend. The Soviets and the Americans — some of them, at least — believed a nuclear war could be won."

"Many of those men were the preeminent military strategists of their day."

Jahandar brushes the comment away with his hand. "To hold such a belief would be naive were it not so reckless." That Tehrani is an academic who has spent no time whatsoever in military service, Jahandar doesn't comment upon. Instead, he chooses to engage his compatriot on territory where he has the high ground: religion. "Less than a decade ago," he says, "I led our nation's clerics in proclaiming that weapons of mass destruction were against Islam."

Tehrani nods sagely, allowing the hint of a smile. "I thought that was just *taqiyya*," he says, referring to the Koran's dictum that lies are permissible when told for the purposes of misleading unbelievers. "As it is written in the Hadith, the Prophet said, 'War is deceit.'" Tehrani's eyes are set deep in his head, framed by wrinkles that suggest constant fatigue. But there's no torpor in his gaze as he lasers in on Jahandar in this moment. "And are we not at war?"

Jahandar considers this for a beat. "There are many forms of war. I would not have us trade the one we're presently fighting for another we have no hope of winning."

Having been involved in politics since the 1980s, Tehrani knows all about the art of the possible. It doesn't take much political calculation to realize that he can't do anything with his country's newly acquired nuclear might while the ayatollah opposes it. He forces a smile and an appreciative nod to hide how frustrating he finds his current circumstances, demonstrating more diplomacy than he thought himself capable of. "Wise counsel, my friend. Extremely wise."

Jahandar sees through this patronizing gesture as if he's looking through a pane of glass. Still, he nods in acknowledgment. The delicate dance of sharing the power of a nation, he decided long ago, is easier with the president of Iran as his ally rather than his opponent. "There are also other reasons for forbearance."

"Such as?"

"For one thing," Jahandar says, "Project One-Eleven is not yet completed. We have nuclear power, yes, but we do not have the means to project it. Tel Aviv is approximately sixteen hundred kilometers away. Without a long-range missile on which to mount our new weapon, all it's good for is blowing up our own country."

Tehrani nods, although he's far more optimistic about Project 111's imminent completion than his supreme leader appears to be. "And?" he prompts.

"I have concerns that the nuclear warhead is designed to fail."

Tehrani is unable to hide his surprise. "And what do you base those concerns on?"

"On that matter, my friend," Jahandar says with an intentionally mischievous smile, "I prefer to keep my own counsel for the moment. Besides, my suspicions may very well be wrong." But Jahandar has lived long enough to know that they never are.

◆

OGC, New Headquarters Building
4:45 P.M. EDT

Alex watches as Gerald wrestles his anxieties into submission long enough to give a presentation on the CIA's cybermonitoring program in China. Code-named MP Hawkeye, the operation utilizes computer hackers working out of Germany and pretending to be Chinese citizens—some patriotic, others less so. Acting as virtual spies, the hackers participate in chat rooms and message boards within China's borders. From there, they do what any traditional CIA NOC does: recruit assets and gather intel.

The one legal issue, and therefore the reason for Gerald's presentation, is that the CIA has been almost exclusively utilizing websites, chat rooms, and message boards set up by Google, an American corporation.

This is by necessity, not choice, of course, because Google is the only Western company that has managed to penetrate China's virtual iron curtain. But many of the servers that keep Google's cyberworld alive are located within the borders of the United States. Meaning that, technically speaking, some of Hawkeye's cyber-activities are taking place in America, thus violating the CIA charter's prohibition against engaging in domestic espionage.

The whole thing strikes Alex as an exercise in debating the number of angels who can dance on the head of a pin. No, it's even more esoteric than that. It's a debate about what constitutes an angel and what could be argued is a pin. But that's why lawyers exist.

Much to Alex's astonishment, Gerald didn't comment on the previous day's excitement or, of greater concern, Alex's part in it. This might have been God's response to the silent prayer Alex made when he saw that Gerald would be involved in this meeting. Or maybe Gerald has more discretion than Alex gives him credit for.

"No e-mail is completely anonymous," Gerald explains to the assembly. "An e-mail, any e-mail, can be traced back to its author, even e-mails sent through so-called anonymous routers. No matter what steps the author takes to cover his tracks, including using anonymous e-mail-forwarding services, there is *always* a trail. *Always.*"

Gerald stops to answer a question from Arthur Bryson about the odds of the CIA's cyber-agents being discovered or, worse, of their cyber-espionage adventures in China being traced back to the U.S. military base in Germany. But the answer doesn't matter. Not to Alex. He's got other things on his mind. And they don't involve Germany, China, or cyber-espionage.

After the presentation, Alex buttonholes Gerald. The geek is eager to make a quick exit from the conference room, no doubt to return to the seclusion of his sublevel-basement office, but Alex's urgency allows no protest. "I need you to follow a money trail for me," he tells Gerald.

"This have anything to do with whatever had you running around the Agency offices like a crazy person?"

"Maybe. I'm not sure." It's an honest answer.

"I gotta tell you, I had to pop an extra Xanax after all that shit."

Gerald is obviously trying to wriggle out of anything Alex has planned, but that isn't happening. "This is important, Gerald. It's potentially very important. Can you help me?"

Gerald thinks for a moment before answering. "Sure. But not here. I'm not gonna go hacking around with one of the Agency's stand-alones."

"You probably couldn't even if you wanted to. There must be a ton of safeguards on those computers."

"There are. You wanna know how I know? 'Cause you're talking to the guy who put 'em there. And even if I hadn't, do you think for two seconds that I couldn't bypass those protections if I wanted to?"

"Didn't mean to offend you, Gerald."

Apparently, the apology is good enough. "C'mon, we'll go to the Internet connection closest to campus."

"And where's that?"

"Where do you think? Starbucks."

The closest Starbucks (not including the franchise that sits in the atrium connecting the New Headquarters Building to the Old Headquarters Building) is across the Potomac in Bethesda. Once there, Alex does his part by providing Gerald with a venti green tea and the routing numbers of the two wire transfers — the one that deposited the small fortune into Harling's account and the other that removed it. It takes Gerald about forty-five seconds to discover that the money came from the same source it was returned to: a two-year-old Internet start-up based outside of Seattle, Washington. "Why is some start-up loaning Harling ninety million dollars?" Alex wonders aloud as he stands behind Gerald and watches the laptop's screen. "Was he an investor or something?"

"Easy enough to check," Gerald says. His fingers dance across the keys of his MacBook Air for a minute, then stop abruptly. "What is it?" Alex asks. Gerald doesn't answer. He sets to work on the laptop again, typing faster, stabbing the keys hard enough to break them, his thumb gliding along the trackpad like an Olympic figure skater. "Gerald," Alex says, but Gerald remains consumed by his work, eyes laser-focused on his screen. Alex tries to follow what's happening on the Air's LCD display, but the images shift too fast for him to keep up. Judging from the expression on Gerald's face, Alex figures that whatever he's finding isn't good.

Alex can't resist glancing around the coffee shop and then over his shoulder and through the windows to the street outside to see if anyone's watching them. That feeling of threat—no longer paranoia, no longer theoretical—is creeping its way back up the center of his body. He's about to tell Gerald to forget it, shut his computer down—better yet, throw it the fuck away—when Gerald looks up from the laptop and turns around to face Alex. "Bud," he says, "you have a very large problem here."

◈

In his time at the CIA, Gerald has picked up a few elements of what's known as tradecraft, the tricks and techniques used in espionage. One of them is the counterintuitive fact that the best location for a private conversation is a public place, preferably an outdoor one. The ambient noises of the outside world—cars honking, trucks driving, people talking, and so on—help to block or at least frustrate most surveillance technologies. As long as one takes precautions against lipreading—by, say, staying in constant motion, pacing back and forth, as Alex and Gerald are now doing—chances of a private conversation remaining private are pretty good.

Right now, however, Gerald moves a bit faster than good tradecraft dictates. It's all Alex can do to keep up with him. "Gerald, will you calm down? Or at least *slow* down?" he pleads, so urgently that he wonders if he and Gerald look like two people in the middle of a heated lovers' spat. Not that Alex cares. He's far, far more concerned with whatever Gerald unearthed during his cybernetic scavenger hunt, which clearly prompted this panic attack. Alex actually has to grab Gerald by the arm and give it a firm tug just to get him to stop walking. When Alex turns Gerald around to face him, he sees a man gripped in a terror that's orders of magnitude more unsettling to him than the anxious expression Gerald normally wears.

"Tell me," Alex says.

That's what Gerald needs. He takes a breath, a deep one, and exhales. "The money…it got wired from and back to—"

"A start-up company," Alex says. "You told me this. So—"

"So it's not a start-up. It's a *front*. It's a fake corporation."

"Set up by who?"

"By *us*."

ELEVEN

ALEX STARES at Gerald, incredulous. "What are you talking about?"

"The front was set up by the CIA. It's a cover for the Agency's black budget."

To Alex, this comes as unexpectedly good news. Despite its name, the black budget is not particularly sinister. True, its existence is highly classified and consistently denied, but it's hardly secret. The CIA's actual working budget is both public and substantial — approximately $55 billion. From that money, which comes with the burden of congressional oversight, the Agency siphons off small amounts — barely more than a rounding error's worth — from its many departments into a secret, black budget for use in its covert operations. Like grains of sand accumulating to make a beach, however, the tiny donations from the CIA's various departments add up to a very significant number.

"Jim Harling was a NOC," Alex reassures Gerald, "so I wouldn't be surprised if he had access to some classified funds, some black-budget dollars. So calm down, okay? All you've unearthed here is the paper trail of a field spook's normal operations." This seems to mollify Gerald a bit. "I wanted to know where the money came from and you found out. And the explanation is totally innocent."

Gerald visibly calms now. "Innocent," he repeats. "Money from a spy's classified bank account is what we're calling 'innocent' these days." The hint of a grin ripples across his face like a mirage. "You ever stop to wonder how the hell this happened?"

"What do you mean?"

"I mean the two of us. Me out of school. You out of your dad's firm. We're about as far away from that shit as you can get. Toto, we are most definitely not in Kansas anymore."

◆

Prince George's County, Maryland
9:00 P.M. EDT

The Awakening is a group of five sculptures created by J. Seward Johnson Jr. The five pieces — a head, two arms, and two legs — are arranged in the ground so as to create an image of a hundred-foot-tall Rip Van Winkle erupting out of the earth. His face is a tableau of agony. The five-piece sculpture is installed at the National Harbor just outside Washington, DC.

Alex stands beneath the right arm, its hand stretching seventeen feet into the air to claw at the sky. He's nursing his second scotch of the night and trying not to think about Jim Harling, Gerald Jankovick, or black budgets. Men in tuxedos and women in evening gowns move around him in the distinct choreography of cocktail parties. Their breath coils in the February air. The heaters arrayed throughout the grounds are apparently doing little to staunch the cold. A brass quintet is arranged, perhaps inappropriately, between Van Winkle's two massive legs, playing a classical piece Alex has no hope of recognizing. Given the current state of health care, the amount of money spent on this gathering for the National Institutes of Health strikes Alex as bordering on obscene.

He doesn't share that observation with Grace.

She's stuck on her refrain about the stakes of the evening; at least, the stakes as she perceives them. "If the NIH doesn't give me this grant, I'm out of funding. I'm destitute."

"Relax," Alex says. "It's not like you're curing cancer or anything." This strikes him as vaguely funny, since that's exactly what Grace is doing, but she's too wound up to see the humor.

A man in his late fifties approaches. He wears a suit that is a decade out of date, even for men's fashion, and he has a ruddy complexion that betrays a weakness for either sun or alcohol. Alex instantly recognizes him as Kurt Langenhahn. Langenhahn is a member of the House of Representatives. Alex is familiar with his face because there has never been an invitation from a political talking-heads show that Langenhahn could turn down.

Langenhahn heads for Grace like a predator and extends his hand, mentally removing every stitch of clothing she's wearing. He flashes a campaign-trail smile that masks none of his lasciviousness. "Congressman Langenhahn," he says. "I serve on the NIH's advisory board."

Grace accepts the offered hand. "Grace Bauer. This is my *fiancé*, Alex Garnett." She leans on *fiancé* for emphasis, but this does not persuade him to remove his gaze from her cleavage.

"Simon Garnett's boy?" he asks, finally looking up, already knowing the answer.

"His son. Yes," Alex says with subtle adjustment.

Langenhahn turns his attention back to Grace. "I've read your funding request. Your research sounds fascinating. Though I've got to confess, I understood only about every other word." Alex thinks Langenhahn might be giving himself too much credit.

Grace maintains her polite mask of a smile and begins to school Langenhahn on the effects of vascular endothelial growth and angiogenesis on tumor development. Alex has heard the spiel before and he's never understood it. He estimates that Langenhahn has even less of a chance of comprehension, seat on the National Institutes of Health's advisory board or not.

As is his custom when he finds himself adrift in the tall grass of medical jargon, he lets his focus drift elsewhere, to the rest of the party.

He sees an assortment of different types: wealthy, academic, medical, political. It takes him back to the salons his mother used to throw — desperate attempts to impress his father, who was always preoccupied, inured to impromptu late-night discussions with the president of the United States.

Grace continues her stump speech for funding, but Alex's gaze freezes at the periphery of the gathering. He spies a solitary man at the edge of the crowd. He wears a black tuxedo and sports a crew cut that suggests a military background to go along with his impressive bulk. He shifts his stance and Alex could swear there's a bulge on the side of his chest right where a concealed gun might be carried. But what's most disconcerting is the fact that the man seems to be — no, *is* — staring directly at Alex. This isn't his imagination, not this time. The man's eyes laser a hole straight through his forehead to the back of his skull. This is no mere *fuck-you* stare. Alex's first instinct is to head toward the man, to confront him, see if he backs off, see what his reaction is, but he's barely taken one step before the congressman stops him. "It's nice to meet you, Alex."

"Same," Alex manages to blurt.

"Your girlfriend's quite the smart cookie. You ever understand a word she's saying to you?"

Alex tries to keep his gaze fixed on his admirer, but good manners draw him back to Langenhahn for a few seconds. "She dumbs things down for me when it's really important." He wills a smile to his face to punctuate the joke, then immediately turns back to the tuxedoed man…who is already gone.

Langenhahn moves off. Alex tries to obscure his unease. "How do you think that went?" he asks Grace.

"Langenhahn's a rubber stamp," she demurs. "He just came over to get a look down my dress."

"Anyone else you need to talk to tonight?"

"No, I think I'm good. Tired."

"Me too."

"The car's still back at the bar," she says. Alex nods. They'd had a drink beforehand, and he'd left the car four blocks away.

"I can go get it," Alex offers.

"I can come with you…"

"Why don't you stay? Mingle for a bit longer. I'll be right back." He seals the promise with a peck on her cheek and moves off. He needs to be alone for a while. He needs to walk off the uneasy feeling the tuxedoed man's dead-eyed stare has left in his gut.

The journey back to the car also gives him time to think. Like a fresh Polaroid developing, his theory of the case finally starts to appear. An ethereal image begins to form, a vague connection between the Fort Eustis troop deployment to Iran and the homicidal fallout of Harling's deposition. At the moment, however, his theory has no basis in fact. Rather, it's the only inference Alex can draw from the evidence he has. *Someone* — possibly the man who called him at the CIA, possibly the man in the tux? — used Harling's bank account as a temporary home for the money being siphoned off the Agency's black budget. Money — particularly government money — doesn't get stolen unless it's going to be spent. And right now, the only use Alex can think of for ninety million dollars in classified CIA funds is the deployment of troops to Iran.

With this idea entrenched, Alex arrives at his Lexus. He gets in and turns the key in the ignition. As the car purrs to life, he hears a voice coming from behind him. "Alex…"

He turns quickly in the voice's direction. This is pure reflex. His head is halfway around before he realizes he's probably turning to face a gun's silencer. So he's relieved to find Gerald. The boy — and he looks very much like a frightened child in the half-light of the car's backseat — looks more stressed than Alex has ever seen him, which is really saying something. "Gerald." Alex exhales. "You scared the living shit out of me."

"Welcome to my world," Gerald mumbles.

"How… how the hell did you get into my car?"

Gerald shrugs. "Cars are just computers with wheels. Here." He hands Alex a manila folder.

"What's this?"

"I followed the money." Gerald sounds distant, like he's talking in his sleep, and Alex wonders if he's taken something stronger than his ordinary antianxiety prescription.

"What money? The money from the black budget?" Gerald just nods. "Is that what this is?" Alex asks, referring to the file.

"This is where I get off, Alex. I owe you and I'm grateful, but I'm also *done*." With that, Gerald starts to get out of the car, but Alex stops him with a hand to his arm. "I'm done," Gerald repeats. He points to the file. "That's everything, all right? Everything I could find. Game over, man." He says this last bit in an affected Southern drawl meant to evoke Bill Paxton in the movie *Aliens*. "Game over."

"What is this?" Alex demands, shaking the file in the air. There's a label printed neatly in Gerald's handwriting. "What is Operation Solstice?"

"It's black, Alex. It's the blackest shit around." Gerald shrugs off the hand Alex has on his arm and opens the car door. "Please," he implores, sounding as young as Alex has ever heard him, "whatever you do next—and for your sake I hope it's burning that file and forgetting all about everything—whatever you do…please leave me the hell out of it." With that, Gerald pushes out of the car, slams the door behind him, and walks off into the night. Alex assumes that Gerald doesn't live in Maryland, certainly not within walking distance of where they are now, but he can tell that getting home is the very least of Gerald's worries tonight.

◆

At the condo, after Alex is sure that Grace is asleep, he sits in the kitchen with his third scotch of the evening. Ignoring Gerald's advice, he opens the Solstice file. His eyes scan the document impatiently, attempting to take the contents in all at once, like a hungry man trying to devour a buffet in a single swallow. The file reveals itself in flashes, words, and phrases jumping off the page:

OVERWATCH OPERATIONAL CONCEPT
Human immunodeficiency virus
Severe acute respiratory syndrome
H1N1
delivery mechanism
biological assassination
The Overwatch
assassination
Overwatch
ASSASSINATION

Alex understands what it says but wills himself to slow down, to turn back to the first page and read the memo in its entirety. Unfortunately, but not surprisingly, the memo's meaning doesn't change with a more comprehensive read. He thinks about reading it again — a third time — but knows he doesn't need to. The language is remarkably easy to follow, the descriptions and plans contained therein are clear and precise. Nowhere in the memo is there an acknowledgment that what it proposes is illegal under two different presidential executive orders and the Biological Weapons Convention: it's a plan for assassination using a bioweapons-grade virus.

TWELVE

THE DAWN arrives in the form of shafts of East Coast sunlight. The condo's vertical blinds carve the beams into claws that rake across Alex's eyes, jolting him out of a deep slumber. It's barely five thirty and Alex wakes to the realization that he fell asleep at the kitchen table, the Solstice file still open in front of him. The previous night's sleep — if it could be considered sleep — was stressed and fitful, plagued by paranoid dreams that could have been produced only by a combination of three glasses of scotch, the file's contents, and an extremely uncomfortable sleeping position. Still, Alex is under no delusion that he dreamed what he read — and reread, to the point of exhaustion, apparently. He knows that everything is very, very real.

Nonetheless, he sits up and reads it again. Just to make sure.

Halfway through his first read, Alex had understood why such operations were code-designated black. The description befits the secrecy in which projects like Solstice are conceived but also conjures up more malevolent connotations. There is a reason, after all, that agents and intelligence agencies that engage in covert behaviors like political extortion, forced coups, and orchestrated revolutions are colloquially said to practice the dark arts. Humans instinctively fear the dark. Our primal selves innately know that nothing good or safe lurks within the shadows. The contents of the Solstice file only confirm that. They also, for once, justify Gerald's anxieties as something more legitimate than neurotic paranoia. His reaction upon uncovering the file last night was, if anything, understated.

As far as black operations go, assassination — known in the intelligence trade as wet work — is considered the darkest of them all. But using a virus, *a disease,* strikes Alex as a particularly stygian blackness. You can shield yourself from bullets. You can protect yourself against knives. Viruses, though, are invisible and, therefore, terrifying. Again, the primal self knows best and is smart to fear disease, particularly the variety for which there is no protection or cure — for example, a virus engineered to be a *weapon.*

Conveniently for Alex, however, viruses fall into his fiancée's area of expertise. Or, at least, close enough to Grace's area of expertise to justify his confiding in her. She slinks out of the bedroom, clearly horrified to discover that Alex spent the night poring over work. Concern shrouds her face. It's nice to have someone who worries about you, Alex thinks. And it's particularly nice considering the kind of danger Alex now finds himself in.

"What's going on? You look like shit."

"Thanks."

"You were out here all night? You slept out here?"

"Fell asleep out here. Actually, more like *collapsed.*"

"What's so important," she asks, her eyes finding the Solstice file and the half-empty bottle, "that it's got you up all night killing half a fifth of scotch?"

"Something medical, it turns out." He gestures for her to take a seat next to him. "I've got some stuff I should tell you."

Grace sits as instructed and Alex tells her everything about the events of the past three days. Laying it all out for her — the suspicious money transfer, the even more suspicious deaths, the threatening phone call, and, finally, Solstice and its plot for bio-assassination — Alex feels like he's back in court delivering a closing argument, summarizing and consolidating all of the evidence for a jury's easy consumption. The only difference is that Alex's case is incomplete; his synopsis of events lacks the cumulative tie-a-ribbon-on-it point that all good summations have.

"He's screwing with you," Grace observes. "This kid —"

"Gerald," Alex supplies.

"This kid Gerald is screwing with you." She closes the file and tosses it onto the kitchen table as punctuation. "This is a joke, right? Did you tell him all the stuff you just told me?"

"Pretty much."

"And then he serves up this." She taps the file. "That kid is fucking with you. You said he's smart, right?"

Alex just nods. He's thinking back to Gerald's high-school computer prank, and a picture of Gerald as an accomplished practical joker is starting to take shape in his mind. He looks again at the file and considers Grace's suggestion. The possibility that Gerald ginned up a fictional conspiracy for his own amusement hangs in front of Alex like a lure, tempting him to grasp it so he can be pulled out of this conspiracy spiral. But there's something he can't discount. "What about the phone call I got?"

Grace raises her eyebrows, incredulous. "You mean the one with the disguised voice? The one that came from *inside* the Agency? The one that *Gerald* told you came from a dusty old file room?" She shakes her head in a way that suggests she finds it adorable that Alex has fallen for this obvious ruse. "That little shit must've been laughing his ass off, getting you to run all around the CIA. You're both lucky his little prank didn't get you fired or shot or worse."

"You're right," Alex admits, grabbing the lure. He thinks for a few seconds, his mind wandering. Feeling Grace's eyes on him, he adds, mostly for her benefit, "I should probably kick his scrawny little ass."

"You'll think of something," Grace answers. "If there's one thing you lawyers are good at, it's payback." She stands up from the table. "I'm gonna get ready for work. I have to e-mail the principal investigator on my grant application. I'm pretty sure the impact scores are out of peer review by now."

Grace moves off, but she doesn't get more than two steps away before Alex stops her. "How accurate was all this?" he asks, almost as an afterthought, holding up the Solstice file. "All the medical stuff in here. Weapons-grade viruses and such."

The question brings the grave expression to Grace's face that she usually reserves for topics like terminal cancer. "Frighteningly accurate." She points at the file. "He's got stuff in there about weaponization of very deadly viruses like Ebola and SARS-CoV and H1N1. He's got data about aerosolization and delivery systems." She shakes her head. "That little prick you're friends with really did his homework. And it sounds like he's smart enough to understand everything he read. He's also a sick fuck."

She leaves Alex with that thought. After a few minutes, he hears the shower running. It occurs to him he should join Grace. But he finds himself unable to look away from the file.

⬥

It takes Gerald fifteen minutes to stop laughing. Alex is standing opposite him in Gerald's office, such as it is, in the bowels of the New Headquarters Building. Here, four stories belowground, there is no sound but the constant hum of the industrial-grade cooling system the CIA uses to keep its massive computer-server farm from overheating. Working constantly, the fans sound louder than a 747's engine, but Gerald's hacking guffaws — periodically punctuated by desperate gasps for oxygen — threaten to drown out even the cooling system's din.

"I can't —" Gerald tries. "You thought —" he attempts. Each time, the statements are buried beneath a fresh layer of hysterics.

"Are you gonna pass out?" Alex asks.

Gerald just continues to laugh.

"I've gotta say, this wasn't among the variety of possible reactions I anticipated here."

Gerald's laughter hits a new level. If this is an elaborate performance on Gerald's part, then his talents would be put to better use by the CIA in Pakistan, Baghdad, Moscow, or any number of places where the Agency could use someone with a good poker face and excellent tradecraft.

"Fuck," Gerald finally manages to croak out, his face as red as a watermelon. "Fuck, Alex, I thought you were supposed to be *smart*. I *owe* you, remember? You helped me out. Do you really think I would doctor all this up to fuck with someone who did me a solid?"

It's a good point. One, Alex has to admit, he hadn't considered.

"Although," Gerald muses, "if I knew fucking with you could've gotten me a laugh like this, it might've been worthwhile." He shrugs. "Thanks for the giggle. It almost makes getting the living shit scared out of me last night worth it. Hell, I wish I *had* concocted it."

"Because then it wouldn't be real," Alex says, completing Gerald's thought.

"Exactly."

Alex looks down at the file in his hand. It feels heavy. It feels heavier than it did than five minutes ago, when he had himself convinced it was a prop in a practical joke. It feels heavier than it did last night when he collapsed on his kitchen table after reading it for the tenth time. The feeling must be written all over Alex's face, because when he looks back up at Gerald, he sees uncharacteristic concern. "You okay, dude?"

"Didn't sleep great last night."

"I'm not surprised." Gerald points toward the file and, with the wisdom of a prophet, advises, "There are ten shredders on every floor of this building. Do us both a favor and drop that into the nearest one. Drop it in, and forget any of this ever happened." Alex looks at the file again. Gerald, sensing Alex's ambivalence, points out, "This shit's way above your pay grade. You're under no obligation to mess with it."

"It's illegal," Alex says. "It's illegal and I'm a lawyer. I'm the *CIA's* lawyer. One of them, at least. And if I've got a client doing something they're not supposed to, I've got an obligation to try to stop it."

Gerald shakes his head with vigor. "You're not representing some DC gangbanger or a Fortune 500 company. This is the fucking Central Intelligence Agency. Even its secrets have secrets. All that happened here is you found out something you weren't supposed to find out. When that happens, you do your best to forget it. When I told you this was above your pay grade, I meant it literally."

"So maybe I just share this with my boss." Alex shrugs. "Send it up the chain of command."

Gerald shakes his head even harder, more in growing anger than any kind of fear. "The people in command already know about it. That's how these things work." Alex isn't so sure that's true, but he lets Gerald continue. "So you'd be telling them *you* know something you're not supposed to. And that comes back on *me*, man. You show your boss that file, he's gonna want to know how you got it. If I'm lucky, I'm only looking for a new line of work. If I'm not, I'm looking for my own lawyer. To defend me against charges I violated, like, fifteen different federal laws." Gerald lets out a derisive snort. "Seriously, for *both* of us, doing anything other than shredding and forgetting is gonna be — I promise you — more trouble than it's worth." The phrase elicits a caustic smirk from Alex. "What's that look supposed to mean?" Gerald asks.

"Nothing," Alex answers. "You just remind me of me."

◆

"Dr. Jafari," Jahandar says, rising from his seat to shake the engineer's hand. "Thank you for making the trip all the way from Darkhovin and joining me in my humble home."

"It is my pleasure, Ayatollah," the head engineer of Project 110 responds with a bow of his head. "It is a great honor."

Jahandar smiles a bit, noting the man's anxiety, having felt the perspiration on his palm when he shook his hand. Conversations are always easier to have with someone who's uncomfortable. Particularly when the goal of the conversation is the procurement of information.

Jahandar waves a hand to offer Jafari a seat. They're in one of the palace's five reception rooms. Although Jahandar refers to it as "humble," he chose the one they're sitting in for its impressive—and, he hopes, intimidating—size and opulence. Antique Persian rugs cover the floor, and museum-quality art and antiques populate the space. Jahandar has never had much use for such trappings, but they do make him appear more imposing. (As if the title *supreme leader* weren't imposing enough.)

An attendant pours glasses of iced green tea from a pitcher and promptly makes himself scarce. After taking a sip, Jahandar breaks the silence. "The work you've done in Darkhovin. Impressive. Most impressive."

"Thank you." Jafari bows his head again.

"And after so much time. How long have you been working on Project One-Ten?"

"Thirteen years, sir. On One-Ten and also One-Eleven."

"There's a Project One-Eleven?" Jahandar asks, feigning ignorance. Over the years, he's found it's useful to give his underlings conflicting ideas about what he does and doesn't know about his government's workings.

Jafari sips his tea and nods. "One-Ten is the construction of a nuclear warhead. One-Eleven focuses on the reconstruction of the nose-cone interiors to accommodate the warhead." He can't help but allow a bit of pride to creep in, adding, "I'm one of only three engineers to work on both projects."

"Well, you've done your nation a great service, Dr. Jafari. This is a remarkable achievement." Once again, Jahandar is sincere, as Muslim law requires him to be. Despite whatever misgivings he may have about using Iran's new nuclear might — and those misgivings are many and profound — there is no denying that Iran's entrance into the nuclear club is a major leap forward for his nation. "I'm curious, though. After thirteen years of work — to say nothing of the many years of work by those who preceded you — after all that time, what was the key to your success? What turned the tide and made such an achievement possible?" Jafari shifts in his seat. Jahandar has made him uncomfortable. He takes another swig of tea, gathering his thoughts. "What was responsible for your breakthrough?" Jahandar presses, filling the silence. "I've always been fascinated by what makes the difference between failure and success." This is not a lie. The only deception being employed now is Jahandar's refusal to fully elaborate on the reasons for his inquiry.

"Some designs recently came into our possession. Blueprints. Schematics. Obtained by the VEVAK."

"From whom?"

"I'm not entirely sure. I wasn't made privy to that information."

"Nor, I suspect, did the VEVAK share the circumstances with you."

Jafari shakes his head. "No, Ayatollah." Then, in an effort to be helpful, he adds, "But judging from the annotations and use of what's known as the customary system of measurements — as distinguished from the metric system — the use of this customary system suggests to me that the schematics were obtained from Americans."

Jahandar nods his understanding but doesn't betray his thoughts. Jafari shifts in his seat again, suddenly uncomfortable at the thought of some nameless, faceless Americans—or any Americans, for that matter—getting credit for an achievement that is rightly his. He leans forward in his chair and tries not to sound desperate. "But the schematics were incomplete. And in any case, only a very…focused mind could glean details that would be of any use to us."

Jahandar offers a characteristic professorial smile. "Of course. You built the tower. These Americans—if that is who it was—merely provided the capstone."

Jafari seizes on this theory, nodding vigorously. "I'd say those schematics saved us a month, maybe six at the outside. I—*we*—would have come to the same conclusions in time."

Jahandar knows this is a lie, but that is between Jafari and Allah. He just nods his head sagely and watches Jafari's body unclench under the warmth of his paternal smile. Behind that smile, however, is a mind hard at work. Jahandar's intellectual capabilities are not insignificant, and at the moment they're all marshaled to assemble the puzzle pieces in front of him. A clear picture is beginning to form. The six American spies who were held at Ardakan Charity Hospital were in possession of schematics and blueprints that made the realization of Iran's nuclear ambitions possible. When the plans were discovered, the VEVAK took them and did the logical thing by turning them over to Jafari and the other scientists and engineers of Project 110. This sequence of events seemed like the will of Allah. This is the way of God: The country's greatest enemy has given Iran the means to achieve its nuclear ascendance. While such good fortune may be the way of God, however, Jahandar knows it's not the way of the world. And that's what troubles him.

THIRTEEN

"It's DONE," Tyler Donovan reports. "He's killed it."

Rykman nods sagely, keeping his own counsel. He's been expecting this moment ever since the fiasco at Ardakan Charity Hospital. A smart warrior knows his enemy and sees their capabilities for exactly what they are, and William Rykman is nothing if not a smart warrior. He knows that Supreme Leader Ayatollah Ali Jahandar is too. Once his operatives had their covers blown by the VEVAK, Rykman knew it was just a matter of time before Jahandar put the pieces together. That same intelligence, however, is not shared by President Tehrani. The man is as dense a leader as Rykman's ever encountered. The Iranian president could be depended on to jump at the bait Rykman had dangled in front of him: a nuclear warhead. Tehrani wouldn't question whether the nuke was operational. He wouldn't wonder why or how American spies could be so reckless as to provide critical engineering information to the Iranian nuclear crusaders working at Darkhovin. He wouldn't suspect his country of being manipulated and, therefore, wouldn't resist the temptation to announce to the world that Iran had finally joined the vaunted nuclear club.

Ali Jahandar, of course, is an entirely different opponent. His request to visit Darkhovin — a trip known to the Overwatch only because of its assets inside Iran — confirmed as much. That Jahandar then felt compelled to meet with Darkhovin's lead engineer was of great concern. The wily ayatollah is figuring out what Rykman is up to. The operational security of Vanguard was clearly compromised and, with it, the project's chances for success. Those chances are still quite good. But *good* is not enough in Rykman's world. He operates the Overwatch in a risk-free environment where there is no acceptable amount of uncertainty. Such is the price of manipulating the course of the entire world.

"Good thing we green-lit Solstice," Donovan observes.

"Copy that," Rykman agrees. "Has the package been delivered?"

"Affirmative," Donovan says with a curt nod. "We got the engineer too."

"Keep him under surveillance to confirm the kill." Dr. Yousef Jafari's death is a reasonable precaution; Jahandar might have shared his suspicions with Jafari, and the nuclear engineer might then have decided to take a more scrutinizing look at the nuclear weapon he and his team had constructed (with the Overwatch's secret help). This would only increase the odds of the Iranians discovering the nuke's imperfections. And imperfections, once detected, could be corrected.

"Eliminate the delivery agent," Rykman says. "Close the loop."

"Copy that," Donovan replies with characteristic obedience. "We have an operative in Syria I like for that. I can have him in-country by tomorrow."

"Go," Rykman confirms as he stands up. "I have to make a call."

Five minutes later, Rykman is at ground level and his phone is doing its work moving through the encryption necessary to initiate a secure call. After a few seconds of electronic machinations, his partner answers. "Yes?"

Assuming, by some miracle of technological legerdemain, an eavesdropper managed to breach the security of the call, he would be rewarded by something approaching gibberish: "Roll-up on Vanguard's almost complete," Rykman reports. "Solstice proceeds apace."

"Do we have someone in Tel Aviv?" Rykman's partner wonders.

"Someone in the Knesset," Rykman confirms, referring to Israel's 120-member parliament. "He's a former Mossad agent. Eight years with them. He's providing Solstice accountability."

"It might be worth letting him know about Iran's Project One-Ten," the partner speculates. "Perhaps there's some usefulness we might wring out of Vanguard after all."

Rykman likes this idea. "We could probably make it look like Solstice was retaliatory," he says in agreement. "Neat and clean. I'll get it done."

<hr />

UNITED STATES DISTRICT COURT, EASTERN DISTRICT OF VIRGINIA
11:00 A.M. EDT

The Albert V. Bryan United States Courthouse in Alexandria, Virginia, reminds Alex of an apartment building in Queens. Although the courthouse was built in 1995, its red-brick façade and low ten-story profile are reminiscent of the dozens of apartment buildings that were mass-produced in the 1950s and 1960s to accommodate the baby boom generation and its need for affordable housing. The building's bottom three floors, with its marbled accents and archway entrances, are the only indication of its function as a courthouse. Otherwise, it looks like the kind of building people live in.

It's also the building in which lawsuits against the Central Intelligence Agency are typically filed. Theoretically, the CIA can be haled into any one of the United States' eighty-nine district courts, but the United States District Court for the Eastern District of Virginia in Alexandria is the one where most lawsuits against the Agency are filed, by virtue of its proximity to the CIA's headquarters — the presumed focal point of any liability — in McLean, Virginia.

Alex finds himself in the courthouse's wood-paneled courtrooms about once a month. He generally appears to argue on what's known as 12(b)(6) motions, referring to the Federal Rule of Civil Procedure that provides for the dismissal of civil lawsuits for lack of merit.

After all, the CIA doesn't pay Alex to investigate clandestine assassination plots. Solstice and Overwatch occasionally have to take a number and get in line behind Alex's day job. It doesn't matter that his life has been threatened. In fact, the sword dangling over his head is the best reason for him to act as if nothing has changed.

Although the assignment of judges is supposed to be random, the availability of judges, which is a function of how government institutions run their courtrooms and manage their dockets, affects the process. Judges with a tendency to permit cases to go to trial often find themselves unavailable to hear motions. This includes motions to dismiss. And the more of those that are granted, the fewer trials they have to preside over. The fewer trials, the more available they are to hear motions to dismiss. It's the kind of feedback loop that accounts for the fact that, more often than not, when Alex is arguing a motion to dismiss, he's doing so before the Honorable Judge Quentin Hotchkiss.

Judge Hotchkiss is an erudite jurist in his midsixties. Alex likes him for his efficiency and sense of humor, the latter being a quality that most judges, in Alex's experience, lack. Alex recalls a time when he was opposing a motion to compel before Judge Hotchkiss. Carl Draper, the attorney for the other side, was accusing Alex of failing to comply with a request for production of documents in violation of federal law. Alex's defense was that the documents his opponent had requested didn't exist. He suspected Draper knew as much but was trying to grind the system. Calling another attorney a liar before a judge in open court is something Alex knew to handle delicately. He said something like, "Suffice it to say, Your Honor, I don't always agree with the factual assertions made by opposing counsel."

Hotchkiss smiled and wryly noted, "I'm sure Mr. Draper would say the same thing about *you* and *your* factual assertions."

"Yes, Your Honor," Alex replied without hesitation. "But I try to limit those instances by confining my assertions to the truth."

Judge Hotchkiss denied Draper's motion, finding in favor of Alex.

Now he is presiding over a similar issue. Alex is trying to dispose of a lawsuit brought by a George Washington University professor who, in addition to his classroom activities, blogs about Middle Eastern issues. The professor's complaint — the legal pleading that commences a lawsuit — alleges that the CIA has been maintaining a file on him as a result of what he posts on the Internet.

In order for a motion to dismiss to be granted under Federal Rule of Civil Procedure 12(b)(6), the judge must presume that every allegation in the complaint is true. With that presumption in place, the question is whether a legal cause of action has been claimed. For this reason, lawyers often call 12(b)(6) arguments So What? motions, as in, "Yes. Everything alleged by the plaintiff is true…but so what?" That's the argument Alex is making now.

"Even assuming for the sake of this motion that the CIA is maintaining a file on Professor Dalton, the existence of such a file wouldn't be a tort" — a legal wrong for which relief can be granted — "and even if it were, there are no damages. Professor Dalton hasn't been harmed — nor has he even *alleged* being harmed — by the creation of a file that may or may not exist."

Judge Hotchkiss nods sagely before looking to Alex's opponent, a scrappy young attorney Alex suspects Dalton recruited straight out of GWU Law School.

The kid, Todd Kessel, does the best with what he has: "The harm, Your Honor, is violation of privacy, which is a legitimate cause of action under the Privacy Act of 1974, 42 United States Code section 552a. As for the issue of damages, the statute provides for a mandatory minimum of one thousand dollars plus court costs."

It's a good argument, but Alex is ready for it: "The existence of a *file*, Your Honor, doesn't per se violate Professor Dalton's privacy, or anyone else's, for that matter. Plaintiff has alleged merely the existence of a file, not any extralegal means on the part of the Central Intelligence Agency to procure the information it contains."

"It's our contention," Kessel fires back, "that when a government agency keeps a file on one of its citizens, that itself is a violation of privacy."

"Cool."

Judge Hotchkiss smiles. "Did you just say *cool?*"

"I'm sorry, Your Honor," Alex says with a grin. "I meant to say, *That's cool.*" He waits a beat for that to land and shrugs. "I've always wanted to argue a case before the Supreme Court. Because that's where Mr. Kessel's incredibly imaginative legal argument will take us." He pauses again before adding, "That is, if you let us, Your Honor." Alex takes care to employ an inflection that conveys his opinion that this would be a terrible idea.

Were Hotchkiss to embark on this perilous legal road, it would inevitably lead to him getting reversed on appeal. (But likely by the Fourth Circuit and long before reaching the Supreme Court.) Alex's argument contains the implied threat of such a reversal, an outcome all judges dread.

Correctly sensing that this judicial math is making an impact on Hotchkiss, Kessel tries to buttress his failing argument. "The CIA's charter prohibits it from spying on American citizens. Why create a file on one of those citizens *if not* for the purpose of spying on him?"

Alex shakes his head with vigor. "For all Professor Dalton knows, and for all he's *alleged,* that file contains nothing but the printouts of his blog posts. If he truly wants to know its contents, his proper remedy is to file a FOIA request," Alex says, referring to the Freedom of Information Act, "*not* a lawsuit in federal court."

Kessel wants to make a point in rebuttal, but Hotchkiss cuts him off.

"Thank you, Counsel. I'll take this matter under advisement, read your briefs, and try to deliver a ruling to you by the end of the month." The court stenographer's transcript of the proceedings will include this statement verbatim, but without the judge's tone, which suggests he's already made up his mind. Alex can feel it too. And he smiles with the inward satisfaction that comes from knowing he's notched another courtroom victory in his belt.

Dr. Edward Dalton, who's been sitting at the plaintiff's table throughout the discussion, can sense the same thing. He shrinks in his chair and looks resigned, albeit not particularly surprised. Before court, Alex did his due diligence and learned — without much astonishment — that this was the fourth lawsuit Dalton had filed against the CIA, and the ninth against the federal government. Dalton has the look of someone experienced at tilting at windmills and losing.

Alex returns to the defendant's table and busies himself with organizing his papers to avoid Dalton's gaze. It's not that he's ashamed at having won the motion — the facts and the law were on his side — but there's an awkwardness that accompanies interactions with those on the losing side of a legal engagement. In this particular case, that awkwardness is coupled with the judgmental stare Dalton has perfected on scores of George Washington University students. Although Alex has angled himself away from Dalton, he can feel the professor's gaze drilling into the back of his head.

This kind of situation is not unfamiliar to Alex. By and large, plaintiffs bringing suits against the CIA are a passionate, idealistic lot. Alex is used to the looks of damnation that come when their dreams of prolonged litigation against America's foremost spy agency are dashed. His standard practice is to ignore them, move on as fast as possible, and hope there isn't a subsequent chance meeting in the courthouse elevator or parking garage.

The professor reaches out and grabs Alex's arm. So much for the avoidance option.

Alex tries to pull away but discovers that Dalton possesses a surprisingly strong grip for an academic. Alex flashes a look toward the bench, searching for Dalton's lawyer, and sees that the man is engaged in some conversation with Judge Hotchkiss's clerk. He turns back to tell Dalton that by touching opposing counsel in this manner, the professor might find himself on the receiving end of a lawsuit, but Dalton gets the first word in. And it's only one word: "Compartmentalization."

Alex had a mental list of things Dalton might possibly say to him — *Fuck you* being at the top — but *Compartmentalization* had not been on it. Alex is caught so off guard that all he can muster in response is a jagged "Excuse me?"

"Compartmentalization, Mr. Garnett," Dalton says. Alex glances again at the attorney. Still talking to the clerk. Still oblivious. "Your argument is premised on the assumption that each directorate in the CIA knows what the other directorates are doing. You assume, in fact, that there is communication *within* directorates. You presume that if the CIA had me under surveillance, that information would be shared with the Office of General Counsel and, further, with you. But the CIA — like any intelligence agency — depends upon *compartmentalization*. Secrets are kept precisely because the left hand *doesn't* know what the right hand is doing. Do you understand?"

Alex swallows, then slowly nods. He understands far more than Dalton realizes.

◈

BEIT RAHBARI PRESIDENTIAL PALACE, IRAN
1635 HRS. ZULU

Jahandar's rib cage heaves hard enough to leave his chest. He's vomiting for the third time tonight. His knees are pained from kneeling on the bathroom tile for the better part of two hours. The worst of it, however, is the headache. His brain feels as though it's swollen to ten times the size of his skull and is trying to claw its way out of his head with every heartbeat.

After he's nearly certain he's finished retching, he reaches out, leans against the wall, and pushes himself to his feet. He'll wake one of the servants and get some aspirin. Maybe he'll swallow it with some green tea in the hope that the warm liquid might do something about the chills coursing through his bones.

He manages to take three entire steps before his stomach lodges a protest, spinning him around and sending him back to kneel before the commode. The attendant, the aspirin, and the tea will have to wait. Again.

OGC, New Headquarters Building
2:15 p.m. EDT

"What can you tell me about compartmentalization?" Alex asks Leah. They're sitting in Starbucks, but not the one he and Gerald used for computer hacking in Virginia. This Starbucks is inside the New Headquarters Building at the CIA. Spies need their caffeine too — and apparently their fast-food fixes, judging by the Burger King and Subway in the NHB's food court.

"What about it?" Leah asks.

"It came up in a case this morning. The Dalton lawsuit." This is not quite a lie. "I got the impression that compartmentalization's gonna be part of their argument and thought I should brush up." This is closer to a lie but still manages to maintain a few kernels of truth.

"There's not exactly any mystery to it, Alex," Leah answers, sipping her latte. "Information is provided intra-Agency on a need-to-know basis. If Dalton wants to argue that information was or wasn't shared within the Agency, that's his right, but he's got to prove it. And as far as that's concerned" — she shrugs — "good luck."

"Right," Alex says as casually as he can manage, "but what if — hypothetically — what if there was a *covert* operation. Something very classified, paid out of the black budget. The need-to-know on something like *that's* gotta be a very, very small group of people."

"So?"

"So is there ever a situation where the Agency personnel behind a covert operation have authority or discretion *not* to report what they're doing?"

"Not to anyone?" Leah's incredulity is obvious. "I don't care how black an operation is, someone in the Agency's gonna know about it. If it's not the DNCS, it's the DCIA." The DNCS is the director of the National Clandestine Service — the operations arm of the CIA. The DCIA is the director of the Central Intelligence Agency, the person in charge of the entire organization.

Leah leans forward and stares directly at Alex with a serious, albeit bemused, expression. "Look, you're still relatively new here, and I know a few months isn't enough to undo years of seeing how the Agency gets portrayed in books and movies. I also know how tempting it is to see conspiracies around every corner — particularly when you're the guy whose job it is to respond to all the lawsuits about those alleged conspiracies." She smiles. "It's like first-year med students becoming hypochondriacs, thinking they're coming down with every obscure bug in their textbooks. But truth isn't stranger than fiction — it's just a whole lot more boring. The fact of the matter is, operations can't be undertaken without the knowledge and approval of the DNCS and the DCIA as well as a presidential finding, which means the president has to have knowledge as well. Bottom line, when you're describing an operation that the DNCS, the DCIA, the DNI, and the president don't know about, you're not talking about a clandestine operation, you're talking about an illegal one. You're talking about *treason*."

Alex nods, his mind besieged by a flood of thoughts. Assassination by presidential executive order is illegal, so if the president was aware of Solstice, that meant he was complicit in breaking the law and was committing treason. And if he wasn't aware, that meant he didn't know what his people were doing. Both possibilities chill Alex to the bone.

"It's been a while since I read Dalton's complaint," Leah says, "but I don't remember him alleging anything on the level of treason or presidential malfeasance. The guy's just pissed off 'cause he thinks we're keeping a file on him, right?"

"Yeah," Alex agrees. "I guess I just wanted to cover all my bases."

Alex's intent is to come off as overly conscientious, but Leah sees past the deception, although she misreads what she sees: "Don't get in the heads of these plaintiffs, Alex," she cautions. "Even the ones who are professors. Believe me, a PhD and tenure doesn't prevent you from claiming membership in the lunatic fringe."

Alex smiles at that and forces a chuckle. But he's burdened by having learned a few things that Leah doesn't know. Not to mention having read a certain file that lays out in great detail a biological assassination scheme that the lunatic fringe could only daydream about.

FOURTEEN

IT WAS in the tea. The green tea Jahandar enjoyed with Dr. Jafari little more than twenty-four hours ago was tainted with influenza A virus subtype H1N1. This particular strain of flu had been weaponized to be 98 percent fatal and hearty enough to live within the *Camellia sinensis* leaves of the green tea for an extended period and strong enough to resist the boiling water it was steeped in. The process took several years and tens of millions of dollars. But time and money are two things the Overwatch has in abundance; the latter is steadily provided by the CIA through the kind of black accounts that Alex unwittingly stumbled upon.

There'd been a recent outbreak of illness caused by the influenza A/H1N1 virus, dubbed "swine flu" by the global media. Given the Koran's prohibitions against the consumption of meat cut from swine, there was a cruel irony to its deployment as a weapon in Middle Eastern countries such as Iran (though the virus is not actually related to the virus that infects swine). But irony didn't play a role in its selection. Rather, A/H1N1 was the virus of choice because of its plausible deniability—it was a naturally occurring pathogen, one with fatal consequences.

Biologic agents like anthrax were more efficient and reliable killers, but in the past decade they had become synonymous with bioterror and biowarfare. Swine flu enjoyed a comparatively benign reputation, although it wasn't always harmless. On January 10, 1977, the *San Francisco Chronicle* reported that CIA "operatives linked to anti-Castro terrorists introduced African swine fever into Cuba in 1971." This wasn't mere conspiracy theory either. The *Chronicle* had a source who claimed that "early in 1971 he was given the virus in a sealed, unmarked container at Ft. Gulick," a detail made damning by virtue of the fact that the CIA operated a paramilitary training center out of Fort Gulick at the time.

The Overwatch avoided suspicion by burying all connections to its operations under several layers of shell corporations, subcontractors, and dummy entities. The project to weaponize A/H1N1 was undertaken in a research lab in a small college in Connecticut and funded by a private donation made by one of Overwatch's many corporate fronts. Even the operative whose responsibility it was to plant the tainted tea leaves in the market that Jahandar's servants were known to frequent had no idea of Overwatch's involvement; he was a local, paid by a "private intelligence group"—less flatteringly referred to as mercenaries—to complete the task.

That man, Sharim Kafir, is now walking through the same Tehran market. He has no idea why he was paid one thousand rials to "enhance" the tea merchant's inventory (he didn't know the tea leaves he planted were tainted, but he had his suspicions); he knows only that the job was easy and the money good. Very good. He has not made the connection between his assignment and Jahandar contracting swine flu. In the past two months, Iran has been plagued by many a spontaneous outbreak of the disease. However, the strain of A/H1N1 at the root of these outbreaks wasn't weaponized. There was simply no need. All that was necessary for the Solstice protocol were other incidents of swine flu infection so that Jahandar's didn't stand out. And although swine flu generally has a less than 1 percent mortality rate, Jahandar's death will be written off as the work of a virulent disease on a seventy-three-year-old body.

Nevertheless, there's a possibility that Kafir might eventually tumble to the connection between Jahandar's death and his own actions with the tea merchant. Rykman's aides calculate this probability at less than 2 percent, but William Rykman lives in a world of absolutes, in a world where one in fifty are unacceptable odds. And so another calculation is engaged in — how much it costs to dispose of a poor, Middle Eastern single man with few social connections and absolutely no personal security. The resulting number is not even a rounding error in Overwatch's budget.

The man for *this* task has no connection to the private security firm that enlisted Kafir. All he knows is that he'll receive one hundred rials for sending a man he's never met before to Allah. He watches Kafir make the last of his purchases in the market and begins following him, careful to keep at a safe remove.

Kafir's route home takes him through a narrow alleyway. The passage between buildings is just narrow enough for the hit man to bump into Kafir and then keep on walking. He's out of the alley and back into the brilliant Tehran sunlight before Kafir's body hits the ground. Once his remains are discovered, the police will note that his wallet — which had just been used to pay for his purchases at the market — is missing; it was lifted by the hit man's hand while the other plunged in the dagger. The missing wallet is all the police will need to write the murder up as a robbery. Mr. Kafir simply chose the wrong alley to turn down on his way home.

The hit man, for his part, is eager to return to his apartment. Although they didn't prevent him from doing his job, chills have plagued his body, and now that the post-kill adrenaline's wearing off, he's feeling the fatigue that almost kept him in bed today. *Damn,* he thinks, hoping that he's not coming down with that swine flu he's been reading about lately.

◈

NEW HAMPSHIRE AVENUE NW
WASHINGTON, DC
8:13 P.M. EDT

"Okay," Grace says, "so we kill someone. Either a terrorist or the head of a terrorist state. We give him SARS or AIDS or H1N1 and we kill him." She pauses for effect, looking Alex in the eyes. "So what?"

Alex has asked himself this question many times since becoming acquainted with Solstice. The question is often posed to the ceiling of his bedroom as he stares up at it late at night or too early in the morning, making sleep frustratingly elusive. "People didn't bat an eye when we killed bin Laden," Grace points out.

"Actually," Alex interjects, "some people did. We didn't give him a trial or even make much of an effort to take him alive." Alex wipes tears from his eyes with the back of his hand. He and Grace are preparing dinner—a Mario Batali recipe Grace has been wanting to try—and the fumes from the onions he's cutting are really starting to get to him. He sets the knife he's working with aside and takes a sip from his wineglass. He goes on: "But bin Laden's death *wasn't* an assassination, at least not technically. He wasn't a head of state or a member of any recognized government. And even if he had been, the president *knew* about the operation that killed him. He authorized it and he monitored it. This Solstice thing…the whole point is that it's so covert that the president, the DNI, and the DCIA don't know about it."

"You *think* they don't know about it," Grace rebuts, jabbing the air with her knife for emphasis. "You don't know for sure. You're making assumptions." Then, lowering the knife to the carving board, she resumes mincing garlic as she continues: "Isn't your train of thought bringing you full circle? You don't know that the head of the CIA *doesn't* know all about Solstice."

"I don't think he does."

"Really?" Grace sounds incredulous.

"What do you mean?"

"I mean" — her mincing takes on a more urgent tempo — "if you can't live with the possibility that the director doesn't know about Solstice, then I respect that. But — and I say this with love —"

"Uh-oh," Alex responds with a smile that says he knows where she's going.

"*But* if this is really some deep-seated, self-destructive way to get yourself fired, then I'd strongly urge you to" — *chop* — "think" — *chop* — "twice." She puts the knife down and fixes him with a look.

Alex grins, somewhat busted. "I've thought about this," he says. "Both possibilities."

"And?"

"And I don't know. I honestly don't." He shrugs with a sincere help-lessness. "But I can't seem to get the idea of taking this to the DCI out of my head. So regardless of the reason, I think this is something I have to do."

"So you're not really asking my advice, are you?"

Alex grimaces, definitely busted now. "It's a bit like a covert assas-sination, honey. If it's happening anyway, shouldn't the president or whoever's in charge at least be brought into the loop?"

"And I'm the president in this scenario?" Grace asks.

"More like the person in charge."

"Even better." And she hugs with a warmth hot enough to cook their dinner.

Alex studies Leah. Leah studies the Solstice file. Her eyes dart back and forth across the pages, but her face remains impassive. She is deliberate in her review, so the process takes an uncomfortably long time. Alex feels his palms getting moist as he waits for a sign that he's crazy, out of work, or both.

After an eternity spent contemplating what his next career will be, he watches Leah calmly set the file down. Maintaining her poker face and keeping her voice level, she says with characteristic dryness: "Well, I think this puts yesterday's conversation into a slightly clearer light..." She gives the file a tap of her finger. "How did you get this?"

"It came out of discovery in the Harling divorce case." Like most good lies, this one is inspired by the truth.

"Documents like this one" — Leah holds the file up — "don't generally come out of a litigation's discovery process." The magnitude of this understatement is hard for Alex to quantify. "How did you get it?" she asks again.

"I can't answer that," Alex says, bracing for the onslaught of Leah's fury. Fortunately, all she does is raise her eyebrows, so he continues. "For the moment. I'd be violating someone's confidence. I'm willing to risk my job over this, but I'd like to avoid widening that particular circle for the time being."

Leah nods, considering it. A few seconds pass like months before she answers. "I can respect that. I also find myself surprised to realize I have some grudging respect for you bringing this to my attention. You could've shredded it or buried it."

"Oh, it crossed my mind," Alex interjects, with a bit more levity than he was really intending.

Leah takes a few more seconds to think, much more comfortable with the silence than Alex is. The file is now resting on her desk and she scrapes a fingernail across it, scratching. "How many copies?"

"That's the only one I have." This is true, but Alex can feel Leah's eyes on him, looking for any sign of a lie.

Leah either believes him or decides to table the issue for another time because she moves on. "First step is to verify that this is legitimate." Alex nods, having anticipated this course of action. "That will be harder to do without knowing where you got it," she adds pointedly. But Alex remains firm. He won't budge on this. "But I'm pretty confident I can do so quietly."

"And then what?"

"Assuming it's authentic?" Leah asks. The silence stretches between them like a chasm. Finally, she answers her own question: "I honestly have no idea."

FIFTEEN

DR. HEERAD Yazdani was the first to arrive. He has been the ayatollah's personal physician for the past thirty-six years and has successfully nursed the supreme leader through countless ailments from shingles to, most recently, a bout with prostate cancer. Given the control the government exercises over the local media, it's not surprising that none of these illnesses made the news. But Yazdani is particularly proud of the fact that Jahandar's medical travails over the years have never been picked up by any international news gathering organizations either. He's also reasonably confident that foreign intelligence services such as the Mossad and the CIA remain unaware of Jahandar's medical history. (Although this belief is in error. In fact, both agencies, as well as Britain's MI6, have detailed files on Jahandar's health, down to his high cholesterol.)

Part of keeping the circle of medical trust closed is limiting knowledge of the ayatollah's heath to his close attendants and Dr. Yazdani himself. Even the oncologists who made the initial the diagnosis of prostate cancer and the ones who oversaw his treatment were reacting to the films and bloodwork of an anonymous patient. Jahandar's current condition, however, so alarms Yazdani that he's taken the unprecedented step of trading security for safety and brought in a consultant, a specialist in infectious diseases. The consultant, in turn, recommended bringing in a team of physicians. There was a direct correlation between the number of medical personnel in the presidential palace and the amount of concern Yazdani had over Jahandar's worsening condition.

Tonight, the palace is filled to capacity. Medical personnel outnumber attendants, staff, and concerned bureaucrats three to one. Everyone speaks in whispers, chattering, gossiping, planning, and debating among themselves and on their cell phones. The building buzzes with a warroom-like intensity. President Tehrani is home, presumably asleep, but six of his eight vice presidents are here, as are three members of the council of ministers and Gholam-Hossein Elham, the government spokesman. Elham's presence, perhaps more than any other person's, signals the gravity of the situation. Elham wouldn't have been invited to this vigil — there is no other word for it — if the government weren't planning on making Jahandar's condition public.

Ayatollah Sattar Namdar watches the activity with a quiet dispassion. He speaks to no one. He doesn't answer his ringing cell phone. He doesn't make eye contact with any one person, although his gaze envelops everyone in every room he enters. Only the six members of the eighty-six-man Majles-e Khobregan, or Assembly of Experts, who are there receive polite nods acknowledging their presence. This may be good manners and better politics, but it's hardly necessary. Although the Assembly of Experts will determine Jahandar's successor in the increasingly likely event that he dies, all of Iran knows Namdar will be the new supreme leader. He's been amassing support and fighting off competitors for the better part of a decade now. He's as close to a supreme-leader-inwaiting as Iran has ever had.

Knowing the inevitability of Namdar's eventual rise to power, the CIA maintains a detailed file on him, including complete psychological workups by three world-renowned psychologists. The only gap in the Agency's preparation for Namdar's election as supreme leader of Iran is that its projections—based on Jahandar's age and health—call for Jahandar to remain in power for at least seven more years. But those projections were made before the ayatollah came down with a case of swine flu that the best doctors—desperately flown in from neighboring countries in vain attempts to save Jahandar's life—have not been able to treat.

Namdar senses the shift immediately. It ripples through the palace, from Jahandar's bedroom to the great hall where Namdar is standing. The whispers he's been listening to all night have become murmurs, and the murmurs have become urgent. He knows it is time.

He quietly moves through the palace. A few of the men assembled take out their cell phones. Others gravitate, as Namdar does, toward the set of double doors that mark the entrance to the supreme leader's bedroom. Dr. Yazdani slips out between them. Yazdani had looked weary—a mixture of concern and fatigue—when Namdar arrived, but now the doctor looks positively ashen, as if he's aged three years in three hours. His eyelids are red and moist. Namdar can tell that the man has been crying. He can also tell that, after thirty-some years of being Jahandar's personal physician, his patient had become a friend. And so, when Yazdani finally speaks—all eyes in the room looking expectantly toward him—he's not able to muster any professional distance nor find the strength to raise his voice above a whisper. But that doesn't matter. Namdar's not the only one who can see that Yazdani is in mourning. Yazdani looks up at the crowd and says, simply, "He's gone."

<hr />

HOTEL MONTEFIORE, TEL AVIV
2300 HRS. ZULU

Mossad case officer Ari Korman likes the Hotel Montefiore because it draws guests from all over the world. On any given night, its bar is packed with women from around the globe. And although he has no explanation for it, many of the women are astonishingly beautiful. Take, for example, the blonde he's currently talking to. She has a lean, athletic body and beautiful white skin that's just beginning to bronze in the Middle Eastern sun. The chances of the girl being Jewish are about as remote, Korman calculates, as the chances of her being older than twenty-one. But his plans for her don't include an interaction long enough for their different faiths to present an issue. Nor do they require that he be fewer than fifteen years her senior. If it's not a problem for her, it's definitely not a problem for him.

And it doesn't seem to be an issue, judging by the way she's smiling at him and the way her hand keeps managing to brush against his fingers. And their flirty banter, while probably the result of the three Manhattans he's bought her, gives him enough confidence to suggest that they might be more comfortable continuing their conversation in her hotel room.

"My friend's up there." She giggles. "I don't think she'd appreciate it."

"She might," Korman suggests flirtatiously. With a lot of women, this crack might earn him a slap or bring an abrupt end to the evening, but intelligence officers know exactly how to read people to determine how far a situation can be pushed.

"That's cute," the blonde purrs, confirming his instincts. "But how about your place instead?"

"Best view of the city," Korman tells her. He has his wallet out already to leave two brown one-hundred-shekel bills.

They're back to his modest flat within twenty minutes. The view of Tel Aviv isn't nearly as grand as he'd advertised, but the blonde doesn't seem to care—she's preoccupied with shoving her tongue into his mouth and rubbing her hands over his toned chest. She's an actress; Korman thinks he remembers her telling him that. From Los Angeles? Maybe. Of more immediate concern is how to most efficiently remove the little black cocktail dress she's wearing. Under the pretext of gentle caresses, his fingers search for her zipper. He finally manages to locate the damn thing and begins pulling it down. However, he doesn't manage to get the dress off before falling unconscious.

The blonde adjusts her dress and looks down at Korman lying on the floor. The sedative has done its work faster than she'd anticipated. He's inconveniently lying in the middle of the bedroom; a more conspicuous position than her operational plan had taken into account. At a hundred and seventy-five pounds, he's too heavy for her to move. Without wasting another second, she goes to the closet and finds the gun safe exactly where the advance team had said it would be. They got the combination right too, of course, and within thirty seconds she's wielding Korman's Jericho 941 semiautomatic in her latex-gloved hand. Now comes the tricky part, but it's not as if she hasn't done this kind of work before. Everything tonight has gone down exactly as her training dictated it would, starting with the moment she drew Korman's eye, letting him come to her, back at the Montefiore. She'd told him that she was an actress. And it wasn't a complete lie.

CIA, New Headquarters Building
6:47 P.M. EDT

In the two days since Alex gave Leah the Solstice file, he's crossed paths with her at a weekly staff meeting, a biweekly resources meeting, and — by his count — no fewer than seven times in the hall and once at the Agency Starbucks. At no point does she mention Solstice, nor does she indicate that she's thinking about it. It's as if their conversation never happened.

Alex is throwing some work-related nighttime reading—a three-inch-thick bound deposition transcript — into his leather messenger bag, getting ready to go home, when Leah swings by his desk. "Let's go," she says, without breaking stride.

Alex drops his bag back on his desk and bolts to keep pace with Leah. "Go where?"

She barely glances at him. "The seventh floor."

Both the New and Old Headquarters Buildings have seven floors, but there's no need for Alex to ask which one Leah means. In the CIA, *the seventh floor* refers exclusively to the top floor of the OHB. Alex has never had occasion to visit said lofty locale, its location being—quite literally—above his pay grade. The seventh floor is the province of directors, deputy directors, and personnel with the word *chief* somewhere in their titles. "Who are we heading up to see?" he asks.

"The DCIA," she answers.

◆

To get from the Office of General Counsel to the DCIA's office, Alex and Leah have to take an elevator down to the ground floor of the New Headquarters Building and pass through the atrium bridging the OHB and the NHB. "Why are we going to see the director?" Alex asks as they ride a second elevator up to the seventh floor.

"You unearth a classified plan to assassinate people with bioweapons and you're seriously asking me that?"

"I meant—I figured if we were going to kick this up the chain that we'd talk to Mr. Bryson about it first."

"He's out of town this week. Conference in Taiwan," Leah says. "But don't worry. I cleared it with him via e-mail."

"You discussed this with him over e-mail?"

"Relax," she reassures him, "we spoke in the vaguest of terms. The *vaguest*," she adds for emphasis.

Alex just nods as they approach the director's outer office. It's past business hours, but the DCIA's assistant is still there. Alex is expecting a middle-aged woman, since that's the cliché, but to his surprise, it's a guy with boyish good looks in his midthirties sitting behind the desk.

"How's his mood?" Leah asks.

"Better than I've seen it in years, worse than I've seen it in months" comes the reply. He then waves Leah and Alex through to the director's office.

Alex takes note of the fact that Leah doesn't have the Solstice file with her. This leads him to believe that Leah has already given it to the director and, therefore, that he's already read it. Which means this meeting isn't about the substance of Solstice but about what, if anything, the Agency plans to do about it. And it's possible that the only thing the director plans to do about it is take Alex to the woodshed over the actions that put the file in his possession in the first place.

The seventh floor is laid out to eschew offices and conference rooms having more than one window. As a result, none of the executives have corner offices. This isn't a function of some attempt at egalitarianism. As with so much at the Agency, the concern is a practical one. In the world of espionage and intelligence gathering, windows are dangerous things. Lips and classified materials can be read and recorded. Conversations can be listened to using high-frequency parabolic microphones. Although Agency buildings are outfitted with a special glass meant to defeat the most sophisticated auditory and visual surveillance technologies, the CIA's institutional philosophy holds it as axiomatic that for every countermeasure that can be deployed, there's a counter-counter-measure capable of defeating it. And if such technology isn't available today, it most likely will be tomorrow. Consequently, secret agents never make assumptions when it comes to security. Which is why, on the seventh floor of the CIA's New Headquarters Building, home to the most sensitive conversations, the reading and signing of the highest classified documents, the offices and conference rooms never have windows on more than one wall. And the view that the DCIA's lone office window looks out on is nothing more impressive than the Agency parking lot.

What the office lacks in terms of picturesque vistas, however, it more than makes up for in size. By Alex's calculation, the room is as big as two offices and at least a third larger than the Oval Office (which Alex has been in several times, thanks to his father). The office is arranged in two halves, with the director's desk (a mahogany monstrosity that's only slightly smaller than the deck of an aircraft carrier) on one side and more casual chairs (all leather and brass nail heads) arranged around a large maple coffee table on the other. The only way the room could look more like an old-fashioned men's club was if it had a deer head stuffed and mounted over a fireplace.

In the absence of a deer head (and a fireplace), the left wall is dedicated to a series of bookshelves festooned with books and mementos in a four-to-one ratio. The opposite wall is the requisite ego wall, replete with various commendation letters, accolades, and photographs of the DCIA taken with the past six presidents and various heads of state.

As Alex and Leah walk in, the DCIA is making his way out from behind his desk. They walk toward one another and meet in the middle of the prodigious office. The director greets Leah with a polite nod. "Leah, good to see you again."

"Director," she answers, "this is the attorney I was telling you about, Alex Garnett."

"Simon Garnett's kid, right?"

"Yes, sir," Alex answers ruefully.

The director extends a hand. "Nice to meet you," he says. "I'm William Rykman."

SIXTEEN

———

DIRECTOR RYKMAN looks down at the Solstice file on his desk and gives it a tap of his finger. "Leah has briefed me, obviously, on what you found here. She also tells me that you're refusing to disclose how you obtained it. I'd like to know this. So, I'll ask you: How did you obtain it?"

Alex shifts uncomfortably in his chair—a third-grader brought before the principal—before providing the answer he'd rehearsed in his head: "With all due respect, Director, I'm sure you know that part of being an attorney is the fiduciary responsibility to keep secrets, be they a client's or the Agency's."

Rykman slaps the notion away with a wave of his hand. "Don't waste my time with this 'fiduciary' bullshit. I asked you a very direct question. I'd appreciate a very direct answer."

"Again, sir, with respect, isn't the file's substance of greater significance than how I obtained it?" Alex is growing more comfortable now, finding his footing, the halo effect of Rykman and his office starting to wear off.

Rykman smiles and softens to take another tact, pulling the velvet glove over his iron fist. "This, I suppose, is what the Jews call chutzpah. You lecturing the DCIA in the DCIA's own office about what's important."

"I'm not trying to lecture you, sir—"

"Where did you get this?" Rykman taps the file again. His tone is even, but forceful. Leah backs him up by leveling her gaze at Alex. The moment that she'd promised, the one that Alex has been anticipating with some dread, has arrived. He's out of options.

For better or worse, he's rehearsed this response in his head as well: "I was following a money trail related to a divorce case I was covering at Ms. Doyle's instruction, because one of the CIA's field agents was involved. The money trail led to an account that I had reason to suspect was related to the Agency's covert budget. And those covert funds were spent in connection with this Solstice project." Alex manages to keep his tone and delivery level, without editorial passion or emphasis. Because he's practiced these lines in his head so many times, it sounds like he's testifying in front of a congressional oversight committee.

"Sounds like a great deal of initiative to take on a simple divorce matter," Rykman observes.

"Well, that's the thing, sir. It stopped being a simple divorce matter — to me, at least — once the case officer in question, James Harling, was killed in a traffic accident one day after this suspicious money trail was uncovered by his wife's divorce attorney. That attorney, *as well as* the driver who allegedly killed Harling, both died within forty-eight hours of each other." Alex is on a roll now, gaining confidence as the evidence stacks up. "So, sir, that confluence of events struck me as suspicious enough to warrant further examination."

"I'd have to agree." Rykman's tone is grave. His face displays the mixture of empathy and detached concern cultivated by oncologists. Alex catches Rykman glancing at Leah, presumably to see if she is already familiar with these gory details; her surprised expression suggesting that she is not is exactly what Alex expects, since he has shared none of this with her. "It goes without saying that we have to take a hard look at the circumstances of these three deaths, particularly that of Case Officer Harling."

Alex nods to suggest he's in violent agreement with this plan, but it's mainly to cover the coldness he feels in the center of his chest. So far, this meeting has played out exactly as he'd expected, all of the chess pieces moving in the ways he'd anticipated when preparing to brief Rykman. But the idea that Rykman might open some kind of inquiry into the three deaths is a possibility Alex had not considered. Any such inquiry would expose Alex's unsanctioned representation of Alan Miller, and then he would have a lot of explaining to do. And he's not sure that any explanation would save his job. For that matter, he could be subject to disciplinary action by the Bar Association and, perhaps, to criminal charges, if he is suspected of having perpetrated a fraud on the court.

"Returning to the file for a moment," Rykman says, "I'm having a little bit of trouble understanding how you could have *obtained* it." He gives the file what must be its hundredth tap. "Things like this aren't kept in a file cabinet."

"No, sir." Alex looks to Leah for some help here, but she acts as if she's not in the room.

"This file must have been hidden under layers of computer security, et cetera. My point being, I find it nigh impossible to imagine that you got it without help."

"Yes, sir. But I'd prefer — I'd appreciate it, sir, if I could keep that individual's name confidential. The person in question was acting under my instruction and if there is to be any disciplinary action taken, I'd like it to be leveled at me and me exclusively. Sir," he adds deferentially, for good measure.

"I'll be happy to keep this name confidential." Rykman is nodding with empathetic warmth now.

"Thank you, sir. I appreciate it."

"What I mean is that I'm happy to keep the name confidential...*between us*." Rykman's face darkens; the velvet glove is thinning, albeit imperceptibly. "Let's skip the 'fiduciary' bullshit this time."

Alex considers the carpet for a few seconds. "Gerald Jankovick," he says.

Rykman smiles, satisfied with his victory. "Now let's turn our attention to the file's contents. They are absolutely authentic." This pronouncement is as unexpected as it is blunt. Alex and Leah instinctively turn to each other, confirming their mutual surprise. Alex had expected Rykman to brush the whole thing off by claiming the file was a research exercise or some Agency strategist's hypothetical flight of fancy. As Rykman continues, however, it becomes clear that Alex's prediction isn't far from the truth: "The Agency explores thousands of different response and preventive-response scenarios. The National Clandestine Service doesn't color within the lines of what's legal when drawing up operational plans. As you are an attorney for the Agency, I imagine that you already know this."

Out of the corner of Alex's eye, he sees Leah's head nodding in concert with his own. "Yes, sir."

"But there is a gaping wide chasm between what's planned and what's *executed*. As an attorney, you know better than I do that there's no law against *thinking* about doing something, even thinking about it in extensive detail and formulating a very thorough plan." Again, the file gets a finger tap. "And that's what we clearly have in this case." Rykman offers up a helpless shrug, as if to suggest that all his power and authority doesn't confer upon him the ability to turn Solstice into something it's not.

"And yet three people — *that we know of* — are dead," Alex says, taking care to keep his tone respectful.

"As I said, we'll be opening an inquiry into those matters. However, that's the purview of the inspector general's office, not the general counsel's." In other words: *Thanks a lot. I'll take it from here. Don't let the door hit you on the way out.*

No so fast, Alex thinks. "I'd like to assist in that investigation, sir. I think, by virtue of my involvement and work to date…I believe I can be of some value," he asserts.

"You're right," Rykman agrees, "that your work here gives you key insights." Alex nods. "But your involvement's a double-edged sword. It also raises issues of impartiality." Rykman lets the veiled accusation land before taking it back. He's feeling charitable today, so he throws in a smile ordinarily reserved for congressional oversight committees. "Our hands remain clean if we let the inspector general's office do its job here."

The smile is undercut by the silence that follows. It's a quiet that says, *This meeting's over*. Rykman waits patiently for Alex or Leah to get the message. It's Leah who picks up on the body language first. "Thank you very much for your time, Director," she says, getting to her feet. "I'll have Mr. Garnett summarize everything we discussed in a memo."

"Let's give that code-word clearance," Rykman agrees, referring to the highest security designation. "I don't want some Agency auditor coming across it and getting the wrong idea, blowing everything out of proportion." There's a slight glance in Alex's direction when he says this, as if to imply that he's guilty of the same overreaction.

Alex weathers this with a pleasant grin and a respectful nod. "Thank you, Director." The belief that Solstice is being swept neatly under the rug is starting to feel undeniable. Rykman's attitude — equal parts patronizing and threatening — is grating on his nerves. Alex's mood isn't helped by the fact that he's kicking himself for ignoring his first instincts and not keeping this whole thing to himself. All he wants to do is get away from Rykman — and, for that matter, Leah, with her unhelpful silence — before he says something that will cost him his job.

Alex looks at Leah and then back at Rykman. He has his head down, reviewing another file and marking it with a pen as if Alex and Leah have already exited the office.

Out in the corridor, Alex waits at the elevator for Leah to catch up to him. Focused on smothering his bubbling frustration, he didn't realize he'd bolted away from her when he left Rykman's office suite. But she doesn't offer an apology for not speaking up, and he knows her well enough not to expect one. Instead, she asks, "How long do you think it'll take you to write all this up?"

The elevator's opening doors spare Alex the burden of answering. They just enter in strained silence. "For what it's worth, you did show me something in there," Leah says. Alex turns to her. "You stood your ground with him. You were articulate. You were assertive, but respectful."

"I'll have a draft of the memo to you by the time I leave tonight." And with that, the elevator's chime announces its arrival at their destination, and Alex walks out, leaving Leah in his wake.

◆

Hotel Kowsar, Tehran
2337 hrs. Zulu

Yesterday was a frustrating day. Everyone in Ayatollah Sattar Namdar's inner circle agreed that his official election as supreme leader was nothing more than a formality, but each day without government confirmation of Jahandar's passing—the blessings of Allah be upon him—was a source of growing concern. The Assembly of Experts might be an academic body composed of *mujtahid*s, Islamic scholars, but its appointment of the supreme leader was a political determination, which made it a political body. And Sattar Namdar knows better than most how vulnerable political bodies are to infection. That's why he's had his closest aides lobbying for him as strongly as decorum permits for the past three days. Not strong-arming, but providing timely whispers in the proper ears, reminders of favors long since bestowed and personal debts heretofore uncollected. Namdar's faith in the ultimate success of these backroom maneuvers was as unshakable as his faith in Allah, but he knew well that while his allies were advocating for him, his competition had friends doing similar work for them. And so, in spite of his faith in both his inner circle and the will of Allah, Namdar finds himself facing another day without even the rumor that the coming dawn will bring his election to the supreme leadership.

In this state of unrest, he finds it heartening to be getting a visit from an agent of the VEVAK. He doubts a member of the intelligence community can offer news of the assembly's decision, but you never know. At the very least, he takes the visit as a sign of respect for the presumptive supreme leader. Perhaps today will bring some favorable news.

He opens the door of his hotel suite. The VEVAK agent he finds calling on him looks young enough to be his youngest son.

"I am Rasoul," the intelligence officer says. "I apologize for calling on you at such an early hour."

"It's no bother at all," Namdar assures him. He waves the young man in.

"Omid Zandi sends you his best wishes," Rasoul says as he enters the suite. "He regrets he cannot conduct this meeting in person."

Namdar smiles inwardly. Naturally, it is Omid who is keeping him informed about events. The VEVAK officer has always been the most loyal of his friends. "I miss Omid. Please tell him that we must have dinner. It's been too long."

Rasoul offers a compliant nod. Namdar gestures for him to take a seat on one of the living room's three chairs, but the man remains respectfully standing. "The reason Omid could not be here in person this morning is that he is preoccupied reacting to new intelligence we recently received. It is this intelligence that he asked for me to convey to you personally. Given its import, he says you will understand why his efforts must remain focused on Iran's response." *This is intriguing,* Namdar thinks. He nods, indicating not only his understanding but that Rasoul should continue. "We have reason to suspect that Supreme Leader Jahandar's passing was not due to natural causes."

"What do you mean?" Namdar is unable to keep the shock from his voice.

"An agent of the Mossad committed suicide less than twelve hours after the Ayatollah Jahandar died. He left behind a note. We are currently working to verify its contents."

"What did the note say?"

Rasoul pauses to take a deep breath. "The note was accompanied by a file outlining how it's possible to eliminate a political target through delivery of an enhanced strain of swine flu."

Namdar works to maintain a stoic expression. "Given that," he says, choosing his words with care, "I would think the appropriate course of action obvious."

Rasoul offers a compliant nod and says quietly, "Acting on this information, we had a series of tests run on the supreme leader's remains." He pauses again. "The results were conclusive for the presence of influenza A virus subtype H1N1. Swine flu."

Namdar nods, his expression grave. The implications of what Rasoul is saying are obvious. "To be clear, Rasoul, you are telling me that the VEVAK believes the Israelis are responsible for the supreme leader's death. That this was an assassination." The idea is so preposterous that Namdar can barely give it voice.

"This is the conclusion suggested by the Mossad officer's suicide note," Rasoul confirms. "As I said, we are working to authenticate the validity of this intelligence."

"But if it's correct," the future supreme leader of Iran notes, "then Israel's actions constitute an act of war." Namdar's tone is grave. Rasoul replies with an equally serious nod. "Does the president know?"

Rasoul nods again. "He has requested that the minister of defense develop a list of military options by the end of today."

Namdar sits. He turns to the window and looks out on Tehran, feeling secure in the knowledge that two things will happen by the end of the week: he will be elected supreme leader, and his country will be at war with Israel. Although neither is absolutely certain, he can feel the tide of destiny moving events. Both outcomes seem likely to him now. What he cannot see, however, is which will happen first.

◆

Washington's National Public Radio station, WETA-FM 90.9, has been a fixture on Alex's car radio since he got the call confirming he had a job with the CIA. The interview process revealed major gaps in Alex's knowledge of current events. So listening to NPR during his commute — when not rolling calls or dictating legal memoranda — has become part of his daily routine. He's glad he's made the effort to stay informed about what's going on in the world that his current employer investigates and protects.

Tonight, however, the radio is only white noise. Alex is still thinking about Rykman and Leah, about bureaucracy and inertia and keeping secrets. While he strongly believes Rykman is actively covering up the existence of Solstice, he is not enough of a conspiracy theorist to think the DCIA is doing it for anything other than politically bureaucratic reasons. As far as he can tell, Solstice is nothing more than an embarrassment to Rykman, another covert flight of fancy cooked up by the Agency's Clandestine Service, like the plan to lace Castro's cigars with a chemical that would make his beard fall out, as the Clandestine Service's predecessor, the Operations Directorate, plotted to do in the early 1960s. But Alex knows in his bones that Solstice is not merely some operational strategist's wet dream, just as he knows that the deaths of Harling, Moreno, Miller, and Zollitsch were not accidental or unrelated. Yet he's truly out of options. He has already taken Solstice to the doorstep of the CIA's highest officer, a man outranked only by the director of national intelligence and the president of the United States. And he has no intention of taking the matter farther up the chain.

But there's one last thing he needs to do. He dials his phone through his car's Bluetooth system. Gerald answers on the first ring. It takes Alex a good three minutes to get past Gerald's now pro forma anxious inquiries, and then an additional fifteen minutes to relay the specifics of his meeting with Director Rykman. Alex could have boiled it down much faster if Gerald hadn't kept interrupting him with questions. But Alex manages to be patient. It's the least he can do, he reasons, still regretting his inability to keep Gerald's name out of the whole thing. Moreover, Gerald has a right to be worried about losing his job in the aftermath — a concern he expresses repeatedly on the call. "If I'm lucky," he says, "and I think we both know I'm *not* — but if I'm *lucky,* they'll just give me a colonoscopy. They're going to go through every keystroke on my computer. They're gonna review every log, every download, every TCP packet."

"Are you worried they'll find something that's a fireable offense?" Alex asks. "Have you been using the Agency network for anything you shouldn't have?"

"I told you," Gerald says, reading Alex's mind, "the Agency's network is *closed*. There's nothing I *could* do."

"Then what are you worried ab —"

"I'll be *under investigation,*" Gerald interrupts. "The subject of an *inquiry.* All they need to do is find something — anything, virtually — that'd give them probable cause to subpoena my home computer. And that's if they're going by the book enough to bother with a subpoena, which is doubtful. Bottom line, Alex, my entire life is gonna be stripped naked in front of them. And that's, *again,* best case — otherwise defined as 'not getting fired.'"

Alex tries not to sigh lest Gerald hear it over the Bluetooth. This is one instance where he feels Gerald is entitled to his neuroses. He didn't ask to be a part of this drama, and it was Alex's failing that he'd given Director Rykman his name. So Alex remains patient, listening calmly and offering the occasional empathetic platitude ("I get it. I totally get it") and reassurance ("It's gonna be fine, Gerald. I promise. I'll make sure it's fine"). But these are empty promises. Alex has as much influence over the Agency's Inspector General's Office as he does over the weather.

"I didn't want to get involved in this," Gerald says, a pronouncement that scrapes Alex's conscience.

"I know," Alex says. "You didn't want to get involved in this. But I forced you to. And I'm sorry. I'm gonna make sure it all works out, Gerald, like I said. But I *am* sorry."

"What'd Rykman say? About the Solstice thing?" Gerald asks, offering an olive branch.

"Pretty much what you'd expect."

"Some analyst's mental masturbation?"

"That's one way of putting it."

"And you know that's bullshit, right?"

Alex thinks on that question, but not for long. All these related deaths, one that utilized a weapons-grade neurotoxin developed at a military base, cannot be explained away by coincidence. "Yeah," he confirms, his voice almost a whisper, "I know it's bullshit."

"I mean, did you ask him how Solstice could be theoretical after what went down in Iran?"

"What do you mean?"

"I read it on Google News, like, an hour ago." Alex can feel Gerald's incredulity over the phone. How can Alex not know about this? "The supreme leader of Iran is dead."

"So?"

"So, do you know what killed him?" Gerald pauses for effect. "Swine flu. An incredibly fatal and, therefore, incredibly *rare* strain of swine flu. Swine flu—"

"Holy Christ," Alex whispers, cutting Gerald off, his hands white-knuckling his steering wheel. "Holy Christ…"

"Swine flu is one of the viruses in the Solstice file." Gerald sounds uncharacteristically calm at this development, as if the degree to which he finds it fascinating eclipses the extent to which he finds it terrifying. "At first, I totally freaked," he admits, "but I figured, if you thought it was a thing—y'know, if you thought there was a connection—you'd call me, like, pronto. But you didn't, so I thought, y'know, coincidence." Gerald takes a long pause. "But you didn't know."

"No, I didn't."

"If Jahandar was killed by Solstice, it's *real*."

That's not all it means, Alex thinks. *It also means that the deaths of Harling, Moreno, Miller, and Zollitsch were murders — assassinations committed on American soil — to cover up the program's existence.*

"Don't panic, Gerald."

"Too late for that, hoss. Way too late."

"When I get back into the office tomorrow, I'll take a deeper look into this Jahandar thing. There might be a perfectly reasonable explanation for it."

"It's cute that you can still say that after all the shit we've learned," Gerald says.

Alex has no rebuttal to that.

◈

About an hour later, Alex's Lexus slides into a parking space in the garage beneath his apartment building. As he gets out of the car, he sees something flash in the corner of the garage. It's a light. Cherry colored. He turns in response, and a second flash of crimson appears to settle on the center of his chest like a landing fly.

Alex instinctively recognizes this red dot as a laser sight and instinctively drops to the garage's concrete floor. As he does, he feels a puff of air along his hairline. The same instinct that just saved his life tells him he just felt a bullet whiz past his head. There's a crackle of safety glass behind him as the rear windshield of his Lexus becomes instantly opaque with impact fractures emanating from a tiny hole directly in the path of where his head had been just seconds before.

◈

NEW HAMPSHIRE AVENUE NW
WASHINGTON, DC
10:43 P.M. EDT

Tyler Donovan has fought in wars and worked covert missions all over the world and he can hardly fathom what he's just witnessed. In all his twenty-eight years—a *lifetime* in the world of the professional military—he's never seen anyone dodge a laser-sighted bullet. All it took was a fraction of a fraction of a second—an infinitesimal gap between his sighting of the target and the twitching of his finger on the trigger—but in that interval, Alex found immortality, at least briefly. And proved to Donovan that he was one lucky son of a bitch indeed.

But luck has a tendency to run out before bullets do. This is particularly true when the shooter wields a M4A1 carbine assault rifle, as Donovan does. He has a standard magazine slapped into it, which means he has twenty-seven bullets left, having spent the first three on a volley that should have blown Garnett back across the length of the parking garage.

Donovan adjusts his aim through the advanced combat optical gun sight to the center of Garnett's forehead. The maneuver flashes the rifle's AN/PEQ-5 carbine visible laser directly into Garnett's eyes. Garnett squints—momentarily blinded—as his hand moves up to instinctively shield his eyes and the second three-round burst comes for his head.

Alex feels the trio of bullets part his hair as he presses his face against the concrete floor, instinctively trying to make himself as difficult a target as possible. Somewhere, someone is muttering, "Jesus Christ, Jesus Christ," over and over again. And then Alex realizes that it's him. He scrambles along the floor. With any luck, all the automotive steel and fiberglass surrounding him will save his life. Safety glass rains down on him like hail.

Bullets whiz past his ears like angry hornets, each one carrying death. Not thinking about the possibility of his hand being shredded by 45-millimeter rounds, he blindly reaches up to grasp the handle of his car's driver's-side door. It doesn't open. But the realization that the car is locked only spikes Alex's adrenaline. His thumb scans the back of the handle, feverishly working to get the keyless entry system to recognize his hand on the lock. It feels like a lifetime — a passage of seconds marked only by the three-shot staccato of machine-gun bursts — before the car chirps and he's able to swing the door open. Bullets slam into the car. Alex hurls himself into the driver's seat, the steel of the open door shielding him as he tries to keep low. He gulps in air as if his lungs were punctured, but the breaths are his most compelling evidence that he's still alive.

◆

Shit, a voice inside Donovan's head screams. He can feel his temper and frustration rise despite his training. The coppery taste of bile infiltrates his mouth as a corner of his mind wonders how anyone could be as lucky as Alex Garnett. This was supposed to be a quick, clean kill, no fuss, no muss, in and out, but it's rapidly turning into a clusterfuck of epic proportions. It doesn't help that those proportions would multiply exponentially should Donovan's bad luck be increased by the arrival of civilians. Then he would truly have a disaster on his hands and would have little choice but to abandon the op. His orders didn't include authorization to engage civilians. No level of collateral damage is acceptable here.

◆

Alex's hand shoots forward to punch the engine's start button. The Lexus's 3.5-liter churns to life. Alex has never heard a more beautiful sound. He throws the sedan into drive and pushes the accelerator all the way to the floor. The car lurches forward—taking out the side-view mirror of a neighboring Ford—and gets only a couple of feet before its front windshield explodes in a hail of gunfire.

Alex should be dead. After all, automotive safety glass isn't bullet-proof. It is, however, extremely resilient, and the Lexus is enough of a moving target that all the bullets manage to do is fracture the windshield into a million pieces. The twin coats of high-impact plastic sandwich the pebbles of glass between them. The result is a latticework of microfractures that cover the entire windshield. What was intended as a safety measure designed to keep shattered glass out of the driver's eyes now completely obscures Alex's view.

So he throws the car into reverse. He whips his head around to see through the rear windshield, only to realize that the initial volley of gunfire that started this nightmare has already done the same fracture-obscuring damage to the back window. Bullets rake the side of the car. Another round explodes the front left tire, causing it to violently lurch forward and skid.

Alex swivels his head back to the front, and his eye catches something in the center of the dashboard. His face lights up. He has an unobstructed view of the Lexus's reverse motion. *It's the feed from the rearview parking camera.* Stomping on the accelerator and clutching the steering wheel, he whips the car around in reverse, using the parking camera to guide himself toward the exit.

In the parking camera's display, he catches a glimpse of his attacker diving out of his way. Alex isn't trying to smash into the gunman, but he wouldn't mind finding pieces of the assailant smeared on his rear bumper and beneath the car's undercarriage when this is all over. For now, he'll happily settle for escaping with his life. He whips the car toward the garage exit. The narrow walls grate against the Lexus's side as the car careens up the garage's exit ramp, scraping the narrow walls and leaving behind a trail of paint on the concrete before belching out from underground as if shot by a cannon.

Cars honk in protest as Alex immediately finds himself in the middle of traffic. But he can't stop. Not yet. For all he knows, his attacker has a car of his own and is following Alex up the parking-garage exit ramp right this moment. Accompanied by a chorus of angry car horns, Alex takes a few seconds to put the car in park — the Lexus sitting, vulnerable, right in the middle of traffic — so that he can shoot his feet forward and kick out the front windshield. He doesn't succeed on the first attempt. Or the second. Or the third. Motorists curse and honk at him until the fourth kick succeeds in dislodging the windshield with an audible pop.

Wasting no time, Alex settles back into his seat and yanks the gearshift into drive. He slams the accelerator and shoots off, leaving behind a shattered windshield and a mob of angry commuters.

SEVENTEEN

GRACE POUNDS on the steering wheel of her Volvo as it creeps along in traffic. A chorus of honking emanates from a few blocks up, punctuating the end of a particularly brutal day. Her eyes are red; her throat raw from protracted sobbing. And the traffic only exacerbates the fury inside her. She took some of that rage out on her steering wheel, but the exercise accomplished nothing except to add a sore hand to her list of woes.

Just a few hours earlier, the NIH denied her research grant. While this had always been a possibility, it never seemed a likely one. A year's worth of work, stress, and sleepless nights rendered instantly worthless. What made the blow particularly shattering was how completely unexpected it was. She didn't think she'd get a decision from the NIH for at least another two months. They gave no more reason for the early execution than they did for their decision.

Her cell rings. She knows it's Alex even before looking at the phone. She decided not to call him with the news when the verdict came down. She wants to be comforted in person. He's probably home already and wondering what's keeping her. She keys the Bluetooth button on her steering wheel and answers in a pained, fatigued voice. "Hey." It sounds like surrender.

"Grace, it's me. Are you all right?" There's so much raw worry in his voice that she wonders if he heard about the NIH's decision already. But he sounds grave. Like he's worried about a person, not a research project. "I need you to listen very carefully…"

"Alex?"

"You can't go home, all right? Do you understand?"

"No." She stops. "I mean, I don't understand. Alex, what's going on?"

"I can't explain right—"

"Alex." She cuts him off, an edge starting to darken her tone. "I've had a really lousy day. The NIH—"

"Grace, *please*," Alex implores. "You *can't* go home. Someone just tried to kill me."

If it weren't for the traffic limiting her car's speed to three miles per hour, Grace would have totaled her car. "What? What are you talking about? Who tried to—someone tried to kill you?"

"You can't go home," Alex repeats dogmatically. "It's not safe."

"You're not making any sense."

"It's not safe."

"Is this—" Grace stops herself because the thought she's having seems so outrageous. "Does this have something to do with the bioweapon thing?"

"Yes."

"Oh my God."

"Yes. I'll tell you about it in person. But you can't go home."

"Then where should I go? Where *can* I go? This is insane."

"Remember that place we'd talk about when we'd talk dirty to each other? Do you remember it?" Grace starts to answer, but Alex stops her: "Don't say it out loud. Just go there. Go there right now. As fast as you can—"

"That won't be particularly fast. I'm stuck in traffic."

"Just — as quickly as you can. I'll meet you in the parking lot."

"Alex, you're scaring me…"

"I know. I'm sorry. Just — it'll be okay. It'll all be all right. Don't worry."

Grace shakes her head in disbelief. "You said someone's trying to kill you."

"I'm fine now. I just want to make sure — I'm just taking every precaution to make sure you're all right."

"What about you?"

"Me too," he says, but that doesn't sound all that convincing. "Now throw your phone out of the window."

"You want me to do what?"

In his own car, Alex drives as best he can without the front windshield. Although the car lumbers along on only three good tires, the wind harshly whips at his face. With its GPS components and cellular technology, Grace's phone is really nothing more than a glorified tracking device. The suggestion that Grace get rid of it strikes him as the kind of sensible precaution that would make Gerald proud.

Shit. Gerald. Alex fights down a new tide of concern.

He calls Gerald and is greeted with only voice mail. *Shit*. He endures Gerald's outgoing message; he waits an eternity for the beep, then forces calm into his voice before speaking. "Gerald, it's me. Alex. Give me a call back soon as you get this. It's important."

Alex catches himself just as he's about to follow his own advice and throw his own phone out the window. If he does, Gerald will have no means of getting back to him. He needs Gerald's help, but more important, he has to tell Gerald that the CIA might have decided to make an attempt on Gerald's life as well.

A wave of nausea hits, making Alex's head swim. Maybe it's too late?

Alex tries to force the thought from his head, but it persists. A few hours ago, Alex was worried about Gerald's job. Now he's worried about whether he'll live through the night.

◆

ENCORE SUITES
WASHINGTON, DC
11:36 P.M. EDT

The Encore Suites is a strip-mall-style motel in one of the seedier sections of Washington, DC. A bend of two-story buildings arcs around the cracked pavement parking lot, inhabited by junkies, hookers, and junkie hookers. A neon sign bathes the area in a sickly pink glow boasting "a TV/AC in every room." Another sign, smaller but equally neon, stresses that the Encore Suites is "an adult motel," as if there were any doubt. The motel is between Alex and Grace's condo and their favorite restaurant. The notion of some anonymous lustful assignation in one of the mirrored-ceiling rooms that can be rented by the hour has always been a favorite mutual fantasy. The motel itself is specific enough, the sex talk private enough, that it's as secure a meeting place as Alex could devise.

He chooses from one of several empty parking spaces. Grace hasn't arrived yet. He looks around and immediately abandons his plan to have Grace check herself in to one of the motel's rooms. He'd rather have her take her chances with the CIA. He rips open his wallet to find a hundred and eighty bucks in twenties and concludes that he'll have to risk Grace using her credit card.

Five long minutes pass before her Volvo rolls into the lot. Panic spreads across her face as she takes in the punctured tire, missing windshield, and unmistakable pockmarking of bullet holes that riddle Alex's formerly luxury sedan. She races to Alex. He sweeps her up in his arms. "It's okay," he assures her. "I'm fine. I'm okay."

174

"What happened?"

"Leah took me to the DCIA earlier this evening. He told me the whole Solstice thing wasn't real, that it was just theoretical. But then the Ayatollah Jahandar — the supreme leader of Iran, a guy who's more powerful than the Iranian president — he *died*. From a rare strain of swine flu exactly like what's described in the Solstice file. I found out about it on my way home, and then when I *got* home somebody tried to shoot me with a machine gun." Alex points to the bullet damage as physical proof. "He did this."

Grace shakes her head in stunned disbelief. "Are you okay? Are you all right?"

"I'm fine. Shaken up, obviously. But okay. Uninjured." She turns away, her mind clearly churning. "What? What is it?"

"This — this isn't going to make any sense..."

"Tonight's set a pretty low bar for sense."

She takes a deep breath. "The NIH denied my grant today. Two months early. No explanation. That's a coincidence, right?"

"I don't know. I'm not sure of anything right now. Except that what's happening here is very real and very serious."

"You have to go to your father." It comes out like a bleat, as if she's been holding the thought in for weeks. "He can help you. He can help *us*. He can find out what's going on, and he can stop it."

"I'm not going to my father." Of this much, Alex is certain. He knows it's irrational, but even with his life at stake, even with *Grace's* life at stake, he can't bring himself to go to his father, hat in hand, and beg for his help. "If what happened tonight happened for the reasons I think, that means the CIA tried to assassinate me on American soil. It means they assassinated the supreme leader of Iran with a *bioweapon*. I don't know what they'll do to my father. I don't know who my father could turn to, who he could trust."

"Or maybe you don't trust your father?"

Alex frowns. "My whole life, when given a choice between the government and me, he chose the government. Every single time. If someone explained to him that I found out something I shouldn't have, and if that person then convinced him that the best way to solve the problem was to make me disappear, I'd be gone. I can't go to my father with this. He might choose them over me."

A range of emotions plays across Grace's face. Fear. Confusion. But disappointment is the most evident. At that moment, Alex realizes he's broken something between them, and he's not sure it can ever be repaired.

He pushes the thought aside. "Drive to Baltimore. Find an ATM and take out as much money as you can. Then try to find a motel, someplace that'll take cash." He gestures to their current surroundings, attempting to sound light. "But someplace a little nicer than this paradise." Grace doesn't smile. "If you can't find a place that's safe and will let you pay in cash, then use a credit card, but only as a last resort, okay?"

"What are you going to do?" There's a coldness in her voice. Or maybe it's just fatigue.

"I probably shouldn't tell you. And you shouldn't tell anyone where you're going."

"I can't. I threw out my cell, remember?"

"Good point."

"I've got my laptop," she offers. "I could e-mail you…"

"No. No, they can track that. Don't even turn your computer *on,* all right?" Grace nods, but the look in her eyes screams that she's just as confused as she is terrified. "Give me twenty-four hours. Then I'll figure out a way to safely get word to you."

"How?"

"I don't know," he snaps, but instantly regrets the outburst. "I don't know," he says again, softer this time. "I'll figure something out. Twenty-four hours." He moves in to kiss her, but finds only a tense cheek to meet his lips.

"Think about calling your father," Grace says.

"I love you" is his only reply. With that, he lets go of Grace and watches her get into her car and turn on the ignition. He watches her until he sees the car's taillights disappear into the traffic.

Then he tries Gerald on his cell again. This time, thank God, he answers. "Alex?"

"Hey, man. You okay?" He tries to sound calmer than he feels.

"Yeah. Why shouldn't I be? What's going on? You've called me like a gajillion times."

Alex dreads the explosion of anxiety that he knows is imminent. "Gerald, someone tried to kill me tonight."

"No fucking way." Gerald sounds genuinely incredulous. "No fucking way," he repeats, but this time disbelief is replaced with his signature move: panic. "Oh my God. *Oh my God*. What are we going to do? What the *fuck* are we going to do?"

Alex can hear Gerald pacing urgently around his apartment. The sound of slamming windows and doors is unmistakable. "I'll tell you what we're *not* gonna do," Alex says as soothingly as he can manage. "We're not going to freak out, okay?"

"Too fucking late, hoss."

"Get it under control, Gerald," he says, more forcefully this time. "You don't want to die? Great. First step is to get your shit together." This appears to calm Gerald down. The hurried sounds of Gerald going into lockdown mode have been replaced with calmer breaths and footsteps.

"Hang on," Gerald says. On the other end of the line, Alex hears the sound of a pill bottle popping open and the telltale shake of capsules. After Gerald swallows, he says, "I've got to get out of here. They could be coming for me next, hoss."

"Relax. If they were coming for you—"

"I'd be dead already," Gerald interrupts. He whispers something Alex can't make out but that sounds like *Shit, shit, shit*. Alex waits for Gerald's pharmaceuticals to kick in.

"I need you to come meet me. My car's totaled. You got a pen?"

"I'm typing it into my phone…"

Of course you are, Alex thinks before giving Gerald the closest major intersection to the Encore Suites.

◆

Tyler Donovan stands at attention and awaits William Rykman's judgment. The equipment and monitors of the Overwatch Op Center hum behind them. It's the only sound in the underground bunker apart from Rykman's disciplined breaths. His gaze hasn't moved off Donovan since the operative relayed the news of Alex's improbable escape.

"This is my fault," Rykman says. These are the last four words Donovan expected to hear, but they serve to untangle the clench in his gut, a little. "I shouldn't have ordered a public operation. We should've been subtler. I let my emotions get the better of me."

"Georgetown PD and the FBI have both been notified. The ballistics are untraceable, but the use of a suppressed M4 carbine should be sufficient to get them scrambling over each other for jurisdiction."

"What about witnesses? Video surveillance?"

"Not my first rodeo, sir."

"Do we know where Garnett is?"

Donovan shakes his head. "A locator wasn't put on his cell because, well, to be frank, we expected him to be dead by now. But if he uses it, we'll be able to pinpoint his location through cell-tower proximity."

"Let's monitor his credit cards as well."

"Already in the works."

◆

Alex leaves his Lexus in the Encore Suites parking lot and walks the three blocks to the corner of T Street NE and New York Avenue. Gerald's Prius pulls up thirty minutes later. Alex gets in. "We should toss our cells," Gerald says.

"I've been thinking about that, but it doesn't matter."

"Dude, those things are tracking devices that make phone calls."

"It doesn't matter if they can track us because they'll know where we're going anyway."

"Where are we going?" Gerald asks, slight desperation in his voice. "Please say Europe."

"Nope," Alex answers. "The Agency."

Gerald blanches. "I don't know if you've been paying attention to current events, but it's the Agency that's trying to kill us."

"We need leverage. We need information to negotiate with."

"Negotiate?" Gerald shakes his head. Alex can see his hands trembling on the Prius's steering wheel. "You can't negotiate with people trying to kill you."

"Well, since the only other option is to go to war with the CIA —"

"What about your dad?" Gerald cuts him off. "That guy's, like, superconnected. Doesn't he have the president on speed-dial?"

"Exactly." Alex nods. "I don't know how far up the chain this thing goes."

"Wait. You're saying you can't trust your own father?"

"I'm not saying he'd sell us out intentionally. We just don't know who he'd speak to, who's involved with whatever is going on here." He watches Gerald take that in.

"Then what do we do?" Gerald croaks like a child lost in a shopping mall.

"We need to find out who's behind Solstice. We know that, we have information we can use. We can threaten to go to CNN with it. We can threaten to pull a WikiLeaks. Intel is our leverage. It's our only insurance policy."

"We've got the Solstice file. That's not enough?"

"Director Rykman has the file now, remember?"

"You didn't make a copy before handing it over?"

"If I'd known I couldn't trust Rykman, I wouldn't have trusted Rykman."

"Good point." Gerald nods. "But doesn't that mean Rykman's behind Solstice?"

"For all we know, he's covering for the person who is. We need to be sure, preferably by finding some evidence to back everything up." Alex sees that he has Gerald's undivided attention. "I remember you said the Agency's network is a closed system," he continues. "So any information—"

"We have to get from on-site," Gerald says, completing the thought. "What information would we be trying to get?"

"We still don't know who transferred the money from the black budget to Harling's account and back. Whoever did that is probably in charge of, or at least neck-deep in, this whole Solstice thing."

Gerald thinks on that for a few seconds. "To move black money around like that, it would have to be someone with top-shelf clearance."

Alex nods. He'd already come to a similar conclusion. "Rykman or one of the deputy directors, most likely. Could you hack into one of their computers?"

Gerald shakes his head. "You're talking about the inner circle of the Agency now. Even if I had administrator access—which I *don't*—I'd need to work off of a direct node."

"I don't understand that."

"I'd have to fake admin privileges. Basically, make the system *think* I'm an IT administrator."

"Okay. I'd think you'd be able to do something like that, no problem."

"It'd be a problem," Gerald insists, "but I'd be able to do it. Probably," he adds. "But, like I said, I'd need to work off of a direct node—a terminal inside one of the directors' or deputy directors' private offices."

Alex deflates. He really thought they had the workings of a plan for a moment. He racks his brain while Gerald drives, the lights of Washington passing by them as he goes through the Agency organizational chart in his head. Then it hits him. He turns to Gerald. "Would the general counsel have the kind of terminal you'd need?"

❖

CIA General Counsel Arthur Bryson lives in Bethesda, Maryland, about seven miles from the Agency's headquarters, in a modest Tudor-style home that he shares with his wife of forty-two years and their loyal German shepherd. Neither his wife nor his dog stir when the phone rings at one thirty in the morning. But Bryson is used to incoming calls at all hours. He looks over to the two phones resting on his nightstand and is surprised to see it's the secure Agency phone that's ringing.

"Bryson," he answers, trying to sound alert.

"Sorry to wake you, sir. But there's a situation developing in Kandahar," says the voice on the other end of the line.

Bryson rubs the sleep from his eyes. "The kind of situation that can't wait for a civilized hour?" Bryson asks, already knowing the answer.

"I'm afraid not, sir. There's an operative who needs to take action pursuant to the DNCS's directive, but we need your signature on a finding, sir."

The voice sounds overly businesslike, considering the late hour. "Who am I talking to?" Bryson demands.

"Alex Garnett, sir. I've got the draft finding right here. All it needs is your seal and your signature."

"The seal is in my office."

At the CIA, Alex nods with a smile. "Then we'll need you to come to the office, sir."

EIGHTEEN

ARTHUR BRYSON is of a generation of men who dress at two in the morning the same way they dress at two in the afternoon, even if they've been woken from a sound sleep thirty minutes earlier. In Bryson's case, this means a neatly pressed Brooks Brothers three-piece suit, conservative tie, and loafers shined to a perfect gleam. Alex, by contrast, looks like he's been scurrying around on the floor of a parking garage.

Alex follows Bryson down the hallway to the older man's office. As they travel, Bryson peruses the intelligence finding that purportedly requires his seal and signature. "Is this your work?" he asks.

"Yes, sir." In truth, it's a finding from 2008 that Alex liberally revised in order to fit his Kandahar cover story and minimize the chances of Bryson recognizing the events from the old case described therein.

"It's good work," Bryson observes, and it's all Alex can do not to laugh.

They arrive at the doorway to Bryson's outer office. Bryson's assistant is not there at this hour to let them in, of course. So Bryson removes his CIA badge — a thin piece of plastic edged in red with a recent photograph of him — and waves it in front of a featureless security panel. The

Agency's pass-card system utilizes radio-frequency identification technology, which means that the badge contains a tiny computer chip along with an antenna that broadcasts a unique signal from the card to the badge reader. All the badge's owner has to do is wave it within the vicinity of the panel, and the electronic locks will disengage.

But the door doesn't unlock.

Visibly flustered, Bryson then does what pretty much anyone else in this circumstance would: he presses the badge to the reader as if the badge's internal antenna will somehow work better with physical contact. This seems to do the trick, as the outer office's locks disengage on his second attempt. Bryson leads Alex though another pass-card-locked door into his private office. By the time they set foot inside, Bryson's already forgotten the glitch that caused his badge not to work on the first try.

What Bryson doesn't know is that on that first attempt, his badge's unique signal never reached the door's security panel. That's because the panel Bryson waved the card in front of was a shell—a mock-up of the card reader that Gerald had placed over the actual panel. Gerald built this false front from spare parts in the space of five minutes for a single purpose: to intercept the unique frequency emitted by Bryson's badge, a practice known to hackers as sniffing or phishing. So while Alex is going through the motions of getting Bryson's sealed signature on a bogus intelligence finding that will be shredded at the first chance he gets, Gerald is hard at work programming a Trojan badge using the cloned frequency from Bryson's.

Alex walks Bryson to the elevator, partially to be polite but mostly to guarantee that he'll be returning home. Bryson gets into the waiting elevator and holds the door open for Alex. "You're calling it a night too, right? I mean, it's practically morning."

Alex shakes his head and holds up the signed finding. "I just want to make sure a scan of this gets secure-e-mailed to Kandahar."

"Suit yourself," Bryson says with a shrug as the elevator doors close.

Alex checks his watch. Bryson was right. Quarter to three in the morning.

◆

Five of three. Alex and Gerald stand outside Bryson's office. Gerald quickly removes the false panel reader and wipes away the congealed rubber cement he'd used to affix it to the wall. He then waves the Trojan badge in front of the reader.

But nothing happens. Confused, Alex looks to Gerald.

"It's the same RFID. It's exactly the same," Gerald says, mystified. He holds the fake badge a centimeter in front of the panel. "Hang on a sec. Just…one…sec…" Alex's eyes dart from Gerald to the pass-card reader and back again, an interminable interval passing before…the panel's internal speaker chirps and the door's lock clicks back with a satisfying *shunk.*

Gerald shrugs. "The plastic on my card might be a few millimeters thicker than Bryson's standard issue. Or the antenna's not as strong. I guess it just needed a little extra time for the signal to get from A to B."

Alex opens the door to the outer office and steps across the threshold. "Well, I guess a little treason's worth waiting for. Will we have the same problem with the inner door?"

"Hope not."

Once inside, Gerald takes his seat at Bryson's computer. The word *computer,* however, is something of a misnomer. There's no hard drive or flash storage device. The machine is a network computer that has no brains — no applications or files — of its own. Its entire technological purpose is to provide access to the Agency's proprietary intranet. A few seconds after the machine is fired up, a username and password challenge appear on the screen. Gerald begins to type furiously. New screens and windows start to clutter the screen with a speed that reminds Alex of a croupier dealing cards in Vegas.

"All right. I'm in."

"That fast?"

"Give me some credit, would you, please?" Gerald sounds annoyed. He continues to type with one hand while manipulating the terminal's mouse with the other. He looks more comfortable than a Cy Young Award winner on a pitcher's mound. "All right. I've got a directory here marked Overwatch."

"What about something called Solstice?"

Gerald shakes his head. "No." His eyes scan the file names cascading down the window open in front of him. "Everything else looks pretty benign." He points at a few of the files, listing off names of directories and subdirectories. "NCS, Strategic Resource Investment, Transnational Issues, Advanced Interrogation Techniques..." Gerald turns around to look at Alex with an impatient glare. "I seriously doubt he keeps everything in a file labeled 'Black Budget Withdrawals.'"

Alex actually chuckles at that. It's true. "Go back to that Overwatch directory." Gerald does and opens it with a mouse click. He's rewarded with a list of what looks like three hundred subdirectories. "Check if there's a Solstice one in there."

"Bingo." Gerald clicks open the subdirectory. There is only a single entry: *K. McCallum.* "That name sound familiar?"

Alex just shakes his head, and that's when he catches a glimpse of a new problem: *There's a cell phone resting on Bryson's desk.* And the sight of it chills Alex to the bone. "Gerald," he manages to say, "you've gotta work faster."

It's because I woke up in the middle of the goddamn night, Bryson tells himself. It's a point of pride for him that he never leaves things behind — his keys, his coat, even an umbrella — so it's particularly galling to arrive at his space in the Agency parking lot only to realize he left his cell phone in his office. It's the first thing he removes from his suit-jacket pocket when he gets into the office every morning. He followed this habit when he went to his desk to get his personal seal to execute the intelligence finding. The frustrating thing is that the trip down to his car and back to his office to retrieve the phone is going to cost him at least fifteen minutes of sleep — every second of which he needs right now, considering he has to wake up for work in a few hours. Hell, he's tempted to leave the damn phone and just retrieve it in the morning, but that would be like leaving an appendage behind. He can't believe it. How could someone of his generation be as attached to a phone as a teenager is these days? So he heads back to his office, returning to the NHB's security entrance, waving his badge in front of the pass-card reader.

The guard on duty looks up from his station's computer screen with a quizzical expression on his face. "Huh. Mr. Bryson, weren't you in your office earlier this evening? Or I mean this morning, I guess."

"Maybe ten, fifteen minutes ago."

"Did you remember to lock your door behind you?"

The doors to high-level offices at the Agency are self-locking, so Bryson is pretty sure he did that by shutting the door behind him. "Yes. Why?" he asks.

The guard shrugs. "According to the system, you're still in there."

❖

In Bryson's office, Alex wills Gerald to type, click, or do whatever the hell it is he's doing faster. There's a good chance Bryson won't return for his phone, either because he'll be too tired or because he'll forget. But Alex doesn't want to wager his career, let alone his continued freedom, on fatigue or memory loss.

Seconds pass like hours. Finally, Gerald leans back in his chair. "Bingo."

Alex instantly unclenches. "Talk to me."

"If I'm looking at this right, the wire transfer to Harling's bank account…it was initiated from *this* terminal," Gerald says, gesturing to Bryson's monitor.

Alex can barely believe it. "You're saying *he* moved the Solstice money?" he asks, unsuccessfully attempting to hide the incredulity in his voice.

Gerald shakes his head. "AIN doesn't match."

"What doesn't?" Alex asks.

"Agency identification number. Every Agency employee's got one. You've got one. It's a seven-digit identification number you get on your EOD." Alex stares back at him. "EOD. That's entry-on-duty date. Your first day of work, basically. I'm not the one who makes the acronyms up, by the way."

"Fine." Alex is getting impatient. "Whatever. Did Bryson move the money in and out of Harling's account?"

Gerald shakes his head and points to the computer screen, which cascades with arcane lines of banking and computer code that Alex cannot even begin to decipher. "See here? The transfers were authorized by AIN four-five-eight-seven-nine-six-three." He points again. "Bryson's AIN is eight-three-nine-six-five-zero-five. They don't match."

Alex reacts like he's been hit with a volt of electric current. He's heard that code somewhere before. He narrows his focus, but digging it out of his memory is like trying to grasp mercury. The harder he concentrates, the more elusive the recollection becomes. CIA clearance codes are all uniquely designated; he has no reason to know an AIN any more than he has reason to know another person's Social Security number. And yet, for reasons that remain frustratingly cloudy in his mind, *this* particular code strikes a resonant chord. He types the code — 4587963 — into his phone before casting another look over at Bryson's, still resting on his desk. "Let's get out of here."

◆

Bryson beelines to his office with the NHB security guard in tow. Normally, it takes a solid seven minutes to get from the security entrance to the seventh floor; you have to take the escalator from the entrance level to the ground floor of the NHB, cross the atrium to the OHB, and go up in the elevators. But Bryson's purposeful strides speak to his determination to shave a few minutes off that time. *Something,* he tells himself, *is fucking going on.*

He reaches the door to the outer office and tries the handle. It's locked, as he knew it would be. He was sure he shut the damn thing.

◆

Inside Bryson's office, Alex whips his head around in the direction of the office's door. It might be a trick of the adrenaline coursing through his body, but he could swear on a stack of Bibles that he heard someone try the handle to the outer door. He looks back and redoubles his efforts on his current task: Removing the air vent that sits directly above Bryson's polished walnut battleship-size desk while avoiding stepping on or jostling any of the pens, papers, or trinkets arranged on top of it. He stretches to reach the vent. He can feel Gerald staring at him with terrified interest. If they're lucky, they have about ten seconds before they get arrested for trespassing and treason.

◆

Bryson and the guard move through the outer office. Bryson waves his badge in front of the security panel on the door to his private office. As with the outer door, this one unlocks without the frustrating delay he experienced earlier, confirming his sense that something is very amiss. He hears the door's lock retract with a pleasing *shunk* and grabs the door handle, gives it a clockwise twist. The door swings open and Bryson blazes in with a full head of steam to find Alex Garnett standing in the middle of his own goddamn office looking guilty as hell.

NINETEEN

ALTHOUGH ALEX doesn't think of himself as an atheist, he doesn't really believe in God. If the question were put to him, he'd describe himself as someone who doesn't often ponder the existence of an Almighty Being, let alone the subject of religion in general. But damn if Alex doesn't find himself praying to a higher power now. He stares at General Counsel Arthur Bryson — a man who reports to the DCIA and the president of the United States — and the Central Intelligence Agency armed guard flanking him, and he prays that neither man notices the air vent above Bryson's desk is hanging down a quarter of an inch. Gerald made it up and into the heating duct with a window of milliseconds before Bryson and the guard entered. Alex spent those milliseconds snatching Bryson's cell phone off his desk. He's waving it in the air now, trying to sound about a million times more casual than he feels. "I realized you forgot this," he says, feeling a cold sweat dampen the back of his shirt collar.

Bryson's eyebrows rise with incredulity. "Really? That seems rather remarkable, given that we left together."

Alex forces a shrug. "Just had, y'know, one of those feelings."

"And how did you get back into my office?" Bryson asks, pinning Alex with a cross-examiner's stare.

"Just walked in. The door was unlocked."

"No, it wasn't." On this point, Bryson is adamant. "I remember closing the door. If not both, certainly at least *one* of them."

"I dunno," Alex responds, trying to sound innocent and at ease, "the doors just opened."

"And you felt compelled to go get my cell phone."

"I thought you'd want it."

"Based on what? Perhaps I *intended* to leave it on my desk."

"Why would you do that?"

Bryson wields the silence between them like a weapon. Alex can feel Bryson's eyes probing him, attempting to see past Alex's dishonesty. "I want this man arrested," he says to the guard.

Alex feels the temperature in the room dive fifty degrees and scrambles to defuse the situation. "I didn't know retrieving a cell phone was a felony," he says with as much good humor as he can muster.

Bryson isn't amused. "Breaking and entering is," he shoots back. "Being in a restricted area is. Treason is."

"Treason? I was just getting you your phone."

Bryson's lips curl into a half grin. Alex realizes a thousand witnesses have seen that exact look from Bryson right before he slips the knife in. The look practically screams *Gotcha*. Bryson points, as if showing a jury. "And why is my computer on, then?"

Alex's vision narrows. He feels the blood drain from his face, making it cold. The world spins off its axis for a few seconds as Alex tries to recover, like a boxer attempting to shake off a knockout haymaker. "Look, I think you're blaming me for something I didn't do."

"I want this man in handcuffs right now," Bryson tells the guard.

"This is all so ridiculous," Alex protests, as if words can keep him from drowning.

"Just take him into custody," Bryson snaps.

"He can't." The statement shoots from Alex's mouth like a gunshot. He's on autopilot now, drinking in a cocktail of instinct, adrenaline, and pure desperation. His argument spills out of him in a torrent. "He's security, not law enforcement. And even if he were law enforcement, he'd need a reasonable suspicion to hold me, and he doesn't have one. And even if he *did*, he's CIA, and the Agency's not chartered with any domestic authority. Bottom line, if you want me arrested, you're going to have to get the FBI's Counterintelligence Division to do it. I'm sure the number for CID is in your phone directory."

The guard turns to Bryson. From the look on the guard's face, Alex can tell he believes everything Alex just said is true. Alex's stomach unclenches slightly. He's staved off execution. For now, at least. Bryson, for his part, swallows bile, tasting copper in the back of his throat.

"You're fired," Bryson says.

It takes Alex a second to realize that Bryson isn't speaking to the guard. That was meant for *him*. Alex's career at the CIA — perhaps his future as an attorney — is over.

"Take his credentials," Bryson instructs the guard. "Walk him out to his car. Watch said car drive off the premises. Do it now."

Alex feels the guard's firm grip on his arm. A light tug pulls him from the office. Bryson's dagger stare doesn't waver until Alex is completely out of sight.

❖

The guard releases Alex's arm once they exit Bryson's outer office. The man doesn't say anything, but his deliberate passivity begs Alex not to make any personal appeals to him. *I'm just a guy doing his job,* the man's face says. *Don't make this hard for me. Don't bring me into this.* Alex doesn't. If there's a higher court to appeal to, this guard doesn't work for it.

On the way out, they pass Leah's office. Her door is shut and locked, but the sight of her name on the placard outside stirs something in Alex. Is it a good idea to make a personal plea to her? Leah could explain everything to Bryson — Solstice, the meeting with Rykman…A quick flash of inspiration as Alex realizes that the attempt on his life earlier tonight might buy him some kind of sympathetic review. He was in fear for his life. He didn't know whom to trust. He wasn't acting rationally…

These thoughts shoot through Alex's mind at the speed of comets. Alex once read a study that showed neurons continue to fire after a person attempts to remember something but fails. That's why one can suddenly think of a name or a phrase hours after having given up on recalling the information.

That's what happens with Alex right now.

And it hits him like a thunderclap.

❖

The guard walks Alex out through the NHB exit, continuing their forced, silent march into the open air. "Thanks," Alex says with a curt wave of his hand.

But the green jacket keeps pace with Alex. "Sorry, but I've got to walk you as far as your car," he explains. "I've got to watch it leave the premises." Alex looks back at him. "Mr. Bryson's orders."

Alex offers up a thin smile. "Get ready to walk, then."

"Excuse me?"

"I took a cab here. And since I can't use my phone on Agency grounds, I figured I'd hoof it out to the highway and call for a ride from there." Alex keeps his gaze level, searching the guard's face for any sign his bluff has been detected. He has no desire to tell the green jacket of his fervent hope that Gerald sped away from CIA headquarters as fast as his Prius could take him.

"I guess I'm walking you out to Dolly Madison Boulevard, then," the guard says, relenting.

Once they reach the main security gate and Dolly Madison Boulevard, aka Route 123, is in sight, the guard holds his hand out to Alex. But it isn't for a handshake. "I need you to surrender your Agency credentials, sir."

Alex just nods. He digs in his pocket for his Agency badge. He wrestles the key to his desk off his key ring and deposits it and his badge in the outstretched palm.

TWENTY

LEAH DOYLE stirs against the warm body of the man lying next to her. He is sleeping soundly as she begins to wake. Her alarm is set for 5:00 a.m., but her sleep cycle is so finely calibrated that most mornings she gets up a few minutes ahead of it. This morning, however, it's the ringing of the doorbell that rouses her.

She sits up, wondering if she's hearing things. Who could be at her door at five in the morning? She slips out of bed, pulling her terry-cloth robe over her naked form. Neither this nor the sound of the doorbell pull the man in her bed from his deep sleep. Leah experiences a twinge of envy; she wishes her slumbers could be that restful.

Cinching her robe closed, she walks to the door of her modest, Colonial-style house. Wolf Trap, Virginia, is a quiet, well-kept neighborhood. She's lived here for seven years. Maybe it's because she feels safe here, or maybe it's because she's still pretty damn tired, but she doesn't bother to peek through the window to get a look at who's outside before opening the door.

"I need to talk to you," Alex Garnett says. He looks as serious as a heart attack. "It's important."

Five minutes later, Leah meets Alex in her living room. She's fully dressed — there was no way in hell she would have a conversation with one of her subordinates in a bathrobe — but by no means as polished as Alex is used to seeing her. He's not surprised to find that she's still attractive — if not more so — despite her lack of makeup and tousled morning hair.

"Keep your voice low, please," she says as they both sit. "My boyfriend's still sleeping."

Alex tries to hide his surprise. It never occurred to him that Leah would have a boyfriend. Like most people, Alex assumed that she was married to her work.

"So?" She stares at him, expectant. "What's so important it couldn't wait till we were in the office?"

Alex doesn't tell her he no longer works for the CIA. The circumstances of his firing aren't why he's here. "I need to talk to you about the money, the ninety million dollars that was wired into Jim Harling's account."

"What about it?" Leah looks genuinely mystified.

"It was used to fund the Solstice project. And Harling ended up dead."

Leah nods slowly. "That's what you told Director Rykman."

Alex locks a stare on Leah. He waits a few seconds to make sure he has her absolute attention before saying, "You wired the money into Harling's account."

"No, I didn't. I can't think of a single reason why I would." She stares back at Alex with complete believability. "Can you?"

"I did some checking and the wire transfer was authorized by someone at the Agency with Agency identification number four-five-eight-seven-nine-six-three."

"That's my AIN."

"I know."

Now Leah is starting to get angry. "And how is it you know my number?"

"You used it in front of me," Alex answers. "You were on the phone with someone when I came in to talk to you about something just after I started with the OGC."

"Bullshit. I'm generally pretty vigilant about not throwing my AIN around in front of people, even fellow Agency personnel."

Alex spreads his hands. "Be that as it may…"

"You're tying me to the death of a case officer." There is steel in her voice.

"I'm not accusing you of anything. All I'm doing is asking what Overwatch is."

"It's a military term. It refers to a secondary military unit that observes the first, usually while executing fire-and-movement tactics. Why?"

"I think you're gonna find that this is the part where *I'm* the one asking the questions."

Alex feels the temperature in the room plummet as Leah sets her jaw. "Alex, you come to my home at five in the morning. You accuse me of God knows what, but whatever it is, it's linked to the death of an active NOC officer. I don't think it's unreasonable for me to ask you to do it without the attitude."

"Who is K. McCallum?"

Leah responds with a look of utter confusion, clearly thrown by both the non sequitur and the name itself. "What does she have to do with anything?"

"So K. McCallum is a woman."

"Yes."

"Who is she?" Leah is silent. Alex's voice finds an edge. "If you need a reason to tell me, it's that you haven't told me a single thing yet that convinces me I can trust you."

"You don't trust me?"

"Who is she, Leah?"

Leah shakes her head and spreads her hands, at a loss. "She used to work in Operations."

"What do you mean, used to?"

"Kate…had some kind of breakdown," Leah answers. "It was bad. Very bad. They had to institutionalize her. She's spent the past three years at the Northern Virginia Mental Health Institute. At least I think she's still there. I'm sorry to say I don't keep close tabs on her."

Alex's eyes narrow. His mind races, trying to fit all the pieces together. Of the hundreds of directories on Bryson's computer, the one marked Overwatch was the only one that contained remnants of Solstice. And McCallum's name was the lone entry in the Solstice directory. There is not a single cell in his entire body that believes these are coincidences. "Did…what did you say her name was?"

"Kate."

"Did Kate have any prior history of mental illness?"

"I doubt it. The Agency doesn't make a habit of employing mentally unstable personnel." She fixes a look on Alex. "Though your behavior is making me question that."

Alex offers up a half smile. *Guilty as charged.* Then he stands. He's gotten as much out of Leah as he's likely to get. "Thanks. I'd better go."

"I'll see you at the office." She says it definitively, but it still comes out as a question.

"I'll see you at the office," he answers, lying through his teeth. He doesn't expect to set foot on the grounds of the Central Intelligence Agency ever again. "Sorry to bother you so early," he says, making his way out.

"And accuse me of murder?"

Alex leaves without rebuttal.

Once Alex is gone, Leah rises to lock the door behind him. She's not exactly sure why, but she's far more unnerved by Alex's visit — and more so by his questions — than she was comfortable letting on.

"Who was that?" asks the voice behind her. It's her boyfriend. She turns around to see him fully dressed, every thread and button in place, per usual. She wonders how much of her conversation with Alex he overheard.

"Alex Garnett," she answers, moving to him. "He's trying to make connections."

"Between?"

"Kate McCallum and this Solstice thing."

He nods his head slowly, saying nothing. Because Leah's boyfriend, CIA director William Rykman, knows more about Solstice than Leah could possibly imagine.

<hr />

Hotel Kowsar, Tehran
1000 hrs. Zulu

Sattar Namdar swallows bile, feeling the bitter taste of anger in the back of his throat. The supreme leader of Iran is also the commander in chief of its armed forces. That army is in the process of gearing up for a massive retaliatory strike against its greatest enemy, and rather than sitting at the side of his country's minister of defense, Namdar is getting secondhand information from a junior intelligence officer. "The engineers believe they've increased the effective range of our Mersad system," Rasoul reports.

Namdar has heard of Mersad. Modeled after the U.S. Hawk surface-to-air missiles, the system previously had an effective range of a mere fifty miles, well short of the thousand plus miles needed to reach Israel. "That's an improvement of several orders of magnitude," Namdar observes with caution after Rasoul tells him the new range.

Rasoul nods. "We've deliberately understated Mersad's capabilities lest the Zionists use it as a pretext to launch a preemptive attack on the republic."

Namdar smiles at this. "So they've no idea of our intentions." There's no judgment in the statement. In fact, Namdar's grin suggests he's pleased with the idea of launching a sneak attack. After all, is that not why the army christened this missile system Mersad? In Farsi, it means "ambush."

❖

Alex navigates the road in his new rental car. He lost an hour walking to a street with enough traffic to offer a remote chance of catching a cab. Even finding an available one took an additional twenty minutes. Then he spent another ten having the cab take him to the closest rental-car outlet, an Enterprise. Although it meant using his credit card, he had to chance it; he had no choice. He needed a workable car, and he couldn't risk contacting Gerald. So Alex gambled and used his American Express to secure temporary ownership of this six-month-old Nissan Sentra, and he's headed south toward the Northern Virginia Mental Health Institute.

❖

THE WHITE HOUSE
7:15 A.M. EDT

The president studies the faces of the men and women in the room. He doesn't need to look at their grave expressions to know they're about to deliver serious news. The assemblage of his secretary of defense, secretary of state, director of national intelligence, and chairman of the Joint Chiefs of Staff is enough. He takes comfort in the fact that if the news were truly devastating, they'd be having this briefing in the Situation Room rather than the Oval Office. With luck, this means there's still time to forestall anything dire. "All right," he says. "This group never convenes for anything good."

SecDef is first to speak. "It's Iran, sir. We're seeing an increase in its military's op tempo. It appears as if they're gearing up for something. Something major."

"And there's no chance this is just a military exercise." It's not a question. The president already knows that this isn't the case.

"The Iranians aren't bothering to disguise it as such," the secretary of state says.

"Obviously, this is a concern," the director of national intelligence chimes in. "We're getting some early traffic out of Tehran suggesting that the Iranians think the Israelis are to blame for Ayatollah Jahandar's death."

"I thought he died of the flu," the president of the United States says.

"Swine flu, yes sir. There's a pretty bad strain of it going around Iran right now. But there seems to be a suspicion on the Iranians' part that this might have been some kind of biological attack."

At this, the president registers genuine surprise. "The Israelis would never be so crazy or so stupid."

"We agree," the secretary of state confirms.

"We're still assembling data," the director of national intelligence adds.

"Assemble it faster," the president orders. He turns to the secretary of state. "And remind Tehrani that it's in his best interests not to lead his country into anything stupid." The diplomat nods as the president thinks. "Who's Jahandar's replacement?"

"The prohibitive favorite is Sattar Namdar," the director of national intelligence replies. "His election isn't official yet, but we believe people in the government are keeping him in the loop."

"What are his politics?"

"Jahandar was very reasonable in comparison, Mr. President."

The president's face darkens. He didn't reach the position of chief executive of the most powerful country in history without knowing how to look deep into the chessboard. Jahandar's death removes a moderate voice from the Iranian government, leaving a more dangerous successor in a position to agitate from a safe distance. Moreover, an assassination carried out against an Iranian head of state by Israel would provide ample justification for a counterattack. The United States would hardly be in a position to condemn Iran when it was constantly threatening military action against Syria in retaliation for chemical weapons attacks against its own citizens. "We can't rely solely on diplomatic pressure," the president observes. "What assets do we have in the region?"

The chairman of the Joint Chiefs is prepared for this question. "The *John Stennis* is currently in the Indian Ocean."

"How soon can you move it into the Gulf?"

"Just waiting on your order, sir."

"Go," the president says. He can only hope that the presence of a carrier strike group in the Persian Gulf will be enough to make the Iranians think twice about doing something stupid.

TWENTY-ONE

The NVMHI is an example of unremarkable 1960s bureaucratic architecture. The expansion and renovation that was done to the place
in the mid-1990s did little to change the fact that the building looks
like the uglier sibling of the Inova Fairfax Hospital, which sits directly
across the street from it. Alex pulls the Nissan to a stop in front of a
third building on the block, a Baptist church. If someone's conducting
surveillance on him, it's better that he appears to be visiting the church
and not the mental health institute. In fact, he takes the added precaution of going into the church, exiting out the back, and doubling
around to enter the NVMHI.

He navigates up to the guard station in the building's nondescript reception area. Having never been inside a mental institute before, Alex
expects to find something akin to a hospital waiting room or the intake
office of a rehabilitation clinic. But the environment is much more like
the jails and prisons he frequented as a defense attorney. The fluorescent
lighting is low and unforgivingly omnipresent. The floors are concrete,
and the walls constructed of cinder blocks held together with cement
and a quarter inch of paint. There's a faint odor that he can't quite

identify but imagines is some type of industrial cleanser, the kind sold exclusively by the truckload.

The overall effect is unrelentingly grim and about as far away from an environment that encourages mental health as Alex can imagine.

The rent-a-cop at the guard station sports an appropriately gray uniform adorned with a gold badge that's meant to suggest the man has some form of legal authority, which Alex knows he doesn't actually possess. Still, the can of pepper spray and plastic zip cuffs on his belt are enough to exert authority when needed.

"Morning. How ya doing?" Alex asks as he flips his faux leather briefcase up on the desk. This was a purchase made en route to the NVMHI — inspiration struck as he passed an Office Depot. He pops open the briefcase's flimsy locks and produces a sheaf of boilerplate legal documents. These too were purchased at Office Depot, Alex having found the one-size-fits-all legal papers — do-it-yourself wills and commercial leases — in aisle 8. He waves them in front of the guard, careful not to offer too close a look. He's completed one of the forms with enough bogus information that it looks legitimate, but he doubts it will stand up to any kind of close scrutiny.

"I'm here to see a Katherine McCallum. She's a patient here. My name's Alex Garnett."

With a practiced apathy normally shown only by employees at the DMV, the guard consults a clipboard for a few seconds and then shakes his head. "I don't see your name here on the visitor log. Visitations have to be scheduled in advance."

"This is kind of a last-minute thing."

"We don't do last-minute here. Not unless you're a family member or one of the patient's treating physicians. You've gotta arrange a visit through one of her doctors." Then he adds, "Sorry," in a tone that suggests he's anything but.

"You don't understand," Alex pleads, trying to sound as pleasant as possible, "this is a special circumstance. I represent the estate of Arthur

Bryson." The guard tries to cut Alex off, but Alex plows through him. "Ms. McCallum stands to inherit three point two million dollars from Mr. Bryson's irrevocable trust." This gets the guard's attention. "But only if she makes her election by" — Alex makes a show of checking his watch — "noon today. Otherwise, the election expires and the money goes to Bryson's sister-in-law." Alex then leans forward and adds with a conspiratorial note, "The sister-in-law is a stark raving bitch. I'd rather see a vanilla-frosted nutbar like McCallum get the cash than her."

The guard considers Alex for a few seconds, measuring him with a look. Then he says, "We don't throw around terms like *nutbar* here, okay?"

Alex nods. "You're right. I'm sorry."

"But the truth is, I don't see how she can legally sign anything. She's not, y'know, mentally competent."

Alex removes another legal document from his briefcase. "That's why I have this power of attorney," he says, holding up what is actually a standard waiver-of-liability form. "Once she signs it, I can make the election for her." The guard thinks on this for longer than Alex is comfortable with. "Look, I represent the estate, but the fact is, if McCallum or any friends or family learn that she had a claim to over three million dollars and *didn't* get the chance to make the election because the Northern Virginia Mental Health Institute didn't allow an attorney access to her…well, that would put you and the institute on the hook, legally speaking."

Alex watches the guard make his calculations. On the one hand, there are the rules the guard is charged with enforcing but that he has no personal investment in. On the other hand, there are the guard's own self-interests to consider. Enforcing the rules isn't worth the headache that would result.

The guard has Alex place his briefcase, car keys, and wallet in a locker that Alex secures with a four-digit code. He asks Alex to remove all staples and paper clips from the legal forms he wants to bring in, but it didn't occur to Alex to fasten the pages of his fake legal documents. The guard asks to review the papers, but Alex is able to wave him off by citing attorney-client privilege, and the guard concedes the point with a shrug.

He waves Alex through a metal detector and into a secure wing of the institute. The interior of the NVMHI is much more Kafkaesque than the comparatively cheerful reception area. Off the narrow corridors are a series of rooms that look like cells, with closed doors and small wire-reinforced windows. A low rattle from worn-out pipes and the churn of an overtaxed ventilation system echo off the cinder-block walls, making for an eerie sound track to accompany the unrelentingly stark environs. Then a chorus of whoops and hollers, punctuated by the occasional grunt or yelp, joins in. It is unnerving, but Alex tries not to react. Still, the guard must have noticed some response because he remarks by way of explanation, "Meds are wearing off."

The guard stops at one of the doors and fishes out a large key ring. He selects a key with surprising ease and unlocks what sounds like a formidable dead bolt. "Can't let you in with a pen or pencil," he says. "When you're ready to have her sign anything, knock on the door. I'll come by with something she can write with."

"Thanks."

The guard opens the door. "Somebody here to see you," he says in a way that sounds neither friendly nor cheerful. *Just the facts, ma'am.* Alex walks in and hears the door close behind him. He looks around the modest room, about half the size of a typical college dorm. The concrete floors of the corridor have given way to brown linoleum. There's a low-standing cot in one corner and a small bookshelf in another. There's a set of folding doors, behind which is a closet, Alex assumes, and a single, ordinary door that probably leads to a bathroom. There are photographs of European cities — Brussels, Florence, Paris, and a few others Alex doesn't recognize — Scotch-taped to the wall above the cot. Some are traditional photo prints while others have clearly been torn from magazines. These are strange accents of décor in an otherwise unadorned room.

The space's lone occupant rises from her cot and stands up to meet him. She wears a modest floral-print dress and looks relatively healthy, despite a complete lack of makeup and the suggestion that it's been several weeks since her long brown hair has seen a brush. Still, there's a distance in her eyes, a lack of affect, either a manifestation of mental illness or a side effect of the medication used to keep insanity at bay. It's with these eyes that Katherine McCallum studies Alex. Her gaze is intense, as if she's trying to fight her way past several layers of sedation to get a decent look at him.

"Katherine?" he asks tentatively.

"Kate," she corrects him. "Who the hell are you?" Although clearly medicated — and, from what Alex can tell, heavily so — she doesn't appear to be insane. Alex's work with the public defenders' office brought him into contact with one or two truly mentally ill clients, and while he's a far cry from a psychologist, Alex is reasonably confident he can tell when someone is, to use the technical term, *nuts.*

"My name is Alex Garnett." Alex speaks slowly, unsure of how much Katherine — *Kate,* he corrects himself — can process. "I work for the CIA." McCallum is more surprised than intimidated. Nevertheless, Alex notices her take a step backward. She seems wary. Looking in her eyes, he senses a fear that talking about the CIA will require more mental acuity than the meds she's on allow her. "I work for Arthur Bryson in the Office of General Counsel. Do you know Mr. Bryson?" Kate stares at him with incredulity but doesn't answer, so he presses on. "Your name was in Mr. Bryson's computer. In a directory called Solstice." Almost immediately, he regrets taking this tack. Talk of computer files and directories probably isn't going to get him where he needs to go with her. "Have you ever heard of anything related to the Agency named Solstice?"

McCallum doesn't answer. The moment yawns. Just when Alex is about to give up, she blurts, "No."

"What about Overwatch?"

At this, McCallum pales. She retreats and sits wearily on her cot. "No," she says again. But Alex knows she's lying.

"You look like that term is familiar to you," he observes, trying to sound as nonconfrontational as possible.

"What are you doing here?" she asks.

"I'm doing some research for Mr. Bryson," Alex lies. "On Overwatch," he adds, hoping to keep McCallum on point.

"I'm not insane" is her only answer. She makes the statement with certainty but without any indication of righteous indignation.

"I believe you," Alex soothes.

"Then prove it. Tell me what you're doing here." She sounds weary, and Alex realizes that as much as he is struggling with her justifiable fears, he's also in a fight against the tide of the medicinal cocktail flowing through her bloodstream.

"I think someone's been killed. Assassinated," he says, switching tactics. "A head of state. And I think it has something to do with either Solstice or Overwatch or both. And," he ventures, treading carefully, "I think you know something that could help me."

"I've never heard of Solstice," she says. Confidence grows in her voice as she continues. "I was in Operations for three years. I never heard anything code-named Solstice. I'm sorry."

"What about Overwatch?"

"Overwatch." The seconds tick by slowly. "Overwatch," she says again, more deliberately this time, "is the reason I'm here."

Alex's eyes shoot wide. "Can you elaborate on that for me?" he asks. The question is broad by design, intended to give his quarry as much latitude as possible.

Sitting on her cot, McCallum appears fixated on a single tile of linoleum. Her voice grows distant; her face tightens as she tries to access painful memories she's long since buried. "HR calls me in for a meeting." She sounds as mystified as she must have been back on the day. "They say that there are complaints about me, reports of erratic behavior." She shakes her head, furrowing her brow, still perplexed after the expanse of years. She speaks in the present tense, as if this were all still happening to her. "They say the quality of my work has been slipping. My divorce is maybe a month old. I think maybe I *am* having problems. That's the thing; they can make you *believe* what they're saying to you. Because they *start* with the truth." She shakes her head as if she's still amazed that she had fallen victim to such transparent machinations. "They want me to sit down with Davis Fordes. That's —"

"An Agency psychologist," Alex supplies, recalling his own interview with Dr. Fordes.

McCallum nods. "He recommends medication. And then a leave of absence. And then…" Her voice cracks; her eyes starting to glisten with tears. "Then he gets Peter — he convinces Peter to —" She stops herself. "No, I shouldn't say that. I don't know for sure if he has been in contact with Peter. But that's how it feels. *That's how it feels.*"

"Peter is your ex-husband?" Alex asks, making the leap.

McCallum nods again. Alex feels her growing slightly more lucid. "Peter had me committed. But the Agency had people — affidavits and incident reports — to back him up. That's why I say that Fordes was involved. Our divorce was finalized. Things weren't so bad between us that he would…do something like this."

While Alex doesn't have any professional experience with involuntary commitments, his instinct is that when those commitments are obtained, they're not easy to maintain. Surely the NVMHI has an army of doctors capable of telling when a patient is truly mentally ill.

Seeing the incredulity on Alex's face, Kate explains, "The meds make me loopy. I don't…advocate particularly well for myself. And the more you say you're not insane, the more people think you *are*. It's like quicksand: the harder you struggle, the faster you sink. It took me a year in here to realize that sane people don't go around telling anyone who will listen how *sane* they are."

Alex nods, having to acknowledge the truth of that. It's a jail with no door, being diagnosed with a mental illness. If there's no x-ray or blood test to clear you, how is anyone to know if you're cured?

"I'll get out of here eventually," she says. It's obvious to Alex that this has been her mantra for years, a promise she made to herself in the name of hope. "Eventually, the hospital will think I'm cured, or the Agency won't see me as a threat and—" She stops herself and nods like she's coaching herself through the moment. "That sounded paranoid. I misspoke. The CIA doesn't determine whether I get out tomorrow or stay here forever." She nods again as if that will cement the thought into truth.

"What can you tell me about Overwatch?" Alex asks her, trying to steer her back on track. "I'll be honest with you, Kate. I've never heard of it before. I don't even know if 'it' is an 'it.'"

Kate lifts her head up, away from the linoleum, and fixes Alex with a deep stare. He does his best to meet her gaze; it feels as if this is a test of his trustworthiness or his capacity to understand.

After a full minute, Kate finally speaks. "There's another agency. A shadow agency." She's adopted the tone of an oracle, distant and omniscient but full of conviction. "A rogue intelligence agency that operates *independent* of the CIA. It's called the Overwatch."

To his surprise, Alex finds himself smiling at her. Too late, he realizes he's doing this to keep from looking as if he thinks she's insane.

"I know it sounds impossible," she allows. "I'm not going to try to convince you that I'm telling the truth. Once people think you're crazy, well, you get used to people thinking you're crazy. You become…accepting of it."

Alex takes a seat next to her on the cot. There's nowhere else to sit down. They sit there, together, looking like two high-schoolers about to make out for the first time. "It's a lot to take in, Kate," he says. "That's all."

"Well, if you can't accept this, then you're going to have a hard time with the next part."

"What do you mean, next part?" he asks.

"The CIA isn't just an intelligence-gathering organization. Like any intelligence service, it also works to influence world events. It doesn't do it as much as it used to, say, during the Cold War, but the CIA will still try to influence the outcome of elections, orchestrate coups, et cetera." Alex nods. Having worked in the OGC to help define when those activities cross over into illegality, he's familiar with this aspect of the CIA's purview. "But the CIA is limited in terms of what it can do. There's congressional oversight. There are executive orders. There's even your office, the OGC, telling field agents what they can and can't do."

"But the Overwatch has no oversight."

"Of course not. How can anyone have oversight over an organization no one knows exists? *Quis custodiet ipsos custodes?*"

"Excuse me?" Alex grows concerned. McCallum is now spouting gibberish.

"It's Latin. A quote from Juvenal's *Satires*. *Quis custodiet ipsos custodes?* Literally translated, it means 'Who will guard the guards themselves?' The Overwatch has no one watching over it. It has no rules governing it. So it can — and does — do anything it wants."

"Like?" Alex has no idea how much of this to believe, but for now he wants to know everything that McCallum will tell him. He'll sort fact from fiction later.

"Well, it's an old example, but a powerful one. Do you remember the Chernobyl disaster?" Kate asks. She's more lucid when discussing events removed from her personal pain.

Alex nods, having been taught all about *Chornobylska katastrofa*, the catastrophic failure of the Chernobyl nuclear power plant in Ukrainian SSR back in 1986. "Are you saying the Overwatch caused the meltdown?" he asks, trying unsuccessfully to keep incredulity out of his tone.

"The USSR's containment and decontamination efforts after Chernobyl virtually bankrupted the Soviet Union. The country lost almost two million acres of agriculture, which was a kidney punch to Russia's economy. And the disaster gave additional political momentum to the policy of glasnost. The combination of these factors led to the end of the Cold War." Reading the skepticism on Alex's face, she adds, "Maybe you need more recent examples." She ticks them off on her fingers with ease: "We invaded Iraq based on evidence of WMDs provided by the Overwatch to the CIA. The Arab Spring flourished because Overwatch's army of computer hackers frustrated the Egyptian government's attempts to cut off its citizens' access to the Internet. China owns sixty-eight percent of America's debt. Ten trillion dollars. What keeps them from calling in those loans?" she asks. "It's not mutually assured financial destruction, like the economists would have you believe. It's the dozens of different ways, covert ways, the Overwatch asserts pressure on the PRC to keep them in line."

Alex takes all this in without accepting or dismissing it. He finds himself unexpectedly intrigued. It's as if McCallum is showing him an alternative version of history, one where world events are caused not by chance or geopolitical momentum, but rather by individuals intentionally pushing invisible levers of power, turning the wheels of cause and effect. World events, he knows, have a way of seeming like fantasy before they become history.

Moreover, there's no question that *something* is going on. The Solstice file, the deaths of Harling, Moreno, Miller, Zollitsch, and Jahandar, and the attempt on his own life are undeniable proof of that. What's also undeniable is the involvement of the CIA. What's the connection between the Overwatch, this other agency, and the CIA?

"The Overwatch has its tentacles in intelligence organizations and militaries all around the world," she says, as if she's sensed his train of thought. "Since the end of the Cold War, the CIA has favored SigInt and ElInt — that's signals intelligence and electronic intelligence — over HumInt, human intelligence. The Overwatch has stepped in to fill that HumInt deficit. And its assets include people inside the CIA. But not just the CIA."

"What do you mean?"

"The members of Overwatch have infiltrated all levels of our military infrastructure. They can use our assets—personnel and equipment—for their benefit." Alex's jaw sets as he remembers the troop deployments from Fort Eustis to the Middle East. But he finds himself shaking his head. The leap from covert action to actual manipulation of the U.S. military seems like a logically impossible one. "It's not that difficult, actually," McCallum notes, reading Alex's skepticism. "All you need is control over one infantry division. A single carrier group. Once something is set in motion, inertia takes care of the rest. Then concern over diplomatic embarrassment or political liability kicks in and cleans up after the fact. And for the really big stuff, there's Agamemnon."

"What's that?"

"I don't think it's ever been used," McCallum replies. "I don't know much about it. It's several feet above my pay grade, as it were," she says, punctuating the statement with an ironic smile. "But rumor has it, the Overwatch has a facility with systems that mimic the Tap-Dance encryption systems of the White House Situation Room. If need be, someone at the facility could issue orders to our military forces, and those forces would believe the instructions were coming directly from the White House."

Alex is stunned. The idea that the most highly trained military in the history of the world could be deceived on this large a scale strikes him as preposterous.

"I'm getting tired," she blurts out. "The medication makes me tired."

Alex nods. "Okay. Okay, just one more question. Let's say all of this is true," he starts, and then immediately regrets his choice of words.

"It *is* true," McCallum snaps, anger finding its way into her fatigue.

"I think Ayatollah Jahandar was assassinated," Alex says, pressing forward. "If this Overwatch was involved, can you think of why it'd want Jahandar dead?"

McCallum looks up at Alex with a clarity he hasn't seen her display previously. She stares as if *he's* the crazy one now. "For years," she says, "there have been forces within the Iranian government agitating for an all-out assault on Israel, a full-scale invasion." She sweeps the air with her hand. "Just wipe out the Jewish State once and for all. Jahandar kept them at bay."

"And you think Jahandar's successor—whoever he is—will move against Israel," Alex says.

"All the models point to an eighty-six point three percent likelihood."

The specificity of the projection catches Alex by surprise. "You sound pretty sure."

"I am."

"Why?"

McCallum shakes her head. "Because I developed the model."

The revelation hits Alex in his solar plexus. "What?"

"I worked in Operations. I was asked to develop a scenario, a model for predicting likely outcomes in the event of the supreme leader's death." Alex stares at her in disbelief. "I was doing work for the Overwatch. That's how I found out about it. That's why I'm in here. I thought you knew all this." Alex just shakes his head. "I'm not crazy," she says, not for the first time. But *this* time, she sounds like she's trying to convince herself more than Alex.

TWENTY-TWO

THE USEFUL thing about computer hackers for an operation such as the Overwatch's is that they can work from anywhere in the world. With access to the Internet, they are as close to anonymous as anyone can be. Even better: with three exceptions, no hacker in the Overwatch's cyberarsenal is aware of the organization's existence at all. The beauty of the hacker community is that the most capable ones care the least about who pays for their services. As long as they receive a prenegotiated allotment of Bitcoin — a decentralized form of digital currency with a market cap of over one hundred million U.S. dollars — they don't care where the money comes from.

Right now, Donovan is working a computer hacker in Belarus who has just pulled Garnett's credit card information from the cloudy mists of the Internet. Via an encrypted instant-messaging platform called BitWise, the Belarus hacker informs Donovan that Garnett's American Express account was most recently accessed by an Enterprise Rent-a-Car in Bethesda, Maryland. It takes only a few keystrokes for Donovan to learn that Garnett is now driving a light gray Nissan Sentra. He thanks the anonymous hacker through BitWise and transfers the prenegotiated

Bitcoin amount into his or her account. Now all that's necessary is for
Donovan to contact a hacker he likes who works out of Hong Kong and
have him forge a BOLO ("be on the lookout for") order and dissemi-
nate it to local law enforcement.

◆

Alex leaves Kate with the promise that he will use all his legal acumen
to win her freedom back for her. But she seems dubious, and Alex has
the feeling that it's not because she doubts his abilities as an attorney.
What she lacks confidence in, he realizes, is his ability to remain alive
long enough to file any kind of legal brief. Alex has similar concerns. If
the Overwatch is even a tenth as powerful as she told him and has even
a scintilla of the resources she believes are at its disposal, then it's extremely unlikely Alex will make it to sundown. After all, what hope does
an attorney have against an organization that's powerful enough to dictate the course of world events and that does so without the rest of the
world knowing?

Alex considers these questions while en route to Georgetown. His
initial instinct is to drive to the offices of the *Washington Post,* flag down
the first reporter he sees, and unload everything he's learned and experienced in a soul-cleansing torrent. Even if it led to a room of his own
at the Northern Virginia Mental Health Institute, at least he'd be doing something. Then he realizes that both Grace and Gerald are still out
there and vulnerable.

Alex considers asking his father for help. He wonders what's keeping
him from making that one simple phone call. Is it dignity? If so, he's
long past the point where that should be a consideration. If Grace had
heard half of what McCallum said and believed even half of *that,* she'd
be telling Alex that whatever his issues with his father were, it was time
for them to take a backseat to stopping whatever the Overwatch was
looking to put in motion with Iran. And she'd be right.

Alex thinks on this for a minute or so before he spots the flashing red and blue lights in his rearview mirror. A Virginia sheriff's cruiser trails behind him. He's been pulled over enough times in his life to know what to do next. He pulls his car to the curb and wonders if, in his distraction, he missed a stoplight or made an illegal turn. Not that he really cares. The thing about global conspiracies, forced civil commitments, and assassinations is that they put little things like traffic tickets in their proper perspective.

Alex puts the Nissan in park and rolls his window down. The clean-cut officer standing over him sticks his hand out expectantly. "License and registration."

Alex dutifully produces his license and the Enterprise agreement. "It's a rental," he notes, but the officer couldn't appear less interested.

"Wait here," the man says, starting to turn away from the car.

"Wait." Alex stops him. "What was I pulled over for?"

"Just wait in your car, sir."

The officer moves away, but the fact that he didn't offer up an explanation for the traffic stop sets off alarm bells in Alex's head. The car idles and Alex gives a moment's consideration to throwing it in gear and peeling out. Initiating a high-speed chase right now doesn't seem like the smartest course. What if the officer had made a simple mistake? But Alex should know by now not to buy into coincidences. His foot hovers over the accelerator as his right hand drifts toward the gearshift. Then the officer returns. "I'm gonna need you to step out of the car, sir," he says in a polite but commanding tone accented with a slight Virginia drawl.

"Why was I stopped?"

"Could you step out of the car please, sir?" the officer says, less patiently this time, with his hand resting on his sidearm.

As Alex sees it, he has three options. He could try putting the car in drive and bolting; he could stay in the car and see if the cop will forcibly remove him; or he could comply and exit the vehicle. None of these choices strikes him as ideal, so he chooses the one least likely to get him shot and reaches for the door handle.

"I'm an attorney," he says, getting out of the car. "I want to know what your reasonable suspicion was that formed the basis for this stop."

"An all-points bulletin was issued for a gentleman fitting your description driving a Nissan," the officer says as if reciting the time of day. Alex's stomach clutches when he turns his head and sees the cop's partner step out of the waiting squad car. Traffic whips past and Alex can see them craning for a view of the roadside drama. Time seems to slow as the adrenaline does its work in his veins. Getting an APB out is nothing, Alex intuits, for an organization that can manipulate the actions of nation-states. "Please turn around and place your hands on the roof."

Cursing himself for not making a run for it when he had the chance, Alex complies, putting his hands on the Nissan's roof. The officer "helps" him do this as his partner rests a palm on his service weapon, which remains holstered for the moment. The cop finishes patting Alex down and says, "Pop the trunk for me, sir."

"What?"

"I'm gonna need to take a look inside your trunk." The officer allows a hint of edge to creep into his voice, speaking more sternly and with greater command.

"I told you, I'm a lawyer. I'm not consenting to a search of my car without a warrant."

"You want us to arrest you, sir? Because we can do that. We can take you into custody and they'll search your trunk at the impound."

Alex is about to tell the officer that he guesses that's just what he'll have to do then when the partner pipes up, standing behind the Nissan now. "We've got something here."

The officer leads Alex by the arm to the rear of the car. His partner points to a few rust-colored droplets on the bumper where the trunk door meets the car's body. "Blood, looks like."

"Pop the trunk," the officer instructs. His partner moves to the driver's side to do exactly that as he notes with professional dispassion, "It seems you've got traces of exsanguination on your car, sir. I believe that gives me and my partner reasonable suspicion to search its contents."

Alex's world spins. He starts to feel light-headed and wonders if that's from adrenaline or the exhaust fumes from all the passing traffic. "There's"—he's grasping now—"there are no exigent circumstances. You still need—" He's about to say *a warrant,* but the trunk pops open and the officer pushes him aside to raise the door. Looking inside, he notes, "We've got trouble here." With that, his head emerges from the trunk and he swivels around to Alex, moving with purpose. "Alex Garnett, you're under arrest," he begins.

"What?" Alex instinctively moves toward the trunk. The officer makes a halfhearted effort to restrain Alex, but the truth is he wants this fucking skel to see what he found.

And the sight turns Alex's blood to ice.

A female form rests in the well of the trunk. She's curled into a fetal position, not moving. There's something about the still of the dead that's unique, a lack of movement not found in the sleeping or unconscious. Without laying a finger on her, Alex knows she is dead. Her long hair falls over her face, masking her features. His fiancée is dead. Somehow, they found Grace. Maybe she didn't throw away her cell phone like he asked. Maybe she was forced to use a credit card. Maybe the Overwatch issued the same bogus APB to law enforcement that they used to snag him. It doesn't matter how, they found her, and now, because of him, she's dead.

Fighting shock and swallowing the impulse to vomit, Alex reaches into the trunk to clear the woman's hair away.

But it's not Grace's face he sees.

It's Leah Doyle's.

◆

William Rykman gave up on love decades ago. His military training made it impossible for him to feel that strongly for another person. At least, that's what he tells himself in his more reflective moments. But there are scores of men with just as much training as himself who are still capable of love; in fact, they have deep repositories of it. No, the explanation for Rykman's lack of love isn't in what he does, it's in what he *is*. While Rykman would never consider himself a sociopath, he has to admit he lacks the capacity for feeling emotion.

Still, Rykman is a man, with a man's physical needs. Being both accomplished and not unattractive, he's had his share of relationships over the years. While one might not expect it, Rykman is drawn to strong, capable women. Women like Leah Doyle. He respected her backbone and was attracted to her intelligence. And she wasn't bothered by his emotional shortcomings, because she was too focused on her work to maintain any kind of sustained romantic relationship. In this, the two were perfectly suited for each other. Mutual respect, mutual attraction, and a shared lack of expectations for anything more.

Then the bitch had to go and fuck it up by asking a million questions.

The nicest thing about being with Leah was that she knew better than to probe too deeply into Rykman's professional activities, even when she was aware that some of those activities—not to mention Rykman's extended absences and late-night meetings—were out of the ordinary, even for a CIA director. But Garnett's visit earlier that morning clearly stirred up something. The irony was that the intelligence and strength Rykman had found so attractive were the same two qualities that kept Leah from buying the usual bullshit Rykman was slinging. He could tell that she could tell that he was hiding something. And once she caught the scent of deception, she would be dogged in ferreting out the truth. And he simply couldn't have that.

She must have seen the shift in his eyes, the coldness that came over him the second he realized he couldn't let her leave the house alive, because she turned from him abruptly with some crap about suddenly remembering something she had to do. She was moving toward the door when he came up behind her.

It had been a long time since he'd killed a woman. He'd forgotten how much lighter they were. He smashed her head into the corner of the granite-topped console table harder than he'd intended to. The resulting crack echoed like a gunshot through the otherwise silent house. He dropped her to the wood floor and watched as she stirred, eyes wide and mouth open. Her body shook from shock. Blood from her head pooled into a shallow puddle on the floor. There was something fascinating, almost beautiful about it.

There were no sirens. Leah hadn't had the chance to birth a scream. No police came. No friend or cleaning lady suddenly arrived and knocked on the front door. And Leah would most definitely not be regaining consciousness, much less getting up, anytime soon. It occurred to Rykman he could stand and look at her for hours.

But he didn't have hours. There was a body to dispose of and containment to handle, and both of those things would take time. So he knelt down on one knee, as if to propose, taking care to avoid the blood, and reached for Leah's face. With a lover's gentle touch, he turned her head toward the floor and into the small puddle of crimson. Then he stood and watched Leah Doyle, attorney for the Central Intelligence Agency, sputter her final breaths into a pool of her own blood.

Once she expired, things happened fast. All it took was an encrypted phone call to Tyler Donovan. He instructed Donovan to add the rental car's description to the BOLO bulletin and then join him at Leah's house. By the time Donovan arrived, the young soldier had gotten word that Garnett's rented Nissan was parked in front of a church near the Northern Virginia Mental Health Institute.

"You want me to get the cops to sit on it?" Donovan had asked.

Rykman nodded. "Have them surveil until Garnett's at a comfortable remove from the hospital."

Donovan stared back with a level of confusion he didn't often exhibit. Until Rykman explained that he'd thought of the perfect place to deposit Leah's remains.

◆

Alex stares at Leah's lifeless face, his eyes finding hers, dull and empty, devoid of anything that could be described as a soul. He feels the two cops behind him. He hears the traffic whizzing past. He feels a vessel in his head throb in unison with his heart, threatening to beat itself free of his chest. And yet, despite this flood of sensory input, Alex maintains no concept of time. He has no idea whether seconds or hours have elapsed. The world is stuck on pause, as if waiting for him to have a sudden flash of inspiration.

And he does.

The idea compels him to bolt forward, out of the cop's reach and deep into the trunk. He lets loose an anguished scream and pulls Leah's still form into an embrace. Tears don't come, but he wails nonetheless, pressing his face against hers. She feels stiff and cold against him. The rust-colored crust of her head wound rubs against his face, leaving ruddy specks of blood. One arm grips the corpse tight as his other hand roams. He bellows apologies for getting her caught up in all of this. He vows to bring her killer to justice. Somewhere, the officer pulls at his shoulder, a hand gripping his biceps, and implores Alex to get himself under control.

Finally, the officer yanks Alex away from the car. Alex's head makes a sound like a baseball hitting a catcher's mitt as it whacks against the top of the metal trunk. The officer catches Alex, grabs the back of his suit jacket, and slaps steel handcuffs around Alex's wrists, then cinches them tight enough to make Alex's fingertips grow cold.

A parade of rubbernecking drivers pass by at a crawl, craning their necks to watch Alex get loaded into the sheriff's cruiser. "Watch yourself, sir," the officer says as he manipulates Alex's head to keep it clear of the car's door frame. But the way he has just manhandled Alex speaks volumes about how little he cares about Alex's physical well-being.

TWENTY-THREE

ALEX WAITS in a featureless interrogation room seated at a Formica table affixed to a concrete floor. A steel loop through which his handcuffs have been threaded protrudes from the table. The carbon steel rubs against Alex's wrists. His skin glows pink with irritation. He doesn't know how long he's been left alone here because the police confiscated his watch along with his wallet, cell phone, keys, and belt.

Finally, a Virginia detective in an off-the-rack suit enters. He has the weathered look of a man who could be either forty or sixty, of a cop who has spent far too long in his job and has seen far too much. With an almost terminal weariness, the detective takes his seat opposite Alex. "You want something to drink?" the man asks in a lilting Virginia twang. "Maybe something from the vending machine? They got Ho Hos."

Alex is too surprised by the questions to do anything other than shake his head.

"Suit yourself." The detective produces a small card from inside his jacket. "I've got to inform you of your rights now." He looks down at the card, but anyone familiar with television could recite what he's about to. "'You have the right to remain silent. Anything you say can and will be used against you in a court of law. You have the right to talk to a lawyer—'"

"I *am* a lawyer," Alex interrupts.

"'You have the right to talk to a lawyer and have him present with you while you are being questioned. If you cannot afford to hire a lawyer, one will be appointed to represent you before any questioning if you wish. You can decide at any time to exercise these rights and not answer any questions or make any statements. Do you understand each of these rights I have explained to you?'"

"Of course I understand them. I understand the Supreme Court opinion that enumerated them. I understand Justice Harlan's dissent and I understand Justice White's dissent. Do *you* understand that—"

The detective cuts him off. "Having these rights in mind, do you wish to talk to me now?"

"Not particularly."

The detective barely shrugs and shuffles some papers in his hand. He selects one and slides it across the table along with a ballpoint pen. "All this does is acknowledge that I've informed you of your legal rights." Alex reviews the form like a good attorney. "Then again, you're a lawyer, so you're not gonna take my word for it," the detective notes, his voice impatient and as dry as sawdust.

Alex finishes reviewing the form's boilerplate and scribbles his name at the bottom. "I want to make a phone call and I want an immediate arraignment," he says as he slides the form and pen back across the table.

"How about we slow down a second," the detective says.

"I'm an attorney. I know my rights. Even if I didn't know my rights, you just did a lovely job of informing me of them. I'm calling an end to this interrogation. If it would help you, I can also request a lawyer. I don't need one, obviously, but we both know you can't continue to question me once I've asked for one."

"I haven't started to question you," the cop protests.

"Phone call and arraignment, Detective," Alex repeats. "You can try to question me and — who knows? — maybe you'll even manage to elicit an answer or two, but we both know there's absolutely nothing I say in this room that a district attorney will be able to use to make a case against me. My suggestion would be that you not waste any more of our time."

The detective studies Alex for a good thirty seconds. "You've got balls, I'll give you that much. Brassy *and* hairy." He stands from the table. "Your funeral, buddy."

"Phone call," Alex reminds the detective, but the man leaves without reply.

◆

Alex estimates that it's around two hours before a uniformed officer comes in. He bends to unlock Alex's handcuffs, noting, "I'm gonna take these off you now. But I'll tell you this once: you make me regret it, you're gonna get yourself hurt."

"I don't want any trouble," Alex answers. "Just my phone call."

"Gotta book you first. Then you can call whoever you want."

The officer walks Alex to a computer that would have been considered obsolete in 2002. He takes down Alex's basic information, including his full name, address, and date of birth, then stands over Alex as he rolls his fingers over an ink pad and a ten card, which will be the official repository of his fingerprints. The mug shot comes next. Alex remains patient throughout the bureaucratic obstacle course. He doesn't have a legal right to a phone call, so he's at the mercy of the police and it behooves him to stay in the officer's good graces.

Mercifully, it works. The officer hands Alex a wet-nap to wipe the fingerprint ink from his hands and walks him to a nearby pay phone. The phone's plastic and metal surfaces are scratched with the jagged initials of former users and pithy observations like *go fuck u*. There are a few stickers advertising the services of bail bondsmen, but Alex has no intention of calling any of them. The officer takes the receiver off the hook and hands it to Alex. "I can't look up any numbers for you and you can only call collect."

"That's fine."

The officer nods and moves a respectful distance away in a gesture intended to suggest privacy while still allowing him to remain close enough to hear every word Alex says. Once the collect charges have been accepted, Alex begins, wondering what the eavesdropping police officer might think about the odd litany of instructions he gives to the person on the other end of the line.

◈

Three hours later, Alex stares at a very haggard-looking Grace. The skin around her eyes is a bright pink, a sign she's done more than a fair amount of crying. He wishes he could run up to her and take her in his arms and assure her that everything is going to be all right. But he's not sure everything is going to be all right. In any case, the uniformed bailiff standing three feet away would tackle him were he to bolt from the jury box where he stands.

Fortunately, the Fairfax Circuit Court for the Nineteenth Judicial Circuit has a night session. Otherwise, Alex would have had to wait until morning to be arraigned. He looks across the wood-paneled room and gives a nod to Grace that he hopes comes off as reassuring, but he's so beyond the point of exhaustion now that he has no confidence his face is capable of conveying anything. In any case, Grace either doesn't see him or pretends not to, because she steadfastly avoids his gaze. Alex cranes his neck to get her attention, but he stops when the bailiff approaches. "Take a seat," he instructs and points to one of the jury box's fourteen blue seats.

Alex does as he's told, but has to stand right back up. "All rise," a second bailiff intones. "Fairfax County Circuit Court is now in session. The Honorable Stephen Wacker presiding. Be seated."

Alex is then forced to endure the arraignments of three prostitutes and an alleged drug dealer before the court clerk calls his case. "Docket ending two-six-seven-seven," the clerk announces. She looks like she just stepped out from behind the counter at the DMV. *"State versus Alex Garnett."* The first bailiff leads Alex out of the jury box and into the well of the courtroom. "Violation of Code of Virginia section 18.2-32," the court clerk continues. "Murder in the first degree."

Alex turns and finally locks eyes with Grace, who wears a look on her face that Alex can't quite read. She appears confused and scared and angry all at once. He just nods to her and offers up a half smile before turning around to address Judge Wacker.

"I wish to enter a plea of not guilty, Your Honor."

Wacker stares down at Alex from the bench. "Do you have an attorney, Mr. Garnett? Do you need the court to appoint you one?"

"I'm an attorney, Your Honor. I don't require legal counsel."

"The lawyer who represents himself, Mr. Garnett, has a fool for a client," Wacker admonishes with a wag of his finger.

Alex ignores this advice. "Your Honor, the only physical evidence against me is the body of the victim allegedly discovered in the trunk of my rental car."

At this, the assistant district attorney, a plump woman in what Alex imagines is her late twenties, tops, stands to object. "Even assuming, *arguendo,*" she says, using the Latin word meaning "for the sake of the argument," "that the defendant's assertion as to evidence is accurate— which it is *not*— that's an issue for the trial court or, at best, the judge presiding over a preliminary hearing. It bears no relevance to arraignment, where the only question is one of bail."

This is an argument that Alex had anticipated and, for the moment, ignores. "The body was discovered pursuant to a warrantless and illegal trunk search. The court is going to rule it inadmissible at trial." Alex's fellow defendants, along with their respective lawyers and the handful of people sitting in the gallery, take all this in with rapt attention. Night court is the province of solicitation and possession cases. It never provides entertainment like dead bodies found in car trunks.

"Once again," the ADA says, "the defendant's arguments aren't relevant to the issue of bail."

"I disagree. The issue of bail is not dissimilar to the question of injunctive relief in a civil case. It's a preliminary step that the court must take in advance of trial. And the court must make those kinds of advance decisions based upon the likelihood of the party's success at trial," Alex says.

"The rules for a preliminary injunction in a civil case don't apply to the question of bail in a criminal one," the ADA rebuts in a tone designed to convey that Alex's argument is nothing other than the lowest form of bullshit.

Wacker muses on the question for some seconds before he delivers his ruling. "Set bail at a quarter of a million dollars bond, one hundred thousand dollars cash." Alex was hoping for less — he's not completely confident he'll be able to scrape together a six-figure bond — but it's better than the alternative. In a murder case where the victim's corpse was found in the defendant's possession, it would have surprised absolutely no one if Judge Wacker had decided to keep Alex in jail without bail.

◆

The bail process takes about two hours. As he waits for the wheels of the probation office's bureaucracy to slowly churn, he begins to hear whispers of news stories. He sees people check for updates on their phones. Bored guards surf the Internet for news. Someone asks if anyone has access to CNN. A terrible sixth sense–like instinct begins to form in Alex's gut. Even before he's able to get confirmation from one of the more connected people around him, he knows this looming event has to do with Iran.

"What's going on?" Alex asks.

The man behind the counter wears a practiced expression of apathy. "Fill this out and sign," he says, handing over a form. He looks like he's dead or at least wishes he were. He taps his finger in four places. "Here, here, here, and here."

Alex takes the pen affixed to the counter with a ball-bearing chain and sets about filling out the form as instructed. "Something going on in the Middle East?" he asks as he writes. The irony is not lost on him. He's gone from working at the heart of the world's preeminent intelligence-gathering organization to scraping for nuggets of news from a minimum-wage probation bureaucrat.

"Something going on with Iran," the man says. "Looks like they're gonna bomb those Israelis." The threat of open warfare between Iran and Israel isn't enough to fracture his indifference. "We're getting involved, of course." The way he says *of course* suggests more than a little frustration that America is heading into yet another dustup in that sandy, too-far-gone region of the world. But then he returns his attention to more pressing matters. "So, you doing cash or bond?"

"Cash," Alex answers. "Well, check." He turns around, scanning the entrance to the cramped office for some sign of Grace. After a few pregnant seconds, Grace enters, waving a freshly inked check. She heads over and hands it to Alex, who passes it along to the bureaucrat.

The man can tell with a glance that this is a personal—not a cashier's—check, and notes, "I've gotta confirm the sufficiency of this account. Whose is it?"

At this, Grace pipes up. "It's mine. Well, ours," she corrects. "It's my check, but it's a joint account."

The man lets out a sigh that Alex correctly takes to mean it's not possible for him to care less. "Wait over there. This'll take five to ten minutes." He points them to some plastic bucket chairs permanently affixed to the wall to their left.

An uncomfortable silence follows. "Thanks for coming," Alex ventures.

"That woman's body was in your car" is the only response he gets. Grace's voice is miles-away distant. This is not going to be easy.

"You know I didn't have anything to do with that." The sentence comes out more like a question than he intended it to.

"I know," she responds, sounding less certain than he'd like.

He looks at her, eyes bloodshot, face pale, and understands she's in some kind of shock. She's acting like this is all some bad dream, and if she just pushes through it, she'll wake up on the other side and discover that her fiancé wasn't shot at last night, that he wasn't just charged with murdering a coworker.

"I knew my father would find some way of locating you," Alex says, trying to push through the fog between them.

"I still can't believe you called him," Grace remarks.

"Neither can I," Alex admits.

"What did he say? What did *you* say?"

Simon Garnett answered the phone with a curt "Hello?"

"Hey," Alex said into the receiver. The cold piece of plastic smelled like halitosis and liquor. "It's — it's Alex."

"Alex." His father sounded surprised. "How are you?"

"Not good. I need your help." Sometimes, it takes only four words to break a vow.

"Of course, son. Whatever you need."

There was such a lack of hesitation in Simon Garnett's voice that Alex immediately felt ashamed. "Thank you." He breathed. "Thanks, Dad."

He couldn't remember the last time he'd called his father that. It felt good to say the word. It was like coming home.

Alex gave his father an abbreviated account of the previous five hours. Habit conditioned him to expect criticism, either for being too curious or for not bringing his superiors at the CIA into his confidence earlier, but no such scolding was forthcoming. His father didn't voice any incredulity at Alex's outlandish claims. "I know this all must sound completely insane," Alex allowed.

"Not to someone who worked in the corridors of American power as long as I did. Truth be told, everything you're telling me connects quite a few dots."

"Really?"

"Really. I accepted as truth the fact that William Rykman is a sociopathic bastard a long time ago. A very long time ago. And if he's at the center of this, then you've got some very serious problems indeed. So what do you need from me? What can I do?"

In response, Alex rattled off a list of assignments. The first was to contact Grace. (A request that should have been of the needle-in-a-haystack variety, except she hadn't tossed her cell phone as Alex had instructed her to. She answered on the third ring.) The other things Alex asked for, however, would be far more difficult to come by. The $150,000 deposit into the joint bank account Alex shared with Grace was maybe the easiest request to grant, but it was by no means easy. Simon Garnett was a man of means, but those means weren't entirely liquid and, therefore, weren't entirely accessible, particularly at a moment's notice. The same could not be said, however, for his law firm's densely filled coffers. After six years of record litigation business, the accounts of Garnett and Lockhart were overflowing with cash. All it took to get the money into the account Alex shared with Grace was a phone call to the firm's managing partner, a man with flexible fiduciary ethics. Simon Garnett didn't even have to explain that the money was so his future daughter-in-law could post his son's bail.

And this action was several orders of magnitude easier than Alex's other requests, all of which had the same goal: stopping a war in the Middle East.

But if the news reports that have been dribbling into Alex's ears for the past forty-five minutes were any indication, his father hasn't had much success.

TWENTY-FOUR

THE 29 Diner is a squat little establishment with a blue roof and a blue-and-white-striped awning. It's fronted by a tall sign that lights up neon after dark boasting that the diner is open twenty-four hours and, below that, a bank of machines offering just about every newspaper printed in the state. It's also a less-than-five-minute drive from the Fairfax County Judicial Center, where Alex's release on bail was processed. No words were spoken between him and Grace in that interval. Alex would like to tell himself it's because they're both beyond exhausted, but he knows the truth. The strain has gotten to Grace, and something has broken under its weight. At the diner, she orders a tossed green salad and he asks for a cheeseburger, but neither is hungry. Alex manages a few bites of his cheeseburger while Grace just rearranges the leafy greens with her fork. Alex keeps quiet to avoid giving voice to the only things he can think of to say, which are all variations on *Don't worry, everything will be all right.* He can't bear the thought of lying to his fiancée on top of everything else.

It's Grace who breaks the silence. "I can't do this anymore."

"Don't worry. It's all going to be okay," Alex reassures her, completely misreading the situation.

"No," she says, shaking her head. "I mean…" Her voice trails off. There are tears in her eyes. An uncomfortable feeling develops in the pit of Alex's stomach. "I mean *this*." She moves her hand back and forth in the space between them.

"Everything is going to work out," he says soothingly, determined to keep the conversation from spiraling to a place their relationship won't be able to recover from. "Look, it's a" — he searches for the right word — "it's a heightened situation." A half snort of a chuckle. "It's a *very* heightened situation. We shouldn't be making these kinds of decisions in the middle of it." He hopes his tone remains calm as he fights back panic.

But the look on Grace's face confirms his instinct that it's not going well. The tears flow freely now, cascading down her face and making her cheeks gleam. In what seems like torturous slow motion, she removes the Harry Winston engagement ring he'd bought her. "You're right. This is a heightened situation," she says. The acknowledgment carries with it a glimmer of hope. "But that's when relationships are tested, aren't they?" She wipes a tear from one eye. "I should want to be with you, to help you, to do whatever for you, but…but all I want to do is run away. You deserve better. You need it."

When Alex speaks, his voice comes out as a croak. "How about you let me decide what I need?" Is there as much edge in his tone as he feels? "Right now, I need you."

Grace shakes her head and places the ring in his limp hand. She closes his fist and holds it in her grip. "I'm so sorry. I can't believe I'm doing this now." Neither can Alex. "But I just feel — I *need* to do this. I need an honest moment between us."

The ring in Alex's hand digs into his palm like a razor. He attempts to process what just happened, but every coherent thought he tries to formulate slips away like sand through his fingers. "Let's just…talk about this after," he says, desperate to say *something*.

◆

Five minutes later, they make their way to Grace's Volvo. Alex can feel the ring in his pocket. It seems to weigh five times the amount that it should. They walk in silence until Alex holds his hand out. She might be expected to give him her hand, but she senses what he's asking for in that way only couples on the verge of marriage can, and she gives him the fob for the car instead.

"So what happens next?" she asks, breaking the silence between them.

Alex knows that she's not asking about the two of them or his legal woes. "I drop you off at my father's. You'll be safe there."

Grace just nods. "I still can't believe you called him." Alex just manages a nod at this, but he's thinking, *Join the club*. "What are you going to do? You said drop *me* off. It's the middle of the night."

What do you care? Alex wants to snap. *You don't get to ask anymore.* But he can't bring himself to say that, so instead, he just replies, "I have to go back to the CIA." Fortunately, Alex doesn't have the burden of explaining how he plans to get on the grounds, because he never told her he got fired.

"Why? Because of what's going on with Iran?"

"Because of everything."

"You mean with Leah?"

"Everything" is Alex's only reply.

◆

Once in the car, Alex works to push aside any thoughts of the death of his relationship. He willfully ignores creeping thoughts of the future. He shuns notions of moving out, of looking for another place; he refuses to deal with any of the logical necessities breaking up with Grace engenders.

He turns on the Volvo's SiriusXM satellite radio, in part to fill the silence between Grace and himself but also to get the latest information on the situation in the Middle East. The television back at the diner was broadcasting Fox News, but there was little information to be had from that source. Before Grace dropped her bomb, Alex had been busy taking comfort in the fact that whatever was happening with Iran hadn't yet boiled over into the type of twenty-four-hour coverage that has the cable news outlets filling the air with talking heads passing off speculation as news just to stay on the topic.

The radio is a little more informative. According to the commentators, the Islamic Republic of Iran Air Force — the IRIAF — is flying what they're calling "exercises" in a manner that's making the Israelis very tense. The one thing all the commentators can agree on is that *tense* is not a good thing where the Middle East is concerned.

"I don't believe this is happening," Grace observes. "It feels like science fiction." Alex just nods. "And this is happening because Jahandar is dead?"

Alex can't believe Grace wants to talk *politics* with him. He wants to scream, to rail at her, to tell her to shut up, that he loves her, that he can't believe she's doing this to him tonight of all nights. "I think it's happening because a lot of people over there have always *wanted* it to happen, but Jahandar kept them in check," he says. "Now that he's gone, the dam has burst."

"They won't really attack Israel. That would draw us into a war, wouldn't it?"

"I don't know," Alex allows. *Shut up. I don't want to talk to you right now. I can't talk to you right now. Can't you see I'm dying here?* "But I don't see how we don't get involved somehow." Nevertheless, Alex holds out hope that his father, with all his friends and enemies, the people who owe him favors and take his phone calls, will be able to at least throw a monkey wrench into the churning gears of war. But he's not optimistic. Which means that any hope lies in Agamemnon.

◈

Two years after the death of his wife, Simon Garnett finally felt comfortable telling people he'd decided it was time to move on from the now far too big midcentury modern home in Bethesda, Maryland. In truth, the huge mansion had lost its appeal immediately after the death of Alex's mother. His son had left for college, and the house was too quiet and too burdensome to maintain by himself. He'd succumbed to outsourcing his wife's domestic responsibilities to a local cleaning lady, but living alone in the home his wife had made for them, where his now-estranged son had taken his first steps and where the love of his life had waged and lost her battle against ovarian cancer, quickly became too painful for him. The penthouse apartment he moved into in the heart of Washington, DC — close enough to work and the thrum of the capital of the world's most powerful city — suited him much better.

Garnett opens the door for Alex and Grace and immediately has to hide his reaction to their haggard appearances. But maintaining a stoic poker face has never been something Simon Garnett has difficulty with. He offers them places to sit and something to drink. Grace takes him up on both — the living room's leather couch and a glass of ice water — but Alex demurs. Instead, he follows his father into the kitchen.

"Have you been able to reach out to anyone?" Alex asks. He sounds more motivated, appears more present and commanding than Simon Garnett has ever seen him.

"I've reached out to several people. A friend in the current administration, someone at State, Neil Henrich at the DOD — you remember him, right?" Alex shakes his head but Simon presses on. "The news isn't good. Everyone's 'checking into it' and will get back to me. They might be shining me on" — Alex finds this doubtful — "or it could be the fact that I was calling them all at two in the morning."

Alex takes in the news, discouraged but not surprised. "Was anyone able to tell you what's going on over there?"

"The IRIAF is flying regular sorties over their southwestern border toward Iraq, which is, of course, in Israel's direction. Iran is claiming they're just flying exercises." Garnett's face confirms he doesn't believe this explanation any more than the Israelis do. "Everyone's waiting on the pass from the next EECS satellite to see what Iran's long- and medium-range missiles might be doing."

"Have you ever heard of something called Agamemnon?" Alex asks.

Alex's father is thrown by the abrupt change of subject. He shakes his head. "What is it?"

"Doesn't matter." Alex checks his watch. It's almost two thirty in the morning. Although he lacks specific information on a wide variety of topics, he can't shake the strong feeling that time is running out. "I have to get over to the CIA," he says. Alex hasn't shared the news of his dismissal with his father either.

"Are you sure that's, well…the safest place for you?" Simon Garnett ventures. "Considering…everything you told me."

To his surprise, Alex wasn't frightened when he was being shot at. He wasn't afraid in the aftermath when he reached the inescapable conclusion that someone wanted him dead. Nor was he afraid when being placed under arrest for a murder he was obviously being framed for. But when Alex looks into his father's eyes — eyes that have seen the way the world, with all its dark and terrible secrets, truly works — he finds nothing but concern and fear, and *that's* when Alex feels the cold hand of terror on the back of his neck.

He forces a smile with the hope that his father can't see through it. He looks over his shoulder to where Grace has curled up on the couch with a drink. Feeling his eyes on her, she looks up, and they stare at each other for what feels like a year. But Alex has nothing to say to her. Perhaps sensing this, knowing this, Grace turns away, looking at anything other than Alex. Alex maintains his gaze long enough to engrave the image of Grace in his mind. Whether it's owing to the state of their relationship or the dangers he's about to face, he doesn't know, but he can't shake the marrow-deep feeling that this might be the last time he ever sees her.

◆

Alex finds his father's BMW 7 Series in its assigned space underneath the apartment building. Before leaving, Alex asked to borrow the keys and his father's cell phone. Walking to the car, Alex scribbles down a few phone numbers from his phone onto his palm before placing the iPhone beneath the right rear tire of the BMW. The Series 7 weighs over two tons—with Alex contributing an additional one hundred and ninety pounds—so his iPhone is well and truly crushed when Alex pulls the German-made automobile out of the garage.

En route to the CIA, he tries one of the numbers he transcribed onto his hand from his now-pulverized iPhone. Gerald doesn't answer, but Alex tells himself this is not indicative of anything dire. He starts to get concerned, however, when Gerald doesn't answer the landline in his apartment either. Fighting a rising tide of concern, Alex tries a third number. He almost didn't write this one down, since the odds of Gerald answering it at two thirty in the morning are slim to none. Which is why Alex is stunned when he hears Gerald answer his direct-dial number at the Agency.

"Hello?" Gerald sounds like the call has stirred him from some particularly deep sleep.

"Gerald." Alex exhales, still surprised to find Gerald at headquarters. But then it occurs to him that Gerald could be taking the call surrounded by a phalanx of eavesdropping CIA security protective officers or Overwatch personnel. This would actually make more sense than the

idea that Gerald had decided to stick around Langley despite their tres-
pass into Arthur Bryson's office.

"Holy shit, Alex," Gerald exclaims. He sounds as surprised to hear
Alex's voice as Alex is to hear his.

"What're you doing still at headquarters?" If Gerald isn't alone, his
reaction to this question will tell Alex as much, particularly since Gerald
can't lie worth a damn.

"I was afraid to go anywhere else," Gerald replies, sounding more
than sincere and downplaying the fact it's been almost twenty-four
hours since the ill-fated incursion into Bryson's office. "I figured the
Agency's just about the safest place for me to be right now. Though,
I've gotta tell you, I've been questioning my assumption that Rykman or
whoever wouldn't try to waste me on Agency grounds. What the fuck
happened to you? I thought you'd come down here or reach out or something."

"I've been a little busy," Alex says. The magnitude of the understatement isn't lost on him. "I'll explain everything in a bit. I'm coming to
you."

"Okay. What's the plan?"

Alex shakes his head. If only he had something remotely approaching
a plan. "I need you to get me on the grounds first."

"What? Just use your badge."

"I can't. It's a very long story."

"Bryson canned your ass, didn't he?"

"Pretty much," he admits.

"Look, Alex," Gerald says, sounding genuinely regretful, "I can hack
you a drive-on, get you in through the visitors', that's easy. That's a matter
of just putting your name on a computerized list. But I can't get you past
the front door. Not at this hour, anyway. The first guard you run into is
gonna ask to see your badge."

"I've got that covered," Alex says honestly. "Just get me past the gate."

"You got it."

"I'll see you in ten," Alex says before ending the call. He follows the Chain Bridge Road as it flows into Dolly Madison Boulevard. Up ahead, the seventh floor of the Central Intelligence Agency peeks above the treetops. He drives his father's car toward the security gate at the visitors' entrance. Those few feet pass under the car's wheels without incident, marking his first time on Agency grounds as a civilian.

TWENTY-FIVE

WHATEVER MAGIC Gerald worked on the computer at the visitors' gate must have been successful, because all Alex needs to do to gain access is flash his driver's license. Fortunately, the guard on duty doesn't recognize him, most likely because Alex hasn't entered through the visitors' gate since his first day at the Agency. Entering as a visitor also pays the dividend of sending him to the visitor lot, which sits just outside the entrance to the Old Headquarters Building, thereby decreasing his chances of running into the guard who escorted him out of the New Headquarters Building less than twenty-four hours ago.

Alex enters the OHB, steps over the sixteen-foot-wide granite emblem of the CIA, and heads for the security gateways — turnstile-like machines with arms that block entry to the building beyond. He selects the one farthest to the left, the one farthest away from the guard station kitty-cornered against the right wall. The green jacket on duty is another unfamiliar face, but Alex gives him a wave as if they're old friends.

"How's it going?" he asks, sweeping a badge over the gateway's RFID scanner. Alex breezes through, heading directly toward the stairs ahead of him. He beelines for the bust of George H. W. Bush at the top of the stairs, almost home free.

"Hang on a sec," says a voice.

Shit. Alex turns around to see the guard approaching him. "Everything okay? I just gotta run to my office to pick up a file." He adds a gesture meant to suggest his office is just a few feet away, as if that matters.

"Can I see your badge for a sec?" the guard asks. *A sec* is apparently his favorite unit of time.

"Is there a problem? 'Cause I'm kind of in a hurry." Alex is wearing his best *C'mon, can't you help a fellah out?* expression.

"System logged you in as Leah Doyle."

"Probably a glitch or something. You should call IT. I think Gerald Jankovick is still working, actually." Alex's mind churns a million miles an hour. *His* badge had been confiscated the previous night. If he turns over the one he's holding now, the guard will instantly see that the photo on the laminated card belongs to Leah Doyle. Which makes all the sense in the world, given that it's her badge. Alex had, to his shame, lifted it off Leah's corpse during his emotional outburst as he embraced her lifeless body in the trunk of his rental car.

"I just need to see your badge," the guard repeats. Alex doesn't move. He can't move. But he doesn't know what to do. The guard, who apparently is not a complete idiot, clearly senses that something is amiss. His right hand is wandering to the SIG Sauer P226 on his holster. "Do we have a problem here?" he asks.

"What's going on?" The question doesn't come from Alex, who for once in his life has no clever argument to Houdini himself out of trouble.

Alex gets a glimpse of a second green jacket approaching. The guard turns to his peer. "I think this joker just tried coming in here with somebody else's badge," he says.

Alex turns and sees the guard more clearly now, and he has to work mightily not to exhale with relief. It *is* another guard. But this one, he knows.

"Alex wouldn't do that," Tom Ciampa answers, walking up to his fellow guard. Nothing has gone right for Alex since the moment he managed to avoid being killed in the parking garage of his own building, but right now he's thankful for all the bad turns he's experienced in the last twenty-four-plus hours, because he has the sense he's about to make a large withdrawal from the karma bank. "Alex is legit. I can vouch for him."

The skeptical guard looks at Ciampa, then over to Alex, and he apparently decides Alex isn't worth getting into a pissing match over. "I'll go call IT. It's probably a glitch," he says, clearly not happy about it.

Once he's gone, Alex looks to Ciampa. "Thanks. I really don't know what was up with that guy."

Ciampa appears to see through Alex with a single concerned glance. "Everything all right with you, Mr. Garnett?"

"Just stressed." This is not an outright lie.

"You take care of yourself, okay?"

"I will, Tom. Thank you." Alex does his best to make it clear he isn't thanking Ciampa just for the friendly concern.

◈

The Overwatch Operations Center is alive with activity despite it being well past four in the morning. This is because in Iran it's nearly one o'clock in the afternoon, and the Islamic Republic of Iran Regular Forces are on high alert. And this heightened military tempo is being matched 970 miles to the southwest by the Tzva Hahagana LeYisrael — Israel's defense forces. The entire Middle East is on a war footing right now. William Rykman smiles. Everything is going according to plan. Years of strategizing, of arranging for contingencies and suffering setbacks, of diplomatic theory and sabotage, are coming to fruition.

At his station, Tyler Donovan jolts as if struck by a wayward electrical current. Rykman takes note of this, as Donovan is the coldest son of a bitch he's ever known, which is really saying something.

"Donovan?"

Donovan leans forward as if the image on his flat-screen computer monitor is going to become clearer or different with proximity. He takes a few seconds to read the screen again before reporting, in a voice more level than his startled expression would indicate, "Sir, the security gateway at the OHB just logged an entry for Leah Doyle."

Rykman instantly understands the reason for Donovan's uncharacteristic lack of calm. Almost as instantly, he knows what's afoot here, but his theory requires confirmation. "Security cameras," he orders.

But Donovan is already working on it. Rykman steps up behind him as the young soldier does whatever young soldiers do with computers these days and waits patiently for the few seconds it takes for Donovan to work his magic. As Donovan manipulates the CIA's security network, Rykman says, "I thought Virginia PD picked Garnett up."

"The sheriff's department, yes, sir," Donovan confirms. He stabs a final button, producing a new window on his monitor. It's a quad-cam feed from the four security cameras monitoring the entrance to the Old Headquarters Building. On two of the video feeds, the face of Alex Garnett is clearly visible.

Rykman's lips curl into a thin, impressed smile. The clever bastard is even smarter than Rykman gave him credit for. In hindsight, he realizes he never should have lost sight of the fact that Alex Garnett is Simon Garnett's son.

"Locate him. Get Agency security on it. They shouldn't have let him get within a mile of Langley. Have them find him and take him into custody. Have them drop him in a hole. I don't care. We just need this little prick shut down for another few hours."

"Roger that," Donovan confirms.

"And get a location on his buddy too."

"Gerald Jankovick."

"Whatever the little shit's name is. Find him and contain him," Rykman says, biting off each syllable. He feels all the heads in the room turning in his direction, not in compliance but in surprise. They've never heard William Rykman agitated before.

◆

"Just stay where you are," Alex instructs Gerald via his father's cell phone. "Just hang right there. You're right: the basement of the CIA is probably the safest place you can be right now."

"Are you following the news? It looks like Israel and Iran are about to go toe to toe. They must be going nutso upstairs."

It's not an entirely inaccurate conjecture. As he wends his way through the OHB, Alex can't help but notice that the entire building looks quite lively for almost four in the morning.

"Do you have any earthly idea what's going on?" Gerald asks.

"I'm piecing it together."

"Don't feel the need to burden me with information," Gerald notes sarcastically.

"The Overwatch is a sub-rosa organization, a kind of shadow agency."

"That doesn't sound the least bit insane." More sarcasm.

"You wanted specifics."

"Okay, assuming for a second you haven't had a psychotic break — which is by no means a safe assumption on my part — what's that got to do with the money transfer out of the black budget and the fact that the Middle East's about to go World War Three?"

"I figure the money's part of Overwatch's endgame. And that endgame involves maneuvering us into a war with Iran. They off Jahandar so someone more militant takes his place, and the first thing he does is start rattling his saber in Israel's direction."

"And if Iran moves on Israel, we have to kick some ass in response,"

Gerald says. "What I don't get is how we could be ready to do *anything* against Iran tonight. Our military's thinner than a fashion model."

Alex's voice grows cold. "The Overwatch has been moving troops into the region for weeks now, if not months."

"Bullshit. They can't move fucking *troops* around."

"All I know is I *saw* a troop deployment out of Fort Eustis to *Iran*. I'll bet every dollar in my pocket that it wasn't the only troop deployment that's been made to Iran or to somewhere near Iran recently. I don't know how they've done it exactly, but I think Overwatch has been putting all the pieces on the board in a very specific way, with everything leading up to tonight."

"That's some fucked-up shit."

"You have a talent for understatement, Gerald," Alex observes as he steps into the elevator and hits the button that will take him to the seventh floor. "I'm headed into an elevator now. I'm gonna lose you."

"Where are you going?" Gerald asks, but the rising elevator severs the connection.

◆

Alex locates G-8 with little difficulty. He's been here before, when Gerald led him to the source of the threatening phone call that was meant, he now realizes, to wave him off the hunt and keep him from digging into matters that would lead him to discover the Overwatch's existence.

Alex is returning to G-8 for reasons not dissimilar to what led him to remember Leah's AIN. In thinking—and thinking and thinking—on Agamemnon and its significance, he realized that he'd seen that name once before: inside the moribund file room located in office G-8.

Alex turns the handle, only to find that the room is locked. "Shit," he curses under his breath. His mind races and he can feel his heart race with it. He thinks, trying to come up with some line or lie that might convince someone in security to open the door for him. Tom Ciampa is probably still in the building, and he seems to be Alex's most viable option. However, he hasn't thought of a convincing line of bullshit. So that remains plan B. He looks around and then, secure in the notion that he's alone, kicks the door in.

Or tries to.

It's a formidable steel-reinforced door with a metal lock. It's not going down without a fight. Alex casts about for something to match the door's strength. He's rewarded with the sight of a fire extinguisher hanging on the wall just a few feet down the corridor. Within seconds, he has the fire extinguisher in his hands and is aiming its base at where the handle meets the door.

His first attempt sounds like a bomb going off. At least, that's how it feels to Alex in the empty corridor with every last nerve buzzing in anticipation of being caught. For all the noise, however, the door just shrugs off the assault. He aims the fire extinguisher a few millimeters away from the door, intending to use its force to pry the handle loose. He tries again, driving the extinguisher down, and feels the handle give. It moves just the tiniest fraction, but it encourages Alex to believe he may actually win this contest of metal against metal. He tries again. The impact echoes loudly in the hallway, but this time Alex doesn't bother to stop to see if anyone's heard him. If someone has, he'll learn soon enough. For now, he just repeatedly assaults the metal handle, putting his weight into it, fueling the attack with all the pent-up stress of the past twenty-four-plus hours, and finally — finally — the damn thing gives. The handle clatters to the floor, leaving behind an empty hole.

Alex inserts two fingers in the hole, ignoring the jagged teeth of metal surrounding the wound, and probes within the lock. He doesn't know exactly what he's feeling around for, but when he touches something that feels metallic and substantial, he curls his fingers to push it up. After three attempts, he feels a tumbler retract with a pleasing *shunk*. The door swings open and Alex kicks the discarded handle into the room, enters, and closes the injured door behind him.

The room is exactly as he remembers it, a museum of dust-covered file cabinets left over from a bygone bureaucratic epoch. He has no idea what such an unremarkable room could have to do with the Overwatch or Agamemnon, but it's desperation time and he's out of options. Moving quickly, he scans the labels. The yellowing on them and the fact that they're typewritten speak to their age, but the cabinets' contents have no more significance to him now than they did when he first raked his eyes over them.

Agamemnon, Alex thinks. *What the hell is Agamemnon?* He consults Google on his father's phone and learns that Agamemnon was the name of the general who commanded Greece's forces during the Trojan War, a bloody and ultimately unnecessary fictional conflict. *Well, that much makes sense, at least.* He consults the cabinets' labels again in the hope of finding something that relates to Greece, the Trojan War, or the like. *Fuck, even Helen of Troy I'll take,* he thinks. But as before, there aren't any names on the file cabinets at all, merely a sequence of alphabetical ranges: *A–F, B, A–G, A–M, D–L, E–M, F–Q, N–O, N.*

Then a gut punch of an epiphany sends him staggering a few steps back: the Overwatch could have learned he'd made it inside and cleansed the room of any evidence, including and especially anything having to do with Agamemnon. It also occurs to him that he's following the rantings of a woman who has been committed indefinitely to a mental hospital. He's about to give up all hope and return to Gerald's basement to figure out his next move when he sees it. The realization is so profound it actually sends a chill up his spine. His eyes dart between the various typewritten labels. Then, in a manic furor, he starts to pull the drawers open again. This time, he does so in a deliberate sequence. First, he opens *A–G.* Then its neighbor, *A–M.* Next, *E–M.* It seems simultaneously insane and eminently logical. He pulls at *N–O.* But it's when he completes the sequence — by pulling at the drawer marked *N* — that it happens: There's a metallic hum. Alex can feel the linoleum beneath his feet vibrate ever so subtly. And then the far wall of the room, to his right…*splits open.*

TWENTY-SIX

"SITREP," says CIA and Overwatch director William Rykman. His voice is cold. He paces around the Op Center in a perpetual circle, hands clasped behind his back. The removal of his Brooks Brothers suit jacket is the only allowance he's made for the stress.

Tyler Donovan is first to speak. "The president just walked into the Situation Room." Rykman is pleased. Things are moving in the right direction. "We've got a line in there, of course."

"Put it up on the big screen," Rykman says, indicating the seventy-five-inch plasma monitor that dominates the room's northern wall. In an instant, the interior of the Situation Room appears on the screen. Their surveillance-camera-quality image looks down on the modest room from above. The president sits at the head of the table, flanked by the vice president, the director of national intelligence, the chairman of the Joint Chiefs of Staff, and the secretaries of state and defense. The video feed plays without audio, but Donovan provides commentary.

"He just asked what our capabilities are to project power into Iran. SecDef"—the secretary of defense—"just told him about our friends from the Seventh Transportation Group being in the region."

Rykman allows himself a small smile of satisfaction. The Overwatch maintained agents within all the major arms of the U.S. military. It was a relatively easy matter to use the Overwatch's assets in the Department of Defense to motivate the transportation group's deployment to the Persian Gulf. The ostensible justification was for the group to assist in training exercises being conducted by the *John C. Stennis* Carrier Strike Group Three (aka CSG-3). The *Stennis's* presence in the Gulf was also the work of the Overwatch. The U.S. Navy maintained eleven carrier strike groups. Redeploying one — particularly to a region as politically sensitive as the Persian Gulf — was no easy feat. Fortunately, however, Rykman has a relationship with the rear admiral who serves as CSG-3's commander. He's been cultivating this particular asset for the past three years, and although the admiral remains unaware of the Overwatch's existence, he's particularly responsive to timely whispers in his ear. Not that a commander can move his carrier group of his own accord, but the commander of the U.S. Naval Forces Central Command listens to his recommendation to occasionally show the flag in the waters of the Persian Gulf. And in the event that he disagrees, well, Rykman has other means of moving the necessary chess pieces on the global board to exactly where he wants them. This is the advantage of being the director of the most powerful U.S. intelligence-gathering organization *and* the director of its most covert agency — a body so covert, so black, that not even the president of the United States knows of its existence.

◆

Alex has never seen anything like it. He stares disbelieving at the fake wall — now retracted in two equal halves — for a few incredulous seconds. He wasn't aware of the slightest seam in the wall, although he has to admit he wasn't really looking for one. Still, the craftsmanship at work here is perfect. The secret door was invisible, and its disappearance reveals a new, surreal obstacle on this journey down the rabbit hole.

He's staring at two interlocked doors.

For a moment, Alex is reminded of the opening credits of the old Don Adams television series *Get Smart,* with its nested series of portals and doors. Next to the doors is a simple panel with a single button at its center. There's something very twentieth-century modern about the design. Alex is tempted to place its construction in the 1980s. He reaches out, presses the button — because why not? — and the doors open. Alex half expects their parting to reveal a third set of doors — after all, that's how it would be on *Get Smart* — but instead he finds a small chamber. No, not a chamber exactly.

It's an elevator.

Alex enters it to find a second panel with an identical single button inside. He gives this one a press as well. The doors close and the elevator lurches downward.

⬩

Rufus Kalin has been serving in the Overwatch for the past eight months. On loan from the U.S. Army, he thought he'd be assisting in some CIA operation. In fact, for the first two of those eight months, he thought that's what he was doing. But after those initial eight weeks, he was "invited to come inside," to use the internal Overwatch parlance. To Kalin's knowledge, which, he has to admit, is probably incomplete and largely incorrect, everyone aware of the Overwatch's existence is in the Op Center right now. This is why the alert that just popped up on his workstation is more than a little puzzling. He checks again and runs a quick systems diagnostic to confirm it isn't a glitch. Only when he's satisfied that it's not does he announce what the computer is telling him. "Sir," he says, swiveling in his Aeron chair to face Rykman, "the G-eight access point has just been activated."

"What?" Rykman looks like he's been hit in the ass with a cattle prod.

"Confirmed, sir. The elevator is on descent." Kalin picks his next words very, very carefully. "Are we expecting additional personnel tonight?"

Rykman offers no reply but the grinding of his teeth.

◆

After what feels like an interminably long interval, the elevator comes to a gentle stop and the doors automatically open. Alex alights and orients himself. What he has just walked into doesn't make any kind of sense to him. He's standing in what looks like a subway station circa 1985. True, there is no signage to indicate an era. In fact, there's no signage whatsoever. But the overall architecture feels like the old Metro stations his father took him to when he was a kid.

Unlike the Metro stations of his youth, however, this one has only one track. He wonders whether he's stumbled upon some vestigial piece of the OHB's construction but then reminds himself that he was able to access the elevator only by making use of what he now considers the Agamemnon pass code.

As in any subway station, there is no means of summoning the next car or train. Alex wonders what his next move is. He glances down at his father's cell phone, thinking this might be a good time to check in with Gerald. But the phone isn't getting a signal here, wherever "here" is.

Suddenly, an electric whine pierces the air. Alex jumps and turns in its direction. He looks to the track, and a lone subway car slides into view. But it doesn't look like a subway car. Not exactly. It's shorter in length and a little squatter. Its large windows reveal no passengers or rail man.

The car comes to a stop. A pair of doors slide open with a pneumatic hiss. Like an invitation. He steps inside. At the edges of the doors are photoelectric triggers that Alex activates by passing through, prompting the doors to close. Alex grabs hold of one of the steel poles and the car surges forward.

◆

"We have enough troops and personnel in Iraq and Afghanistan," SecDef says, "and the Seventh Transportation Group has the necessary vehicles and equipment with it. Bottom line, we should be able to cobble together a modest invasion force."

"I'm not sure which I find more troubling, 'cobble together' or 'modest.'" This draws a few small chuckles in the Situation Room, breaking some of the rock-solid tension. But the president is serious. He isn't going to war on the cheap.

"What I mean, Mr. President, is that if need be, we can assemble an invasion force on the order of what we went into Iraq with back in '03."

"That doesn't comfort me much," the president retorts.

"We still took the country, sir."

The president nods. "What about air options?"

"We've got Carrier Strike Group Three in the Gulf right now. They've got Carrier Air Wing Nine with them and four strike fighter squadrons. They fly the F/A–Eighteen C Hornet and the F/A–Eighteen F Super Hornet."

"When can you get them up and flying?"

"As soon as you give the order, sir."

"Mr. President," the secretary of state chimes in, "something to consider: if we start flying fighter jets over Iran's airspace, they're going to view that as an extremely aggressive act."

"Not unlike the aggressive acts Iran is directing against Israel, one of our most important allies and our *only* ally in the region?" the chairman of the Joint Chiefs chimes in.

"All I'm saying is, if our air force finds itself in an engagement with the IRIAF, this could very quickly — *very quickly* — escalate into a shooting war with Iran."

"A shooting war with Iran is what we're looking at in the event that Iran goes through with its apparent plan to attack Israel. Maybe a few

F/A-Eighteens in their airspace will make them think twice about their intentions." The president takes a beat. "Start low-level reconnaissance flights along the Iraq-Iran border."

◆

"He just committed air assets," Tyler Donovan reports less than a second later. "Sorties along the border."

Rykman nods, satisfied. He sees several paths to war now. With the U.S. military putting skin in the game, he knows inertia will do most of the work for him. All it takes is one shot for a cascade of military reaction and counterreaction to plunge the United States, Israel, and Iran into war. He knows most people would never understand the degree of satisfaction this gives him. Only a bloodthirsty sociopath, conventional wisdom says, would agitate for war. He doesn't covet war for the sake of war. But he remembers when the U.S. embassy in Iran was overrun in 1979. He remembers the hostages who were taken, how impotent the crisis made America appear to its enemies. He remembers the assassinations of Israelis by Iran in 2012. He remembers the series of bombings that followed shortly thereafter in New Delhi, Tbilisi, and Bangkok. Most important, he knows better than almost anyone on the planet the extent of Iran's passion to join the club of nuclear-weaponized nations. Iran is a terrorist country that has been allowed to exist for far too long. Rykman is an extremely intelligent man and knows more about geopolitical realities than most heads of state. But he could never fathom why his government chose to invade Iraq and Afghanistan and leave the much greater threat of Iran untouched.

But that's all going to change tonight. And it makes William Rykman smile.

TWENTY-SEVEN

THE SUBWAY car comes to a gentle stop and the automated doors swish open. On the other side of the doors, Alex finds another platform virtually identical to the one he just left. The only difference is the mouth of a long tunnel-like corridor opposite the platform. He walks toward it, checking his father's phone again. Still no reception. He pockets the phone and ventures into the dark corridor. The only lighting comes from a line of fluorescents strung overhead. They illuminate the walls of rough-hewn rock, suggesting that this space was dug directly into the ground. Pipes run overhead parallel with the fluorescent lights, bolted directly to the rock face.

As Alex moves deeper into the tunnel, he begins to hear faint sounds, the hum of electronics and the murmur of voices. He quickens his pace. The sound of his loafers on the floor abruptly changes from the soft *thwap* of shoe sole on rock to something less organic, more like a chime. He finds himself on a steel-mesh gangway, metal stairs descending on either side of him. The space the gangway looks down upon seems about the size of a small movie theater. In the center is a glass-enclosed conference room, complete with a polished walnut table and rolling Aeron

office chairs. Built into the top of the conference table is a metal door —
which, judging from the circular dial at its center, is some kind of safe.

The area outside the conference room is ringed by bleeding-edge
computer workstations, each equipped with a trio of flat-screen monitors aglow with information. Crew-cut men and a token pair of women,
all in conservative business suits, manage their respective workstations.
At the far end of the room is a massive screen whose display is currently
divided into a series of video feeds: CNN's broadcast, a cornucopia
of satellite imagery, and, astonishingly, what looks like security camera
footage of the White House Situation Room. Alex recognizes the president and the secretaries of defense and state. He recognizes the room itself from news photographs and, although it's changed somewhat, from
the time his father gave him a tour of the facility when he was eight.

There's a man standing in front of the huge screen. He's facing away
from Alex and he's backlit by the video unfolding in front of him, but
it's obvious from his body language that he's in charge.

Alex is so focused on the surreal surroundings that it takes him a moment to register that his presence has gone undetected so far. He reaches
inside his suit jacket for his father's phone. With luck, he can snap off
a few photos using the phone's camera and then turn tail and go back
from whence he came. He snaps off the first shot without incident, then
works to operate the digital zoom to get a better glimpse of Mr. Big, but
his view is obstructed by the conference room's glass enclosure. Slowly,
he maneuvers around the gangway for a better angle, taking care to minimize the noise of his footfalls. But with each step, the sound of his shoes
on the metal appears to grow louder. He prays that the height and ambient noise from all the computer and video activity will cloak the sound
of his movements.

He aims the phone again at a more promising angle. Mr. Big ac-
commodates him somewhat with a slight turn of the head, offering a
three-quarter view that is better than nothing. Once Alex is properly
zoomed in, what he sees makes complete sense.

Director Rykman is in the center of all this.

After all, the attempt on his life was made mere hours after Alex tried, and failed, to blow the whistle on Solstice in Rykman's office.

Alex takes the picture and considers taking another when he hears the click. The sound is unmistakable to anyone who watches movies or TV: the telltale *shik-shak* of a semiautomatic weapon being tromboned. Alex turns in the direction of the noise to see the man who was able to sneak up behind Alex while he was playing photographer. He has a Glock 19 in a two-handed grip and the gun is leveled directly at Alex's head. The coldness in the man's eyes confirms that he not only knows how to use the weapon but also will do so without hesitation before or remorse afterward. There's a look on his face that strongly suggests Alex's presence is the exact opposite of unexpected.

Rykman leads Alex into the conference room and closes the door. All the computer chatter and random noise from the outer room immediately disappear in the soundproof space. "Have a seat," Rykman says. Alex doesn't move. "Sit down," Rykman orders again in a more commanding tone. Alex sits. Rykman paces. Slow. Methodical. "I'm afraid I can't let you out of here at the moment, Mr. Garnett. We have a delicate operation under way."

"Orchestrating a war between the United States and Iran?"

"All wars are orchestrated, Mr. Garnett. Have no illusions about that. Even our involvement in World War Two, considered history's most noble war, came about because FDR suppressed the intel we had that the Japanese were about to attack Pearl Harbor in order to orchestrate our getting into the war."

"That conspiracy theory's been debunked. But then, I didn't come here to debate history with you, did I?"

"Why did you come here, Alex? Do you mind if I call you Alex?"

"You tried to kill me last night. Or have me killed, I guess is the more accurate way of putting it. Because I found out about Solstice."

Rykman shakes his head. "No. Because you were a rogue element in an equation I need to maintain strict control over. It was absolutely nothing personal. No one man's life, including my own, isn't expendable in this endeavor."

"Invading Iran." Alex meets Rykman's dead-eyed stare, reducing all his machinations to a pair of words, both of which drip with disapproving judgment.

"I'm not going to debate policy with you, Alex. Suffice it to say, we should have invaded Iran in 1979 when they committed an act of war and took sixty-six innocent hostages. Don't believe the rhetoric. I'm the director of the Central Intelligence Agency and I'm here to tell you that Iran has always been more dangerous than ten Iraqs or twenty Afghanistans."

"I've got no problem with us going into Iran," Alex asserts. "And maybe I don't even have a problem with assassinating Jahandar, even though we both know it's illegal." He pauses. "What I have a little bit of a problem with, however, are the murders of Jim Harling, Evelyn Moreno, Alan Miller, Brenda Zollitsch, and Leah Doyle. You've killed more Americans than Jahandar did."

Rykman's eyes blaze. Alex can see he's struck a nerve. "I told you," Rykman says, almost snarling, "no one isn't expendable. No one." Then, as if to make the point, he turns and looks out of the conference room. Alex's eyes follow and his heart skips a beat.

He sees Gerald.

The kid—and in this moment, he looks very much like a kid—is standing on the other side of the soundproof glass. He's trembling. His eyes gleam with tears threatening to spill forth. A man in a dark suit with a military bearing to match his crew cut stands behind him. Gerald's eyes find Alex's and make a silent plea. *Whatever they want you to do, whatever they want you to stop doing, please…please…just listen to them, do whatever it is they want.*

"Let him go," Alex says through clenched teeth.

Rykman just shakes his head. "Mr. Jankovick is my insurance policy."

"Against what?"

"Against you."

"Let him go and I'll keep my mouth shut."

"The book on you is that you're a better negotiator than this." Alex looks at Rykman, quizzical. "I let him go today, what, you think I can't kill him tomorrow? Or maybe you were thinking I'd just give you my word?"

"You could," Alex allows. "But there's no word you could give me that I could trust."

"Attaboy."

"I guess your only move here is to kill us both," Alex says. To his own surprise, he's not frightened. He's not sure why — maybe it's the fact that at least all the lies and uncertainties are gone — but he's grateful for the inner calm. It gives him focus. With adrenaline blazing through him, the entire world seems sharper now.

"I don't want to kill you, Alex."

Alex shoots Rykman a dagger stare. "Really?" His voice drips with incredulity. "I guess it was someone else who tried to have me killed, then."

"You've shown me quite a bit of sack and ingenuity since then," Rykman admits. "Moreover, our operation in Iran is much further along — and, therefore, in a much less vulnerable state — than it was in thirty-seven hours ago. Even if I were to let you walk out of here with my untrustworthy promise you won't come to any harm, I doubt there's much you could do to stop the wheels that are currently in motion."

Alex has to acknowledge the truth of that. Fortunately, his goals are a bit more humble than stopping an international military conflict. All his focus now is on bringing Rykman and the Overwatch to light. He wants to drag Rykman and his minions in front of the flashing cameras and omnipresent microphones of media scrutiny, senate subcommittees, and a marathon of criminal trials culminating in his lifetime imprisonment in a supermax control-unit federal prison. This much must be obvious, or maybe Rykman can just read it on his face. "And I don't think prison is in my future either, if that's what you're thinking," Rykman observes.

"Well, I'm a licensed attorney. And you might find circumstances to be a little different once someone informs you of what the laws against murder, assassination, conspiracy, and treason are."

"William Donovan was a lawyer too. Did you know that?" Alex nods, unsure of Rykman's point. He thinks of the statue of William "Wild Bill" Donovan in the lobby of the Old Headquarters Building, directly opposite the chiseled stars—currently 107—on the Memorial Wall featured in so many Hollywood movies. Donovan was considered the father of America's intelligence-gathering agency. "President Roosevelt directed Donovan—who, in addition to being a lawyer, was an army colonel at the time—to draft a plan for a national intelligence service."

"What does this have to do with anything?" Alex snaps impatiently.

"Everything" is Rykman's answer. His voice is threatening and cold. "Donovan helped create the Office of Strategic Services, the OSS, which was a precursor to the CIA. Through Donovan, the OSS crippled Nazi Germany from the inside out, ran Operation Paperclip, kicked the Japanese out of Burma..." Rykman looks at Alex to make sure he understands the magnitude of Donovan's and the OSS's accomplishments. "The OSS not only made history, Alex. It changed it." He shrugs. "But the price of success is envy. So the likes of General MacArthur and J. Edgar Hoover leveraged President Truman into signing Executive Order 9621."

Alex nods to indicate his understanding although he doesn't know what Rykman's point is. "The order dissolved the OSS. Liquidated it, essentially."

"But why would President Truman dissolve America's first intelligence-gathering agency, particularly given its enormous success during World War Two?" With this, Rykman moves to the center of the conference table and bends to twist the combination dial for the safe embedded into the tabletop. After a few spins of the dial, the metal door pops open and Rykman reaches into the table's depths and produces a single sheet of paper, yellowed with age. "Truman's signing of Executive Order 9621 made sense out of his *contemporaneous* execution of *another* order — Executive Order 9621-*X*." He holds up the weathered typewritten document, nearly seventy years old, and hands it to Alex.

Alex scans the ancient presidential order, although by now he has a good idea as to what it states. As he reads, Rykman continues, "You're looking at one of only two copies in existence. The other copy is entombed in the hollow cornerstone of the CIA's Old Headquarters Building."

Alex finishes reading and sets the paper down. He glances up to find Rykman staring straight at him, looking as if he's just laid out a royal flush, aces high. "As you said, you're a lawyer. You understand what 9621-X does, don't you? You grasp its legal import?" Alex just nods. "It reconstitutes the OSS, resurrecting it, effectively, as the Overwatch." Rykman takes the order and restores it to the safe. As he swings the door shut, he adds, "President Truman believed in an intelligence agency free of the kind of political and interagency territorial squabbles that led to the OSS's public demise. He wanted an agency that could do what it needed to do, unfettered by congressional oversight, in the interests of the United States. Bottom line, Alex, everything the Overwatch has done, everything it's doing right now…it's all legal."

TWENTY-EIGHT

Bullshit, Alex thinks. Fortunately, he still retains enough self-control not to give that thought voice. His mind spins while he struggles with the one thing he wasn't expecting. That the Overwatch and all its actions were illegal was the one thing, the *only* thing, Alex could count on. The law was always something he took for granted, a means to an end, a path to employment, yet in this case, it insidiously wormed its way into his thoughts as something more: the guiding principle, the constant star, navigating him through this entire mess. The law draws a bright line between right and wrong, and Alex had been sure he stood on the right side, looking heroically over the line at the Overwatch on the other side.

But that was never true.

The seconds drip by, molasseslike, seeming like minutes; minutes seeming like hours. If Rykman is telling the truth, then Alex is the traitor, the criminal, in this scenario. He looks over at Gerald, an unwitting pawn in the drama playing out. In that regard, the only difference between Gerald and Harling and the rest of them is that Gerald's still alive. But probably not for very much longer.

"What about murder?"

"Excuse me?" Rykman asks.

"You've racked up quite the body count. And that's just the people I know of, so I'm guessing *tip of the iceberg* is something of a massive understatement." Alex meets Rykman's gaze. "What, you assume some secret executive order gives you the authority, the right, to murder people indiscriminately?"

"It gives me the authority to act in the interests of the United States. When a *state* kills, it's not murder. It's policy."

"Sounds like a good argument for agency oversight to me."

"I'm not here to debate policy with you, Alex." Rykman's voice is dispassionate and level.

"Then why are we here? Because I've gotta tell you, if you're gonna kill me and Gerald, I'd just as soon you got on with it. I've got zero desire to be around while my country gets dragged into a war a handful of guys, or maybe just one guy, come to think of it" — he points to Rykman — "thinks is a good idea."

Then a new epiphany hits Alex. A new piece of the puzzle slides into place: "The president doesn't know about the Overwatch. Does he?"

"No oversight means no oversight. Truman never went to college. He had no command experience in the military. He knew, better than anyone, the folly of someone like him having *oversight*" — the word is slathered with contempt — "over the decisions made, deemed viable and prudent and in this country's best interests, by someone like me."

Alex has represented enough genuinely bad people in his day to know better than most the validity of the truism "Every villain is the hero of his own story." He's witnessed villains' genuine remorse too, but such regret, by its nature, always comes after the fact. In the moment, all tyrants believe themselves to be on the side of the angels. But Alex's experience is limited to criminals, street thugs, white-collar hustlers, and abusive husbands. He's never come eye to eye with a zealot, with a man who believes in the righteousness of his actions with religious fervor.

Until now.

"Like I said," Rykman remarks, "I'm not here to debate policy with you."

"Well, if you're not going to debate me and you're not gonna kill me, then what are we doing here?"

"When you found your way to the Op Center, I thought it was rather impressive. An unexpected annoyance, to be sure, but you've managed to piece together something that no one else in nearly seventy years has been able to." Rykman glances at Alex, studying his reaction. "I typically draw my personnel from the military, usually straight out of West Point or JSOC, the Joint Special Operations Command, men who know how to keep secrets."

And who follow orders without question, Alex thinks.

"It's a small pool of qualified personnel, you can imagine," Rykman continues.

Alex can't stop himself from asking, "What happens to the guys you tell about the Overwatch who turn you down?" He has a feeling he already knows the answer.

Rykman says nothing. He just offers a slight shake of the head, confirming Alex's suspicion. These failed applicants meet with accidents of the variety that befell Jim Harling. "My point being, Alex, I can't exactly put an ad in the newspaper. When I see talent — and I see talent in you — it's in my best interests, and those of the Overwatch, to act on this opportunity."

"You're offering me a job." Alex's incredulity is obvious. Rykman nods, as if he thinks giving Alex the chance to join the very organization he's trying to bring down is an excellent idea. Rykman's bearing suggests that attempting to employ a man one just tried to kill is the most sensible thing in the world. "If you can't beat 'em, join 'em," Alex comments.

"Wake up to current events, Alex. You *are* beaten. As you pointed out, my only other move here is to have you eliminated."

"What about Gerald?"

"We'll cross that bridge when we come to it. But let's focus on you for the moment." Rykman leans forward, serious as a heart attack. "Do you know what it is I'm offering you here?"

A variety of potential answers come to Alex's mind: *Damnation.*
Guilt. The opportunity to be a part of something that I know in my soul is
wrong. "Let's go out on a limb and assume that I don't," Alex ultimately
selects.

"I'm offering you the chance at something your father never had.
Access to power, the levers of power that he couldn't fathom because
he didn't even know they existed. That's *true* power, Alex. Power that
doesn't require legal authority or public awareness. Power on its own
terms, derived from its own manifest destiny."

Taking in Rykman in this moment, feeling the man's fervor, Alex
realizes that he's witnessing something few people get the chance to
see: the true William Rykman — the king who sits atop a throne no
one knows about, drunk with his own power. Yet although Rykman
stands before him, stripped naked, his most private truths revealed, the
observational door swings both ways. Rykman has read the CIA's psychological workup that was done when Alex joined the Agency. He
knows exactly the right buttons to push. "Your entire life, you've been
an ant, scurrying to find a little patch of sunlight outside your father's
looming shadow." Perhaps realizing he's coming on too strong, Rykman
quiets, adopting a more Zen-like tone. "This, Alex, is your chance. To
be your own man with your own achievements." Then the Zen devolves
into something that sounds almost like apathy. "I'll be very interested to
see whether you take it."

Alex nods. He looks to Gerald, who's still standing outside the glass
enclosure of the conference room, still looking terrified. Then he looks
past Gerald, to the facility surrounding them. The entire area hums with
more than electrical power. Alex thinks he can almost feel the global
power Rykman's describing and offering. The power to literally make
history. All the more tempting is the fact that it's legal.

"It's funny you should mention my father," Alex says, speaking slowly.
"We get our values from our parents, don't we? It probably shouldn't be
surprising that the law is the way I determine the difference between right

and wrong. I learned that from my dad." He pauses. "You're right. My whole life's been about trying to get out of my father's shadow, be my own man. Well, how about this?" He looks at Rykman, eyes blazing with a passion he's never felt before. "My father was wrong. Just because something is legal doesn't make it moral. Just because you have the authority doesn't mean you have the right." Rykman stares back in disbelief. Alex imagines he himself must have had a similar look on his face when Rykman was taking him through the Overwatch's history, and he finds a sliver of the moment to enjoy the irony. Alex stands from the table, rising to meet Rykman face to face. "You're committing murder and treason, and a thousand secret executive orders wouldn't make it otherwise."

Rykman considers Alex for a long moment. "All right," he says. His voice is raised barely above a whisper. "I respect that. Even though it means I can't let you leave this building alive."

◆

Alex leans forward and meets Rykman's ferocious stare with a fury of his own. "If you've got so much fucking legal authority," he spits, "why do you need to kill me to shut me up?"

"OpSec" is Rykman's cold reply. Operational security.

"Bullshit."

"The Overwatch is a black agency. Our power would be diminished if we had to operate in the light."

"Well, I certainly fucking hope so."

Rykman shakes his head, confused. What the hell is that supposed to mean? But Alex offers no explanation, at least not with words. Instead, he leaps across the table and tackles Rykman. On some level, he knows this is suicide. Even if Rykman is unarmed, Alex is certain the same can't be said for the Overwatch personnel outside, including the one guarding Gerald. But surprise is his only advantage. Acting unexpectedly is his only weapon.

Rykman roars with indignation as Alex feels himself collide with the older, bigger man. The momentum of the tackle sends them both tumbling backward, crashing through the glass wall of the conference room. They fall at Gerald's feet as glass rains to the floor all around them. The man guarding Gerald reaches for his weapon.

Alex acts on instinct. He's eye level with the guard's ankle and his first impulse is to yank it toward him, so that's what he does. The man topples like a redwood. Gerald, sensing this is his window, elbows the man, driving his arm straight into the asshole's jaw. By this point, his Glock 23 has been liberated from its holster, but the tumult frustrates the guard's grip, and as he falls back, the gun leaps out of his hand and clatters to the floor.

Rykman works to scramble to his feet, but Alex surprises him with a kick to his gut that buys him a few more precious seconds. He feels something whiz past his ear. Only then does he realize that the other Overwatch personnel are shooting at him. He remains focused on the wayward Glock, resting motionless on the floor like a promise.

Gerald, also acting on instinct, kicks the Glock in Alex's direction. The firearm skitters across the facility's concrete floor. There's a millisecond where Rykman catches a glimpse of the gun and reaches for it just as Alex does. Alex's head collides with Rykman's shoulder on their mutual descent, but Alex has a fraction of a second's head start. His fingers find purchase on the weapon and manage to curl around it as he brings it up in the direction of Rykman's head.

Alex hears a loud gunshot. But it's not from the Glock, it's just the latest in a fusillade of weapon fire. Somehow still alive, Alex shoves the business end of the gun against Rykman's temple and yells as loud as he's capable, "Weapons down!" This stops the shooting, but Alex's whipping glance around the space reveals a room still full of armed men. "Put your guns on the fucking floor!" he screams. Without waiting to see if they'll comply, he points the Glock downward. He's never held a Glock before, much less fired one, and he silently prays its previous owner disengaged the safety when he unholstered the weapon. Apparently he did, because the .40-caliber gun belches forth a bullet. The Glock 23 has a short-recoil design that keeps it from flying out of Alex's inexperienced fist. The report resounds loudly in the tense chamber, and the noise is followed quickly by Rykman's voice. Even a military man of Rykman's training and fortitude isn't immune from yelling in agony as a bullet rips through his thigh.

Just as quickly, Alex brings the Glock back up so that it's level with the phalanx of men he's trying to keep at bay. "Next one goes in this motherfucker's head!" he yells. Although Alex has no experience with armed standoffs and hostage crises, the situation is merely a negotiation in its purest form, and negotiating is something that's virtually second nature to him. It doesn't hurt that he was a participant in a not dissimilar standoff fairly recently.

Alex looks around the room, at the men and all the guns they still have trained on him. They haven't shot him dead yet, however.

Next to him, Rykman writhes in the grip of Alex's free hand and winces in a special kind of pain. His blood leaks profusely into his pant leg and onto the concrete beneath his feet. Alex is concerned Rykman will bark the order to end him and is surprised when the command doesn't come. Maybe William Rykman isn't quite as ready to die for his cause as he appears.

"Clear the room," Alex says. His voice is quieter now but his tone is no less commanding. "Clear the room and lock the door." He's assuming there's only one point of ingress and egress to the facility. "Do it now."

Alex sees some of the men look for an answer in Rykman's eyes. "Go ahead, Donovan," Rykman says. "There's nothing these pricks can do to stop what's going to happen." As Donovan reluctantly leads the Overwatch personnel out of the Operations Center, Alex prays this is not the case. Otherwise, thousands of people — potentially hundreds of thousands, possibly millions — will die. And the body count will start with him and Gerald.

TWENTY-NINE

ALEX HEARS the heavy metal door to the Op Center slam shut with pneumatic precision. He estimates that he and Gerald have about five minutes to do whatever it is they're going to do. After that, he fully expects to die badly. He releases Rykman to one of the nearby chairs, the man gripping his wounded leg. "Give me that," Rykman growls, pointing to an extension cord on one of the workstations. Alex hesitates, and Rykman adds, "For a tourniquet, you little shit. Or you might as well just shoot me in the head."

Alex just nods and tosses the cord over. Rykman catches it and starts tying it around his thigh, above the bullet wound, to stanch the prodigious bleeding. As Rykman does his work, Alex whips back around toward Gerald, who's staring at him in wide-eyed amazement.

"Holy fuck, dude. You're like a fucking badass."

"Gerald, you've got to find a way to contact the White House."

"What?" Gerald is paralyzed.

"Focus," Alex snaps. "These guys have Tap-Dance encryption capabilities." At least, that's what Katherine McCallum claimed, and he hopes she's right. "They mimic the White House's systems. It's one of the tools these assholes have to manipulate the military into doing their bidding."

"You don't know what you're talking about." Rykman grunts. Rage fills every pore on his face. But instead of dissuading Alex, this tell convinces him he's on the right track.

"Do it, Gerald," Alex orders. "Get on their system."

"And do what?"

"I want to talk to the White House."

Gerald's eyes shoot even wider and Alex is relieved to see ambition replace shock on Gerald's face. This would be the mother of all computer hacks. The kid actually breaks into a grin. The hunter has the scent. He moves with purpose to the closest workstation. "I'm going to tear your skin off in strips," Rykman hisses. Gerald freezes.

"Don't listen to him, Gerald," Alex advises, walking over to Rykman. "Get to work. We don't have a lot of time."

"Damn right, you don't," Rykman spits. "My men are armoring up right now. Kevlar. High-powered rifles. You fucks won't last the next ten minutes."

Out of the corner of his eye, Alex sees Gerald hesitate, struck motionless by Rykman's threat. "Shut up," he orders Rykman, and backhands his face with the Glock, hoping to knock the bastard unconscious. But all it does is make Rykman grunt in pain and bleed from his mouth. The man's about to bark some epithet, but Alex adjusts his grip on the Glock — holding it by the barrel — and swings the butt of the synthetic polymer-coated gun into the back of Rykman's head. Alex has seen this done in the movies and been told that it works because the back of the skull is where the brainstem is.

This time the blow does its job and Rykman slumps out of the chair, unconscious.

"Seriously, dude, badass," Gerald repeats.

"Just really pissed off. Where are we?"

Gerald is in his element, working tech magic on the keyboard. He's thrown his work up onto the room's big screen, and the massive plasma updates with new overlapping windows and cascading lines of impenetrable computer code. "There isn't any outflow from this facility to the

White House's Situation Room," he says as he types. "Basically, these guys can see the White House, but the White House can't see them."

This much is consistent with what Alex witnessed earlier. "Gerald, you've got to—"

"I've got a work-around," Gerald interrupts. His fingers don't leave the keyboard as he types furiously. "Their Tap-Dance connection goes to the Pentagon, however, like you said. And the Pentagon can talk to the White House. They've been talking to them all night, in fact. So basically, what I'm trying to do is jump on to the DOD's connection through what they're using here." Gerald looks like a kid in a candy store on Christmas morning. "I'm hacking the fucking Pentagon, dude. I'm ascending Mount Everest."

Alex breathes a sigh of relief and shoots another look toward Rykman. The asshole stirs but remains unconscious for now. "Ascend faster."

"Alex," Gerald says, "I think I've got it. Get ready to talk to the president."

The president is in the eighteenth month of his administration, and the tension in the White House Situation Room has never been higher. It feels like he's spent a lifetime in the room, but it's been only a few hours. When he walked in, he was greeted by a handful of people. Now, the three-hundred-square-foot space is standing room only, packed with military, diplomatic, and political personnel of every stripe. Every man and woman is a trained professional. They all go about their business with stoic efficiency, but the tempo of their work and the urgency on their faces speaks to how tense they feel, a testament to how close the United States is to the brink of war.

In the past three hours, two of Israel's F-14D Baz fighter jets— American-made Boeing F-15 Strike Eagles—have been shot down by Iran's newly completed Bavar-373 long-range air defense system. In retaliation, the Kheil HaAvir — the Israeli air corps — launched bombing raids on a heavy-water plant in Khondab and a missile research and development facility in Khuzistan. These air strikes involved flying sorties through the airspace of Syria, Jordan, Iraq, and Saudi Arabia — none of which are known for their warm feelings toward the State of Israel. In the White House Situation Room, the director of national intelligence briefs the president on the gearing up of the militaries of all four countries. It's long been an axiom of American foreign policy that were Israel to make a move on any of its neighbors, reflexively or preemptively, it would be the tipping domino that would lead to the collapse of the entire fragile region.

The president came into office hell-bent on avoiding the third rail of diplomacy that was the Middle East. He'd watched his predecessor get mired in two separate wars there — conflicts that did nothing other than cost American lives and create fresh breeding grounds for new terrorists who would cost even more American lives. No, he vowed, he wouldn't get sucked into a war that would make the wars in Iraq and Afghanistan look like petty dustups. But now, as dawn breaks over Washington, DC, he finds himself on the cusp of a moment that threatens to define his presidency. The momentum that Rykman set in motion — indeed, has been counting on — is gathering speed. With casualties on both sides, it will become exponentially harder to get control of this situation.

"What pressure can we bring to bear — economic, diplomatic, political, it doesn't matter to me — to keep Israel's and Iran's neighbors from getting involved here?" he asks. The question is posed to the director of national intelligence, but it's actually for the entire room.

"We're talking to Syria, Iraq, Jordan, and Saudi Arabia through back channels, but the truth is, Syria's in the same boat as we are," the secretary of state answers.

"Meaning that their alliance with Iran will obligate them to come to Iran's aid if Israel's counterattacks reach a crisis point," the president says.

"Yes, sir."

"And the Saudis are going to feel the heat once this starts to look like Israel is killing Arabs," SecDef chimes in with characteristic bluntness.

The occupants of the room soberly nod in agreement as the stark reality of what they're facing sinks in. To be sure, this is not the first time the world has faced the specter of a Third World War. Nor is it the first time such a threat has come from the Middle East. It isn't unprecedented for the United States to feel the need to apply carrot-and-stick pressure to stay Israel's retaliatory hand, as President George H. W. Bush and his cabinet did when Iraq lofted SCUD missiles toward Israel during the First Gulf War. The world waited to see whether Israel would respond in kind, waited with the same breathless, fearful anticipation that fills the White House Situation Room at this moment.

"What are we doing to keep Israel from making a counterstrike if this thing reaches a tipping point?" the president asks, recalling the forty-first president's efforts.

The secretary of state leans forward to answer. "The usual entreaties, Mr. President. But this is a very different situation from Desert Storm."

The president nods. He certainly didn't need to be told that. But still…"You need to get on a plane. Right now. Do whatever you have to, promise whatever you have to…threaten, I don't care, but do whatever you can to keep Israel from escalating this thing."

The secretary of state nods. "Given what Iran is doing, Mr. President…it may not be up to Israel."

Just then, the plasma monitor at the head of the room flickers. What was previously a hard-line video feed to the Pentagon is replaced with a jumble of pixelated static. The White House chief of staff orders an aide to see what he can do about restoring communications.

Then Alex Garnett's voice fills the room.

On the large screen in the Overwatch Op Center, Alex watches as the president, his cabinet members, and his staff react to his unexpected and disembodied voice. "Mr. President, my name is Alex Garnett. I'm an attorney for the Office of General Counsel for the CIA." Alex can see a trio of aides rush out of the room, no doubt hell-bent on figuring out what the hell was going on, but he stays focused on the president, who looks uncharacteristically confused. He leans forward and asks a question, but whatever he's saying is lost in a cloud of garbled static. "Gerald—"

"Something's wonky with the signal," Gerald reports. "Remember, this is a work-around and—"

"I need to hear him, Gerald," Alex snaps.

"I'm *trying*."

Alex lowers himself to the microphone Gerald jury-rigged and speaks with as much command as he can muster. "Mr. President, Iran and Israel have been manipulated into a conflict with each other." Onscreen, the president furrows his brow. This confirms that although Alex can't hear the president, the president can hear him. And although Alex can't understand the president's garbled response, the man's incredulous expression screams that he finds what Alex is saying preposterous. "I know how this sounds, Mr. President. But Ayatollah Jahandar's death was an assassination. He was murdered with a weaponized strain of swine flu."

Alex watches the video feed as the White House Situation Room explodes, everyone talking at once, stunned expressions and wild gesticulations. Through it all, the president stays calm, though his face says he remains highly suspicious. Alex presses on. "I believe Iran is under the impression that Jahandar's death was orchestrated by the Israelis." This is conjecture on Alex's part, but it seems reasonable. Jahandar's death and Iran's military aggression are no coincidence. "But it wasn't, sir. *We* killed Jahandar." The static-filled audio feed from the White House grows louder as everyone in the Situation Room talks over one another. But then Alex loses visual. A uniformed navy officer strides into the room and beelines for the video-conference camera. Within seconds, the man's ministrations to the camera—no doubt trying to figure out how the secure connection to the Pentagon has been compromised—completely blocks Alex's view.

"I'm standing in a CIA facility at this very moment." This last part is, if not an outright lie, a severe stretching of the truth, but Alex has a high enough mountain to climb. One step at a time. "Mr. President, this facility will prove to you beyond all reasonable doubt that everything I'm telling you is true." Then he turns to Gerald. "Can you send them our location or something?"

Gerald, still hard at work at the computer terminal, shakes his head. "We're too far underground. I can't get a cell signal, so I can't get a GPS location on my phone." He works the computer for a few seconds—his fingers flying across the keyboard—and adds, "I'm trying to send them a data packet instead. Hopefully, they can trace us through the IPX they're using here."

Alex doesn't know what an IPX is but Gerald's use of the word *hopefully* is what concerns him. Hope is something he has in very short supply. The other thing he lacks is time. To his right, Rykman stirs, threatening to shake off the grip of unconsciousness. Alex's voice finds a new level of urgency as he returns his attention to the microphone. "Mr. President, this facility is an underground bunker about fifteen miles from CIA headquarters at Langley. But of greater concern is what's going on in the Middle East. Sir, Iran needs to know it is taking action based on *fabricated* intelligence."

Suddenly, Alex's entire world goes white. Someone shoves white-hot needles into his ears. The room around him swims, rotating off its axis, as his inner ear struggles to regain equilibrium. He's confused, deaf, blind, and disoriented. His hands shoot out in front of him in a vain effort to quiet the vertigo seizing him. It's all he can do to stand up, as his ears report an incessant high-pitched whine.

The M84 stun grenade is little more than a magnesium-and-ammonium-nitrate pyrotechnic charge encased in a thin aluminum housing within a perforated cast-steel body. When detonated, the charge produces what's called a subsonic deflagration. But the grenade's nickname — "flash-bang" — is far more descriptive of its capabilities. The flash is brighter than six million candelas. The bang is louder than a hundred and seventy decibels. The flash ignites all the photoreceptor cells in Alex's eyes, rendering him effectively blind. Normal sight will return to him in five seconds, but the stun grenade is merely the opening salvo in this attack.

The tear-gas canisters come next. If Alex weren't deaf, he'd hear them clattering their way down the Op Center's metal staircase en route to the floor, spraying phenacyl chloride. His hands reflexively shoot up to wipe tears and gas from his eyes. He staggers in Gerald's direction.

The realization that Rykman is not where he used to be comes two seconds too late.

Without warning, Alex is slammed into one of the Op Center's workstations. A kidney protests in searing pain as Rykman delivers a solid jab into it. The DCIA throws a flurry of punches, yelling a variety of obscenities. Alex kicks his foot forward to catch an advancing Rykman in the chest, buying himself three seconds to look over at Gerald, bending over and coughing violently.

A gunshot. Gerald snaps back. He flies toward the floor, leaving behind a comet trail of red mist. He lands on the concrete with a sickening thud, a wet slap as if his body were nothing more than a sack of raw meat.

Alex doesn't have a millisecond to react to the horror of what he's just witnessed because this first volley is followed by a series of gunshots. He feels bullets surge past him and is seized with violent clarity: He needs to get close to Rykman. The attack is the work of Rykman's men. They retreated only to take up the arms they're now using to try to kill him. The only chance Alex has of surviving the next sixty seconds is if he gets close enough to Rykman that the Overwatch personnel won't risk a shot for fear of hitting their boss. With every ounce of strength he possesses, Alex launches himself against Rykman and the two men tumble to the floor like clumsy lovers.

Rykman lands on top and presses all of his considerable weight — one hundred and seventy-five pounds, most of it muscle — down on Alex. Alex tries to fight back but finds himself gasping for air. Rykman removed the makeshift tourniquet from his thigh and is now repurposing the cord as a garrote, tightening it around Alex's throat. Alex's eyes bulge. His lungs scream for air. His jaw is open wide, but he can't draw a breath. All he can see is Rykman's wild eyes and clenched teeth. It's a terrifying sight — not one of rage or vengeance, but of raw homicidal intent. Then this image — so vivid only milliseconds ago — starts to lose color. Everything around him is bathed in a ruddy gray. His hands flail at Rykman's eyes in a last-ditch effort at survival, but they miss their intended target. A realization begins to overwhelm him that this is how he's going to die.

THIRTY

HE'S A smart little shit, Tyler Donovan thinks as he looks down the Schmidt and Bender 3–12x50 Police Marksman II LP scope of his M40 sniper rifle. From his vantage point atop the stairs looking down on the Op Center, he has a clean shot at Alex. Or he would if the bastard hadn't been smart enough to get within inches of Director Rykman. Or maybe the lawyer isn't smart so much as lucky. Just as he'd been lucky back in that parking garage. Donovan's not an accomplished marksman by any measure, but he'll be damned if he's going to let Alex slither out of his gun sights again. Clouded by his own resolve, Donovan doesn't think to let Rykman finish choking the life out of Alex. He wants the satisfaction of ending this asshole himself. Alex's proximity to Rykman complicates matters, sure. Is it as clean a shot as he'd like? No. But circumstances in combat are rarely ideal and the cloud of tear gas is dissipating rapidly. Looking at Alex's head framed in the illuminated reticle of his scope, Donovan is confident he can make this shot without striking his boss.

◆

Through the literal fog of the clearing tear gas and the figurative one of bloodcurdling rage, William Rykman has never felt so satisfied. He's about to crush the threat Alex poses as firmly as he's crushing his windpipe. Before Donovan and his men's counterassault, Rykman had been stirring back to consciousness. He'd heard enough of Alex's conversation with the White House Situation Room to reason that the wretched little computer geek figured out a way for Alex to communicate with the president. It seems like Alex got out enough information to compromise the Overwatch. But containment will be tomorrow's problem. There are numerous options at Rykman's disposal for dealing with this kind of breach in operational security. They range from classic plausible deniability to the extreme step of bringing the president into the fold of secrecy. And if the president won't recognize the necessity of the Overwatch's patriotic mandate, well, there is an even more extreme step available.

For the moment, the only person Rykman is going to kill is Alex Garnett. The little shit's eyes are beginning to roll up to the back of his head, exposing a white that bespeaks imminent death.

❖

Tyler Donovan's index finger curls around the trigger of his M40 and begins to apply the four pounds of pressure that will send a single 7.62x51mm NATO round into Alex's head at the speed of 2,550 feet per second. Alex won't feel anything. He'll be alive one moment, dead the next. Like throwing a light switch.

❖

There are no words for Alex's last conscious thought. The instinct that causes his fingers to jut out and dig into Rykman's thigh is purely survival. It takes two beats of his heart—an eternity, given the circumstances—for Alex's thumb to find its target. But fortunately, Rykman's bullet wound is right where he remembers it being.

The reflexive howl of agony is its own reward. Alex might die, but he's not going gently into that good night. *No fucking way.*

◆

Through his scope, Donovan sees his boss snap his head back. The man's in obvious pain, but the action has the benefit of clearing Rykman's head from Donovan's shot. A sniper rifle does not a sniper make, however. Donovan may have the equipment, but he lacks the training. It takes two full seconds for him to recognize that his shot is pristine and pull the M40's trigger. In that interval, Alex reaches up and yanks Rykman downward, intending to head-butt him, but the maneuver pays a much more valuable dividend.

The rifle cracks with a commanding report. The top of Rykman's head is ripped off his skull, like the lid on a can of dog food peeling back. Alex is hit in the face with a spray of blood and tissue. He doesn't have time to think about this now. He's too busy barrel-rolling away from Rykman's corpse. His attacker isn't limited to a single bullet, and therefore, Alex is still facing the threat of death.

He comes up from the roll and looks around. The first thing he sees with any clarity since the flash-bang did its work is a phalanx of Overwatch personnel arrayed against him. Three men spill down the metal staircase clutching semiautomatic handguns. Another man at the top of the stairs holds some kind of rifle. Alex ducks for cover before the shot is taken. A computer monitor explodes directly behind him. As he finds with all of his victories, the relief of the moment is short-lived. The trio of Overwatch agents surrounds him, and he's under no illusion that they plan to take him alive.

"Freeze!" It's a very loud bellow, but strangely, it doesn't seem to come from any of the men. "Weapons down!" This is also odd. Alex is unarmed. "Drop 'em!" the voice continues. "Drop 'em now!"

Alex stares at the three men in total confusion. Who's talking? And how can he drop a weapon he doesn't possess? The surreal moment lasts for a few seconds as the three men slowly lower their guns to the concrete floor. To say this is unexpected is a massive understatement, but Alex doesn't have time to process it. A new group of men — a second group? Alex can't be sure — swarm the area. They all have guns of their own, and they wear the dark green suits of the Agency's security protective service. "Down on the floor!" one of them barks. "Down on the floor!" Alex begins to raise his hands in surrender. He doesn't want to have survived the past ten minutes only to be shot by his own cavalry.

EPILOGUE

"THIS ISN'T a negotiation," the president of the United States says. "There has already been too much loss and too much bloodshed on both sides of this conflict." This is true. In the past thirty-six hours, the Israeli and Iranian militaries have inflicted a lot of damage on each other. The casualties won't be fully known for another three weeks, but the CIA estimates that they number in the thousands. It's only by dint of the work of the State Department and the presence of the *John C. Stennis* in the Persian Gulf that the United States has been able to keep Iran's allies from entering the fight. If they had, or if Iran's ability to project power in the region through means other than its air force and Mersad missile system had been more effective, the death toll would have been worse. Far worse. "In fact, sir, the CIA informs me that yesterday Iran attempted a nuclear attack on Israel by flying a nuclear warhead on a MiG into Israel's airspace."

"That's a very dangerous accusation, Mr. President," the State Department official says, translating for the newly elected supreme leader of Iran on the other end of the phone. "If there were any merit to it, then I imagine that Israel would be sitting underneath a mushroom cloud." Both men know why it isn't: the bomb failed to detonate. Neither, however, knows the reason why. The knowledge that the nuke would most likely fail to work was known to only two men, both recently dead.

"As I said, sir, I'm not on this call to negotiate with you. Nor am I interested in dissuading you of truths we both know. Among those truths is the fact that the Israelis had no part in, or responsibility for, your predecessor's unfortunate death."

"Or so you have claimed," the translator says for Namdar. "But you have offered no proof of this either."

"Ayatollah Namdar," the president says, clutching the phone receiver tight, "believe me when I tell you that any such proof would include evidence of Iran's culpability in the deaths of six Americans." He doesn't bother to specify that the six Americans he's referring to are the six Overwatch agents held hostage and murdered during an ill-fated rescue attempt by the U.S. Special Forces. Nor does he volunteer that he knows about the hostages thanks to Tyler Donovan's detailed account of the Overwatch's activities. His only concern at the moment is making clear to Namdar that Iran is engaging in a game of diplomatic brinksmanship: to exonerate Israel, the United States is willing to admit the existence of Solstice, but it will also place the loss of six American lives on Iran's doorstep in the bargain. "I might also remind you, sir, of America's military capabilities thanks to the presence of a carrier strike group in the Persian Gulf and our ability to rapidly redeploy our troops in Iraq and Afghanistan."

"Are you threatening military action against my country, Mr. President?" the translator asks on Namdar's behalf.

The American president's reply is quick. "I'm expressing my fervent hope it won't come to that."

There is a long pause on the line. Finally, the president hears a flood of Farsi and the translator says, "My predecessor did many things right, Mr. President. He also left room for much improvement. One of those areas is the relationship between our two countries. It is my hope that my election as supreme leader will mark a new chapter in the relationship between our two nations. The easing of sanctions, for example."

The president looks up at the roomful of staff and cabinet members looking on. It's obvious to everyone that Namdar has offered a way out of the present conflict. And it's equally clear that the president is going to take it. "I agree that would be an appropriate way to signal an evolution of our relationship, Ayatollah." He waits for a few seconds before adding, "Though obviously we could not contemplate any such step while your country is on a war footing with one of our closest allies."

A long silence from the Iranian end of the line. Finally, the translator speaks up. "As you said, Mr. President, perhaps there has already been enough bloodshed."

The president smiles and exhales. He releases a grip on the telephone that he hadn't realized was so tight until this moment. "Our State Department will be in touch with your diplomats. Thank you, sir." With that, he sets the receiver down, and the room explodes in applause.

◆

The Learjet 85's twin Pratt and Whitney PW307B engines spin up as the jet taxis down the runway. The plane's lone passenger settles in for his transcontinental flight. As he watches the terminal of Ronald Reagan Washington National Airport recede in the distance, he reflects on the events of the past two days. William Rykman is dead. Tyler Donovan and the other Overwatch personnel are being held in an FBI safe house in McLean, Virginia, according to his sources in the current administration. But he has no concern about exposure. Donovan and the others have no idea of his existence. That was a secret his partner, friend, and coconspirator William Rykman took to his grave. The only person who can offer any kind of meaningful operational intelligence is lying in the morgue at Georgetown University Hospital. The CIA and the president's administration will handle containment for him. The existence of a rogue or shadow intelligence agency is a secret the government will go to extraordinary lengths to protect. This is particularly true given the delicate cease-fire the president recently negotiated with Iran.

This is not to say that the Overwatch hasn't been dealt a crippling blow. Its infrastructure has been exposed and, along with it, a treasure trove of intelligence that highly trusted analysts within the CIA will be combing through for years. Then again, the discoveries they make will be reburied for fear of causing embarrassment. Fallout will be reduced to whispers in the corridors of power, past and present, as word reaches the president and his successors that they weren't always as in control of world events as they'd thought. There will be questions and inquiries and threats of FBI investigations and congressional hearings, but it will all amount to nothing. As far as anyone knows, the Overwatch died with William Rykman. Sure, its operatives remain in place throughout the world, but apart from the men currently in federal custody, they are all freelancers. For all the operatives know, they work for a bank account.

He still has access to the levers of power that chart the course of the world. Without the Overwatch, he'll just have to lean against those levers a bit harder. It's not as though he isn't willing to or doesn't know how. But right now his primary concern is leaving America behind. As the East Coast becomes obscured by the clouds at thirty thousand feet and the steward brings him a glass of red wine, he thinks about how nice it is to be heading home.

Even paranoids have enemies, Alex thinks as he enters Gerald's room. Gerald had been almost prescient in his anxiety, as if he'd known the situation Alex had dragged him into would end badly for him. But *badly* is relative. Getting shot in the shoulder is still preferable to being dead.

Barring some unexpected complication, Gerald will get discharged from the hospital today. He sits up in his bed as Alex comes in and looks genuinely happy to see his friend. Are they friends? Gerald hadn't given it much thought until now, but he supposes that they are. What else do you call two people who have been through so much with and for each other? And isn't paying a visit to a hospital room something friends do?

"How's it going?" Alex asks. There's a free chair on the side of the bed, but Alex remains standing.

"Shoulder's stiff. Docs say it could be like that for a little while. Beats the alternative, though."

"I'm thinking you owe me one hell of an 'I told you so.'"

"Getting shot wasn't what I was so worried about. To be honest with you, dude, if I'd known that was on the menu, I would've told you to go find yourself another computer jock."

Alex smiles. "Fair enough."

"FBI's been by plenty. And CIA security," Gerald says, changing the topic.

"I just got out of a marathon session of interrogations and interviews myself," Alex says. "Otherwise, I would've been here sooner."

"I expected them not to believe a friggin' word I said, but they just took everything down, no trip to the funny farm."

Alex thinks of Katherine McCallum. With luck, Gerald's not the only person getting discharged from a hospital today. In the midst of all the questioning he'd undergone at the hands of the CIA and FBI, much of which took place with him strapped to a polygraph, he'd insisted they look into her situation and get her out of that mental hospital posthaste. The alternative, Alex had threatened, was Alex marching into open court with a petition for a writ of habeas corpus to get her released. Not unexpectedly, this had worked quite well.

"So what's gonna happen now?" Gerald asks. "One of the docs here told me you got arrested for Leah's, y'know…" His voice trails off. Unable to say *murder.*

"The FBI is getting into it since she's a federal employee. *Was,*" Alex corrects himself. "But one of Rykman's lackeys is cooperating, they tell me. He's the one who put her…remains in the trunk of my car. His testimony should exonerate me."

"What about the rest of this shit-burger? These guys were operating under the CIA's nose. I mean this literally."

"It was actually a few miles underground, away from Agency HQ. But I take your point." Alex sighs, contemplating the long road that lies ahead for them. "We'll both be enjoying a closed-door congressional hearing or two, I suspect. The administration is treading very carefully here. They need to put their arms around this, but at the same time, there are too many political and diplomatic ramifications if it all gets out in the open."

Gerald's head bobs in agreement. "Meet the new boss, same as the old boss."

"Speaking of, you've still got your job at the CIA if you want it. In fact, they tell me that you're gonna be getting the Intelligence Medal of Merit." This is the CIA's award for "the performance of especially meritorious service or for an act or achievement conspicuously above normal duties which has contributed significantly to the mission of the Agency."

"I'm probably lucky to still have a job," Gerald allows. "What about you?"

That's a question Alex doesn't know the answer to. "I'm supposed to sit down with Bryson tomorrow to discuss my options."

Gerald shakes his head. "I thought he was in cahoots with Rykman. He had computer access to that Overwatch directory," he reminds Alex.

"I told Security that. Apparently, Rykman co-opted the high-level access of a lot of people so nothing could get traced back to him." Alex thinks primarily of Leah Doyle. Rykman used her security code to move the money from the black budget into Solstice. Leah said as much when Alex confronted her, but Alex had to admit that her suspicions had been correct.

"Okay, so if Bryson says he wants to take you back, you gonna do it?"

Alex turns to the window and remembers when Rykman invited him to join the Overwatch rather than destroy it. The choice had been between what was legal and what was right, and it made Alex aware of the gulf between law and justice. He wants to work to narrow that gap, to help the law do a better job of achieving justice. Can he still do that at the CIA? He isn't sure.

For one thing, it's hard to make career decisions while the rest of his life is in such upheaval. He'd returned home from his inquisition at the hands of the CIA and FBI to discover that Grace had efficiently boxed up all her belongings and moved out. She'd left behind a note full of explanations and apologies and regrets, but the words never coalesced into anything more than written static. It is so strange. Last week, Alex had a job and a fiancée. How quickly life turns.

Despite it all, he's never felt more serene. This is a paradox it will take Alex months to unravel, but when he does, he'll realize it hearkens back to that defining moment in the Overwatch Operations Center. His entire life has been spent in the emotional and professional shadow cast by his father. He believed the only way out of that darkness was to eclipse his father's achievements. And in Rykman's offer, he discovered a way to do that, to have access to power his father never had. When faced with it, he realized he didn't need it after all. And the epiphany was like unlocking a thousand shackles. He could finally be his own man.

"Are you gonna come back to CIA or not?"

Alex turns away from the window and looks at Gerald. He smiles with a lightness of spirit Gerald hasn't seen from him before.

And he shrugs.

◈

A coffee place struck Alex as an odd choice for this not-quite reunion, but at least the venue is neutral ground. Sitting alone with his espresso, he thinks back upon the length and breadth of their relationship. He wonders what went so wrong and when. There was love once, and genuine affection. But relationships have a way of dying on the vine. Although Alex cast himself as the aggrieved party, he knows there's really no one to blame. These things happen, and if there is any chance of reconciliation, the healing has to begin with letting go of the blame.

He feels the presence of someone else at the table and stands. "This is a nice place," he allows. "Good idea."

"Yeah, I like it," comes the reply.

They sit down and for a moment neither is sure what to say. Alex swivels his small cup of espresso one rotation before venturing, "I'm glad we're doing this. I want to fix things between us."

"So am I. So do I." A pause. "I've been thinking about it. A lot, in fact. I'm really sorry. This all started with me. I think I wasn't — I think I didn't rise to the challenges of the moment. I think I was weak."

"Thanks. Seriously," Alex says. "But I've been thinking about it too. And we shouldn't do the blame thing. We should just, y'know, move forward."

"I'd like that. I'd like that very much." And for the first time since childhood, Alex sees his father smile.

ACKNOWLEDGMENTS

Writing a novel, particularly a first novel, takes a village. In writing this one, I am indebted to a veritable city. My thanks to them cannot be conveyed properly—and are presented here in chronological order of their assistance.

It all began with my then-manager, now sister-in-law, and sister-in-fact, Lisa Guggenheim (née Lisa Santos), who kicked this whole thing off when she called to tell me that "the CIA has a legal department," knowing all the while that she was planting the seed for this novel. Her advice, feedback, and help throughout the development of the story were invaluable. Bottom line, there would be no *Overwatch* without Lisa.

Nor would *Overwatch* have taken the form of a novel had my friend and not-nearly-frequently-enough collaborator Michael Green not advised me to spend some unexpected free time between gigs on "something [you] wouldn't ordinarily write."

Lindsey Allen, Emily Silver, and Alisa Tager were the first people to read the manuscript in its zygote stage. Their thoughts were helpful, and their encouragement to keep going was critical.

Ian Tuttle was kind enough to provide me with a tour of CIA headquarters and to not have me arrested for loitering in my car for twenty minutes in the visitors lot afterwards, scribbling down all the information I had stored in my short-term memory. (No cell phones or cameras are permitted within Agency HQ.)

As she so often has on other projects, Louise Byer at Westlaw buttressed my atrophying legal research skills with relevant and useful case law.

Erin Malone, my book agent at WME, uttered the words every author longs to hear from their agent: "Yeah, I can sell this." More important, however, she did.

Joshua Kendall, Wes Miller, Tracy Roe, Michael Noon, and Garrett McGrath at Little, Brown and Company were more than editors, they were educators, teaching me things about prose writing I'm embarrassed not to have known already.

My assistant, Grace DeVoll, served as a *de facto* additional editor. Her sharp eye and sharper pen helped take the manuscript to much loftier heights. She also kindly lent her name to Alex's fiancée, taught me that there are two e's in "fiancée," and finally convinced me to use the Oxford comma. (Happy now, Grace?)

I'm breaking with chronological order to save a special thanks for last. Peter M. (he's asked that I not use his real name) is a former nonofficial-cover officer for the CIA and wrote up extensive notes on the completed manuscript, providing much of the authenticity of the Agency and its inner workings. My artistic license is freshly laminated, however, and I have occasionally strayed from his good counsel, primarily in the service of getting Alex back into headquarters after having been fired.

About the Author

Marc Guggenheim practiced law at one of Boston's most prestigious firms before leaving to pursue his dream of becoming a writer. In the past decade, he's written for television (*The Practice, Law & Order, Brothers & Sisters, Arrow*), feature films (*Green Lantern, Percy Jackson: Sea of Monsters*), graphic novels (*Spider-Man, Wolverine, The Flash*), and video games (*Call of Duty 3*). He lives in Los Angeles with his wife, two daughters, a dog, a cat, and a turtle (which may or may not be alive at the time of this writing).

MULHOLLAND BOOKS